SANNAH AND THE PILGRIM

SUE PARRITT

ODYSSEY BOOKS

Published by Odyssey Books in 2014

ISBN 978-1-922200-14-3

www.odysseybooks.com.au

National Library of Australia
Cataloguing-in-Publication entry

Author: Sue Parritt
Title: Sannah and the Pilgrim / Sue Parritt
ISBN: 978-1-922200-14-3 (pbk)
ISBN: 978-1-922200-15-0 (ebook)
Dewey Number: A823.4

Cover designed by Elijah Toten

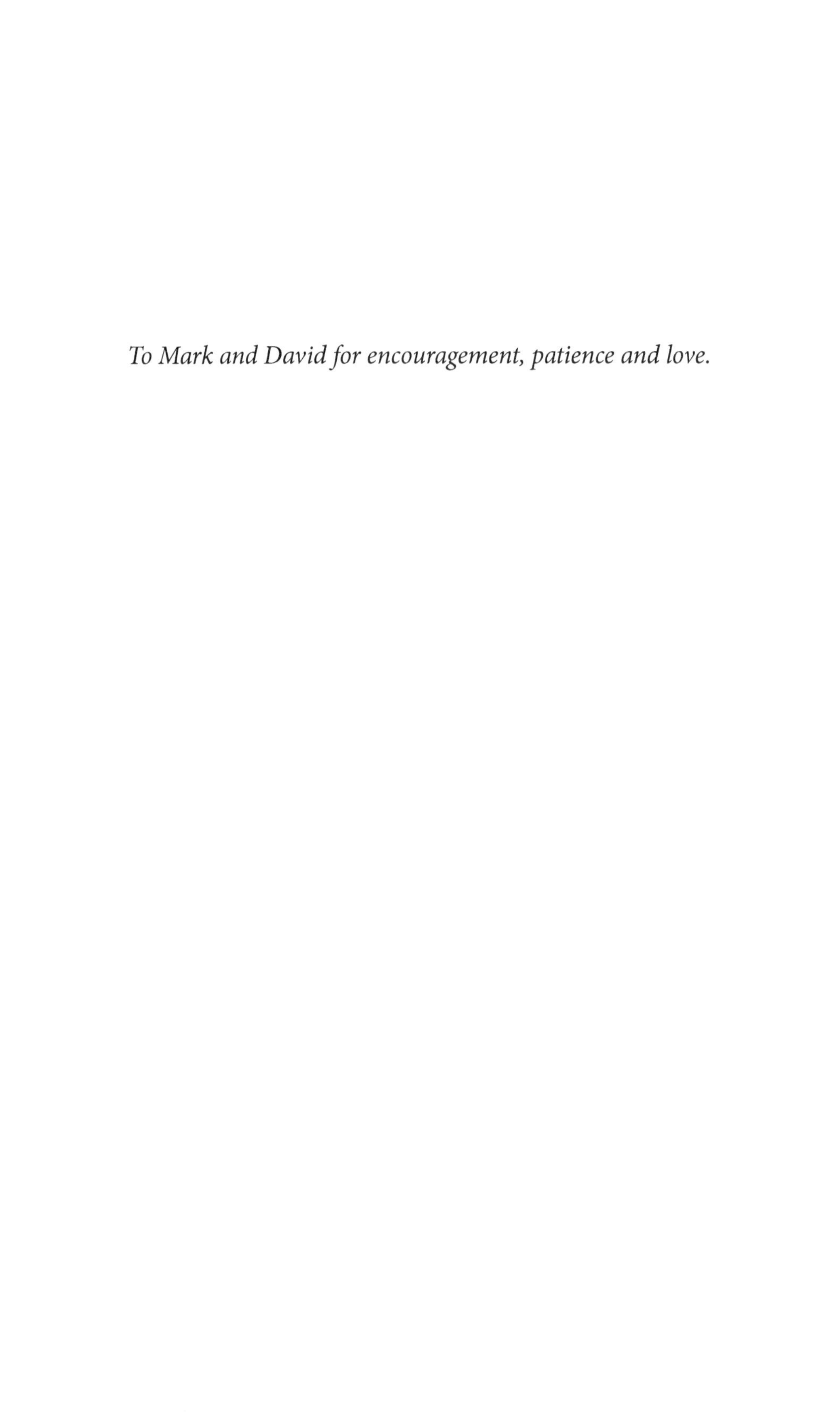

To Mark and David for encouragement, patience and love.

PART I

SANNAH THE STORYTELLER

CHAPTER 1

She woke with a start from dream shadows, her body rigid beneath the thin sheet, her mind sharpened by a potent sensation of fear. Wide-eyed she peered into darkness and saw only a thin beam of light surrounding the door panel. Her hands groped under the pillow and retrieved a knife and thigh-band. She attached them hurriedly before grabbing the crumpled robe draped over her bedside stool. Flimsy fabric slung around her shoulders, she crossed the chamber and waved her left hand towards the light. The door panel, made of moulded recycled plastic, as were all the dome's fittings and furniture, slid silently into the wall.

Steep stone stairs lit by light-strips above the handrail led to her living chamber and kitchen, built at ground level. Bounding up two steps at a time, she paused at the top for the wall lights that were activated by body heat to illuminate the windowless space. Everything remained as she'd left it: cloth floor-cushions scattered around a low table, program-packs stacked untidily on shelves, head-cloth and sandals discarded by the kitchen door. She approached a square pad embedded in the curved concrete wall, raised her right index finger and waited a moment for the lights to dim before moving further into the chamber, her bare feet making little sound on the cool stone floor. Head pressed against the main door, she listened for unfamiliar sounds, but heard only the wind gusting around the hillside drying her carefully nurtured plants. The cover-strip, a thin piece of plastic inserted in the door panel halfway up, opened at a touch of her hand. She peered through the slit in the door, blinked as her eyes adjusted to brightness, and discovered at once the reason for dark dreaming. On the edge of her domestep, a bundle of white cloth huddled in a shady corner away from the glare of afternoon sunlight.

'What the Sun do you think you're doing sleeping outside in daylight?' she called as the door panel opened. 'You're lucky a trooper didn't catch you.'

The stranger rose stiffly, smoothing crushed cloth over long limbs. 'I'm just a weary traveller seeking a place to stay,' a male voice answered.

'For how long?'

'A couple of nights.'

She glanced at his dusty sandals and soiled robe. 'Then why didn't you call through the sound-grill?'

'The what?'

She pointed to a small aperture halfway up the wall to the left of the door. He stepped forward, peered, nodded. 'I did knock a couple of times.'

'I wouldn't have heard you downstairs.'

'Sorry.' He pushed the dirty head-cloth away from his face and turned towards her, sea-green eyes glistening as he offered an apologetic smile. She had never seen such intense eye colour, and sensed mysterious depths behind the brilliance. For a few moments he held her gaze, then blinked and appeared to be focusing on a point above her head.

'You'd better come in,' she said, stepping back into the cool dome. The door panel closed behind him.

'Wait over there.' She gestured towards the floor-cushions. 'I'll fetch some cold water. You must be thirsty.'

In the adjoining kitchen she listened to the *slap-slap* of his sandals on the stone floor, pondering why he'd arrived in daylight and why he hadn't called through the sound-grill. 'Strangers', the term members of the clandestine group the Women's Line applied to political prisoners on the run seeking assistance, usually came during the night, mingling with the crowd in the marketplace for a while before making their way to her isolated white dome high on a hill overlooking the village. Occasionally she observed them making small talk with the stall-keepers, purchasing token items to prevent a trooper's eyes lingering too long on travel-scarred clothing. She always knew who they were even if her friend Fley, a Line leader, hadn't told her to expect anyone. Certain gestures betrayed them: eyes flicking over the produce, hands picking up inferior pieces, fingers fumbling in money-belts.

She filled a large tumbler from the cooler water jug and returned to her living chamber.

'Welcome to my dome, stranger,' she said, giving the customary greeting. 'I am Sannah the Storyteller.'

The man nodded, slowly unwound his long head-cloth and shook out shoulder-length black curls. 'I am Kaire.'

'Where have you travelled from, Kaire?' she asked, noting the unblemished ivory skin taut over high cheekbones, the small pointed nose and naked chin.

'Sky z59.'

'Is that a village?'

'We call it a community.'

'I see. And what is your rank?'

'I am a pilgrim.'

What an absurd statement, she thought.

'You know the term?' he asked.

'Of course.'

'Then you'll understand why I've come to your world. All my life I have dreamed of making this journey.'

'You must have lost your way. This is no sacred place where pilgrims gather. This is the Brown Zone, northern Australia, the area reserved for people like me.'

'What do you mean, people like you?'

'Brown-skins, descendants of environmental refugees from drowned Pacific islands.'

'Pac-if-ic,' he repeated, pronouncing each syllable as though savouring the sounds.

She handed over the tumbler. 'Drink, we can talk later.'

'Thank you.'

He must be parched, she thought, watching him drain the tumbler in a few gulps. A glance at his money-belt confirmed it was too small to contain a water vessel.

'Most refreshing,' he said, handing back the tumbler.

She placed the empty tumbler on the table and turned to face him. 'Now perhaps you can tell me why you walked up a steep hill to my dome in fifty degree heat instead of sheltering in the shade down in the village?'

'I looked around the village for somewhere to stay but everything seemed closed. Then I noticed what looked like a temple at the top of a hill. So I decided to climb up and see if anyone was inside. But there was no sign of life up here either, so I lay down in the shade and fell asleep.'

'Of course there's no one around, it's the hottest part of the day!'

'As I thought,' he murmured. 'Siesta.'

She fingered the knife through the folds of her robe, considering her next move. She had assumed he was a stranger seeking sanctuary for a few nights while arrangements were made to pass him down the Women's Line to safety in Aotearoa, but his odd remarks suggested ignorance of northern life. His accent was also unfamiliar, lacking both southerners' clipped consonants and the slur of the northern vernacular. Although it was possible he had come from another country, few travellers visited Australia and they never journeyed alone.

'Now Kaire,' she said firmly, 'to return to the question of your rank.'

'I told you I'm a pilgrim.'

'Stop playing games. What is your rank?'

'I am a senior pilot.'

She nodded. 'Merchant ships, passenger ships, riverboats?'

'Er, passenger ships.'

'Thank you.'

The Women's Line had never sheltered a senior pilot before. High-ranking officials were seldom incarcerated in northern prison domes. Whatever their crimes against the state, position and wealth generally ensured they were remanded in the less harsh surroundings of southern penitentiaries. She would have to tread warily; an escapee from the south should not have known hers was a safe dome. The Women's Line confined their seditious activities to the Brown Zone and the area close to the border with the Asian Zone. 'So, Senior Pilot Kaire, what are your plans?'

'Nothing specific. I thought I'd stay here for one or two days and then move on. I'll probably head for the coast. I should like to observe the ocean.'

He obviously knows the protocol, she thought. 'This ocean offers solace,' she answered, stressing the last word.

'Solace,' he repeated dreamily, 'the warm embrace of sky and stars.' Pale cheeks flushed, green eyes stared into space.

She frowned, perplexed by his odd remark. It would be better for Fley to deal with this senior pilot.

'I think a person of your standing would find more suitable shelter down in the village. I can arrange it.'

'Don't trouble yourself, this is fine.'

She smiled, then pressed her palms together beneath her chin, the Brown Zone gesture of welcome. 'As we say here, Senior Pilot Kaire, my dome is yours for today.'

'I'm very grateful for your hospitality.'

'And now I expect you'd like to bathe?'

'Yes please, the dust has infiltrated every pore.'

'The bath chamber is downstairs. Come with me.'

He followed her down the stairs to the small sleeping chamber deep in the cool earth, and stood in the doorway while she selected a clean robe from the dozen or so hanging from a rail beneath a wide shelf running the length of one wall. All her robes were made of lightweight cotton, some plain-dyed, others decorated with swirls of vibrant colour. Simple garments designed for coolness and ease of movement, no buttons or clasps, and gathered at the waist by a money-belt or sash—they were the standard dress worn by both female and male Brown-skins.

'Here, this should fit.' She held out a pale blue robe but before she could hand it over, he had untied his robe, slipped it from his shoulders and dropped it to the floor. Astonished by his bad manners she stepped back a pace, her eyes travelling down his body, riveted to the pristine whiteness. The usual signs of hard physical labour and the livid welts of prison dome torture were absent; his torso was satin-smooth, dark nipples the only embellishment. Puzzled, she ventured lower, noted the complete lack of pubic hair minus the shadow usually present if skin had been shaved, his penis flaccid against the fold of thigh and his long slim legs tapering to slender ankles. Apart from the black curls brushing his shoulders, his skin seemed as smooth and unblemished as a newborn baby lifted from the womb by a surgeon's gentle hands.

Her eyes flicked back to his flat abdomen. First glance had not deceived her. He had no navel.

'Have you a towel?' he asked, reaching for the robe.

'In the bath chamber.' She gestured towards a door panel at the rear of the chamber, activating the opening device. 'Take your time, there's plenty of water.'

'Thank you, Sannah the Storyteller,' he said, making a small bow. He headed for the shower, leaving her free to retrieve the palm-sized communicator lying on her bedside cabinet. The moment he turned around to step into the shower, she secured a perfect digital image of his head and shoulders.

Back in the kitchen she opened a wall panel and descended the few steps to her small store. Glass jars of all shapes and sizes lined the shelves. Lifting a jar labelled 'rice', she carefully extracted the old communicator used exclusively for Women's Line business and pressed the opaque central screen. It remained blank. Frowning, she shook the device vigorously. The letters LLF appeared on the screen.

'Yes, Sannah,' Line Leader Fley answered sleepily.

'I have a visitor.'

'I'm not expecting anyone. Male?'

'Yes, Senior Pilot Kaire.'

'Code?'

'Sky z59, a new one on me.'

'Me too, I'll run a trace.'

'There's something else. He has no navel.'

'There could be a monitoring device in his abdomen. Examine the area thoroughly.'

'I'll use the sleep spray. He seems very tired.'

'Too risky. The residue from this latest batch remains on the skin for some time. Use your charms instead.'

'Are you sure?'

'Sometimes rules have to be broken. Meet me this evening at six in the schoolyard.'

For a few moments Sannah stared at the blank screen, pondering Fley's instructions. Then she remembered her interrupted dream, a soft tangle of limbs, sweet sensation swelling. The anticipation of delight suddenly eclipsed by apprehension, an eerie sense of another's presence. She shuddered, re-wrapped the communicator, and thrust it deep into the jar.

The cooler fruit box contained several mangoes. She selected the least damaged and carried it to the bench. A platter of sweet mango and a tumbler of spiced nectar should put her visitor in the right mood.

But when she returned downstairs, robe pushed back over her shoulders to reveal the swell of ample breasts, she found him curled in the middle of her bed sound asleep. Standing beside the bed, she watched him sleep. His red lips were slightly parted, dark curls rested against a smooth cheek, almost translucent eyelids were tightly closed. It was difficult to believe he could be an imposter. No trooper would act in such a relaxed manner on an official visit to a Brown-skin's dome. But if the governor's men hadn't sent him and he wasn't a prison escapee, his sudden appearance belied rational explanation.

Men came to her dome for two reasons, sex or sanctuary. Rarely both—she tried to keep Line rules. Sex provided excellent cover for sanctuary: the whole village was aware Sannah the Storyteller enjoyed many lovers and no one, not even the troopers, questioned the men who climbed the hill path to her solitary white dome.

Cautiously she raised the sheet and folded it back. Red lips closed, her long white fingers brushed the pillow. She held her breath, waiting for eyelids to flutter, bright eyes to question her activities. Nothing stirred save his chest rising and falling in the rhythm of deep sleep. Leaning over him, she brushed his abdomen with the tips of her fingers and, pressing gently, moved in small circles across the smooth surface. She encountered neither the hard edge of a monitoring device nor a thin line of scar tissue.

Replacing the sheet, she picked up his robe and head-cloth and carried them into the bath chamber. A touch of her palm closed the door panel. On the floor near the shower, lay his leather sandals and money-belt. Kneeling on the cool tiles, she spread out his robe. Thin cloth slipped through her fingers, its colour and weave similar to those worn by her people. His head-cloth was fashioned from the same fabric, a single strip held in place by a leather clasp. Discoloured and cracked, the clasp could have belonged to any villager in the north.

She pushed the clothes aside and reached for his money-belt. Unlike the clasp, this leather was soft and new. It also lacked any motif, often an indication of a person's status or locality. Had it been purchased in a hurry, the buyer unwilling to wait for the craftsperson to add a distinctive design? She lifted the flap and tipped the contents onto the shower mat. A few old coins, a pebble, a dried flower, a transparent tube containing white tablets—these were commonplace items and no cause for concern, but where was his identity disc? She shook the money-belt, groped around her feet, in the folds of her robe, on the woven mat. Nothing. She sighed and began to replace his belongings in the money-belt. This was a dilemma for the Women's Line; without identification, counterfeit or genuine, the man Kaire did not exist.

CHAPTER 2

Down in the village the evening siren screamed, its clamour rising from the valley floor up the steep slopes of Storyteller's Hill. Sannah stretched her limbs, stiff from hours leaning against the shower wall trying not to fall asleep. She hadn't dared venture upstairs to the living or kitchen chamber, not with an unverified stranger on the other side of the thin partition. Opening the door panel a fraction, she peered into her sleeping chamber. Senior Pilot Kaire continued to sleep, clearly unperturbed by the siren sounding. Relieved, she closed the panel and stepped into the shower. The cool water calmed her nerves but the wash gel seemed to chafe her skin and the towel felt rough when she dried herself. These were signs she could not ignore, every sense amplified a second flush of fear.

Dressed in a white night-robe tied with a braided blue sash, she picked up the message board lying on the bedside table, keyed 'Gone to the village to buy bread, back soon,' and propped it against the lamp.

The dying rays of day illuminated the path as she entered the school-yard where Fley stood in the shade of a play shield. The older woman raised her hand in greeting before ambling over to a nearby seat.

'You look tired,' Sannah remarked as Fley settled her bulk on the bench.

'I didn't get to bed until three,' her friend replied with a yawn. 'But I don't suppose you've had much sleep either with a man in the dome.'

'No, but not for the reason you're thinking.'

'Don't tell me your seduction technique failed?'

'I didn't have the opportunity.'

Fley became serious. 'Tell me about your visitor.'

Sannah had just described Kaire's appearance and was about to mention his odd behaviour when loud voices and heavy footsteps emanated from the rear of the school dome. 'I'd better go,' she said, reaching for her basket.

'No, stay. We're just having a chat before work, if they ask.'

As she spoke, two troopers emerged chasing a young man wearing only a loincloth. All three jumped over the low wall surrounding the schoolyard and disappeared in the direction of the medical dome next door.

'Flin,' said Sannah. 'Always in trouble, that one.'

Fley nodded and sat back on the bench. 'So is this senior pilot seeking sanctuary?'

'I'm not sure. He doesn't behave like an escapee, or a trooper for that matter.'

Fley looked thoughtful. 'He could be a Security Department official masquerading as a traveller. What does it say on his ID disc?'

'Couldn't find it.'

Fley frowned. 'None of this makes any sense. We weren't expecting anyone for some time after the last fiasco. It took me ages this morning to convince the river women not to bail out.'

Sannah shivered. 'And now this.'

'We must stay calm. I know it's been tough but the only thing that matters is that the Women's Line remains intact. I'll uncover the truth about your curious visitor. I'm running a nationwide trace on his code right now. Get hair and skin samples to me as soon as you can. But first you'd better arrange a fake ID in case it's needed.'

'Is it still third dome, second row?'

'Yes. Go straight home afterwards but don't hand over the disc. Wait until I contact you. In the meantime get whatever information you can from him.'

Sannah nodded.

'What hour is the Tales?' Fley asked.

'Five.'

'Good, that gives me plenty of time to make further inquiries.' A child wandered into the schoolyard, trailing a stick in the dust. 'I must go, children to teach,' said Fley, levering herself from the bench. 'Till the Tales, friend.'

Sannah smiled. 'Till the Tales.' She remained seated; it would be unwise to appear in a hurry at this hour.

As she walked away from the bench towards the schoolyard gate, a familiar voice called out to Sannah.

'Greetings Trooper-in-Charge Wurn,' she answered, turning around and raising her right hand level with her cheek.

'What are you doing in the schoolyard?' he asked, leaning over the wall.

'Enjoying the evening air.' She smiled, walked towards him, hips swaying. Reaching the low wall, she bent forward, caressing the smooth stone with her free hand. 'Can I expect you after the Tales?'

'Unfortunately I won't be back in time. I have to visit a river village.'

She sighed, relieved he would be occupied throughout the coming night.

'I'm sorry,' he murmured, misinterpreting. 'Maybe next week?' The palm of his hand brushed her cheek.

'I do hope so.' She straightened up. 'Well, I can't stand around here chatting, I have provisions to buy. See you later.'

'Undoubtedly.'

She watched him stride down the path leading to the medical dome, his short tunic displaying broad shoulders and firm thighs to full advantage. They had been lovers for some time. He treated her well and seemed genuinely to care, while her own feelings wavered between desire and unease. Experience had taught her to tread carefully where White men were concerned. Most troopers regarded Brown-skins, especially women, as an inferior group to be controlled with a heavy hand. Although Wurn treated those under his control with reasonable fairness, permitting adequate meal breaks and restricting dangerous daylight work, in one area he remained inflexible: insisting one's identity disc be carried at all times. He treated breaches harshly, imposing the maximum fine, and persistent offenders were thrown in the village prison chamber for up to a week.

The marketplace was thick with villagers eager to purchase before the goods had been picked over and further damaged. The best produce bypassed Brown Zone villages destined for White Zone markets. Insufficient rainfall in southern Australia and the Isle of Tasman had precluded agriculture of any kind for centuries, but the White inhabitants had no intention of moving north. Water and insect-borne diseases flourished in northern heat and humidity, and cyclones and floods were prevalent. Life expectancy for Brown-skins was around ninety years, while southern Whites could anticipate at least a hundred and twenty in their hot, dry climate. A long healthy life was essential if they were to retain supremacy over the more numerous Brown and Asian Australians.

After a long wait at the baker's stall, with the delicious aroma of fresh bread tormenting her empty stomach, Sannah left the marketplace, her fingers tearing at thick crust as she wound her way through narrow streets to Eran the Recorder's dome. Only when she reached the domestep did she stop chewing, wiping her mouth with the end of her head-cloth before addressing the sound-grill.

'Enter, Sannah the Storyteller,' Eran answered formally.

The door panel opened revealing a dark-skinned woman in her thirties sitting at a work-module, a recycled-plastic desk with inbuilt computer, scanning rows of figures from a metal strip into a small screen.

'I'm sorry to disturb you, do finish the line,' said Sannah, stressing the last word to explain the nature of her call.

'No problem, I have many more lines,' Eran replied.

'I need an ID disc,' said Sannah quietly, positioning herself directly behind Eran's chair.

A slim container rose from a concealed compartment beneath the work-module. Thin fingers glided over a small screen.

'Details,' Eran said in a low voice.

'Male, about twenty-five, name is Kaire.'

'An old name, *Kaire*, isn't it?'

'I imagine so.'

'Rank?'

'Senior pilot.'

'Any distinguishing features?'

'Er no.'

'I won't be a moment. Help yourself to a drink.' Eran indicated a stone jug to her right.

Sannah drank slowly, savouring the ice-cold water. Even in darkness it would be a long hot climb up the hill path and she couldn't afford to dawdle with Senior Pilot Kaire alone in her dome.

'All done.' Eran held out a small silver disc.

'Thanks.' Sannah slipped the disc under the loaf in her basket.

'No problem. See you later. I must get back to work now.'

Sannah smiled. 'Goodbye. Till the Tales, friend.'

Eran repeated the customary farewell for that day of the week before turning back to her screen and retrieving another figure strip from the plastic box on her work-module.

Sannah almost collided with her lover as she stepped into the street.

'Greetings Trooper-in-Charge Wurn,' she said, hurriedly raising her hand.

'So we meet again. What brings you to Eran the Recorder?'

'Thirst. It's hot tonight, don't you think?'

'No more than usual in these parts. Why didn't you buy a drink at the marketplace?'

'I ran out of tokens.'

He leaned forward, poked the bread in her basket. 'You could have bought a smaller loaf and saved a token for a drink.'

She noticed the disc was protruding from under the loaf on her side. Her fingers tightened around the plaited handle. 'Now why didn't I think of that?'

'What distracted you?'

She adopted a seductive pose, and reached out to run her fingers up and down his bare arm.

'Next week, I promise,' he murmured.

'I'll be waiting.' She smiled. 'Must go, it's a long climb to my dome.'

'And worth every step.'

'I'm delighted you think so.' She turned and made her way up the street. At the corner, she waved in case he was watching.

Hot breeze ruffled stagnant water as Sannah walked beside the canal. Stray curls clung to her sweat-soaked neck. She pushed them back under her head-cloth and was reminded of intimate gestures made with tenderness. Her lover, Wurn, always lifted her thick tresses away from her neck after making love so he could kiss the warm skin beneath. For a moment, a smile brushed her lips, and then she quickened her step, grateful for a clear starlit sky. There were no lights at this end of the canal and she dare not risk a fall. It could be hours before anyone discovered her here; the rough narrow path was little used, though she found it a useful shortcut especially after curfew. Troopers tended to avoid this part of the canal, the stench from polluted water proving an effective deterrent.

Before long she reached the light that marked the beginning of the hill path and turned for home. Halfway up the steep slope, she heard a volley of high-pitched noises that appeared to be coming from the cleared area in front of her dome. Stepping into the shadows at the edge of the path, she listened carefully. Half-singing half-whistling, the sounds resonated around the hillside.

'Who's there?' she called.

'Coo-ee, coo-ee.'

'Give the greeting,' she demanded.

'Coo-ee, coo-ee.'

She strode towards the group of large boulders balanced precariously on dry soil a short distance ahead. The sounds faded. Her right hand gripped the knife hidden beneath her robe and quickly freed it from the thigh-band. Pebbles skidded down the slope.

'Give the greeting,' she repeated, but this time there was no response. She searched thoroughly but found no one hidden behind the boulders. Puzzled, she rejoined the path. Her knife remained unsheathed.

She was within sight of her dome when the sounds began again. They were closer now, too close to chance a sprint to the domestep.

'Show yourself,' she ordered. 'I am Sannah the Storyteller.'

'I am Kaire the Pilgrim,' came the reply. Kaire moved away from the shadowed domestep.

'What do you think you're doing, running around making strange noises?'

'A greeting, that's all. I saw you coming up the path.'

'What were you doing outside?'

'Just looking around.'

'You could have slipped on the slope. There's no light around the back.'

'Don't worry, I haven't been far. That would be foolish at night when I don't know the area. You can take me down to the village in the morning.'

'We won't be going anywhere in the morning.'

'Why not? Do you intend to keep me captive in your dome?'

'Of course not, but I must obey the curfew.' She crossed to the entrance and pressed her palm against a clear panel. The door opened.

Entering the dome, she quickly unwrapped her head-cloth and discarded dusty sandals. Cool air embraced hot skin and she shivered beneath her light robe.

'Sit down while I prepare a meal,' she said to Kaire, still standing near the door. 'No doubt you're hungry?'

He smiled. 'Thank you, but I've already taken sustenance.'

In the kitchen she checked the cooler but a platter of mango and another of cheese remained untouched. Curious now, she checked the jars on the bench. Flour, rice, sugar, tea, nuts, dried fruit, all appeared undisturbed.

'Are you sure you don't want anything?' she called.

'A drink would be pleasant.'

She filled two tumblers from a jug and set them on a tray beside cheese and fruit. The fresh loaf, its chewed end hastily trimmed, completed her preparations.

For a few minutes she ate steadily, conscious only of texture and taste. Hunger appeased, she looked up and reached for her tumbler. Kaire sat quietly sipping his drink, his eyes riveted to her platter.

'You may talk while I eat,' she said, wishing he would overcome his reticence and accept some food.

He pointed to a piece of cheese. 'Is it hot or cold?'

'Cold of course, I keep cheese in the cooler.'

'And this one?' He indicated a slice of mango.

'The mango's also cold.'

'And this?' A pale finger brushed the bread she held in her free hand.

'Why all the questions? Haven't you eaten these foods before?'

He shook his head.

'Then you'd better try some.' She broke off a piece of bread and handed it to him together with a small slice of cheese.

He studied each piece intently before placing both in his mouth at once. Almost immediately he gagged, and spat the half-chewed food onto the floor.

'What the Sun are you doing?' she cried, disgusted.

Racked with coughing, Kaire could not answer.

'Have a drink.' She reached over and held the tumbler to his lips. 'Better?'

He nodded and drank deeply. 'I do apologise. Where are your cleaning materials? I must clear up this mess.'

Poor man, she thought, *he's starving, couldn't wait to chew the food properly.*

'I'll clean up. Help yourself to the rest of my meal. And this time chew it well.'

Returning from the kitchen with a cloth, she noticed he had eaten very little. 'Don't you like my food?'

'It's …' Kaire beamed. 'I don't know how to describe it, it's fantastic.'

'But you've hardly touched it.'

He took a tiny piece of mango and placed it carefully between his small teeth. After several exaggerated jaw movements, he stuck out his tongue, removed a strand of fruit fibre with his finger and proceeded to study it. On her knees, cloth in hand, she pondered the unusual eating habits of the inhabitants of Sky.

The dome wall communicator flashed and buzzed. She hurried across the chamber to answer it. 'Sannah the Storyteller.'

'Greetings, this is Fley the Instructor. Is your visitor still with you?'

'Yes.'

'It appears he's a traveller from the far south. Awaiting confirmation.'

Sannah glanced at her pale-skinned guest.

'Bring him to the Tales,' Fley continued, 'and take him to the trooper dome afterwards to register.'

'Wurn may not be back by morning.'

'No matter, just get him away from your dome.'

'Will do.'

'Talk to you later. Till the Tales, friend.'

The connection closed before Sannah could repeat the phrase.

Deep in thought, she returned to her floor-cushion and slipped the soiled cloth underneath.

'You have no visual display,' he remarked.

'No, they're not common in these parts.'

'Too expensive?'

'Yes, for my people. The troopers have them, naturally.'

Kaire nodded. 'So who's the commander here?'

'Trooper-in-Charge Wurn.'

'I should like to meet him.'

Sannah hesitated. What was this southerner playing at? He must know the rules. All travellers, irrespective of rank, had to register their arrival in a Brown Zone village with the trooper-in-charge.

'I believe he's away at the moment, but I can take you to the trooper dome later. The trooper on duty will be happy to sight your identity disc and arrange an interview later.'

'I have no identity disc, as you would have discovered when you searched my belongings.'

'I'm sorry about that, but I was disturbed by your sudden appearance. White travellers are rare in the Brown Zone and recently there have been several breakouts from prison domes further north. Mostly White prisoners I believe. As you know, harbouring an escaped prisoner is a capital offence.'

'I assure you I'm a free man, and as for my lack of identity, that's easily explained. My identity disc is with the rest of my travelling gear, in my backpack at the bottom of your filthy canal. I slipped on the path, dislodged my backpack and it rolled into the water.'

'You expect me to believe that? Perhaps it's time I called a trooper.' She leapt to her feet and ran over to the communicator.

'I don't want to get you into trouble,' he said mildly. 'Let me explain the situation to the troopers. I come in peace, to live among your people for a while and absorb the mysteries of this place. I bear no arms as you already know, and I carry no deadly diseases.'

She turned away from the communicator, retraced her steps and stood over him, hands on hips. 'Then what are those tablets I found in your money-belt?'

'Sustenance. They keep me alive.'

'So what's wrong with you?'

'Nothing, I'm in peak physical condition, otherwise I couldn't have undertaken this journey. Everyone in my community takes sustenance.' He glanced at her platter. 'Sustenance is our mango and cheese.'

'You take tablets instead of eating? Why?'

'It saves time, energy. Isn't that the way of all advanced societies?'

'Not this one.'

He frowned. 'I'm confused. This is obviously not a primitive society—your communication device and cybernetic door panels prove that. But I've seen nothing else to indicate advanced technology—no transportation system for instance.'

Sannah pondered her response, reluctant to divulge information Kaire should have already known. On his journey north he must have noticed the solar trains, and the riverboats piled high with goods.

'From which direction did you enter the Brown Zone?' she asked finally.

'East.'

'Are you sure?'

'Yes. I travelled across a desert, then a plain, through a mountain pass, up into a range of hills and down into this valley.'

'That's not possible. No one comes to the Brown Zone by that route. It's desolate country abandoned decades ago. The desert has reclaimed all territory west of the range.'

'It's certainly arid out there. In three days I met no one and the only sign of habitation I found was an abandoned dome a good half-day journey from this village. I sheltered there for a time.'

'From the troopers?' she ventured, considering the possibility Fley had been given incorrect data. The derelict farm dome had not been used to hide escapees for some time but Kaire could have known of its existence.

'I sheltered from the sun. Travelling in your country is exhausting. I'm unaccustomed to such heat.'

'Enough, you speak in riddles. Save your story for the troopers, they will discover the truth.'

She turned on her heel and marched back to the communicator. But as she reached out to press the panel, a hand touched her shoulder. She tensed, waiting for the hard edge of an eradicator to push into her back.

'Truth is never absolute,' he said calmly. 'It depends on the mind-processes of speaker and listener. I am Kaire, a pilgrim from a place called Sky z59, but if you choose not to believe me then my words carry no meaning and an identity disc cannot prove their validity.'

She turned slowly. 'I don't suppose a few hours will make any difference. Under the circumstances it might be best to wait till Trooper-in-Charge Wurn has returned.'

'Thank you, I am truly grateful.'

They moved back to the floor-cushions and continued their meal in silence.

When they had finished, Sannah stacked platters and tumblers onto the tray. 'I have to prepare for the Tales and would appreciate not being disturbed for several hours. You may use my sleeping chamber. If you want some entertainment, there's a screen on the wall opposite my bed. Numerous interactive and passive programmes are available.' She smiled. 'You see we are not a primitive people.'

CHAPTER 3

At the rear of the dais, half-hidden by shadows, Sannah perched on a stool, watching villagers file into the community dome. One by one, they took their accustomed places on the old wooden benches arranged in semi-circles either side of a wide aisle. Once seated, conversation ceased, hands rested on knees, eyes focused on the dais. Near the entrance, the trooper on duty lounged on a padded seat, seemingly indifferent to those around him. A lazy individual, Sannah knew he welcomed this early morning shift as an opportunity to take it easy or even sleep. The villagers never caused trouble during the Tales, for she could weave a spell around the dome with stories of lives long ended, distant catastrophe and distant redemption.

When everyone had settled, she stood up, glided to the centre of the dais, the white robe rustling around her bare feet, gold ankle chains gleaming in bright dome light. Tilting her face to the domed white ceiling, she raised her arms in a wide arc until her palms touched.

'Praise the Nocturnal Life Project that protects us from the sun,' she cried. 'Praise moon and stars.'

'Praise the great White government that takes care of us,' the villagers chanted in response.

'Praise the Tales that teach us truth.'

'Praise the Tales.'

She lowered her arms, surveyed the expectant audience. 'This morning, I continue the Journey Tales that we may be reminded of the great gift our ancestors were given when hope, like their island homes, had vanished beneath the blue Pacific.'

Several villagers cried out and ripples of sorrow flowed through the dome like the waves that once washed island shores. Sannah glanced at Senior Pilot Kaire sitting in a front row aisle seat. He appeared uneasy, eyes flicking from left to right, fingers twisting the edge of his robe. *Perhaps he's unaccustomed to public displays of emotion*, she mused, waiting for calm waters.

'The gift of land,' she continued, 'the gift of life: precious, priceless, the reason for our people's continued existence.' She paused, walking to the edge of the dais. 'But first I return to the distant past, for we must not forget our people were latecomers to this great White land.' Raising her arms to embrace the island continent, she fixed her gaze above the rows of white robes, the familiar brown faces. 'In the southern ocean lay an immense continent,' she began, slowly lowering her arms, 'sweet fruit in her orchards, grain in her fields, sheep and cattle on her inland plains, fish in her waters. A bountiful and beautiful country, but by the mid-twentieth century, a country lacking a viable population. Although numerous migrants had arrived in the years since the original inhabitants—White explorers from Europe who had sailed into Botany Bay—many more brave souls were needed to develop the vast tracts of virgin land. Advertising campaigns began in earnest, urging Europeans to join the Australian family and make a home under clear southern skies. Thousands of men, women and children answered the call, fled the stink of death, the smoking ruins of Europe, the ash-filled sky. Crammed into narrow cabins, they crossed the wide oceans, meagre belongings in the hold, abundant hope in their hearts. They came seeking freedom from war, depression, deprivation. The peace had promised prosperity and progress but instead, victor and vanquished alike knew poverty and powerlessness.' She hung her head for a moment, then raised it and looking directly at the audience, said passionately, 'So the great White migration began and the land flourished as never before. Cities pulsed with energy, smooth highways teemed with traffic. Rail tracks rang with the rhythm of countless trains carrying minerals and other produce from the interior to the ports. Wharves piled high with containers awaited ships from all over the globe.'

She smiled at the audience. 'The people, too, flourished and before long their lifestyle was the envy of others in less affluent countries. Migrant workers watched their children playing in the sun and gave thanks for the opportunity to build new lives in a golden land.'

Her robe rustled as she moved a few paces to the right. 'An opportunity to begin again must never be taken for granted,' she instructed, her voice firm. 'We must continue to give thanks as our ancestors did following their own migration a hundred years later. They appreciated the immense generosity shown by the Australian government at a time when due to protracted inter-racial tension usually only White migrants were admitted. They accepted that as Pacific environmental refugees, they must live in a designated zone and be closely monitored.' She paused as her training dictated, allowing the familiar rhetoric to pervade already malleable minds.

The trooper snored loudly. *No need for him to change his ways*, she thought. White skin ensured high status. Her brown eyes blazed as she watched his large belly rise and fall, the white tunic shifting over fleshy thighs. Tossing her dark curls, she turned her attention back to the audience.

'We must never forget the loss of our ancestral islands could have been avoided. The responsibility rests entirely with our people. They populated the Pacific without regard for the limitations of fragile coral islands, over-fished and hunted island fauna to extinction. And when they had ruined one island, they moved on to another and another, until all that remained were sand-blown specks. Little wonder Mother Nature punished them by drowning their islands.'

'Sins must be punished,' the villagers chanted.

'All Brown-skins have inherited that fatal flaw,' she thundered, 'therefore we must obey our White masters at all times.'

'White way is right way. White way is right way,' came the habitual response.

Sannah bowed her head. The villagers followed suit. After a lengthy pause for reflection, she raised her head and said gently, 'Let us return to the Tale. There are many more wonders to explore in the marvellous twentieth century.'

A hundred heads rose, a collective sigh coursed through the dome.

An hour later, perspiration running down her face, Sannah brought the Tale of the Great Migration to a close and retreated to the rear of the dais. Roused from sleep by her dramatic conclusion, the trooper yawned loudly and stretched his limbs. Silence blanketed the dome; the people sat motionless, heads bowed.

The trooper stood and marched down the centre aisle, his heavy boots striking the concrete floor like hammers. Reaching the dais, he jumped up and swung around to face the villagers.

'Praise the Tales,' he proclaimed, his voice gruff.

'Praise the Tales,' the people responded.

'Be gone to your domes. The sun is rising and all must seek shelter from damaging daylight.'

The villagers rose as one and began to file out of the dome. Sannah moved forward to face the trooper, her left palm raised.

His hand was clammy as he performed the ritual greeting, prolonging, deliberately it seemed, the moment of contact.

'You are well, Trooper Areth?' she asked politely.

'Fit to take on anything or anyone, and don't you forget it, story-teller.'

She flashed a brilliant smile. 'Even a vigorous Brown woman?'

He laughed heartily, exposing strong white teeth. 'I like a woman of spirit. How about a drink at Clar's? My shift's over in a few minutes.'

'Sorry I can't today. I've got to visit the trooper dome.'

He snorted and dropped her hand.

'I bid you farewell, Trooper Areth.' She swept from the dais, white robe swirling.

'I'll have you one night, whore,' he called after her.

In the small chamber behind the dais, she quickly unfastened the storyteller's robe and golden sash and hung them in the small cupboard reserved for her use. She had just finished fastening her own robe when the outer door panel opened and Fley bustled in, obviously agitated.

'Where's that disc?' Fley flopped onto the bench next to the cupboard.

'In my sash. You said hang on to it till you'd received confirmation. Where have you been? I thought I'd see you here before the Tales. I'm taking Senior Pilot Kaire to the trooper dome in a few minutes.'

Fley took a deep breath. 'Something about the original trace just didn't seem right and your subsequent message about his lost backpack confirmed my suspicions, so I sent an all-village alert. I've been waiting for the other Line leaders to get back to me. The response was unanimous. There are no southern travellers in this zone at present.'

Sannah sat down next to her friend. 'Someone's lying, but we can't afford to wait for truth to surface.'

'Exactly. We have no choice but to hand him over to the troopers immediately. The Women's Line must not be put in jeopardy.'

'I've arranged to meet him in the marketplace. If I leave now we should be rid of Senior Pilot Kaire in about ten minutes.'

But there was no sign of Kaire at the agreed meeting place. Sannah retraced her steps in case he had misunderstood her directions but still failed to find him. Perhaps he'd ventured to the trooper dome alone, confident his missing ID would be overlooked given his high rank. Somewhat relieved by this thought, she decided to return home and headed for the open area surrounding the closed-up stalls.

'Over here, Sannah.'

She turned to see Kaire sitting on the ground a short distance away beside old Fen's cart.

'What the Sun are you doing?' she called, hurrying over.

'Enjoying more wonderful mangoes.' He pointed to several discarded stones.

'You were supposed to meet me opposite the trooper dome.'

'My apologies, but I couldn't resist these. The stallkeeper gave them to me. He said they were leftovers.'

She glanced around. What had happened to Fen? He usually kept his cart in the small yard behind his dome.

'Where's the stallkeeper now?'

'Gone to visit his granddaughter. He said he'd pick up the cart later.'

'Right. Well, we'd better get going.'

'Oh, I don't mind waiting for him. I'd be happy to push the cart to his dome. It's the least I can do.'

Whoever heard of a southerner offering to help an ancient Brown-skin? she thought, bemused once more by his odd behaviour.

'We can't wait for Fen,' she said firmly. 'We must go to the trooper dome now. I have to return home before seven.'

Reluctantly Kaire abandoned his half-eaten mango.

The night shift had almost ended when they entered the trooper dome reception chamber. Behind a work-module, a young trooper lounged on a chair, yawning.

'Greetings, Trooper Roa,' said Sannah. 'I bring a traveller to register.'

The trooper stretched and ambled over to the counter. 'Trooper-in-Charge Wurn has only just returned, storyteller. He won't want to see anyone now.'

'Perhaps you could make an appointment then.' She smiled sweetly.

He pressed the counter pad. 'Step forward, traveller.'

Sannah stood aside.

A loud beep-beep sounded from behind the counter. Trooper Roa glanced at the visual display communicator.

'Yes, sir, I'll send her in.' Looking up, he pointed at Sannah. 'Storyteller, approach the security pad, Trooper-in-Charge Wurn wants to see you right now.'

Sannah hurried over to a door in the far wall and waited a moment for the pad to register her presence and release the door panel leading to Wurn's chamber.

'Who's the man you were talking to just now?' Wurn demanded the moment she entered the chamber.

'A traveller, sir. He arrived in the village yesterday morning.'

Wurn turned to his visual display communicator and pressed a panel on the screen. A frown creased his broad brow. 'I have no record of any traveller.'

'He's registering now. He came to my dome seeking shelter from the sun so I offered him hospitality for the day.'

'I see. And what has he been doing since nightfall?'

'When I told him you were away, he decided to share breakfast with me and …'

'And more besides, I imagine,' Wurn interrupted, his mouth tightening in a sneer. 'Many hours have passed since last evening, storyteller. Did he tell you of his travels as you rolled together on the bed?'

'No. He was exhausted, he *slept* in my bed.'

'For nearly twenty-four hours? Do you take me for an idiot?'

'Of course not, sir. The traveller slept half the day, had breakfast with me and then returned to my bed to sleep most of the night. After that he attended the Tales.'

Wurn thumped the work-module with his fist and roared with laughter. 'Strange as it may seem, storyteller, I do believe your explanation. The indignation in your voice cannot be denied, my dear.'

Sannah hung her head as though embarrassed. The trooper-in-charge got to his feet and walked around his work-module. Arms tight around her waist, he kissed her passionately.

'I think you've missed me,' she murmured when he finally released her.

'It's been nearly a week, Sannah. I must come to your dome soon.' His voice was now kind, rich and warm.

'Come whenever you like, you know you're always welcome.'

'Too much work, that's the trouble.'

She stroked his cheek. 'Get someone else to do it, spend a little time with me.'

'I wish I could.'

Her fingers slipped under his tunic, slid between his firm thighs. 'Leave the work soon, lover.'

'I will, I promise.' His wrist-communicator buzzed. 'Oh, what the Sun now?' He raised his arm. 'Yes, Roa?'

Prudently, Sannah withdrew her hand and backed away.

'Send him in at once.' Wurn turned on his heel and marched back to his work-module.

'I'd better leave.'

'No, stay, I won't be long with this traveller.'

She nodded and retreated to a bench at the rear of the chamber.

The door panel opened and Kaire stepped into the chamber. Without a glance at Sannah, he strode across the chamber to the work-module.

'Greetings, Trooper-in-Charge Wurn. I trust we can resolve this matter quickly?'

'That depends on your explanation.'

'I have already told your officer how I came to lose my identity disc. All I ask is some assistance to retrieve my backpack from the canal. I'm certain I can locate the spot where it fell.'

Wurn consulted his VDC. 'Senior Pilot Kaire from Sky z59,' he read slowly and deliberately, 'visiting the Brown Zone to absorb the culture and environment.'

'That is correct.'

Wurn raised his head. 'In all my years as a trooper, Senior Pilot Kaire, I have never heard of anyone wanting to study this inhospitable region or its primitive people.'

'I assure you, sir, I have permission from my commander to undertake research here. My disc will confirm this.'

'The name of your commander?'

'Breta.'

'Very well, I give you twenty-four hours to find your belongings. I'll organise a couple of field workers to come and help you search the canal.'

'Thank you, sir.'

Wurn nodded. 'In the meantime I shall make my own inquiries. And I must warn you, senior pilot, should you fail to produce an appropriate disc I won't hesitate to confine you to the prison chamber.'

'I'm sure that won't be necessary.'

The door panel opened. 'Twenty-four hours, Senior Pilot Kaire. I bid you farewell.'

Kaire turned and almost ran out of the chamber. The door panel closed behind him.

For a few minutes, Wurn sat drumming his fingers on the workmodule, his expression part annoyance, part concern. 'I sense this traveller may be troublesome,' he said finally, beckoning Sannah to his side. 'I want you to keep an eye on him. Accompany the field workers to the canal. You may ignore the curfew today.'

'I'm happy to help, but why not assign one of your troopers?' she asked, longing for a good sleep after the previous day's interruption.

'I'm not wasting a trooper's time.' He reached into a small drawer, retrieved a small communicator and handed it over. 'Report anything unusual and don't put yourself at risk. There could be weapons concealed in his backpack. Communicate with me directly if you need assistance, whatever the hour.'

'Yes, sir.' She pocketed the communicator and turned to leave.

Behind her Wurn leaned back in his chair and slapped his thigh. 'Come over here, my dusky beauty. I have a few minutes to spare.'

CHAPTER 4

Sandwiched between waist-high brown grass and a strip of polluted water, Sannah stood on sunbaked earth, head-cloth pulled tight across her mouth. Her hands and arms were scratched from hours rummaging around in nearby bushes. She had felt awkward sitting idle in the shade while others toiled and had soon joined in the search. Further along, near the concrete barrier marking the end of the canal, Kaire dragged a long pole back and forth, creating deep furrows in the viscous black water. On the opposite bank, two field workers lay exhausted among a tangle of sun-dried grasses, their hair and loin-cloths matted with debris. They had scoured the water for seven hours but found no trace of a backpack or anything else belonging to Kaire. Sannah knew this failure should be reported and Kaire returned to the trooper dome immediately but she wanted to make use of his remaining hours of freedom.

Pulling her head-cloth aside, she called, 'Thanks guys, that was a great effort. Get on home now and have some rest.'

The young men struggled to their feet, crossed the concrete barrier and disappeared into long grass. Sannah waited a couple of minutes before joining Kaire.

'We need rest too, and food,' she said, reaching out to grab the pole. 'I've arranged to go to my friend Fley's dome. It's not far from here.'

'Do as you like, I'm going to search along the banks again.' Pale fingers lifted her hand from the pole.

She tried a different tack, warning him of dehydration and heat exhaustion. He responded by moving further along the bank.

'Well don't blame me if the sun fries your brain and you fall in the canal,' she shouted, stomping off, dust flying from her sandals.

'Oh, all right,' he called, lifting the pole and tossing it in the grass. 'I'll come.'

She turned and flashed a brilliant smile.

She guided him over rough ground to the junction of the jetty path and the short track leading to the southern fields. By following the edge of the fields, they would reach Fley's dome in a few minutes. But as they turned onto the track, she noticed a trooper leaning against a boulder a short distance ahead. Reluctant to waste time explaining to him her reasons for being outside in daylight, she took Kaire across a patch of brown grass and skirted the school dome instead.

Fley was waiting in the open doorway. She gave the formal greeting and hurried them inside. 'Make yourself comfortable traveller, while Sannah and I fetch some drinks. The meal will be ready shortly.'

'Thank you, Fley the Instructor,' Kaire replied, bowing in her direction before heading for the floor-cushions.

Fley turned to the nearby wall monitor. 'Some entertainment for your enjoyment, traveller,' she said, raising her hand. Thunderous orchestral music reverberated around the chamber. 'I'm so sorry.' She waved her hand frantically. 'I must have accidentally altered the volume when I was cleaning.' The volume decreased and became a pleasant background sound.

'That's better, so sorry.' She hastened towards the open door panel leading to the kitchen where Sannah could be seen pouring drinks.

Standing at the bench, protected by the music-generated security screen, Fley quickly shared the latest information received from Opal, the chief technician at the island spotter station and a valuable member of the Women's Line. Opal's report had stated that although no alien vessels had been sighted in southern Brown Zone waters in recent days, it was still possible Kaire had come over ocean. The report also said that his ship could be moored up one of the creeks near the border, which would make his claim to have walked for several days before reaching Village 10 credible. Opal had concluded her report by advising that no local craft used those creeks as they contained sandbanks and submerged rocks, so his ship would not have been spotted.

'The mystery deepens,' Sannah remarked, picking up the tray of drinks.

'Wait.' Fley opened a drawer, pulled out a sachet and poured the contents into one of the tumblers.

Sannah watched blue crystals dissolve in the amber fluid.

'We show great interest in his journey,' said Fley, 'almost excitement, explaining we never travel far from our home villages. We smile sweetly, encourage, express amazement at his exploits, tease out information.'

Sannah nodded and walked into the living chamber.

Kaire had drained his tumbler and set it on the low table. 'Magnificent. I've never tasted anything so silky smooth.'

Fley smiled. 'Another one?'

'Maybe later.' He fiddled with the hem of his robe. 'I, er, I'd like to ask your advice, Fley. If this afternoon's search also proves fruitless, Wurn will throw me in prison. What can I do to convince him I'm a genuine traveller?'

Fley made a show of considering the question. 'Well, there is a strategy I use when dealing with children's dilemmas, but I should stress I've never tried it out on adults.'

'I'll try anything to avoid imprisonment.'

Fley settled back on the floor-cushion. 'Initially I find it helpful if the child relates how the problem developed. Goes back to the beginning in order to solve the end as it were.' She paused and smoothed her robe. 'Perhaps you could tell us why you came to our village?'

He frowned. 'I really can't imagine how that will help find a pack sunk in the canal.'

Fley smiled indulgently. 'Oh, you'd be amazed how background information can help a seemingly insolvable problem. Why don't you start by telling us what prompted your journey?'

'Very well.' He gave a nervous cough. 'I, er, I've been fascinated by this place ever since I started studying twentieth and twenty-first century history programmes when I was twelve. They fired up my imagination and by the time I reached sixteen I'd exhausted the supply of relevant material in the data hub. It was then an idea began to evolve, to travel here and see for myself the home my ancestors had left ages before.'

'The Brown Zone isn't the place to find your roots, Kaire,' said Fley. 'Apart from troopers, all Whites live in the south and have done so for many generations.'

'Why is that?'

'For someone who professes to have studied this place you know very little,' Fley remarked. 'Since the twenty-fifties, skin colour has determined where one may live in this country.'

'The programmes must have been wrong,' Kaire said, half to himself. 'I remember reading about apartheid in South Africa but I can't recall any reference to such a system in Australia.'

'That's because successive governments denied apartheid existed here,' said Sannah bitterly. '*Our* history programmes state the government policy of 'race zoning' was simply a system designed to assist migrants settle in. Strange it still exists two hundred years after immigration ceased.'

'Leave it, Sannah, we're here to listen to Kaire's tale.' Fley leaned forward. 'So what happened after you'd decided to travel here?'

'Obviously at sixteen I couldn't make such a journey so I studied hard and three years ago was promoted to senior pilot. By then I felt I possessed the skills to take me on my pilgrimage. For that is what it had become—I felt compelled to visit the place where my people began.'

'So why wait three years to undertake this pilgrimage?' Sannah asked.

'I knew it would be difficult to obtain permission for my voyage. You see, Sky People never travel backwards …'

'Backwards?' Fley interrupted. 'Time travel is impossible!'

'I mean, we never retrace our steps. Sky People are explorers, forever seeking new destinations. Our voyages are legendary.'

Fley turned to Sannah. 'A community of pilots. Fascinating, don't you think?'

'Absolutely. So how did you get permission to travel here?'

'I mentioned the idea to my supervisor and the officer in charge of the Pilot Unit. Both were against it. We honour the past, they said, but we do not seek a return to it. All life must evolve in order to survive. So

I sought an audience with the commander and was astounded when one was granted. He heard me, the first person in all my life to really listen and understand where my words came from. He gave permission for an eight-month voyage with a crew of two.'

Fley frowned. 'A crew of two, eh? You arrived alone. Where are your fellow travellers?'

'No one wanted to accompany me. Commander Breta was reluctant to force anyone so he said I could travel alone in one of our new ships. They're designed for solo long-haul voyages.'

Sannah started, remembering the trooper dome meeting and the commander's name that Wurn intended to check. 'How long did it take you to travel here?' she asked.

'About six months.'

Sannah and Fley exchanged glances. They had heard storms lashed all the world's oceans but six months seemed an inordinate amount of time to travel by ship, even allowing for bad weather.

'Where is your ship now?' Fley asked.

'Several thousand kilometres west of here. I can't give you the precise location without my communicator, and that's in my backpack.'

'How convenient,' Sannah retorted.

Fley glared at her, then turned back to Kaire. 'Why did you leave your ship so far away?'

'I found a good docking place so I decided to explore the country in my land transporter.'

Sannah raised her eyebrows. 'You didn't walk then.'

Fley put her hand on Sannah's arm. 'Where is this land vehicle now?'

'I left it on a hillside camouflaged with foliage. I'd seen signs of life in the valley below but didn't want to draw attention to myself so decided to continue on foot.'

Sannah looked at Kaire's empty tumbler. Had the veritas crystals lost their potency through lengthy storage? Beside her Fley stared at the floor as though uncertain how to proceed.

'Tell us about the journey from your ship,' said Fley finally, her voice quiet but firm.

He told them about the desert, the sand that made the transporter sluggish, and the heat that even penetrated his sealed capsule. How just when he was beginning to think the desert would never end, clumps of brown grass had appeared, then a few dead trees. There had been no signs of habitation, present or past. Eventually the plains had given way to a mountain range covered with grass and bushes. Driving parallel to the slope, he'd discovered a track littered with slabs of grey rock, and followed it through the range and down a steep slope. At the bottom of the slope the track had petered out, so after some deliberation he'd turned north and climbed into a range of hills. High on a ridge he'd stopped to survey the surrounding country and saw a river meandering through a broad valley, fields dissected by canals, clusters of white buildings and in the distance, a blue ocean.

After hiding his transporter, he'd continued on foot, his silver backpack crammed with sustenance tubes, water flask, communicator, computer strip and a change of clothes. The journey had been more difficult than he'd anticipated, the heat intense, the descent into the valley hindered by thick undergrowth that tore his bodysuit and scratched his exposed hands and face. The sun had made his head ache and his lightweight boots proved no match for rock-strewn terrain. As the day progressed, he had become anxious, distances appeared greater than he'd calculated and water failed to slake his thirst. What a relief when he'd emerged from tangled bushes onto a patch of dusty ground leading to a dilapidated stone dome. He'd crawled through an opening into what he imagined was once a living area, although it contained no trace of the previous inhabitants. Exhausted, he'd collapsed on the floor and fallen asleep.

When he awoke night had fallen and he'd considered moving on but soon dismissed the idea, given his unfamiliarity with the country. Instead he'd explored the dome using the beam from his communicator to light the way. In a room built below ground, he'd discovered a robe, a pair of leather sandals and what looked like a scarf tucked inside a small chest of drawers that had fallen on its face. Beneath the rusting bed-frame he'd found an old leather clasp, which had proved useful to fasten the scarf around his head, giving some protection from the sun. He'd also found a few old coins. The moment it was light, he'd set off again towards the cluster of white buildings the communicator advised him could be reached in five hours at average walking speed.

Although the village, like the isolated dome, was deserted, there were at least signs of recent habitation. Behind a stall in the market-place, Kaire had found the money-belt he now wore and, thinking it would be more convenient to store his sustenance where he could eas-ily reach it, transferred several tubes from his backpack. When he said that in hindsight he wished he'd transferred his communicator and ID as well, Fley smiled ruefully and remarked this error might cost him dearly. Then after listening to the reasoning behind his climb to San-nah's dome, she suddenly terminated his monologue, saying he'd given them plenty to think about and disappeared into the kitchen to fetch food and drink.

The meal passed slowly, Fley urging Kaire to eat all manner of fruit, cheeses and several portions of the rich sweet bread normally reserved for special occasions. Sannah winced as Fley refilled his tumbler for the third time. Liquor might loosen his tongue more than the veritas crystals but she felt he had already consumed too much. His normally pale cheeks were flushed, his speech blurred. Before long he would either fall asleep or become incoherent.

'Enough, don't you think?' she whispered, touching Fley's arm.

'I wish I'd had this on my trek,' said Kaire, lifting the tumbler to his lips.

'I don't think so,' Sannah replied. 'It promotes sleep, not energy for walking.'

Kaire yawned. 'I do feel a bit tired.'

'Why don't you go down to my sleeping chamber and have a rest before returning to the canal?' Fley suggested. 'We'll clear away the dishes while you sleep.' He smiled, levered himself from the floor-cush-ion and made his way unsteadily down the stairs.

In the kitchen Fley washed platters and tumblers while Sannah dried and put them in the cupboard beneath the bench. Neither of them spoke for some time; Kaire's tale had alarmed and confused them.

At last Sannah asked the question rolling around both their heads. 'What went wrong with the veritas? That was the most unlikely tale

I've ever heard. No one dreams of visiting a deprived country—some pilgrim he is. He must have come from the south.'

'Then why haven't we received any warnings from our people at the border crossings?'

'He could have deliberately bypassed the border.'

'That would explain his arrival from the west but it doesn't explain why no one saw him. No unknown vehicle has been sighted west of River Village 5 in the last couple of weeks.' Fley leaned heavily against the bench. 'No warnings, no belongings, no known location code. It doesn't add up.'

'Unless the veritas did work and he *is* from over ocean.'

Fley was about to respond when the sound of boots crunching on the gravel path filtered through the tiny sound-grill she had secreted in the outside wall where the cupboard joined the floor. Below the kitchen, a small chamber had been excavated years before, accessed from a concealed door at the rear of her sleeping chamber. This served as a secure space for Women's Line business.

The footsteps faded and were replaced by heavy breathing. 'Day patrol,' Trooper Areth announced through the entrance sound-grill. 'Storm's approaching from the west. Close all vents.'

'Thank you,' they chorused.

'Who's with you, instructor?'

'Sannah the Storyteller and the traveller, Kaire.'

'Three in the bed. Isn't it a bit crowded?'

'We've given the traveller the bed,' Fley replied calmly, 'as is our custom.'

'Liar, I know you Brown women and your idea of hospitality.'

They remained silent. To respond would only antagonise.

'Sorry to interrupt, girls,' Trooper Areth called. 'I'll join you another time when I'm not so busy.'

Sannah listened to his footsteps and raucous laughter as he moved away from the dome. He appeared to be crossing the schoolyard so should be well away from Fley's dome by the time she emerged with Kaire. Although Wurn had given her permission to be outside during daylight, she preferred to avoid Areth in case he insisted on accompanying them to the canal. Should Kaire's belongings surface, she wanted an opportunity to look them over before returning to the trooper dome.

'Even if Kaire is a genuine traveller,' said Fley wearily, 'his lack of ID is no concern of ours. Besides, should you fail to find his pack this afternoon, if he cooperates, his white skin may yet save him from a lengthy stay in prison.'

Sannah nodded. 'Come on, let's grab some sleep while we can.'

An hour into the second search, Trooper Areth reappeared, ostensibly to warn them to take shelter from the fast approaching storm. Sannah was using the pole and Areth made a show of helping her lift it out of the water. Putrid debris clung to net and pole. He grimaced.

'Shall I leave it here, sir?' asked Sannah.

'No, take it back to the trooper do—'

'I'll bring it,' Kaire interrupted, stepping forward and taking the pole from Sannah. 'I'm going to check close to the banks again while it's still light.'

Areth turned to face him. 'No, you're coming with me.'

'Your trooper-in-charge gave me twenty-four hours to find my belongings.' Kaire retorted. 'Fourteen hours remain before I have to produce ID.'

Areth pushed Sannah out of the way, wrenched the pole from Kaire's hands and threw it into the canal. 'Fourteen, ten, two, what's it matter? You don't fool me, mate. Nothing down there 'cept a load of shit.' Pulling an electronic wristband from his tunic pocket, he quickly fastened it to Kaire's wrist. 'Best come quietly, mate. Those bands can give a nasty shock.'

Kaire looked pleadingly at Sannah as Trooper Areth pushed him along the path.

CHAPTER 5

Trooper-in-Charge Wurn rolled away from his lover and lay back against the pillow. 'Now my dear, I'm afraid we must return to the business I mentioned earlier.'

Sannah allowed a sigh to escape her lips and stretched her cramped limbs. 'Surely a trooper would be better placed for this important task?'

Wurn shook his head. 'I prefer to keep this unofficial at present. I've made some discreet enquiries, therefore I know this so-called pilot I have in custody isn't a prison escapee. No trace of a Commander Breta or a place called Sky either but they could be deliberate fabrications to disguise his real reason for being in the Brown Zone.'

'Perhaps he's been sent by a hostile foreign power.'

'Most unlikely my dear. A spy from over ocean would hardly risk exposure by claiming to have lost his ID. But don't worry, I'll uncover the truth about him and I'm determined to do it without bringing in the Security Department. Arrogant bastards, think they're the only ones with brains in this bloody country.' He thumped the mattress with his fist.

'Hush, don't spoil our beautiful afternoon.' She reached out and stroked his arm. 'I'll show him around, though I can't imagine he'll reveal anything useful to me.'

Wurn smiled and turned to face her. 'My dear, with your honey tongue you can charm anyone into saying anything.' He caressed her cheek and slid closer. 'Honey tongue, honey skin.' Fingers travelled south, lingering on warm breasts.

'Business over?' she asked.

'Almost.' He rolled a nipple between finger and thumb. 'I'd like to reward your cooperation in this assignment. So, my dear, if you uncover Kaire's true identity, I'll try to arrange an early release for your daughter from her working party.'

Sannah embraced him passionately, the image of her beautiful daughter Pia dancing before her eyes. Like other fifteen-year-old Brown-skins, Pia had been sent north to an agricultural working party three years earlier and had two more years to serve. It would be wonderful to have Pia home again, but Sannah queried whether Wurn really had the authority to secure a worker's release. Whatever the outcome, this assignment would at least provide an opportunity to meet with island members of the Women's Line.

The riverboat made slow progress down the canal, stopping every few minutes to disgorge passengers, mostly workers from the processing plant returning home after a long night shift. Sannah sat silently among them, half-conscious of the drone of conversation and the slap of water against the hull. This latest journey troubled her, not least because of the eradicator concealed in her money-belt beneath her message board and travel authorisation strip. By contrast, the visits to downstream villages the previous week had been a welcome change from every-night duties. Kaire had given her no cause for concern; on the contrary, he'd proved a good companion, interested in all she showed him and grateful for her company. She had looked forward to their subsequent trip to Island 1.

Then two nights ago Wurn had ordered her to come home and await further instructions. She'd returned Kaire to the trooper dome, but Wurn wasn't around and hadn't left a message for her to wait so she'd gone back to her dome. Shortly after her return, Wurn had arrived, out of breath as though he'd run all the way up the hill path. After drinking copious tumblers of water, he'd announced in a voice she hardly recognised his urgent need for her beautiful body. Their lovemaking had been rushed, lacking the preliminaries he usually enjoyed so much. Afterwards he'd held her in an embrace so tight she could scarcely breathe, all the while professing words of love interspersed with bursts of anger about impending loss. Puzzled, she'd tried to reassure him she knew how to look after herself, but he'd remained agitated and suddenly insisted they go outside.

In the shadow of the small trees at the rear of her yard, he'd given her a smaller version of the eradicators all troopers carried, saying he now suspected Kaire *had* been sent by a foreign power. Although Australia had long been left to her own devices (scarce mineral resources and encroaching desert had consigned international trade to a file on a history disc), certain neighbouring countries coveted the sparsely populated and fertile northeast coast. Dispatching a White official to the Brown Zone in the guise of a traveller could simply be a ploy to ensure unrestricted access to northern villages.

The riverboat was approaching the end of the canal. Sannah inhaled sea air, tasted salt on her tongue. Dismissing Wurn's qualms, she turned to her companion. 'Did you ever see such a beautiful sight, Kaire?'

'We're going out there?' he asked, staring at undulating blue water dotted with white caps.

She pointed to a large island in the eastern part of the immense bay. 'That's Island 1.'

'How many people live over there?'

'A few hundred—there are several villages. Once they were fisher people, now they serve as spotters.'

'What are they looking for?'

'Foreign vessels. This area is off-limits.'

'Why?'

She explained the dangers of the open ocean, the numerous reefs and countless submerged wrecks, the pirates from Asia that frequented these waters, hoping to commandeer any vessels in the area.

'I trust the spotters will recognise this ship!'

She laughed. 'Riverboats don't venture into open sea. I've arranged for us to spend the day sleeping at the inn. The sea-craft leaves at five.'

Kaire looked thoughtful. 'Sleeping during the day and working at night—has this always been the custom here?'

'Surely you've heard of the NLP?'

He shook his head.

Genuine ignorance or a desire to discover her opinion? she pondered.

Her eyes flicked over his youthful countenance: green eyes sparkling with health, unblemished skin, glossy black hair—he had not suffered two decades of darkness, this traveller from the place called Sky z59. A country, a zone, a village, she did not—*could not*—believe existed. Sky was above and beyond, blue-black firmament, backcloth of day and night.

She withdrew her gaze, selecting her words carefully. 'The Nocturnal Life Project was introduced here in the Brown Zone twenty years ago to improve productivity. It's been fairly successful, especially in the agricultural sector. Cooler night temperatures ensure field workers remain focused. Less heat stress equals more work, to put it bluntly.'

'Makes sense I suppose.'

She turned away, lifting her face to bright morning light.

Island 1 sparkled in early evening sun: patches of green ringed with white; splashes of turquoise, yellow and brown; vibrant colours assaulting the senses. The light intensified as the sea-craft neared high sand cliffs.

'It's a desert,' cried Kaire suddenly. 'Why have you brought me to this desolate place?'

'There's nothing to fear. What you see are sand dunes. Beyond the dunes are green fields, lakes and palm trees. This place is beautiful.'

'I apologise, I'm not familiar with island terrain.'

Sannah smiled. 'The island is a sanctuary for me.'

'Do you visit often?'

'Whenever I can.'

'Have you considered moving over here?'

'That isn't an option. I am the storyteller for Village 10.' She moved to the rail, turning her attention to the fast approaching land.

A small group of women had gathered on the jetty to meet the sea-craft. Fley's communication had aroused considerable curiosity among island members of the Women's Line. An unidentified traveller from an unknown place with a strange name and skin as pale as moonlight. Who could resist being late for work to greet this man? The trooper on duty would reprimand them but there would be no long-term recriminations. Trooper Cron was a weak man, and the women understood his needs.

A petite woman of middle years stepped forward as Sannah and Kaire disembarked. 'Welcome to the island, Sannah the Storyteller,' she said formally.

'Greetings, Maris the Spotter,' Sannah responded, raising her left hand. 'We must meet after the Tales,' she added in a low voice.

'We look forward to the Tales,' Maris replied.

Sannah stepped aside. 'May I introduce Traveller Kaire?'

'Welcome, Traveller Kaire,' said Maris, giving a slight bow.

'Welcome, Traveller Kaire,' the other women chorused, staring at the visitor with undisguised interest.

'A dome has been prepared for you,' said Maris. 'Follow me, it's not far.'

Reluctantly the island women stepped aside. 'Till the Tales,' they called as Maris escorted the visitors along the jetty.

The quayside was crowded with passengers waiting for the signal to board the sea-craft for the return journey. Maris skirted the throng, leading Sannah and Kaire up a narrow flight of steps onto a crushed shell path. After a short walk inland through palm groves and thin windswept scrub, they arrived at an isolated dome set among tropical foliage.

'No one will disturb you here,' said Maris, activating the door panel. 'Jade the Storyteller is away for a few nights.'

'When she returns, please thank her for the use of her dome,' Sannah replied.

Maris nodded and turned to Kaire. 'If you wish to rest before the Tales, the sleeping chamber has been prepared for you, sir, and there are fresh towels in the bath chamber.'

'Thank you for your hospitality,' Kaire responded.

Maris bowed and turned to leave.

'Kaire, you bathe first,' said Sannah casually. 'I'm going for a short walk with Maris. She wants to show me a new palm grove on the ocean side.'

'That suits me, I could do with a shower. My skin feels sticky.'

Sannah smiled. 'It's the salt air, the wonderful breath of the sea.'

Outside on the path the two women embraced warmly.

'Fley's message implied problems with the traveller,' said Maris. 'Is that why you're here?'

'Yes and no. Wurn asked me to bring Kaire to the island and show him around, so Fley thought it would be a good opportunity for other Line members to speak to him, observe his reactions to the spotter station and so on.'

'What do *you* think? Is he a genuine traveller or a government agent?'

'I honestly don't know.'

'I sense he could be from over ocean,' said Maris as they turned onto the path leading to the beach. 'If storm damage forced him to abandon ship and he entered these waters in a small landing craft, it's possible we missed it.'

'Then why not ask the *Liberty* to scan for a damaged vessel on her return journey?'

Maris slowed her pace. 'The *Liberty* is three nights overdue, Sannah, and we've had no word from the Kauri coast.'

The two women walked on in silence. The Line had lost two ships during the past year due to severe storms. Now the *Liberty* was the only vessel they possessed capable of making the journey to Aotearoa. If they were to continue sending escapees from political prisons to the settlement—a village established on the Kauri coast fifty years before by invitation of the Aotearoan government—a ship was essential.

Suddenly Sannah grabbed her friend's wrist. 'Suppose Kaire's ship intercepted the *Liberty,* and captured and interrogated her crew. Then he came to Village 10 posing as a traveller to obtain more evidence about the Women's Line.'

Maris frowned, shaking her head. 'An interesting idea, but I fear your imagination has led you astray. The *Liberty* may be small, but she's well equipped to defend herself. Had she been intercepted, Jade would have risked sending me a message.'

'Yes, yes of course she would. Forgive me, I'm not thinking straight.' She released Maris's arm and turned away.

'What is it, Sannah?'

'Ever since Kaire arrived I've struggled to quell the fear. I sense its presence even during meditation when I reach the inner place of still-ness. It lurks within and without, ready to pounce.'

'This is serious. I haven't seen you like this for years. What has this man done to you?'

'Nothing, he has done nothing. He's a pleasant, helpful, courteous young man. A perfect guest.'

'Then what are you afraid of?'

'The truth behind his tale.'

'The Women's Line will uncover the traveller's truth,' said Maris, squeezing her friend's shoulder. 'And who knows? It may even prove useful.'

Sannah managed a fleeting smile. Linking arms they walked on towards the ocean.

After a short walk along the beach, Maris departed, leaving Sannah sitting at the foot of a small tree, waiting for sunset to shade the cloud-less sky. As day transmuted into brief tropical twilight, it became impos-sible to resist the allure of deep ocean. Quickly discarding robe and sandals, Sannah waded towards the waves until they broke against her sweaty body, thick foam surging between her thighs. Inhaling deeply, she plunged into cool water. Beyond the breakers she swam effortlessly, relishing solitude and freedom. The ocean contained no boundaries, no troopers, no restrictions; she could swim forever, governed only by tide, wind and her own strength. Freedom here, too, from the golden sash that proclaimed her role as storyteller. Naked she was nameless and ownerless, a brown body caressed by silk-smooth water.

A full moon guided Kaire's footsteps along the beach. Sea wind stung his face and grains of sand grazed his sensitive skin, but he refused to turn back. Two hours had passed since Sannah had left the dome with Maris. He was reluctant to contact anyone in the village and raise the alarm unnecessarily. Sannah had said she was familiar with the island and may have simply decided to walk along the beach after visiting the palm grove.

A flutter of white cloth caught his attention. Running up the beach, he discovered a robe tied to the branch of a small tree, and at its base a pair of sandals. There was no sign of Sannah, no sound save the pounding of waves on sand, the cry of the wind.

'Sannah, Sannah!' he yelled, racing towards the ocean.

At the water's edge, he paused, called her name again and listened in vain for a response. Hitching up his robe, he waded cautiously into the dark ocean, gasped as swirling white water foamed over his legs and torso. Reluctant to proceed, he stepped back, tripped on a half-buried rock and fell headlong into damp sand. Scrambling to his feet, he tried to brush the sand from his hair before grudgingly retracing his steps.

'So you like the ocean after all,' said a voice from somewhere behind him.

'Sannah?' he queried, flicking wet curls from his face.

'Did you enjoy your swim?'

'I was worried about …'

'I'm not surprised,' she interrupted. 'It's dangerous swimming in these waters at night unless you know the currents. You should have told me you wanted to swim.'

'I was worried about *you*.'

'Why? I'm a strong swimmer.'

'You had been gone two hours. I was concerned for your safety.'

'The ocean is written in my history,' she said as she reached his side. 'I am at peace in her embrace.'

'Embrace? Not what I'd call pitting your strength against surging salt water.'

'Come,' she said grasping his hand, 'we must return to Jade's dome and dress for the Tales.'

They walked up the beach to the tree, Kaire gripping her hand tightly as though afraid she would disappear into the ocean again. *How strange*, she mused, *a man who commanded a ship yet appeared frightened of the ocean.*

'Such a beautiful night,' she exclaimed, lifting her face to the ebony sky. Reaching out, she untied her robe and slipped it around her shoulders.

Kaire turned his head, gazing wistfully at distant stars.

'Your wet robe must be very uncomfortable.' She touched his shoulder with cool fingertips.

'I can put up with it,' he replied, conscious of her warm breath on the back of his neck.

She slackened the sash around his waist and eased the robe from his shoulders. 'Pale as moonlight,' she murmured, her lips grazing damp skin.

He attempted to pull the robe back around his shoulders but she peeled away the cloth until both sash and robe fell to the sand.

'You are too beautiful to hide,' she murmured, her sea-softened hands meandering over his body, tracing the outline of bone and muscle, down to the crack of white buttocks.

He trembled.

'Don't be afraid, I won't hurt you.' Her fingers slid between his thighs.

'Why are you tormenting me?' he cried, pulling away from her.

'Don't I give you pleasure?'

'Yes, yes, as never before.'

'Then why resist?'

Despite his misgivings, he turned back to her beautiful body.

CHAPTER 6

Situated inland on the shores of a deep fresh-water lake, Village 12 was the largest settlement on Island 1, with a hundred domes radiating in semi-circles from an arc of white beach on the northern shore. Beyond the beach, a small promontory thrust into still blue water; at its head the white community dome shone like a beacon. Light spilled from the open doorway as a throng of blue-robed islanders entered for the Tales. In the middle of the dome, Sannah and Kaire were already seated on the central bench reserved for guests. A commotion drew their gaze to the end of the aisle where seven light-skinned children with blond curly hair were jostling with one another for places on the small front benches. Several island women soon intervened to restore order and Sannah observed Kaire's growing curiosity as the children reluctantly obeyed their mothers. Later no doubt, she would have to explain Trooper Cron's penchant for island women, and his complete disregard for mixed-race procreation rules. She thought of her tall golden-skinned daughter, a living reminder of her long-dead partner. How he would have rejoiced to see the beautiful woman Pia had become.

'Silence,' ordered the trooper on duty, rousing Sannah from contemplation. 'Silence for the music-makers.'

'Music?' Kaire whispered in her ear. 'What about the Tales?'

'Wait,' she mouthed as conversation and movement ceased around them.

A drum roll shattered the silence. A second drum roll followed, then the softer, sweeter sound of a pipe. Two drummers and four pipers, wearing waist-tied blue sarongs with garlands of white flowers around their necks, made their way slowly down the side aisle. Smothered with perfumed oil, their bare arms and torsos glistened in the bright dome light as though they had just emerged from the ocean. Reaching the dais, they split into two groups: drummers to one side, pipers in a small arc in front.

After a few moments, the sole female piper stepped forward, lifted her instrument and began to play a slow, haunting piece evoking the sounds of ocean and wind. Almost immediately the audience began to sway and moan. Currents of warm air drifted through the dome, flowers danced on the piper's breasts, white-laced waves rose and fell to rhythm of the sea.

Sannah felt Kaire's hand stroke her arm, heard a slow inhalation as he slipped beneath the surface and dived towards dream.

A palm-fringed island swam before his eyes. Entranced, he watched small Brown children play in shallow water, splashing one another, laughing, teasing. Close by, a group of women sat on a white beach mending fishing nets, chatting among themselves, pausing occasionally to check the children had not ventured too far into the water. Beyond the still lagoon, fishing boats rocked on a turquoise ocean swell.

'Harmony,' whispered a voice in Kaire's head. 'Clean air, clean water, plenty of fish.'

'Come closer,' he called. 'I can't see you.'

'Palm groves and vegetable gardens, food for everyone.'

'Where are you?' he asked, reaching out to touch the invisible.

'Untainted water, unblemished fruit on the trees, full-grown yams in the sweet soil.'

'Who are you?' he cried, arms flailing.

'I am the spirit of islands past and present. I am Mother and Father, the key to all life.'

'No, that's not possible,' he sobbed, his mouth filling with fluid, his lungs aching for air.

Strong arms lifted him as he surfaced, gasping for breath.

'Don't be alarmed,' Sannah whispered. 'The music can have this effect sometimes. Just take a few deep breaths.'

Slowly his breathing returned to normal.

'That's better. No harm done. Now you shall hear tales of islands past and present.'

He grabbed her arm. 'Don't make me dive down there again. I can't swim. I'll drown this time.'

'Hush,' she reprimanded, 'you'll miss the Tales.'

He sat back in his seat and mouthed, 'Sorry.'

At the rear of the dais, the music-makers sat cross-legged, instruments at their feet. In the centre someone had placed a stool but there was no sign of a storyteller. Sannah speculated on who would take Jade's place today, there being no other official storyteller on the island.

'Praise for the Tales,' said a voice behind her.

Turning her head, she was surprised to see Maris making her way down the aisle to the dais.

'Praise for the Tales,' the audience replied.

'Jade,' hissed a solitary voice as Maris climbed the steps to the dais.

Others took up the cry and the name reverberated around the dome.

'Silence,' yelled a trooper, rising from his seat by the entrance. 'Let Maris the Spotter speak.'

'Thank you Trooper Innis,' said Maris sweetly as the din subsided. She moved to the centre of the dais. 'Island people, tonight our beloved storyteller Jade cannot be here. She is with three spotters investigating the sighting of an alien vessel near the southern beach. She volunteered to help as sickness had reduced available personnel. The Tales could not be postponed for we have an important visitor.' She indicated Kaire with a broad sweep of her arm.

Those in front turned around to look at the stranger. His pale cheeks flushed.

'Traveller Kaire is interested in all aspects of island life,' Maris continued, 'so please make him welcome during his visit. Tonight I shall be your storyteller and as is appropriate for our visitor,' she paused to smile in Kaire's direction, 'I shall give a condensed version of our island history.'

A murmur of approval filled the dome. Maris waited a few moments for the audience to settle before raising her arms and drawing a circle in the air.

'Once we Brown people were islanders,' she said, lowering her arms slowly, 'scattered over the wide Pacific, living out our lives on a multitude of islands. Coral islands, sand islands, rock islands—these were our homes in ages past. We were fisher people, drawing many creatures from the generous blue ocean. Palm trees ringed the shores of our islands; we ate their fruit and drank their sweet milk. Gardens surrounded our villages; we grew vegetables and kept livestock. Some of our people undertook long voyages to distant islands. Sea-craft such as we have never seen and cannot imagine carried them across the ocean. Some returned to tell of their travels, others remained to people uninhabited islands.

'Wet season, dry season, wet season, dry season. For thousands of years we endured, a maritime people living in harmony with sea and soil.' Maris smiled then bowed her head.

'Twenty-twenty,' she cried, her head jerking upwards. 'Twenty-thirty, thirty-three, forty, forty-two, three, four, five—the ocean rose, inundated our islands, drowned our livestock. Cyclonic winds tore our palm trees to shreds, destroyed our houses, salt water tainted our gardens. Season after season, year after year, tsunami, death and devastation, until we were forced to flee all the small islands.

'We became wanderers, searching the ocean for new island homes. Some of the larger islands had been spared total destruction and for a time we were welcomed, the people content to share the harvest of sea and soil. Then the ocean rose again and storms battered the large islands. The people said it was our fault, they said we newcomers had angered our Mother and Father.'

Kaire's fingers clutched at Sannah's arm and she felt his body tremble. Keeping her gaze fixed on the storyteller, she gently rubbed warmth into cold flesh. *A sensitive soul, this pale-skinned pilot*, she mused, *perhaps exile also loomed large in the history of his people.* Apart from near neighbours, she knew very little about other countries. It suited the government to keep Brown-skins in relative ignorance. Education inevitably led to complex questions, questions the ruling Whites preferred not to answer.

'War broke out,' cried Maris, 'fishing boats lay idle on the beaches, weeds strangled village gardens. Many were killed, many starved. The survivors fled and sought sanctuary on the island continent. The government of the time called us 'environmental refugees' and housed us in temporary camps while they considered the situation. Later they allowed us to work as market gardeners and fisher people, supplying produce to the large urban areas that existed in those days. After several years we were given permission to stay permanently and allowed to leave the camps. We were given land to establish villages near the fields and waterways, in order to be close to our work.

'Years passed, we grew accustomed to the new land and no longer yearned for distant islands. Long before we heard the news, we knew in our hearts return was impossible. The ocean had triumphed, all our island homes had vanished beneath the waves.' Maris walked to the rear of the dais, head bowed. The audience waited expectantly for the familiar finale. 'Now we are island people once more,' she cried, spinning around, 'praise the great White government for allowing us to live on this beautiful island.'

'Praise the great White government,' the audience responded.

'Praise the Tales,' Trooper Innis called.

'Praise the Tales,' the people intoned.

'Be gone to your domes, the sun is rising.'

The islanders filed silently out of the community dome.

At the base of the promontory, Sannah and Kaire left the main path to the village and headed southeast following a narrow track through windswept bush. Walking in single file confined conversation to brief directions when the track divided, or warnings to take care where recent rain had exposed tree roots. The bush petered out after a while, replaced by newly planted palm groves. Here the track was wide enough to walk side by side so Sannah pointed out the different varieties of tropical ferns and flowering shrubs growing parallel to the palms. Kaire appeared indifferent to their beauty and kept his eyes fixed on the track.

'What did you think of the island Tale?' she asked finally, hoping to discover the reason for his atypical silence.

'Bizarre,' he answered curtly.

'In what way?'

He looked up, glancing sideways as though unwilling to meet her gaze. 'Primitive music obviously designed to induce a hypnotic state and the Tale itself, a weird concoction of fact and fable, similar of course to the Tale you told.'

Sannah considered her reply. She had no desire to antagonise or confirm his accurate analysis. 'The oral tradition has always played an important role in the history of my people,' she said proudly. 'Fable, myth, story, whatever name one applies, elucidates the past, enabling a better understanding of present realities.'

Green eyes widened, a smile flickered across his face. 'Spoken like a true politician, storyteller.'

'My people take no part in politics, we prefer a more traditional lifestyle.'

He shook his head and reached out to pluck a scarlet flower from a nearby hibiscus. 'For an exotic Pacific beauty,' he said, handing it over. 'May I one day earn your trust.'

She twirled the flower in her fingers before tucking it behind her ear.

Back in Jade's kitchen, Sannah prepared drinks, sprinkling yellow crystals in the tumbler intended for Kaire before returning to the living chamber.

'Maris has provided the best,' she remarked, handing over the tumbler. 'I'm sure you'll like it.'

Kaire sipped the cool golden liquid. 'Magnificent!'

'A little fruit as well?'

'No, thank you, this is the taste I wish to dream of.'

She smiled, sank down on a floor-cushion beside him and stretched sensuously, her toes pushing against the low table. 'It's a warm morning,' she said, loosening her robe.

'Yes,' he conceded with a sigh, kicking off sandals and wiping beads of perspiration from his forehead with the back of his hand.

'It would be much cooler in the sleeping chamber.'

'I don't want to sleep yet.'

'There's entertainment downstairs.' She grabbed his hand and pulled him to his feet.

Deep in the cool earth, she sat at a small table anointing her naked body with liquid from a stone jar. Delicious perfume filled the chamber. She heard his sigh, rose without a word, and climbed into bed beside him. Throughout their brief union she studied his face, her hands moving automatically over his smooth body. At the climax, he cried out, a spiral of sound twisting between them. She waited silently for desire to drain, eyelids to droop and close.

Moving hurriedly, she checked pupils, pulse and heartbeat for the telltale signs. The sunflower crystals had taken effect; Kaire would remain dreaming for several hours. Flinging on her robe, she hurried upstairs and abandoned the dome to the hush of day.

Outside a small dome on the edge of the village, Sannah paused to catch her breath before speaking into the sound-grill.

'Enter Sannah the Storyteller,' answered Line Leader Maris, releasing the panel.

Several women were already seated around the table in the living chamber. Sannah took an empty floor-cushion next to Maris.

'I apologise for the delay. The sunflower took much longer to work than I had anticipated.'

'Ah, the vitality of youth,' murmured a young woman.

'We welcome Sannah the Storyteller from Village 10 to our little gathering,' said Maris, lifting a small black box from her lap. She scanned each face to invoke a security screen before placing the box on the floor. 'I have grave news,' she began, voice wavering, hands gripping the edge of her robe. 'We have word at last of the *Liberty*.'

Fear glazed four pairs of eyes.

'Two nights ago a cyclone struck the Kauri Coast. Fortunately the villages sustained minimal damage but the huge seas created havoc for shipping. The *Liberty* capsized and sank within minutes. Several crew members and two escapees managed to launch the lifeboat and reached shore safely.' She hesitated, looking down at the floor. 'Jade was not among them.'

Hands reached out, palms pressed, an unbroken line of sorrow.

'Let us give thanks for the life of our beloved Jade,' Maris continued, struggling to control her emotions. 'Though she has been taken from us, the memory of her courageous deeds will live forever in our hearts. No law or trooper could crush her spirit—she was an example to us all. And we shall not be crushed under the weight of our grief, the Line must continue. Jade lived and died so that some day our people might know liberty.'

'Jade knew the truth,' cried Sannah, 'and the truth will set us free.'

The other women nodded in agreement.

Minutes passed, silence permeated the dome. Sannah longed to enfold Maris in a warm embrace but this was neither the time nor the place for personal grieving.

'Our Kauri friends have offered to build us another ship, but that will take time,' said Maris, her voice steady now. 'Under normal circumstances we could simply defer operations until the new ship's ready but there's talk of tightening security at the northern prisons. We've also received some disturbing information from our contact in security. Apparently the department is so concerned about the number of escapees in recent months, they've decided to build new prisons solely for political prisoners in the northwest desert.'

Desert. Each woman felt the fear rise up in her throat, saliva dry in her mouth, muscles knot in limbs and abdomen. Even if escape from these new prisons were possible, no one could live for long in the desert. Endless red sand dunes, devoid of food or water, nowhere to hide during the day from blistering heat and sleek silver trooper cars. Desert prisons could mean the end of the Women's Line, the passing of a dream.

Sannah alone heard another word and its meaning struck her a blow so powerful she almost cried out. *Betrayal, betrayal, betrayal*—the word juddered in her head, a hammer striking home truth. An image flashed before her eyes: a traveller emerging from the desert, a man calling himself pilgrim, who professed total ignorance of her people and her land, a man whose youthful appearance camouflaged knowledge and power.

'We must move quickly,' said a young woman named Desi.

Maris raised her hand. 'Before we consider our options, I must tell you these new prisons are to be built entirely underground to minimise the possibility of escape. Tunnels will connect each prison and there will be only one entrance at ground level.'

'Are we certain the information is authentic?' asked Sannah.

'Obviously the file has been verified, Sannah,' Maris answered curtly. Rebuked, Sannah bowed her head.

'We must ensure the most vulnerable prisoners never reach the desert,' Maris continued, 'so northern Line leaders are preparing a list. Any questions?'

'How much time do we have to organise breakouts?' asked Desi.

Maris sighed. 'Until construction begins, we can only guess the timeframe.'

The women exchanged glances. The task seemed hopeless; political prisoners were held in all six northern prisons.

'Now, is there anything else we need to discuss?' asked Maris, aware it was now an hour after curfew.

A stocky woman with short spiky hair leaned forward. 'Just a reminder to be on our guard if we meet that weird White traveller Sannah's brought over.'

'I was ordered to bring him here, Opal,' Sannah retorted, annoyed by the implication. 'Wurn asked me to find out why Kaire's visiting the Brown Zone.'

'The few travellers I've met were keen to talk of their adventurers,' said Maris mildly. 'Why don't you invite him to the spotter station, Opal? Express interest in his journey here while you're showing him the equipment.'

'Oh, all right, but I would prefer him to come alone.'

'Tread carefully,' Sannah cautioned. 'He's unlike any White man I've ever known.'

'And you have known many,' Opal muttered.

Sannah stiffened, glaring at Opal.

'It's time you were gone to your domes,' said Maris. 'The day patrol will be around shortly. I'll advise you of the next meeting when I've communicated with Fley.'

The women rose and left the dome singly at two-minute intervals.

'A word,' Maris called as Sannah, the last to leave, reached the door.

Sannah turned around. 'I'm sorry, Maris, but Opal just winds me up.'

'It's nothing to do with my sister,' said Maris, closing the door panel. 'I sense something is troubling you.'

Sannah hesitated, glancing around the chamber as though the other women were still present. 'Kaire said he came from the desert and now this prison plan has surfaced. What if our contact in the Security Department has been discovered and deliberately fed information in order to flush out anti-government agitators?'

'It's possible.'

'But you don't believe it?'

'No. Her scanner isn't linked to any other equipment and the copy she made of the file was transported by hand to the border group. Besides, so far the Line has failed to find anything to connect Traveller Kaire to the government.'

'Wurn hasn't found any link either, but …' Sannah's voice trailed off.

'Try to remain calm, Sannah, and don't forget, your trooper-in-charge is our ally at the moment. While you feed him scraps of information about Kaire's reason for visiting the Brown Zone, be they true or false, he'll continue to seek your help, which in turn keeps us in the loop.'

Sannah nodded. 'I'll do my best.'

Maris patted her arm. 'You'd better go now.'

'We've done nothing but Line work. Can't I stay and comfort you for a while?'

'Later. I need to be alone now.' Maris lifted a trembling hand to wipe away a stray tear. 'Alone with my memories and Jade's spirit.'

'She's free now.'

'Free as the birds that once followed our fishing boats,' said Maris wistfully.

Sannah leaned forward and kissed her friend's cheek. 'Be gentle with yourself and allow time to grieve.'

Maris raised her hand. The door panel slid open, revealing bright sunlight and cloudless blue sky. The palm trees Jade had planted many years before swayed in the ocean breeze. As she entered the palm grove, Sannah turned and waved but soon realised Maris could not see her. Grief had finally broken through. Her friend stood on the domestep, shoulders heaving.

CHAPTER 7

The spotter station had been built on a massive rocky outcrop at the northern tip of the island. From this vantage point spotters could observe both ocean and bay. Constant surveillance was essential along the Brown Zone coast. Pirates from neighbouring countries frequently entered these waters to raid merchant ships leaving mainland ports laden with produce for southern markets. At present, the escalating number of breakouts from northern prisons also concerned the authorities, as they believed most of the escapees were leaving the Brown Zone by sea. Recently a small, unidentified vessel had been spotted in northern waters but had eluded capture by a patrol boat. All spotter stations had since been ordered to increase surveillance.

Opal was proud of her position as chief technician. She had worked hard, studying night and day to pass the required examinations. Since her appointment, she had taken great care to maintain friendly relations with the troopers, but this did not mean pressing her brown flesh to their pale hides. Such activities she abhorred and willingly left them to others like Sannah. Opal preferred to use her wits and natural sociability to gain the troopers' trust and friendship. The men sent to guard the island were coarse, tough and not usually endowed with great intelligence. So occasionally when an alien vessel had been spotted, she would invite a couple of troopers to the spotter station (off-limits to all except spotters and the island trooper-in-charge) where she would demonstrate the obliteration equipment. Her guests would roar with delight when she blew a pirate ship out of the water.

In her free time, Opal often drank with troopers in the village inn, taking part in gambling and cracking crude jokes to cultivate mateship. Consequently, she rarely had to account for her movements around the island. She also acquired information useful to the Women's Line, for the men were careless with their remarks, particularly after several hours at the inn.

This morning Opal was alone at the spotter station, having despatched her assistants to the southern end of the island to investigate reports of an unidentified vessel sheltering in one of the coves. She sat facing her equipment, the programme set on automatic, her mind preoccupied with the White traveller. He was due to arrive within the hour and although they had not yet spoken she knew instinctively his intellect would match hers. She didn't expect a battle of wits but sensed it would be difficult, if not impossible to extract anything valuable from him, especially as both Fley and Wurn had failed in this regard.

The security system announced an unidentified person near the entrance. Glancing at the monitor, Opal saw an unfamiliar pale face and released the panel. 'Enter Traveller Kaire,' she said in a friendly tone, addressing her wrist-communicator. Before long he stood before her, a tall slight figure, white hands clasped over his money-belt.

'I greet you, Opal the Technician,' he said formally.

'Welcome to my station, Traveller Kaire. It's an honour to have a visitor from southern parts, a rarity around here I can tell you. Now what can I show you?'

Kaire glanced around the chamber. 'Well, first of all, I'm not certain what you do here, so perhaps you could explain?'

'I'd be pleased to, pull up a chair.'

'Thank you.' Kaire removed his head-cloth and shook out his long black hair. 'That's better, I'll never get used to this heat and humidity.'

'You're from far south then. Let me guess, the Isle of Tasman?'

'No, I'm from Sky z59. I'm not familiar with this Tasman.'

Opal stiffened. Everyone in the Brown Zone knew the name of the island south of the continent where the central government was located, even if it was out-of-bounds to all but high-ranking Whites.

'Sky z59', she said slowly. 'Can't say I've heard of that either so we're equal on that score. Never mind about geography, I want to show you the surveillance equipment.' She turned to the monitor. 'Ocean five six zero.'

An immense screen rose from behind the monitor, displaying an undulating mass of glistening blue water.

'Oh my stars!' Kaire cried, clutching his stomach.

'Does the ocean disturb you, traveller?'

'No, no,' he answered quickly, 'but I find the intensity of light troublesome after weeks in the gloom of a prison chamber.'

'Light is life, Traveller Kaire,' Opal said solemnly. 'You would do well to remember that.'

'I came to your land in search of light and life, but I have found a people shrouded in darkness.'

'Surely you understand the reasoning behind the NLP?'

'I wasn't referring to the Nocturnal Life Project,' he retorted, suddenly determined to speak his mind. 'I'm talking about apartheid, troopers ruling so-called inferiors, children in labour camps, travel restrictions. Why don't you people attempt to alter the situation? Haven't you ever heard the term revolution?'

Opal sat back on her chair, noting the blush creeping over pale cheeks, the flash of anger mirrored in staring green eyes. 'You're not from the south, are you?'

'No, I told you, I'm from Sky z59.'

'And that is where?'

'Many months travel from the Brown Zone,' he replied carefully.

Opal pressed a panel on the console to dim the screen. 'Why did you come to this country?'

'I came to observe your way of life, to increase my knowledge, satisfy my curiosity. I have tried to explain this to Sannah, Fley and Trooper-in-Charge Wurn, but no one believes me.'

'I believe you.'

'Thank you.' He sighed. 'Then perhaps you can clarify something?'

'I'll do my best.'

'Have you any idea why I have been brought to this island?'

'No idea, my friend.' She looked up, smiled. 'I may call you friend?'

'Of course.'

'I can make some discreet inquiries if you like.'

'That would be most helpful.'

She touched a pad and restored the screen. 'Now I must resume surveillance.'

He nodded, turning to face surging blue water.

'Zoom three zero zero,' she commanded. A small white dot in the centre of the screen instantly became a ship. 'No problem here, Kaire, this is one of ours, a patrol boat. See the blue and white emblem on the bow?'

'Yes. But tell me, why do you use ships for coastal surveillance when you have all this?' He indicated the banks of monitors around the chamber.

'This is a spotter station, we're not permitted to capture. We relay the position of any alien vessel to the patrol boat troopers and await instructions.'

'So the troopers decide whether to seize a ship and her crew?'

'Yes, although my orders are generally to destroy the vessels. My equipment can blow a ship sky high. You should see the explosions, they're quite spectacular.'

Kaire blanched. 'And the crew?'

'The patrol boat sometimes picks up suspected fugitives but pirates are expendable.' She turned to face him. 'I hold the record for pirate ships in these waters,' she said proudly.

Kaire rose abruptly and began to pace the chamber, holding his head in his hands.

'Are you ill?' Opal asked anxiously.

There was no response. She hurried to his side. 'Are you ill?' she repeated, standing in front of him to block his path.

He struggled to push past her but she stood firm, her stocky frame filling the narrow walkway between the banks of monitors. 'Kaire,' she said gently, 'tell me what's distressing you. I have medication here that can ease pain.'

'Not this pain,' he answered at last. 'This is the pain of disbelief, the pain of abhorrence.'

'I don't understand.'

'The messages I'm receiving are causing me acute distress.'

'Messages from your communicator?'

'No, no,' he cried, covering his eyes with his hands.

Opal seized his hands and pulled them away from his face. 'Who is sending you these painful messages,' she demanded.

He began to shake violently. 'You are,' he answered and fell in a heap at her feet.

It was an hour past curfew so Sannah would have some explaining to do if a trooper saw her. She walked briskly; Opal's message, although a little vague, had come with an urgent tag. After leaving the village, she headed straight for the coast then took an abandoned path that climbed up over the cliff face, disappearing periodically where erosion had eaten into the rock.

By the time she reached the spotter station two hours later she was exhausted. Breathing heavily, she stood on the pad waiting for Opal to admit her.

'Security clearance complete,' the system announced, releasing the door panel. 'Enter Sannah the Storyteller.'

'You look dreadful,' Opal exclaimed as Sannah staggered into the control room. 'Are you ill as well?'

'No, but that path's a killer. I'm not used to walking that far in daylight.'

'Sit down. I'll fetch you a drink.'

'Where's Kaire?'

'I put him in my rest chamber.'

Refreshed by the drink and the cool interior of the station, Sannah soon recovered. 'Now tell me what really happened. Your message wasn't clear.'

'I didn't want to alert anyone else as I'm not certain what we're dealing with here. In the middle of a conversation about my duties, Kaire stood up and began pacing the chamber, cradling his head in his hands. When I questioned him, he said he was receiving painful messages. I asked who was sending them but he collapsed before he could answer. He's been unconscious ever since.'

'You've checked …?'

'Of course,' Opal interrupted, 'and there's no sign of a cerebral implant.'

'Did you do a full body search?' Sannah asked tentatively.

Opal nodded. 'I noticed his navel was missing, which means there could be a communication device under the skin. But I couldn't feel anything and there's no scar tissue.'

'I know that, I examined him weeks ago.'

'I trust you reported it to Fley.'

'Of course.'

'And?'

'We haven't had an opportunity to pursue the matter.'

Opal sighed. 'Then we should do a more comprehensive examination now while we have the opportunity.'

'What do you suggest? We can hardly approach a White physician.'

'A friend of mine works in our medical dome. She has access to body scanners. I'll ask her to bring one up to the spotter station, say there's a problem with my digestive tract. Nothing serious but I want it checked quickly so I can recall my assistants if I need treatment at the medical dome.'

'A good idea, but shouldn't we wait until evening? We don't want your friend to be intercepted by a trooper.'

'There'll be no problem about curfew; she'll come in the trooper car. That's the usual practice here for day medical problems. And don't worry, the trooper will stay in the car. He can't enter the station without my permission.'

'I didn't realise you possessed such power.'

'Security is of prime importance here,' Opal replied curtly, turning to her communicator.

Ette the Healer found no trace of non-human material either on or beneath Kaire's skin. She suggested transporting him back to the medical dome for further tests but Opal was reluctant to bring his condition to the troopers' attention. The fear of unidentified disease carried by travellers remained paramount in Australia, especially among Whites, despite the passage of time since the last great epidemic. Ette could offer no medical explanation for Kaire's comatose state; his pulse, heartbeat and blood pressure appeared normal. If he didn't regain consciousness within two hours, she promised to return with medication to revive him.

When Ette had departed, Opal returned to her duties in the surveillance chamber, leaving Sannah to watch over Kaire. After a few minutes Sannah noticed a hint of colour on his smooth forehead.

'Wake up, Kaire,' she said, raising him gently to an upright position. His eyes remained closed and she was about to lay him back on the pillow when he stirred slightly and snuggled against her breasts, his lips nuzzling her robe.

'Kaire,' she said softly, 'it's Sannah. Can you hear me?'

Her question remained unanswered, his only response probing fingers pushing her robe apart. He began to suckle and she smiled, remembering her daughter's tiny pink lips and soft golden cheeks. 'Who are you?' she asked the man-child nursing at her breast.

Soon she became aware of movement, eyelashes fluttering against her skin, legs stretching. 'Kaire, can you hear me? It's Sannah.'

'How did you get here?' he asked, struggling to sit up.

'Lie still, you've been unwell.'

'What do you mean?'

'You fainted in the surveillance room. Opal carried you to her rest chamber and then contacted me. You've been unconscious for hours.'

'No, you don't understand. I had no choice, I had to shut down.'

'Shut down?'

'Sky defence mechanism.' He glanced furtively around the chamber. 'This place is evil,' he whispered. 'I can't stay here.'

'What happened this morning?'

'I learned the purpose of this station. Opal is a murderer. She kills fugitives and pirates.'

'What are you talking about? She's a technician. This is a spotter station.'

'Spot and destroy.'

'No it's a surveillance station. Government patrol boats deal with unauthorised vessels. Opal can't be held responsible for the troopers' actions.'

He drew a hand across his forehead. 'Perhaps I misunderstood. I felt very hot when I arrived. The trooper car cooling system had broken down.'

'I trust Opal offered you a cold drink?'

He shook his head.

'No manners, that woman. I'll fetch you a drink now.'

'I'm not thirsty now.' He leaned forward and kissed her lips.

'Waking the patient with a kiss,' Opal remarked from the doorway. 'Unorthodox medicine, whatever would Ette say?'

'I have recovered now,' said Kaire brightly. 'It was the heat. I apologise for any inconvenience I've caused. We can continue our conversation if it's convenient.'

'I'm afraid it isn't,' Opal replied. 'I have an important report to prepare.' She smiled. 'But I'm sure we can arrange another visit.'

'Thank you.'

'Sannah, I'll see *you* in the surveillance chamber in five minutes when you're properly clothed.' Opal turned abruptly and left the chamber.

Kaire leaned towards Sannah. 'Is she angry because I kissed you?' he asked in a low voice.

'No, it's not that.' Sannah fastened her robe. 'She's upset. We, she received distressing news last night. A friend has died.'

'I didn't realise. I wouldn't have come if I'd known.'

'Don't worry about it, Opal invited you here. Now try to get some rest.'

'Not here, I can't stay here.'

'You know the rules, we can't leave until late afternoon.'

'I beg you,' he pleaded, clutching her robe.

'I'll see what I can do.'

Sannah closed the door panel behind her and walked down the corridor to the surveillance chamber. 'You wanted to speak to me?' she asked from the open doorway.

Opal remained hunched over her equipment.

'Opal?'

'In a moment, I'm communicating with the patrol boat.'

'Sorry.'

'No sightings at all today, Trooper Dene. Yes, I was aware of the cyclone in southern waters. We were indeed fortunate it missed us. No, Trooper Dene, I have had no communication from Jade the Storyteller. Report 2 terminated.' Opal placed the communicator back on the bench below the surveillance screen.

'What will you tell the troopers when it becomes obvious Jade isn't coming back?' asked Sannah, walking into the chamber.

Opal swung around. 'Allow me to deal with it. A drowning will be reported, that's all you need to know. Now, about your behaviour.'

'My behaviour?'

'With Traveller Kaire. Your intimacy was observed, Sannah. How could you engage in such acts when he has yet to be medically cleared? Who knows what diseases he's carrying.'

'We each have our ways of using White men to help the Women's Line,' Sannah answered carefully. 'I don't question why you drink and gamble with the troopers.'

'I …' Opal began. 'Oh, forget I asked, this is a difficult time for all of us.'

'Especially Maris.'

'I'll take care of her.'

'I know you will.'

Opal turned back to the screen. 'Ette should investigate Kaire's collapse as soon as possible. A seasoned traveller doesn't faint away like a weak woman or become nauseous at the sight of ocean rollers. I can call for the trooper car now.'

'I thought you didn't want to alert anyone?'

'There's nothing amiss with him now. I'll ask Trooper Robi to deliver him to the medical dome and advise him it's the next place on Kaire's itinerary.'

'All right. I'll stay here till curfew's over and then make my way back to the village.'

'Go with Kaire, no need for you to waste time here.'

'Won't the trooper wonder how I got here?' asked Sannah.

'No, his mind will be focused on the end of his shift and the game we've organised. Trooper Robi is a good mate, he never asks awkward questions.'

'I'll go and tell Kaire we'll be leaving soon.'

At the medical dome, Ette the Healer subjected Kaire to numerous tests but could find no evidence of any known disease. She concluded his collapse had been caused by heat stress and recommended he carry water at all times. As for his lack of a navel, she remained perplexed and eventually asked him directly.

'I've looked like this for as long as I can remember,' he said, patting his smooth stomach. 'It's quite common in my community.'

Ette was forced to conclude it was a localised genetic abnormality.

CHAPTER 8

The riverboat pilot guided his craft towards the jetty, taking care to avoid the weed that grew in abundance around the ancient piles. The journey from the coast had already been delayed by a sandstorm whipped up by strong easterly winds. Both passengers and crew were keen to return to their domes as more storms were expected later in the morning.

Sannah leaned on the rail watching her village emerge from the early morning mist, relieved to be home at last. The island visit had unnerved her. Jade's death, the loss of the *Liberty*, Kaire's collapse at the spotter station … each incident had ignited another flame of fear. She wanted to immerse herself in tales, forget the grim present for a while.

'Isn't that Trooper-in-Charge Wurn?' Kaire asked suddenly, pointing to a figure leaning on the jetty rail.

She followed the line of his finger and shuddered, recalling the purpose of her travels. Despite Wurn's confidence in her, she had failed to uncover anything new about Kaire.

'I don't imagine he's come to ask how we enjoyed our excursion,' she said quietly.

'Well, I won't be so cooperative this time. I intend to request another search of the canal.'

'He may not agree to that.'

'Then I shall ask to speak to a higher authority. Travellers must have some rights in this country.'

She smiled. 'I suggest you mention Officer Keo of the Security Department. Wurn and Keo are the best of enemies.'

The riverboat locked onto the jetty. Sannah lost sight of Wurn in the crowd and dismissed his presence as coincidental; he could easily have detained them as they disembarked. At the end of the jetty she steered Kaire away from the main route to the village and cut across a patch of sodden ground to the canal. A pungent odour hung in the sultry air; they did not linger.

Beyond the concrete barrier that indicated the end of the canal, the narrow path petered out in a patch of waist-high grasses.

'Watch out for rocks in here,' Sannah called, pushing through the grass. 'Only a few metres of this, we'll soon reach the hill path.'

Suddenly she crouched down in the grass and motioned Kaire to her side.

'Get down,' she whispered. 'There's someone sitting beside the path up ahead.'

'Is that a problem?'

'Could be. Wait here.' She loosened the knife from her thigh-band and crept forward. Reaching the patch of low scrub bordering the start of the hill path, she cautiously raised her head.

'Welcome home,' called a familiar voice.

Sannah ran towards the path where Fley sat in the shade of a large boulder, a basket at her feet. 'What the Sun are you doing here?'

'Resting my weary bones before attempting the hill path. What have you done with Kaire?'

Sannah gestured towards the grass. 'He's back there, waiting while I discover who's planning to waylay us.'

Fley smiled. 'No harm intended, I assure you. I heard the riverboat siren and wanted to be certain our paths crossed. I knew you'd go straight home as it's almost curfew.'

'Why didn't you meet us at the jetty or communicate?'

'Personal contact seemed the better option.'

Sannah leaned forward. 'Is something wrong?'

'No. But we do have what you might call an interesting development.' Fley extended her hand. 'Help me up, I've been sitting too long.'

She grasped Fley's wrist and hauled her upright. 'Well, what is it?'

'Yesternight I discovered a couple of my students playing with some unusual objects.' Fley bent and picked up her basket. 'I believe Kaire's belongings have surfaced.'

Sannah activated a security screen as they sat around her low table finishing the cold drinks she'd brought from the kitchen.

'Now I've caught my breath,' said Fley, placing her tumbler on the table, 'I'd like to share my news.' She looked over at Kaire, seated opposite. 'I have in my possession some items I believe belong to you.'

Kaire leapt to his feet. 'You've found my backpack?'

'Not exactly.' Fley turned to the basket beside her and took out several narrow tubes and a small sealed package. 'Do you recognise these?'

Kaire leaned over the table. 'Yes, the tubes contain tablets called sustenance, what you call food.'

'And this?' She passed him the package.

He quickly broke the seal, extracted several small discs and a tiny black strip. 'At last, proof of my identity.' He handed them to Fley.

Fley studied the discs, turning them over, holding them up to the light, tapping them with her fingertips. The metal was unknown to her, the symbols on each disc meaningless. She passed the discs to Sannah and picked up the black strip. Devoid of markings, it resembled the recycled strips used by village recorders. 'Do any of these contain your identity?' she asked.

Kaire pointed to the black strip. 'All the information you need is on my computer strip.'

Fley looked puzzled. 'This gives you access to a computer?'

'Yes, but it also works independently. Allow me to demonstrate.'

Fley passed him the computer strip, staring incredulously as he pressed his lips to the smooth surface. The device glowed green. 'Can you both see the screen?' Kaire asked, turning the strip towards them.

They nodded, watching, mesmerised, as a face materialised—a face that looked remarkably like an older Kaire.

'Greetings,' said a voice similar to Kaire's. 'My name is Breta. I am the Commander of Space Station Sky z59.'

Sannah and Fley exchanged glances.

'Pilot Kaire, one of my senior pilots, has requested permission to visit Planet Earth for a few months and this has been granted. He carries no weapons, either on his ship, his land transporter, or his person. He is interested in experiencing your way of life first-hand before continuing his primary voyage. Rest assured he comes as an observer only and will not disturb Earth-life in any way. He is twenty-six years old and in peak physical condition. Medical examination will substantiate this. Although Pilot Kaire has developed a fascination for Earth through many years of study, I must stress that we at Space Station Sky z59 generally have no interest in your planet. We are primarily concerned with the exploration of galaxies far from Earth and its neighbour moon. However, we would welcome contact with you. Pilot Kaire will advise how this can be achieved. We Sky People are descended from a group of scientists comprised of representatives of all races, who left Earth in the twenty-two thirties to search for a new unspoiled home. After a fifty-year sweep of nearby galaxies failed to find a planet capable of sustaining human life, the surviving travellers decided against returning to Earth and instead re-colonised an abandoned space station. Since then Sky z59 has served as both a home and a base from which to launch our craft. Sky People remain convinced other living planets exist and dedicate our lives to this search. I leave you with this message: Earth and Sky—one universe—one people—one creator. Message created Earthyear 2399.'

Sannah sat motionless, her mind filled with images of spaceships, moon buggies, white-suited astronauts leaving the first human footprints on alien soil. Historical matter, consigned to discs for use in school domes. The promise of life elsewhere in the universe, the solution for an overpopulated and damaged planet had been a beautiful dream, but a dream shattered long ago by the harsh realities of environmental and economic disasters.

She glanced at the computer strip still held between Kaire's fingers, blank now except for a tiny green dot. 'An incredible tale, Pilot Kaire, but one I find hard to believe.'

'I do not believe the tales you tell,' Kaire countered. 'In fact, I know they are a distortion of historical fact.'

'Tales always contain a grain of truth.'

'So you admit to tampering with the truth?'

She bristled at his harsh tone. 'I don't create the tales, I'm only the storyteller.'

Beside her, Fley continued to stare at the floor, seemingly lost in thought or perhaps unwilling to participate in a heated exchange.

The computer strip slipped from Kaire's fingers and lay inert on the table. 'I get it, the storyteller's function is to tell lies.' Pale fingers grasped the edge of the table. 'Lies that convince the oppressed their situation is hopeless, irreversible, the fault of some imagined deity.'

'Imagined deity? What the Sun are you talking about?' Sannah retorted, her voice rising sharply. 'You know nothing of Brown Zone life.'

'Enough, Sannah,' Fley scolded, slapping the palm of her hand on the table. 'Explain your statement, Kaire.'

'I was referring to the bizarre beliefs I've heard expounded here. Punishment for the sins of past generations, an inherited flaw that justifies servitude; songs to appease the ocean and encourage the soil to produce healthy crops; hypnotic music to make the audience receptive to untruths. Your people are led to believe a deity called Mother Nature caused Earth's oceans to rise up, crops to fail, diseases to multiply.' He leaned across the table. 'Come, Fley, do you take me for a fool? It's Earthyear 2399, I'm sure you know as well as I do what caused climate change and subsequent environmental chaos on this planet.'

'Greed, corruption, hatred, war,' said Fley quietly. 'The vices of the human race. These are what destroyed the paradise we had.'

Kaire sat back on his floor-cushion. 'So why do Storytellers tell lies?'

'We have no choice,' replied Sannah bitterly. 'Our government considers the Tales an essential element of Brown Zone administration. Storytellers are trained to deliver a distorted version of history, which warrants our people's continuing low status in Australian society. A constant diet of such tales reinforces White superiority and ensures compliance.'

'What about children?' Kaire turned to Fley. 'Are they also fed propaganda in the guise of facts?'

Fley nodded.

'So how did you two learn the truth?'

Fley fiddled with her robe. Sannah squirmed on her floor-cushion. 'Well?'

Fley looked up. 'Suffice to say some of our people possess authentic knowledge and pass it on to others.'

'One day all our people will know the truth,' said Sannah passionately. 'Then liberty will be within our grasp.'

Kaire picked up one of the tubes, twisted the base and extracted a slim cylinder, which he shook vigorously. 'Good,' he murmured as a red glow spread over the cylinder. 'No damage from the water.'

'That isn't sustenance,' cried Sannah. 'Are you threatening us?'

'It's a communicator, not a weapon.' Kaire handed it to Sannah. 'I can use it to help you pass on knowledge.'

Sannah frowned. 'How?'

'On Sky z59 we have meteorological records, scientific reports and media reports dating from Earthyear 2020 to 2230. Documented facts on global warming, climate change, glacier and ice cap melt, inundation of low-lying coastal regions and islands, loss of major cities, increases in tropical diseases. In fact, everything you need to banish ignorance. If I explain your situation to Commander Breta I'm certain he would agree to transmit the relevant programmes.'

'Your commander's message said you would not disturb Earth-life,' Fley reminded him.

'I know, but how can I remain a dispassionate observer now that I understand what's going on here? Let me help enlighten your people. Then they will no longer submit meekly to tyrannical troopers or swallow Storytellers' lies. Revolution need not be a long time coming.'

'Oh, if only change were that simple,' Fley muttered.

'You underestimate me,' he persisted. 'I can help your people in numerous ways. In my ship I have highly sophisticated technology that could be used to monitor trooper movements and infiltrate their communications systems.'

'We'd be one step ahead of them at last,' said Sannah excitedly.

Fley glanced at the cylinder still glowing in Sannah's hand. 'How do we know your communicator isn't recording everything we say in order to report back to the Security Department or Trooper-in-Charge Wurn?'

Kaire sighed. 'You don't, and I'm not sure anything I said would convince you my offer of help is genuine. All I can ask is that you trust me.'

Fley remained silent, eyes fixed on a point above his head, one hand cradling her chin, the other tucked under her large stomach. Beside her, Sannah struggled with conflicting emotions as the atmosphere grew thick with tension.

Fley moved her hands, smoothed her robe. 'Your assistance would be much appreciated, but I must ask you not to communicate with your commander until I've conferred with others.' She looked into his eyes. 'Kaire, you aren't the first person wanting to effect change here.'

'I thought as much. You have my word I won't contact Commander Breta, but if that's not sufficient, keep my communicator until a decision is made.'

Fley nodded. 'It won't take more than a few hours.'

'Right. Soon as you give the word, Fley, I'll visit the trooper dome and present my credentials.'

He placed the communicator on the table.

'It might be better if you didn't mention Sky z59,' said Sannah. 'Both troopers and the government are paranoid about aliens.'

'I am not an alien.' Green eyes flashed fury.

'Sannah means foreigner,' said Fley quickly. 'White Australians always think foreigners want to take over the country or impose their culture.'

'I've come to observe and learn. You heard Commander Breta.'

'Observe and learn,' Sannah muttered to herself. 'A scholar from over ocean.'

Both Fley and Kaire looked baffled.

'Would it be possible to alter your identity files?' she asked.

'I'd need authorisation from Commander Breta, but I don't foresee any problems.'

'How long would that take?'

'Two hours at most.'

'Good. The sooner you're officially registered the better.'

Fley scratched her head. 'Sannah, what are you proposing?'

'A little role-play,' she answered mischievously, her dark eyes shining.

Fley reached out for Kaire's communicator and slipped it into her pocket. 'I'll accompany you to the trooper dome this evening and explain how I discovered your belongings.' She levered her bulk from the floor-cushions and picked up her basket. 'Now I must get home before the day patrol comes around.'

'Stay here,' said Sannah. 'It's too late to risk the hill path. If Trooper Areth's on duty he's bound to check here first. It amuses him to wake me by shouting through my sound-grill.'

'Thanks.' Fley smiled and sank back down on the floor-cushions.

When at last they were alone, Kaire pulled Sannah into his arms. 'I need you storyteller,' he murmured. 'Tell me a tale of silken thighs and moist hot lips.'

'Sleep is what I need right now,' Sannah replied, planting a chaste kiss on his forehead and detaching herself from his arms. 'But tomorrow, I promise you, when stars dust the night sky, tales will flow sweet as honey.'

True to her word, after dealing with trooper dome business, Sannah returned to her sleeping chamber and employed her skills in the art of lovemaking. The joining of bodies was an easy task for her: lips, hands and limbs all moved to her command. She was a perfect pleasure machine, finely tuned, able to adapt to the other's flesh. Traveller or trooper, friend or foe—she could accommodate them all.

But these couplings meant nothing—they were simply an extension of her role as storyteller. Within her dome she deliberately created an atmosphere of calm contentment; gentle words pacified, fingers caressed world-weary flesh, honeyed tongue soothed away cares until the other was putty in her hands. Lulled into security her lovers forgot rules and regulations, the barriers of race and class tumbled as they lay their heads on feather-soft breasts. Loose-lipped they poured out troubles, fears and secrets while she stroked their fevered brows and murmured lines of sympathy. When the time came to leave, her lovers sighed and promised a swift return before walking out into the nightly struggle of Brown Zone life.

Sweet lies she told, sweet dreams she supplied. She was the storyteller.

So why, she asked herself as she lay naked on the bed waiting for Kaire to return with cold drinks, had she abandoned her long-held role tonight? Down in the normally cool sleeping chamber, the atmosphere was thick and moist, the aftermath of passion not the usual perfunctory sex. Her skin was damp with the heat of it; her hair stuck to neck and forehead. Between her thighs sweetness oozed, his fluid and hers blended, a powerful concoction. Intermittently her body shuddered and sensation overwhelmed. Aftershocks—mind and body reliving those all too brief moments of ecstasy, her sated flesh yearning for more. She marvelled at these sensations, her ability to feel so intensely.

Kaire was the stuff of dreams—young, beautiful, passionate. And innocent, for he was unschooled in Brown Zone ways. Lies, deceit, violence—these were not part of his experience. From what he had said as they walked down the hill path with Fley, she sensed his life had been an ordered one, or was until he arrived in Village 10. An innocent abroad, he wandered wide-eyed through the chaos of maltreated Earth.

Questions swirled in her mind: What did he hope to find in this hostile environment? Could Australia be the homeland of his ancestors? Commander Breta had said Sky People had no interest in Earth, so why was Kaire attracted to a doomed planet?

Nothing made any sense. She didn't understand why long-dormant emotions had stirred. Despite a reasonable day's sleep, her weary body yearned for rest but slumber would be a long time coming, for now the fear was thickening in her.

'Help me!' she cried, burying her face in the pillow. 'I am the storyteller, but I have no tales for him.'

CHAPTER 9

The communicator reverberated through the dome. Reluctantly Sannah left her bed and made her way upstairs. The message panel flashed red, indicating an urgent call.

'Sannah the Storyteller,' she answered formally.

'Get your Brown butt down here,' ordered Trooper-in-Charge Wurn. 'There are questions I want answered.'

'Yes, sir, I'll be there in twenty minutes.'

The connection closed. She stood by the panel pondering what could have caused Wurn's brusque tone. The last time they met, he'd been perfectly amiable—he'd even apologised for neglecting her since her return from the island and promised to visit soon.

'Who was it?' Kaire asked the moment she returned to the sleeping chamber.

'Wurn. I've been summoned to the trooper dome.'

'I sense trouble.' He jumped out of bed. 'I'll come with you.'

'No, it's better if I go alone.'

'Then I should contact Fley.'

'No sense in alarming her. I'll call in at the school dome on my way back.' She turned away and headed for the bath chamber. 'I'm just going for a quick shower.'

When Sannah emerged from the bath chamber, Kaire had dressed and stood near the bed, his hands clasped around his communicator.

'Take this,' he urged, pressing it into her hand. 'I don't trust Wurn.'

'How do I activate it?'

He twisted the cylinder and pointed to a red dot. 'Press three times to contact me on my computer strip.'

'Thanks.' She turned to retrieve a robe from the rail.

'There's something else, Sannah.'

'Yes?'

'I love you.'

She stood facing the rail, one hand clutching her robe, the other curled around his communicator. How many lovers had whispered those words in the heat of passion? How many times had she smiled in response, thanked them with sweet kisses, sweet lies? Those three words symbolised happiness, hope and the possibility of a brighter future. For others, perhaps, but not for the storyteller—hers was a world of make-believe. Love affairs were part of the illusion, a brief respite from reality, but were shattered in the fierce light of day.

'Many men have uttered those words,' she said wistfully, turning to face him, 'but I have only known true love once.'

'Twice, this makes it twice.' He bent down, gently kissing her lips.

'I must go now,' she said softly. 'Trooper-in-Charge Wurn is waiting.'

She draped her robe around her body, secreting the communicator within its folds.

'Go carefully, my love,' said Kaire, standing aside to let her pass.

At the western edge of the marketplace, Sannah encountered an inebriated Trooper Areth. After greeting him formally she hurried away, but he followed her through the maze of stalls, calling out insults, lunging at her whenever the crowd impeded her progress. At last she reached the path leading to the trooper dome, gathered up her robe and sprinted to the entrance.

Once inside, the trooper on duty ordered her over to the security pad. The panel opened immediately.

'You took your time,' Wurn snapped, grabbing her wrist and pulling her inside his chamber.

The panel closed behind them and Sannah heard the faint whirr of a security screen. After pushing her into a hard plastic chair, Wurn retreated to his upholstered multi-position swivel seat.

'I have a few questions, storyteller,' he barked, pounding the work-module with his fists, 'and I expect truthful answers. This is no time for tales.'

'No, sir.'

'A few weeks ago a death occurred on Island 1, a drowning near the southern beach. Trooper Cron forwarded the report to me as you were visiting the island at the time. The victim was Jade the Storyteller. A friend of yours, I believe?'

Sannah sat motionless, her eyes riveted to the hard line of his jaw. 'Yes,' she answered after a lengthy pause, 'Jade was a good friend.'

'Did you meet with her during your visit?'

'No, she was away helping the spotters investigate the sighting of an alien vessel, I believe.'

'That's correct.' Wurn sat back in his seat and flexed his thick fingers. 'No body has been recovered. Don't you think that odd?'

'Not particularly, the currents in that area are very strong.'

'So you're prepared to accept that Jade drowned?'

'What are you implying?'

'Answer my question.'

'Yes, I accept Jade drowned.'

'And yet the sea was calm that night.'

Sannah remained silent, hoping to avoid further discussion.

'Let me show you.' Wurn turned his monitor to face her. 'Records for the last two weeks. No storms in the area, no reports of rockslides or other seismic activity. The rest of the spotter party returned safely. Their report of Jade's death was submitted without delay. Unfortunately I don't believe it.'

'May I ask what the report said?'

'It maintains Jade slipped and fell through a crevice into a blow hole.'

'There are several along that coastline.'

'Yes, and Jade would certainly have known their location.'

Sannah shrugged. 'Accidents happen.'

'You can't offer any other explanation?'

'No, sir. I didn't see or communicate with members of the spotter party either before or after Jade's death. Trooper Cron can confirm my movements on the island.'

Wurn's features softened. 'I suppose it could have been just an unfortunate accident.' He sighed. 'I must admit I'm in no mood to stir up trouble and I'd prefer not to leave any loose ends.' He leaned across the work-module. 'I've been transferred, Sannah, I leave in two nights.'

'Two nights!'

'I'm as shocked as you are, my dear. I had expected to stay here for another month at least, but the trooper-in-charge of Village 300, Asian Zone, has fallen ill. I'm to replace him immediately.'

'I shall miss you, you're a good man, Wurn.'

'And you are a good woman, Sannah. I'll take fond memories with me.'

She smiled. 'Has a new trooper-in-charge been appointed yet?'

'Transferring your affections already?'

'Of course not, I'm just curious.'

'Trooper Gage from Village 400, Asian Zone, but he can't take over for a few weeks. Trooper Areth will take charge in the interim.'

Sannah stiffened. 'Areth!'

'You have nothing to fear from Areth, my dear. He's not interested in women, White or Brown.'

'I beg to disagree.'

'Sannah, I've seen him with my own eyes. I assure you Areth is a man-lover.'

'Then why does he claw at my skin every time we meet?'

'Perhaps you misunderstand his gestures.'

'Misunderstand, never. I know what men want.'

'Of course you do, my dear.'

'But I don't want him,' she added in a small voice, 'under any cir-cumstances.'

Wurn sighed, stood up and walked over to her chair. 'It distresses me to see you upset,' he said, placing his hands on her shoulders and dropping a kiss on her forehead, 'so I'm going to send you away until Trooper Gage arrives. You can visit the river villages for a few weeks. I'll activate an order now. Take Senior Pilot Kaire with you. He can interview some river people for his research on the NLP. But make sure you steer him towards reliable villagers, these academic types can cause trouble if given free rein. The last thing I need is a central government inquiry into a region I've just spent years administering.'

'I'll make sure he doesn't interfere in things that don't concern him,' she said, remembering an incident the previous year when Wurn's attention had been drawn to the river. A trooper had found two escapees from a medium-security prison dome hiding aboard a riverboat headed for the port. The men, Brown Zoners with a long criminal history, had tried to implicate the boat's pilot, Borne the Transporter, maintaining he was part of a clandestine group helping prison escapees flee the country. Borne had been subjected to lengthy interrogation but managed to convince Wurn he knew nothing of such a scheme. The two escapees had been eradicated soon afterwards but despite extensive covert investigation the Women's Line had failed to uncover the source of the leak.

'Take care, my Brown beauty,' Wurn murmured in her ear.

Sannah looked up and smiled. 'I thank you with all my heart for giving me leave to visit the river villages. I'll never forget this kindness.'

'Think of it as a parting gift, dear woman,' he answered, kissing her gently.

Deep in thought, Sannah walked away from the trooper dome, ignoring the sounds and smells of the busy marketplace. A change of command could prove problematic for the Women's Line; Wurn had been a liberal ruler. If the new trooper-in-charge were keen to impress his superiors, long-abandoned regulations could be enforced, minor misdemeanours punished. They would all have to be vigilant in the coming months.

CHAPTER 10

A trooper car transported Sannah and Kaire to the produce terminal where they boarded a fully laden riverboat destined for the river villages. Along the river, five communities had been established for over a century to farm the rich alluvial soil. Crops were transported by riverboat to Village 10's produce terminal where they were either loaded onto merchant ships for the journey south or taken straight to the adjoining processing plant.

Sannah was pleased to discover the pilot was her old friend Borne. The crew was busy checking the cargo of building materials destined for River Village 3, which gave her plenty of time to visit the control chamber and catch up with Borne's news. Since her last visit to the river, Borne and his partner Cela had been blessed with twins, a rare event in Brown Zone villages these nights. Multiple births flouted the one child policy applicable to Brown-skins and strictly enforced by the White authorities. If discovered during pregnancy, excess fetuses were compulsorily aborted. Cela had been fortunate; the White physician in charge of the village medical dome had been taken ill during her pregnancy and was not replaced for some months. The Brown healers left in charge had gleefully ignored the two images evident on Cela's scans.

Towards midnight, the riverboat was nearing River Village 2 where Sannah wished to disembark, so she left Borne to supervise docking and went in search of Kaire. She found him sitting on the main deck with one of the crew, laughing and talking loudly. An empty bottle of tropica rolled around the crewman's feet.

'Go and grab your pack, Kaire,' she said curtly. 'We'll be docking in a few minutes.'

'Prefer to stay here.' Kaire picked up the bottle. 'Great stuff, tropica. Nothing like this on Sky.'

Sannah extended a hand and hauled him to his feet.

'Oh my,' Kaire exclaimed, clutching his head. 'Stars all around, just like in space.'

Sannah turned to the young man sprawled on the deck. 'Sorry about this, he's not used to strong drink.'

'No problem, I love to see Whites lose control,' he said, reaching for the empty bottle and tossing it into the water. 'He's full of shit but it sure was entertaining.'

Sannah glared. 'I don't think Borne would approve of your drinking on duty. I'd get back to work if I were you.'

A high-pitched siren arrested further conversation and sent Kaire sliding to the rail where he vomited into the brown water.

Night descended over the river as Sannah propelled Kaire along the jetty. She had to get him to the inn, out of sight before a trooper spotted them and began to ask awkward questions. Her travel authorisation strip might be genuine but she didn't want to be accused of deliberately intoxicating a government official.

The village hummed with activity now daylight curfew had ended. Sannah took Kaire's hand as they neared the marketplace. She couldn't risk losing him in the crowd. Docile now, he trotted along beside her like a well-behaved child. He hadn't spoken at all during their walk from the jetty and had kept his head down, eyes focused on the path.

A fruit stall piled high with colourful produce drew Sannah's attention. She noticed the queue was fairly short, decided a few minutes delay wouldn't hurt and steered Kaire towards it.

'Why have we stopped?' he asked. 'I thought we were going to the inn.'

'I have to see a friend first.'

'Here?'

'She's the stallkeeper.'

Kaire looked across to the stall. A large woman was serving a customer. 'Your friend is pale like a trooper,' he remarked loudly.

'Hush.' Sannah jerked his arm. 'Keep your observations to yourself. It's rude to discuss mixed parentage.'

'Sorry.'

They shuffled forward.

'Two mangoes and a few bananas please, Haika,' said Sannah.

The stallkeeper looked up, dropped her tongs and seized Sannah's hand. 'My dear friend, what brings you to the river?'

'I'm escorting a southern scholar,' she answered, indicating Kaire.

Haika selected the least damaged fruit and placed it in Sannah's basket. 'Come to my dome at five, we can share the dawn meal.'

'I look forward to it.' Sannah smiled and handed over a token.

Hours later, when Kaire had slept off the effects of tropica, Sannah took him for a walk beside the river well away from the crowded village. Moonlight guided their steps for there were no lights on the edge of these flood plains. The river drifted by, tranquil now after the passage of numerous craft.

'It's so peaceful tonight,' she remarked. 'The field workers must be busy elsewhere.'

'Elsewhere,' Kaire repeated, tilting his head to the night sky.

'Are you thinking of the world you left behind?' she asked, drinking in the beauty of distant stars.

'Some of my friends will have already embarked on their primary voyages,' he said wistfully. 'They'll be sitting at the controls of their ships, savouring the splendour of space. A million stars illuminating the ebony sky, vapour clouds drifting around unidentified planets, the eerie light of a distant sun. And somewhere out there, a living planet: green lands, blue seas and white clouds waiting for our people. Exile is a lonely existence but the history of grim centuries propels us onward. To return to the Mother planet would be absurd. She is dying, raped by her rapacious children.'

'Evolving, not dying,' said Sannah, looking down at living water bathed in silver moonlight. 'If we can learn again to live in harmony with soil, sea and sky, there will always be a place for us on Mother Earth.'

A phosphorescent insect brushed Kaire's upturned face. Startled, he stepped back from the bank into a patch of long grass.

'I hope you're right,' he said, reaching for her hand. 'But whatever happens in future years, I'm glad I came here now. I have no regrets.'

'No regrets,' she murmured as they sank down to a soft bed of rain-washed grass.

Sannah paused to catch her breath before addressing Haika's sound-grill. Her friend lived with partner Rive in a small dome built into a steep hill adjacent to a banana plantation. Looking across the small garden to the river below, Sannah noticed a riverboat making its way upstream. *A perfect place to observe any unusual activity on the river,* she thought.

'What a magnificent view,' said Kaire, joining her in the shade of the dome entrance. 'Well worth the climb.'

'Definitely. And there's good quality fruit next door too.' She indicated the plantation. 'Wait until you taste it.' She turned to the sound-grill and gave their names.

The panel opened instantly. Haika stood in the doorway, her left hand raised. 'Greetings, Scholar Kaire and Sannah the Storyteller, welcome to my dome.'

'Thank you, Haika the Stallkeeper,' Kaire replied, inclining his head.

Haika stood aside to let them pass. 'Make yourself comfortable and listen to some music while I fetch the food.' She waved her hand towards the screen on the opposite wall. 'Rive will be up in a moment, he's just showering.'

'I look forward to sharing a meal with you both,' said Kaire politely. 'I've already tasted your fruit and may I say it's delicious. I've never tasted such sweetness.'

'Thank you, sir. I trust you'll enjoy the meal I've prepared this morning.'

Sannah smiled, knowing her friend would have selected the very best bananas from the plantation for her guests.

'I'll help you carry the platters,' she said, following her friend into the tiny kitchen adjoining the living chamber.

'Why have you come to the river villages?' Haika asked, her voice muted even though the music programme automatically activated a dome-wide security screen.

Sannah explained the imminent change of command in Village 10.

'It seems we shall all be closely watched in the coming months,' said Haika. 'There's been increased traffic on the river in recent weeks including large numbers of troopers. The riverboats have all been heavily laden. Rive says the cargo is predominantly building materials and drilling equipment. At River Village 5 it's loaded onto land carriers, which depart in a westerly direction. The old super-path cuts through the range due west of there so it seems more than likely they're heading for the desert.'

'The prison building plan must be going ahead sooner than we thought.'

After the meal, Rive began to gather up tumblers and platters, but Sannah made no move to assist him. The information about recent river traffic had reinforced the plan she'd conceived during the climb to the hillside dome. Conversation regarding riverboats had led to discussion of other modes of transport, with Kaire clearly determined to prove the superiority of his land vehicle over trooper cars. Sannah had learned that apart from the capability of much greater speed, the all-terrain transporter also contained a scanner to pinpoint geological features both above and below ground. With a range of a thousand square kilometres, it would be possible to scan the northwest desert for evidence of a building project if Kaire agreed to retrieve the transporter and travel further inland.

'Why don't you leave that until after curfew?' she suggested. 'Let's go outside and enjoy the light while we can.'

Rive left the pile of dishes and followed her outside to a small rocky outcrop overlooking the river.

'Do you ever tire of this view?' she asked.

'Never, but you haven't brought me out here to admire the river, have you?'

Sannah shook her head. 'I want to ask a favour.'

'Go ahead.'

'I need transport upriver.'

'No problem, I can take you to all three villages.'

'I need to be taken as far upstream as possible.'

'Can you tell me why?'

'I want to retrieve some equipment hidden in the hills.'

Rive raised his eyebrows. 'I can transport you as far as River Village 5. Beyond that the river's too shallow for riverboats. But I can get a message to Sheela, and ask if young Ro can take you further upstream. His small craft is suitable for navigating the upper reaches.'

'I don't want to put your grandson at risk.'

'You won't. If he's ordered to shore for any reason, you have permission to be on the river. Besides he's a born riverman, knows every twist and turn, every concealed landing place.'

'Good.' She looked beyond the river to distant hills emerging from early morning mist. 'The hills northwest of River Village 5 … how long would it take to reach them on foot?'

'It's a fair distance, say two or three days if you travel during the cooler hours.'

'We can take our time. I have permission to be away for three weeks.'

'You're taking Scholar Kaire?'

She paused, considering her response. Fley had stressed the importance of concealing Kaire's true identity, even from other Women's Line members.

'He won't be a problem, Rive, I know how to handle White men.'

Rive grinned and turned his attention to the river.

CHAPTER 11

Troopers were much in evidence at the various landing places on the journey upstream. Rive's boat was a familiar sight on that stretch of the river so they passed by unimpeded, troopers barely acknowledging its passage. A short distance beyond River Village 5, Rive cut the engines and drifted as close to the bank as he dared. Before long, a small punt piloted by a fair-haired boy skimmed across the water and drew alongside the riverboat. Sannah and Kaire emerged from the stern cargo hatch and slipped over the side into the punt. In the control chamber, Rive opened a side panel and exchanged a few words with his grandson before restarting the engines.

Sandbanks made navigation tricky as they travelled towards the hills but young Ro was well acquainted with the river and already a skilled pilot. After an uneventful journey, he deposited his passengers on the riverbank some ten kilometres northwest of his village.

Early morning mist dissipated as they walked away from the river, following a narrow path Rive had told Sannah led to a deserted dome. They planned to shelter there during the hottest part of the day, resume their journey in the late afternoon and continue until nightfall. Sannah would have preferred to travel under cover of darkness but considered it too dangerous. She was unfamiliar with the country beyond the river and Kaire's communicator could only guide them in the right direction. Human eyes were needed to negotiate the huge boulders, tangled undergrowth and shifting sands Rive had said typified this region. There were no villages or prison domes in the vicinity so they were unlikely to encounter troopers during their daylight trek.

After three hours brisk walking through bone-dry country, they spotted a dome in the distance.

'Thank the stars for that,' Kaire exclaimed. 'I don't think I could cope with much more of this glare. My head's pounding.' He slackened his pace and wiped his face and neck with a corner of his head-cloth. 'Do you think we'll find any water in there?'

'I doubt it. Rive said the dome hasn't been occupied for years.'

'I can see why. Is all the country away from the river like this?'

Sannah scuffed dry soil with her sandal. 'This is a vast brown land ringed by a narrow strip of green. Every year the desert moves closer to the ocean. Some day I fear this entire continent will consist of nothing but sand.'

'Surely something can be done to halt the desert's progress?'

'I'm afraid not. The damage was done centuries ago. Europeans ruined this country when they cleared the forests and introduced sheep and cattle. They should have listened to the land.'

'We should all have done that.'

'We?'

'My people also played their part in the decimation of this planet.'

'Do you know where on Earth your ancestors came from?'

'I have no idea.'

'What about their names, their language?'

Kaire shook his head.

'How sad to have no history, no stories of past good times, no knowledge of what made you.'

The abandoned dome sat on a low ridge surrounded by drifts of sandy soil. The entrance door panel yielded easily to a few gentle prods, its locking mechanism long since disconnected. Inside, the chambers were much as the former inhabitants had left them but there was no sign of food, drink or clothing.

'I'd hoped to find some stores here,' said Sannah, dumping her backpack on the dusty floor. 'We could do with extra.'

'Don't worry, I have plenty of sustenance in the transporter.'

Sannah grimaced at the thought.

'There's nothing wrong with sustenance,' Kaire retorted, grabbing her waist and pulling her towards him. 'It made me what I am and you don't seem to object to that.' He kissed her fiercely, his dry lips grazing her mouth.

'No, Kaire,' she reprimanded when he finally released her. 'We must eat and then rest. We have many hours of walking ahead of us.'

'Hard woman,' he muttered.

They slept fitfully on the sagging bed, conscious of every creak and groan as it shifted beneath them. Below ground the air was thick with the dust they'd disturbed and numerous insects scuttled around the floor. By late afternoon they were on their feet again and heading towards the distant hills.

Walking at a steady pace, they paused only occasionally to drink from the water flask. The ground remained dry with sparse vegetation. There was no sign of water or any trace of human activity, past or present. No birds flew across the clear blue sky and not even a lizard skittered across the burning soil.

The landscape altered as they climbed into the hills; sandy soil giving way to smooth rock, mineral-stained and pockmarked. A hot wind blew incessantly across the ridges, drying their skin and increasing thirst. When the sun began to sink behind the hills Sannah resigned herself to spending the night huddled on exposed rock. There seemed little chance of finding shelter on these slopes.

'Another half hour and we must stop,' she called to Kaire, who was lagging a few metres behind. 'We can't risk a fall in the dark.'

'Give me a moment, I need to relieve myself.'

She sat down, grateful for a brief rest. After a few minutes she turned around, expecting to see Kaire right behind her. The hillside was deserted. Puzzled, she cupped her hands to her mouth and shouted his name repeatedly but only the echo of her voice reverberated around the ridge. *How odd*, she thought, *no sound of feet slipping, no cry for help*. Scrambling to her feet, she began to search the smooth rock for large crevices.

Suddenly she heard her name and saw his head and shoulders emerge from the rock a few metres up the slope.

'I've found water,' he called.

The crevice, just wide enough for an adult to slip through, opened out to a broad granite shelf littered with large boulders. She followed Kaire to the shelf edge and stared with disbelief at the scene below. A series of curves and ridges wound down a narrow chasm to a small pool, dark with deepening shadow.

At the water's edge, she kneeled and scooped a handful into her mouth. It tasted sweet; the pool was probably fed by an underground spring. She filled the water flask before peeling off her dusty robe and joining Kaire in the pool. Together they splashed and laughed like small children.

Cleansed and refreshed, they sat beside the pool eating the last of the fruit strips and cheese. Darkness soon enveloped still water and black boulders pressed against night sky.

'I saw a cave further up,' she said, reaching for her robe. 'That would be better than sleeping out in the open.' She rose and hoisted her back-pack.

'I could stay here forever,' said Kaire with a sigh. 'I never thought to experience such beauty.'

'You'll change your mind in a few hours. The sun will bake this rock come morning.'

'I know, but it does no harm to dream of a perfect world.'

'Light breezes, warm sun, gentle rain.'

'Tell me a tale of such a place, storyteller.'

'Later.' She moved towards the cave.

He hurried to join her. 'Weave your words around me,' he whispered, his breath tickling her cheek. 'Tell me a tale of Aotearoa.'

She answered quickly, drawing her mouth over his, flicking her tongue over moist flesh. Hands stroked his smooth chest, soft thighs pressed against firmness. The backpack fell to the ground. Releasing his mouth, she sank to the smooth rock, pulling him with her.

In the shallow cave, Sannah lay still beside her sleeping lover, her thoughts swirling. She wanted to believe Kaire's odd question had been prompted by curiosity alone—perhaps he had read of Aotearoa during his study of Earth's history and wanted to visit now he was close by. But why did he imagine she was familiar with that country? Her people had come from other, smaller islands. This he knew, this he had heard during the Island Tales. She wanted to trust him completely as Fley appeared to but experience had taught her otherwise. Hours passed. She longed for dawn, for the opportunity to locate his land transporter. Then perhaps, she would learn more truths about this mysterious man.

Early in the morning they emerged from the cave and trekked north along the smooth granite ridge. In places the rock had weathered, several times they narrowly avoided slipping on loose pebbles. Grasses grew in the cracks between slabs of rock and lichen laced the base of deep depressions. As day drew to a close, foliage disappeared and a hot wind flung dust in their faces.

'How far now to your transporter?' she asked when they stopped to rest in the shade of a boulder balanced precariously on the steep slope.

Kaire consulted his communicator. 'About twenty kilometres north-west.'

Sannah peered into the distance. The rocky slopes extended as far as she could see. This wasn't the landscape *she* would have chosen to begin a trek on foot. 'Why did you decide to leave the transporter in this difficult terrain?'

'I didn't come this way. The landscape will change soon I imagine. I left the transporter on the side of a low ridge covered with short brown grass and a few small bushes.'

'Were there any trees?'

'None living.'

She sighed. 'It's as I feared, the desert has crossed the Divide.'

'What's the Divide?'

'A range of hills that separates the fertile coastal strip from the arid interior.' Her fingers brushed the dry rock. 'Long ago the slopes were covered with forest, creeks flowed year-round and birdsong rang through moist mountain air. It was a magic place they say. A place to restore body and soul.'

'Yes, I have experienced such environments.'

She stiffened. 'How is that possible?'

'Haven't you ever heard of Computer Generated Environments?'

Sannah shook her head.

'Sky people find CGEs essential to maintain psychological stability as we live in a completely manmade environment. I don't think you are able to understand how different our worlds are.'

'You're right, but if your people have known no other life, wouldn't it seem normal?'

'Of course it seems normal to us,' he replied, 'but one can't help but wonder what it would be like to have a real experience of the environments on Earth, to crave the texture of a leaf, the breath of wind.' He sighed and rose to his feet. 'It will soon be dark. We must press on and find a less exposed place to rest.'

But darkness descended swiftly and they were forced to spend the night huddled on the naked hillside, buffeted by desert wind.

By early morning the wind had abated, easing their climb along the ridge. After several kilometres, the granite petered out and the landscape became as Kaire had recalled. He scanned with his communicator frequently, remarking with relief on the diminishing distance. But with only a few hours' walk remaining to reach the transporter, a high-pitched whine suddenly replaced the communicator's muted hum.

'What the Sun?' Sannah covered her ears with her hands.

'Distortion.' Kaire adjusted the controls until the noise abated.

'What do you think caused it?'

'External influence, I imagine—metallic perhaps or magnetic. I've managed to override the interference.' He smiled. 'Not far now. I'll just scan again to ascertain the transporter's exact location.'

Sannah flattened a patch of grass with her feet and sat down. Idly she twisted a brown stem around her fingers, remembering childhood games, grass rings, flower bracelets. The grass cut into her hand and wincing from the pain, she watched a single drop of blood roll across her palm.

'Stop scanning, Kaire,' she demanded, leaping to her feet. 'Stop at once.'

'Don't be ridiculous, I'm getting a perfect signal.'

Launching herself at his stooped figure, she threw him to the ground. The communicator flew from his hand and rolled away down the steep slope.

'Lie still,' she hissed, pushing his face into a thick mat of grass.

He struggled to raise his head.

'Still, I said.' Her strong arms pinned him to the ground. She listened carefully, hearing only the wind whining through long brown grass, the rustle of leaves in a nearby bush. 'We're safe now,' she whispered, releasing him. 'The danger has passed.'

He raised his head slowly, spitting out pieces of grass and soil. 'What danger?' I saw nothing and heard nothing, either before or after you attacked me.'

'I didn't attack you, I was protecting you.'

'From what?'

'I heard something down in the valley. It could have been the wind but I …' She showed him the smear of blood across her palm. 'This is a sign I can't ignore.'

'Superstitious nonsense,' he muttered half to himself.

'No, a premonition.' She hesitated, pondering how much to reveal. 'I've had them before, in dreams.'

He looked puzzled. 'But you weren't sleeping just now.'

'No but …' How to explain what she didn't fully understand? She took a deep breath. 'The first time, I woke with a start, convinced a riverman's son, a boy I knew only by sight, had been seriously injured on the canal. Discrete inquiries confirmed the accident had occurred at the precise moment of my dreaming. Several months later, I woke screaming, reeling from graphic images of my friend Nami, crushed beneath a trooper car. That evening, news of Nami's death buzzed around the marketplace. After this, I determined to suppress my subconscious and began to experiment with mind-altering drugs. But the premonitions persisted, proving correct every time, and I began to dread going to bed at day. In desperation I booked into the medical dome for a cerebral health test. The results revealed nothing abnormal. The medical officer recommended a holiday and despatched me to the rest and recuperation centre on Island 3.'

She paused, leaned towards him, and said softly, 'On the island I abandoned myself to the ebb and flow of the ocean. Healing waves washed over me and eventually I was able to acknowledge and accept the gift of prophecy, if that is what it is.'

Kaire scrambled to his feet. 'So you believe it was this psychic power that warned you of imminent danger?'

'Yes. I believe there are troopers down in the valley.'

'I've never believed in the supernatural.'

'Then how do you think I knew you were sheltering outside my dome?'

He shrugged. 'You heard a noise, opened the door and found me.'

'No, I woke with a start, and knew immediately someone was outside.'

'I'm not entirely convinced, but whatever the cause of your apprehension we'd better go and retrieve my communicator and then get going.' He began to walk down the hill, eyes fixed to the ground.

'Come back,' she cried, running after him. 'The troopers could be tracking it.'

'Unlikely. It would take sophisticated technology to track my signals and I haven't seen any evidence of that in the Brown Zone.'

'What about the interference, that could have been troopers?'

He froze in mid-stride. Unable to stop the downhill momentum, Sannah ran into him and they fell to the ground, a mass of flailing limbs. Tangled together they rolled down the steep hillside, coming to rest in a clump of bushes.

'What is it?' Sannah asked when she had caught her breath.

'I thought I heard a high-pitched noise coming from down in the valley.'

Sannah raised her head slightly and saw Kaire's communicator lying in a patch of dry grass just beyond her reach. She gestured towards it but he made no attempt to move.

'Listen, there it is again,' Kaire said softly.

'I can hear a bird calling, that's all.'

'It's not a bird, it's someone whistling.'

'How can you be certain?'

'Whistling always hurts my ears.'

'I've never heard a trooper whistle.'

'It may not be a trooper.'

'Who else would be this far west?'

'I don't know but you were right. Please forgive me for doubting you.'

She smiled, resisting the urge to kiss his mouth.

Suddenly they heard three short, sharp whistles followed by a long answering trill. Grasses rustled in the breeze and insects buzzed as they strained to hear the sounds of human movement.

'Can we get going?' Kaire asked after a few minutes. 'Whoever's down there doesn't appear to be coming this way.'

'No, we stay here. I can still sense their presence.' She pressed the palms of her hands into her forehead. 'Heading this way, two of them.'

They both heard the swish of dry grass, the murmur of conversation. A wide strip of sunlight penetrated the bushes illuminating their light-coloured robes. Exposure was imminent.

'Hold on a minute,' said a young man's voice from the slope below. 'What's this?'

'Put that box down,' ordered a second, more mature voice. 'Put it down slowly, it could be a tracking device.'

A beam of light shot through the grass.

'I said slowly. The fucking troopers will know our exact position now.'

'Sorry, Gers.'

'How many times must I tell you not to use my name? Come on, we gotta get out of here before they find us.'

'Coming.'

The voices faded but just when Sannah thought it was safe to move, a cry of pain broke the silence enveloping both hillside and valley.

'I imagine Gers or his companion fell over,' she said softly.

Kaire nodded. 'My communicator won't be much use now. That flash of light we saw indicates the remote receiving device is broken.'

'They did us a favour then.'

'I don't follow …'

'The troopers won't be able to track us any further. I just hope we can locate your transporter before they come looking for those two.'

'Don't worry, we'll be safely aboard before then. I managed to get a preliminary reading before you knocked the communicator out of my hand.'

'Sorry about that, but it seemed the only way to stop you.'

'Forgiven. Fortunately I have a spare communicator in the transporter.'

They backed out of the bushes and began to climb, but then loud groans and a string of expletives sent them scurrying back to the relative safety of the bushes where they lay motionless waiting for the thud of footsteps. No one approached. Puzzled, Sannah slowly parted two low branches and peered out. There was no sign of the two men. Then the voice of the one called Gers floated across the valley, fainter this time.

'Come on, mate, get up. We can't go back to the desert. You know as well as I do they weren't going to let us builders leave when the prisons are completed.'

A high-pitched hum suddenly echoed through the valley.

'Oh my stars, what was that?' asked Kaire, wincing from the pain in his ears.

'Detcom, it's a personal detection device implanted under the skin of all prisoners. Escapees have to slit their skin to deactivate it. The fall must have re-activated it. I'd say they're at least five hundred metres away now.'

'Can they hear us?'

'No.'

'But the troopers will hear, won't they?'

'Yes. Freedom is a feeble flame for some.' She crawled out of the bushes and started up the steep slope.

CHAPTER 12

The silver transporter, cylindrical with two transparent dome-shaped bubbles one behind the other, ascended the ridge at high speed. Kaire was determined to put as much distance as possible between them and any troopers in the vicinity. Behind him, Sannah slumped in the passenger seat, exhausted from their daylight scramble over the hills. She had taken several sustenance tablets but hunger pangs still rumbled around her stomach. Above her head sunlight flashed across the bubble, increasing her discomfort.

In the end the transporter had proved simple to locate, the foliage Kaire had used as camouflage mostly disappeared, blown away by the strong winds that blew constantly around the hills. The exposed passenger bubble had been visible from a fair distance even to Sannah's untrained eyes. Fortunately, close inspection revealed no one had tampered with the vehicle and despite the presence of fine dust coating the exterior Kaire had managed to start the thrusters after only three attempts. The transporter had moved slowly at first but quickly gained velocity.

'Are you feeling all right?' he asked suddenly.

'I'm okay. Just not used to travelling at such high speed.'

'High speed! Compared to my ship this is walking pace.'

'Walking pace will do me!'

Kaire laughed and turned back to the control panel.

They sped west, dry soil churning beneath wide wheels, smothering the empty land with a blanket of dust. Sannah calmed her nerves by focusing her attention on the intelligence gained from the fugitive prison builders. It had come as no surprise when Gers had said the construction gangs would be the first inmates. The government would hardly risk details of the new prisons reaching the villages; there had been too much leaked information in recent months. The complex must be almost due for completion, she surmised, which meant political prisoners could be transferred soon. The Line would have to move fast. No plans had been made to sabotage one or more of the transports but Fley said the subject had been mooted during recent Line leaders' communications. Before long, the Line would know the new prisons' exact location and could calculate the route the transports were most likely to take.

Kaire had readily agreed to scan for signs of underground structures once they were well away from possible trooper interference. After their almost-encounter with the prison builders, there had been little point in disguising why desert scanning was needed. However, Sannah had not disclosed the possibility of intercepting prisoner transfers. Line operations of that magnitude must remain secret.

Extensive scanning and subsequent interpretation of data would take several days, according to Kaire. This didn't present a problem, they weren't expected back in Village 10 for two weeks, but Sannah remained reluctant to transmit either the prison builders' information or the desert location despite Kaire's repeated assurances his communicator was secure.

'When scanning is completed, how long will it take to get back to the village?' she asked, considering it might be better to return home early.

'Depends how far west we travel but probably no more than a couple of days.'

'That's incredible.'

'No, just advanced technology.'

'How long do you intend travelling today?'

'Until nightfall.'

She glanced at her timepiece. 'That gives us about two hours.'

'We'll both need a break by then.'

'Yes, it is rather cramped in here.'

'Two hours more, then we'll stop for exercise and sustenance.'

'Will you start scanning tonight?'

'No, it would be safer to scan in daylight, scanning beams are visible for a considerable distance at night.'

'I doubt there's anyone out here.'

'What's the rush? I thought you wanted to stay away the full three weeks.'

'I must speak to Fley as soon as possible.'

'No problem, use the transporter's communicator.'

Sannah hesitated. 'I need to speak to Fley in person.'

'How many times do I have to tell you my communications system is completely secure?'

'I'd rather speak to Fley in person.'

'Oh, I get it, you're concerned I'll overhear confidential matters. Sannah, I am your friend. I want to help your people. What must I do to convince you this is my truth?'

'It's not that. I *do* believe you but …'

'But what?'

'It's too risky to involve you in this. You could be killed or worse, imprisoned for the rest of your life. What would your commander do if he lost a senior pilot?'

Kaire swung around in his seat, gripping the headrest until his knuckles turned white. 'He would do nothing.'

'Surely he'd send another ship to investigate?'

'Aren't you listening? I said he would do nothing. I am but one among many.'

Her gaze shifted from hunched shoulders to pale face and what she saw disturbed her, for his eyes betrayed immeasurable sadness. 'Maybe, but you are important to me.' She stroked his cheek. 'I need to return home as soon as possible because I believe the desert prisons could soon be ready for inmates. Why else would those builders have escaped? Once your scans have confirmed this, my er …' She paused, needing a moment to choose her words carefully. 'My group will make certain arrangements.'

He nodded. 'Don't worry, we'll set off the moment I've finished.' He turned back to the controls. 'I'll activate the automatic pilot pro-gramme so I can analyse the information while we travel.'

She leaned forward, wrapped her arms around his shoulders and kissed the back of his neck.

'Alas, we shall not go anywhere at all if you distract the pilot,' he remarked in mock-serious tone.

'I do beg your pardon, Senior Pilot Kaire,' she replied, releasing him. 'I promise not to distract you until we get home.'

Kaire's scan of the northeast desert revealed the presence of an extensive underground structure with tunnels running close to a long-abandoned uranium mine. Surface construction appeared minimal.

As promised, Kaire restarted the thrusters as soon as the onboard computer confirmed the data load. He had decided to risk transporter travel to within ten kilometres of Storyteller's Hill, using darkness and the hills west of Village 10 as cover. Sannah, familiar with these hills, advised he should find somewhere to conceal the transporter on the western slopes. To ensure no one observed this unorthodox return, he planned to send a false storm alert to the village's trooper dome, plus a message advising they were returning early due to his suffering heat stress and would be catching the first riverboat they encountered heading for Village 10.

After twenty-four hours' continuous travelling, they were now approaching high ground. Kaire dimmed the lights and set the night vision. The instrument revealed a range of hills covered with dense medium height foliage, dissected at intervals by deep gullies.

'You'll need to take extra care further up or we could fall into a gully,' Sannah warned as the transporter began to climb the lower slopes. 'They're broader near the top.'

Kaire reduced speed. 'Would it be possible to conceal the transporter near the summit?'

'Yes, the shrubs are quite thick in places.'

'Right, let's go and take a look.'

'I said take care!' she cried as they emerged from the scrub onto a narrow strip of stony ground barely wide enough for the transporter.

Kaire laughed. 'Leave the driving to me. I'm going to follow the edge of this gully, much easier than pushing through bushes.'

Sannah gripped the seat and forced herself to remain silent.

Before long they were compelled to make a detour where a recent storm had eroded the slope. Thick foliage slowed their progress for a while but eventually gave way to sparse scrub. They climbed steadily towards the summit, small branches scraping the transporter's side, stones rattling against the base. Then without warning, the ground gave way and they found themselves lurching over a gully rim. Kaire fought to control his vehicle as it skidded down the steep slope. A tangle of bleached roots finally broke their fall. The transporter shuddered and stopped.

'I think we've found our hiding place,' he announced.

'But how will you ever get it out of here?'

He shrugged. 'I'll find a way.' He glanced at digital figures flashing on the console. 'Approximately two hours' walk to your dome. We must get going, I've arranged a dust storm for five.'

Gratefully, she lifted the bubble and clambered out into the dry gully.

The storm siren sounded as they reached the rear path leading to Storyteller's Hill. The back route had not been used for some time; the path was overgrown and petered out altogether two hundred metres from Sannah's rear boundary.

'Congratulations,' she called over her shoulder. 'Right on time.'

Kaire checked his timer. 'Accuracy is vital in space. There's nowhere to go if you miscalculate.'

'So how did you figure out the journey to Earth?' she asked, slowing her pace so he could catch up.

'The planning took years. I had to decipher old programmes, some of them damaged, some clearly distorted. Occasionally I had to theorise.'

'Did you have any idea where you would land?'

'No, that part was conjecture.'

'What a shock it must have been to find yourself in such desolate country.'

'The landscape improved immensely once I reached the storyteller's dome,' he said, leaning towards her and kissing her softly on the mouth.

They climbed in silence, each absorbed in the closeness of the other. Above their heads the soft light of dawn began to paint the night sky. Before long the dome materialised through the half-light.

'Home at last,' Sannah murmured.

'May I call it home too?' he asked tentatively.

'For as long as you wish,' she replied, reaching for his hand.

CHAPTER 13

Down in the village, long after the lovers on Storyteller's Hill had fallen into a deep sleep, Fley tossed and turned, Sannah's unexpected message echoing in her head. Given Sannah's intention to remain absent during the whole of Areth's brief tenure as acting trooper-in-charge, Fley couldn't imagine why her friend had returned home early. Life in Village 10 had become intolerable since Wurn's departure, with Areth making extensive use of his position by enforcing regulations long overlooked during his predecessor's administration. Field workers now toiled for an extra hour each night, irrespective of weather conditions; troopers made nightly visits to the school and medical dome, supposedly to check on the wellbeing of pupils and patients; and travelling to the islands had been restricted. The Women's Line had already been forced to postpone one planned meeting on Island 1.

Soft light suffused the chamber as Fley waved her hand over the bedside lamp. Easing herself out of bed, she made her way up the stairs to the living chamber.

Several minutes passed before Sannah answered the communicator. 'I received your message,' said Fley quickly, dispensing with the usual greeting.

'It's two in the afternoon, Fley, did you have to wake me?'

'Is it?'

'What's wrong?'

'Nothing. I just wanted to invite you to breakfast.'

'But I've already told you I'll meet you at the school dome after I've reported.'

'Oh, do come for breakfast first, dear, I've been up half the day making date rolls especially for you.'

'You know I don't like ...' Sannah began, then remembering Fley sometimes stored her Line communicator in a jar of dates, added brightly, 'Of course I'll come. See you later.'

After Fley's communication, Sannah slept fitfully, her mind a mass of conflicting thoughts. Eventually she got up at four, leaving a message board text advising Kaire she had decided to report early and would return soon. The hill path was in shadow at this hour so with luck she wouldn't be observed. It could be difficult explaining to a trooper why she found it necessary to visit Fley before reporting.

Safely down in the village, she avoided the marketplace by skirting behind the community dome and between the store domes. At the junction with the school path, she made sure no one was around before running across open ground to Fley's dome. The door panel opened as she reached the entrance.

Fley was waiting at the top of the stairs and signalled Sannah to follow her. 'I do hope you like the date rolls,' she said loudly as Sannah traversed the chamber.

'They're delicious,' Sannah replied, flicking her hand in the direction of the wall monitor to increase the volume.

Shadows danced on walls and ceiling as they entered the concealed space behind the robe-rack in Fley's sleeping chamber. Fley secured the panel and sat down heavily on a wooden bench placed against the wall. 'Areth's running the village like a prison dome,' she said. 'He's imposed all the old rules and there's no lenience if they're broken.'

Sannah sat down beside her. 'I'm not surprised, a man like Areth was bound to demonstrate his new authority.'

'You don't seem overly concerned, but I'm not going to take any chances with that maniac.'

'Neither am I, in fact I'll do my best to avoid him.'

'Then why the Sun did you come back early?'

'I'll explain if you give me a chance.'

'Sorry.'

Sannah took her friend's hand. 'I have news concerning the desert prisons.'

'From the river villages?' Fley interrupted. 'I've heard nothing from Haika.'

Sannah related the prison builders' conversation and her subsequent decision to return to the village once scanning had been completed.

'I'll communicate with the others now.' Fley reached into her robe to retrieve the communicator used exclusively for Women's Line business.

'I'll go and report.' Sannah rose to her feet. 'You can brief me later.'

The trooper dome was a hive of activity, unusual for so late in the afternoon.

A junior trooper dealt with Sannah, asking few questions and entering her data without hesitation. There was no sign of Acting Trooper-in-Charge Areth.

By contrast the marketplace was almost deserted apart from stall-keepers. The few customers appeared to be in a hurry, making their purchases and then scurrying away in the direction of their domes. No one returned Sannah's greetings.

'What's going on, Fen?' she asked at the vegetable stall. 'Where is everyone?'

'We're afraid to be seen gossiping in a public place,' he replied in a low voice, 'for fear the troopers will accuse us of inciting trouble.'

'Have there been arrests?'

Fen looked around furtively. 'Yes. Fuerte the Tailor, Timp the Labourer and several field workers.'

'And their crime?'

'Loitering in the marketplace with intent.'

'But we always gather here. This is our meeting place.'

'No longer, Sannah, and you would be wise to remember that. Timp was forced to work three days in the quarry as punishment.'

'Thanks for warning me, Fen.' She pointed to some blemished tomatoes and zucchini. 'I'll take those.'

'Three tokens please.'

'Three for these poor specimens!'

Fen shrugged. 'Take it or leave it, the rest has gone south.'

She handed over the tokens.

'Enjoy your meal,' Fen intoned, placing the produce in her basket.

Two troopers entered the marketplace from the northern perimeter as Sannah crossed to the baker's stall. She noted the flash of colour reflected on their white tunics at regular intervals. *Active eradicators,* she thought, *that's unusual for marketplace duties.* Approaching the stall, she selected her bread quickly, exchanging only necessary dialogue with Ingle the Baker. Then she slipped through a narrow passageway between two stalls that led to the first store dome. After making sure she hadn't been followed, she skirted the dome and headed for the canal path, having decided to take the shorter route home.

Stars flecked the night sky and a bright moon illuminated the unlit canal—even the polluted water looked less foreboding in the silver moonlight. She walked at a steady pace, swinging her basket, her spirits light despite Fley's disturbing news and the dreary experience of the marketplace. High on the hill waited her lover, in whose arms she could forget the myriad problems of Brown Zone life. He'd be awake now and no doubt hungry. She envisaged the look on his face as he lifted the loaf from her basket and smelled its freshness. Kaire the Sky Explorer had become fond of old-fashioned Earth food.

A small splash roused her from reverie. Carefully she made her way to the edge of the canal and peered into the water. Nothing stirred the smooth surface. A piece of earth must have broken away from the bank further upstream, she concluded, returning to the narrow path. She hurried towards the light marking the beginning of the hill path.

'What a beautiful night, storyteller,' called a familiar voice from the canal.

She spun around saw a small punt gliding towards the bank, Areth at the helm.

'It is indeed, sir, I'm enjoying my walk home from the marketplace.'

The punt rubbed against the bank. 'I trust you also enjoyed your visit up river, storyteller?' He jumped out of the punt and ambled towards her.

'Yes, thank you, it was good to see old friends again.'

'And the scholar, he found the visit interesting?'

'Yes. He particularly appreciated the hospitality.'

'I, too, appreciate river people's hospitality,' he said, increasing his stride, 'but no one can compete with you, storyteller.'

Instinctively, she drew her basket up to her chest. She wanted to run but forced herself to remain still, refusing to give him cause for aggression. He drew closer, so close he could have touched the basket. She gripped the plaited handle. He smiled, revealing large stained teeth, then turned his head slightly and appeared to be studying the night sky.

'It's been pleasant talking to you, Trooper Areth,' she said, backing away slowly, 'but now I must return to my dome. I have much to prepare for the Tales.'

'I said, no one can compete with you, storyteller,' he repeated, his eyes fixed on the stars and moon.

'I'm pleased you find my tales interesting. Goodnight then, till the Tales.' She set off towards the hill path.

But before she had taken three paces, a powerful hand grabbed her neck, ripping her flimsy robe. Swinging her around with his other hand, Areth slammed her head against his chest. Her basket fell to the ground.

'You can't refuse me now, storyteller. Lover-man Wurn has flown away.'

It was useless to struggle—at more than twice her size Areth could easily overpower her.

'My dome is much more comfortable than this stony path,' she said, pushing her pelvis against him. 'I can soon dismiss the scholar.'

'Silence, storyteller, I'll tell you when to speak. Down in the dirt where you belong.' He pushed her to the ground and brandishing a long-bladed knife, stood astride her, pinning her robe to the path with his heavy boots. Breathing hard, he cut her sash and flicked the robe apart. 'Hot and brown and soft,' he mocked, nicking her nipples with the tip of the blade, 'just like spoiled overripe fruit. Storyteller, I spit on your stained skin.'

A stream of spittle landed between her breasts and trickled down to her belly. Raising his right foot, Areth ground the saliva into her abdomen, grit trapped in the sole of his boot grazing her soft skin. Blood trickled from her damaged breasts.

'Stained skin deserves to be split,' he said, scuffing his boot clean on the grass. 'That's what I told my father the day he brought his Brown lover into our White home, fucked her in the bed where I was born.' He spat again, watched blood and spittle merge around her nipple. 'Tonight, Brown-skin, you're gonna realise how much power there is in pure White flesh. Tonight, storyteller, you're gonna beg for mercy when I invade your spoiled Brown body.'

Meticulously he wiped the blade clean on her robe. Sannah made a grab for the knife but the seasoned trooper anticipated her action and whipped it away, laughter gurgling in his throat. Then to her astonishment, he turned the knife on himself and slashed his tunic from waist to hem.

'Look at my body, storyteller,' he ordered, sheathing his knife, 'and remember, White flesh, White dominion.'

CHAPTER 14

Kaire paced around the living chamber, anxious for Sannah's return. She should have been back hours ago. It didn't take long to report to the trooper dome, only a few minutes more if she had decided to visit the marketplace before returning home. Earlier he'd considered calling Fley to see if Sannah had called at her dome, but thought better of it, knowing neither woman would appreciate his intrusion if they were discussing important business. A glance at his timepiece increased his disquiet. Fley would have been teaching for at least an hour, more than enough time for Sannah to climb the hill path.

Unsure whether to call the school dome, he decided it would be prudent to wait another hour before alerting Fley. His mouth felt dry so he strode into the kitchen to pour himself a tumbler of fruit juice. The jug yielded a mere mouthful and a search of the cooler yielded only a few wizened pieces of fruit. Then he remembered the fruit powder Sannah kept for emergencies so he headed for the store and began rummaging among the dusty jars.

'Jupiter,' he exclaimed as something sharp sliced into his naked foot. Bending down to examine the wound, he discovered Sannah's knife protruding from between two jars. He felt fear slither over his skin as his fingers touched fresh blood. Sannah needed help, his own blood a signal: he must act at once. Dripping blood on the stone floor, he backed out of the store and grabbed his communicator from the kitchen bench.

'Village 10 school dome,' answered a male voice. 'Please state your child's identity code.'

'Fley the Instructor,' said Kaire, struggling to remain calm.

'The instructor is teaching at the moment. I am Ranu the Athlete, can I take a message?'

'No, put me through now.'

'That's not possible. If you could give me your name, I'll inform the instructor you called.'

'Scholar Kaire.'

'Transferring you now, sir.'

Rough fabric chafed Kaire's thigh as he ran down the hill path. On impulse he had taken Sannah's knife, attaching it to his leg with the straps he'd watched her tighten on many occasions. This was the first time he had carried a weapon and he pondered how he would react if called upon to use it. Sky training hadn't prepared him for physical confrontation. Conflict in his world was resolved through mediation. He'd also taken the communicator retrieved from the transporter, which although less sophisticated than the one destroyed by the prison builder, at least possessed a cloaking device.

At the bottom of the hill path, he paused beneath the light to adjust the coarse straps. Shadows flickered around his feet, a warm wind ruffled his loose robe, and from a nearby bush came the sound of scratching followed by a series of low growls. He shivered, Earth night noises disturbed him. Hurriedly he re-tied his robe and turned towards the village, but he had only walked a few metres when a burning sensation assaulted his chest. Pain spread down his abdomen to his groin and soon he was doubled over in agony. Determined to ignore this sign of weakness, he took a few deep breaths and continued his journey. But the pain persisted, travelling down his legs until they buckled beneath him.

Lying on the hard earth, he considered whether his collapse had been engineered, a slow-release muscle inhibitor perhaps, for it seemed someone was determined to prevent him from reaching the village. Between waves of pain he became aware of a human voice; faint yet persistent, it came from the direction of the nearby canal, a plaintive cry for help.

'Sannah,' he cried, and the moment he spoke her name the pain subsided. Scrambling to his feet, he returned to the crosspaths and raced through long grass to the canal. The sound spiralled when he reached the water's edge—now he knew for certain she was close by. 'Sannah,' he called. 'Sannah, I'm coming!'

There was no response. Was he running into a trap? How many troopers lay in wait, Sannah their captive, forced to cry out and lure him into their clutches? He slowed his pace and withdrew the knife. The cries intensified, swirling around him like invisible bands of pain. 'Sannah,' he yelled, plunging into the tangled grass bordering the canal path.

He almost collided with her prostrate body. He could not determine how long she had been unconscious, but something told him it was more than the few minutes it had taken him to run from the cross-paths. 'A simple message would have sufficed, my love,' he whispered, tenderly brushing soil from her face before lifting the communicator to his lips.

The four women responded instantly to Fley's communication, leaving work, dome and marketplace, risking punishment if their absence was noted. Making their way separately to the canal, they assembled as instructed on the jetty where several punts were moored. Troopers used them to cross the canal or travel downstream and it only took seconds to unfasten one. The small punt glided along the canal, the only sound the swish of paddles dipping into black water.

'Over there,' said Payr the Healer, spotting Kaire's white robe.

Minutes later, the women had secured the boat to the bank and were running across the grass towards Kaire.

'How is she?' Payr asked.

'Still unconscious but breathing evenly.'

'The bleeding?'

'Stopped.'

'Good.' Payr kneeled beside Kaire and ran her hands over Sannah's bloodied body. 'No broken bones,' she said with relief, 'just bruising and small cuts.'

'There are more cuts on her legs,' said Kaire, lifting Sannah's robe.

Payr parted Sannah's thighs and gently touched her bruised flesh. 'It's as I feared, she's been raped.'

'Raped!' Kaire cried. 'Are you certain?'

'Yes. Now if you would move away, please, we must get her back to her dome.'

Kaire swayed slightly and fell sideways onto the dry grass, his head spinning and heart racing. He lifted himself back to his feet and steadied himself as two of the women began to carry Sannah up the hill path. Payr spoke quickly and seriously as she instructed Kaire to go ahead and prepare medicaments in the dome. As he ran up the hill path, he felt relieved to be away from them, their stoicism in the face of this tragedy both disturbed and intimidated him. He was also acutely embarrassed by his own lack of control. No doubt the women considered him contemptible, a puny White male incapable of coping with Brown Zone atrocities.

As his steps took him closer to Sannah's dome, he resolved to take her away from her appalling world. In the vast unpeopled reaches of space he could keep her safe. Together they would explore the galaxies, find a new planet where love was the dominant emotion, not hate.

After a second communication with Kaire, Fley decided to delay climbing the hill path until school had finished for the night. Right now Sannah needed rest, not a Line leader demanding answers to difficult questions. Pocketing her communicator, Fley hurried to the staff chamber for the midnight meal.

Ranu looked up from his platter as she entered. 'Tough evening?' he asked, noting her strained expression.

Fley nodded.

'Scholar Kaire sounded extremely agitated. Did he upset you?'

'It was my fault, I forgot to give him some statistics. I've sorted it out. I don't think he'll report me to the troopers.'

'All the same, you look as though you could do with a decent break. Why don't you go to the inn and have lunch? I'll help the schoolyard minder keep an eye on the children.'

'Thanks, Ranu, that's an excellent idea.'

Outside Clar's Inn, a few patrons were seated at tables enjoying drinks in the cool night air. A stallkeeper raised his hand in greeting. Fley smiled but did not linger. Inside, two old men appeared to be sleeping in a shadowy corner; behind the bar, the innkeeper tidied tumblers.

'What brings the instructor to my inn at this hour?' asked Clar.

'I've had a dreadful evening.' Fley collapsed on a stool. 'Those children will be the death of me. Appalling behaviour, I can't think what got into them. A large tropica please.'

Clar reached for a bottle, filled a large tumbler and handed it to Fley. He waited for her to drain the tumbler before leaning across the bar. 'Your students weren't the only ones playing up this evening. Areth was in here earlier.'

'Causing trouble?'

'No, but I had to call the trooper car to take him home. Areth can't hold his drink like he used to.' He glanced around. 'Our acting trooper-in-charge was celebrating,' Clar continued in a low voice, 'told me he'd conquered the storyteller tonight. It must've been quite a session—you should've seen the scratches on his face and his torn tunic.'

'I would call it rape,' said Fley quietly.

'Oh, come on, Fley, we all know Sannah's game for anything and anyone. She probably needed a bit of persuading, that's all.'

'How would you feel if Areth raped your beautiful daughter?'

The innkeeper shuddered. 'But Askus is only a child.'

'Take care of her.' Fley rose from the stool. 'Goodnight to you, Clar, I must return to the children.'

But Fley did not take the direct route to the school dome. Instead she walked through the marketplace and headed towards the cluster of domes where the troopers had their quarters. She had no idea what she was going to say to Areth. Most likely he remained comatose and wouldn't even hear her voice at the sound-grill, and even if he were awake, he would be unlikely to admit her. A formal complaint would have more effect, she decided; rape was viewed as a serious offence even if the victim was a Brown-skin. The new trooper-in-charge wouldn't risk a riot by ignoring her complaint. At the very least there would be an inquiry.

Her footsteps faltered. To her left was the path leading to the school-yard, to her right the path to Areth's dome. *Personal feeling must be cast aside*, she told herself, knowing if she abused Areth either verbally or physically, it would lead to arrest and imprisonment. Wearily she took the left-hand path.

'Turn around, Woman of the Line,' said a sharp voice when she had walked a few paces.

'Who's there?'

There was no response. Fley peered into the shadows but couldn't see anyone so continued to plod up the path, thankful when at last she reached the gate in the schoolyard wall. Breathless, she leaned on the gate.

'The time is ripe, Woman of the Line,' said the same voice. 'Turn around.'

Instinctively Fley reached under her robe and unclasped her knife. 'Who's there?'

'Turn around, your sisters cry out for retribution.'

Fley walked back down the path and continued up the other.

Areth's dome was in darkness and it took her several moments to locate the sound-grill. 'Fley the …' she began, her voice trailing off as she noticed a tiny shaft of light above her head. The dome entrance hadn't been completely sealed. Tentatively she moved her hand across the panel. The door opened, revealing the thin strip of light that surrounded communications equipment. She waved her hands towards it. No ominous alarm erupted and there was no sign of Areth in the living chamber. Discarding her sandals, she padded across the chamber to the stairs. From below came the sound of heavy breathing interspersed with loud grunts. She descended soundlessly, paused by the open sleeping chamber panel and peered inside. A bedside lamp threw shadows on the wall. Areth lay on his back asleep, a rumpled sheet covering the lower half of his naked body. Fley made her way towards the bed, knife raised.

Bloodshot eyes opened at the sound of her footsteps and stared in disbelief. 'What the Sun?' cried Areth.

A blade sliced into his right arm. He tried to grab the knife with his left hand but Fley anticipated his action and quickly backed away from the bed. Clutching his bleeding arm, Areth struggled to sit up. Fley rushed forward and stabbed him in the chest. He opened his mouth to scream but no sound emerged; heavy limbs shuddered briefly and were still.

'This one's for Sannah,' said Fley, grabbing the sheet and flinging it aside. She raised her knife for a final thrust. A lump of pink flesh slid across a thick thigh, leaving behind a crimson trail. Satisfied, she wiped her blade clean on the white sheet and walked out into the night.

Deep in the cool earth of Storyteller's Hill, Sannah lay somnolent in her bed, bathed in soft lamplight and the comforting balm of friends. Time would heal her wounds, for flesh was resilient and she was healthy. Mind-lesions were not so easily repaired and would remain with her forever, deep, dark crevices haunting the interminable daylight hours. She had been defiled; the role she played so willingly, compromised by the brutality of rape.

For many years she had employed her craft, grateful for voluptuous breasts, fleshy lips, flashing eyes. Some would call her whore but she didn't consider herself in those terms and unlike those who loitered around inns and wharves, she never demanded payment for her services. To her, sex was like storytelling, an art form that required practice to improve performance. Her rewards for this dedication were manifold: sometimes she received information vital to Women's Line work, sometimes she rejoiced in the results of her pleasuring, very occasionally she welcomed a little love. But now it was time to abandon her role as pleasure-giver, comforter and lover. Split skin couldn't be reconciled with gentle caresses or passionate couplings.

The other role she played in village life, weaving an intricate web of tales as dictated by her White masters, had also taken years to perfect. But from this night forward she would spin with a different thread. Sannah the Storyteller no longer had any substance; her tales had ruptured, seeped into the dry earth along with blood, semen and saliva. She was done with lies; sweet or sour they couldn't obscure reality. Whatever the risk, she would dedicate the rest of her life to dispelling myth for truth that would engender liberty in the end.

Night travelled towards dawn. Women friends slipped away as she entered the healing sphere of sleep. Dreams would not disturb her rest for she was an empty vessel. When she awoke, metamorphosis would be complete and hope would be thickening in her as she embraced a new role.

PART II

SANNAH THE TRUTHTELLER

CHAPTER 15

At dawn a siren reverberated through the village. In the market-place, stallkeepers and customers raised tired eyes to a pale blue sky. Whispers of cloud greeted their gaze and a gentle breeze bathed their faces, no portent of storm. Fearful now, the villagers turned their heads in the direction of the trooper dome and watched in horror as twenty troopers in full riot gear emerged from the main entrance and ran into the marketplace.

'Remain exactly where you are,' bawled Trooper Xan, a senior officer notorious for his vicious disposition. 'My men will conduct a weapons search. Untie your robes and empty baskets and money-belts.'

The villagers obeyed instantly, remaining silent as troopers moved amongst them examining piles of belongings, deliberately stepping on any food items, and kicking aside baskets. Several knives, two daggers and an ancient laser gun were discovered, their owners ordered to lie face down on the ground. A baby began to whimper. His mother rocked him gently but the whimper soon erupted into a scream.

'Keep the little bastard quiet, that noise gets on my nerves,' a nearby trooper ordered, ripping the mother's robe from her shoulder and shoving the baby to her breast with the sharp edge of his eradicator.

Waves of fear surged through the crowd and parents scooped up their small children.

'Silence,' roared Trooper Xan, raising his weapon and discharging it into a nearby stall. Fragments of fruit and vegetables spattered the ground.

Trooper Roa, standing beside the baker's stall, picked up a loaf, threw it to the ground and crushed it with his boot.

'Trooper Roa,' yelled Xan.

'Yes, sir.'

'As you appear to have nothing worthwhile to do, take the owners of these weapons to the trooper dome and charge them.'

'Right away, sir.'

'And Trooper Roa.'

'Yes, sir?'

'A first-year trooper does not possess the authority to destroy village supplies.'

'No, sir. Sorry, sir.'

Trooper Xan turned back to the crowd. 'There will be no more trade today. Return to your domes immediately and remain there until advised. Dome to dome communication is forbidden.'

The villagers began to disperse in an orderly fashion, all except for an elderly man who remained behind his ruined stall, too distraught to move.

Trooper Xan moved towards him. 'It was a small price to pay, Fen,' he said, prodding a shattered mango with his boot.

'What do you mean, sir?'

'Surely you possess a small knife to cut up your produce?'

'Yes, sir. My five work knives are kept behind my stall in a box on my cart.'

'Then you won't mind if I count them?'

'Not at all, sir.'

Trooper Xan strode through the debris to the small cart Fen used to transport his produce from storage dome to marketplace. He opened the box.

'One, two, three, four, five,' he counted out loud, running a finger over the blades.

'May I go to my dome now?' asked Fen.

'Oh, I don't think so. I'll need to test these. I may as well take them now, don't you agree?' He closed the box. 'Then I'll know if I can eliminate you.'

Fen blanched and began to shake.

'Don't look so worried, stallkeeper, I meant eliminate you from my list of suspects.'

News of Areth's murder had spread through the village within an hour of Fen's release from the trooper dome. The troopers were far too busy interrogating other weapon owners to escort one old man to his dome. Taking a circuitous route home, Fen called at dome after dome to report the murder. When he reached his own small dome on the outskirts of the village, he carefully descended the steep steps leading to the storeroom beneath his sleeping chamber. Behind the sealed door panel, he activated his ancient communicator and contacted his daughter on Island 1. Maris hastily forwarded a coded message to all local members of the Women's Line, cautioning them to be prepared for reprisals and increased trooper activity.

Payr the Healer received no such warning. Heading home along the canal path, she spotted a trooper in the distance, realising as she drew nearer that he was wearing riot gear. Repeated flashes confirmed her fears; his eradicator was in active mode. Her fingers tightened around the medical bag.

'Good morning, Trooper Roa,' she said brightly, raising her free hand in greeting.

'It is not a good morning, healer,' he replied, blocking her way.

'Trouble in the village?' she asked, remembering the solitary siren. She had assumed it was another false storm alert.

'Big trouble,' he answered, waving the eradicator in her face, 'and you'd better have a good alibi.'

'For what?'

'I ask the questions, remember that.' He pointed the eradicator at her chest. 'What are you doing out after morning curfew?'

'I've been attending a patient. I heard the siren and thought I should wait a while before returning to my dome.'

'Who was the patient?'

'Sannah the Storyteller.'

'What's wrong with her?'

'She tripped and fell on the canal path on her return from the marketplace this evening. She managed to get home but then she vomited and suffered severe head pain. Scholar Kaire contacted me and asked me to visit. He was concerned she might have a concussion.'

'I see. And now you're returning home via the same path? Rather stupid wouldn't you say?'

'It's light now.'

'Yes, and you're required at the medical dome immediately.' He lowered his weapon and stood aside to let her pass.

'Are you sure? Jules the Physician should be on duty now, my shift doesn't start until midday.'

'The physician is at the morgue conducting a post-mortem.'

Before Payr could ask who had died, Trooper Roa had departed and was racing along the canal path towards the hill path light.

A voice boomed through the sound-grill, waking Kaire with a start. He hadn't expected anyone, even a trooper, to pay Sannah a visit before the dome communicator relayed an all-clear bulletin. The siren had been followed by an order for villagers to return home and remain inside until further notice. Like Payr, Kaire had presumed severe storms were expected. So after waiting for the sleeping draught Payr had given Sannah to take effect, he'd settled down on a couple of floor-cushions to grab some sleep.

'Unseal your entrance,' Trooper Roa repeated impatiently.

Kaire fastened his robe and hurried to the front entrance.

'Greetings, Trooper Roa, what can I do for you?'

'Where's the storyteller?'

'In her sleeping chamber, she's been injured in a fall.'

'So Payr the Healer informed me when I met her on the canal path.'

'Sannah remained unconscious for a considerable time but fortunately she doesn't appear to have sustained any serious head injuries.'

'Good, then she'll be able to answer my questions.' He pushed past Kaire and strode across the living chamber to the stairs.

'Why the Sun would a first-year trooper need to question an injured woman?' asked Kaire, hurrying after him.

Trooper Roa halted and turned to face his superior. 'Sir, I don't think you understand the situation. My commanding officer has ordered me to search this dome for weapons and question the storyteller concerning her movements yesternight. There's been trouble in the village.'

'What trouble? Why didn't Trooper Areth inform me?'

Roa leaned forward. 'Areth is dead, sir, murdered in his dome this morning. Trooper Xan is now acting trooper-in-charge.'

Kaire clutched the stair rail.

'I understand this has come as a shock, sir. Perhaps you should go and sit down. This won't take long.'

'No, I'm coming with you.'

'Of course, sir.' He winked. 'I understand your desire to guard your property. After you, sir.'

Small stones rolled down the hill path as Trooper Roa descended at high speed. He had been shocked by the storyteller's appearance. Her injuries were genuine but not consistent with a fall and she'd been rather vague when asked the time of her accident. He should have stayed and searched the dome for weapons but Scholar Kaire's belligerent attitude during the interview had set off alarm sirens in his head. The scholar had seemed more than possessive over the storyteller. It had been obvious he wanted to protect her from unwelcome questions.

Reaching the first row of domes, Trooper Roa noticed a figure in the distance leaning against the low wall surrounding the inn. He imagined it was a colleague bored with patrolling empty paths. Increasing his pace, he waved his arms frantically to attract attention.

Trooper Hild took a last swig from his flask and replaced it in his tunic pocket. Perspiration rolled down his neck and his head itched beneath the heavy riot helmet. Cursing the sun, the villagers and his commanding officer, he began to walk slowly towards the marketplace. At least he would find a little shade there and maybe a place to sleep among the abandoned stalls.

'Hild,' yelled Roa with all the breath he could muster. 'Wait.'

Trooper Hild spun around, eradicator flashing in his hand.

'Roa,' he exclaimed as the young trooper ran full-pelt towards him. 'What the Sun's happened?'

'Hild, you must help me. We must get back there quickly.'

'Where?'

'The storyteller, she's been in a fight. She's the one who murdered Areth.' Roa clutched his side. 'He's involved too,' he added breathlessly.

'Who?'

'The southerner, Scholar Kaire.'

Trooper Hild pulled out his flask. 'Drink this and then explain everything slowly.'

Sannah slept peacefully, the trauma of the previous evening buried deep, at least for a few hours. The news of Areth's murder had dissolved anger and hatred and replaced them with indifference. Emotionally and physically exhausted, she refused to expend energy on past events.

Beside her Kaire lay wide awake, deeply troubled by Trooper Roa's visit. How long could he shield Sannah from troopers' prying eyes and probing questions? If only he could persuade her to leave the village, seek sanctuary in a more enlightened society. But deep down he knew she would never willingly abandon her people.

'Unseal your entrance,' an unfamiliar voice called through the sound-grill, banishing contemplation.

Kaire reached under the pillow for Sannah's knife.

'Unseal your entrance,' the voice repeated. 'We have orders to escort the storyteller to the trooper dome for questioning. Resistance is futile, the dome is surrounded.'

'Do as they ask,' said Sannah sleepily, 'and put the knife away.' She closed her eyes.

'Unseal the entrance, Scholar Kaire.'

Kaire slipped the knife under his robe and left the sleeping chamber.

The door panel slid open, revealing Roa and another trooper Kaire didn't recognise. Two eradicators were pointed at his chest, and he glanced around for signs of other troopers.

'I told you this would be a simple exercise,' Trooper Hild muttered to his colleague.

'You can put your weapons away,' said Kaire, realising he'd been duped. 'I'm not going to interfere.'

Trooper Hild smiled. 'Thank you, sir, but I must ask you to hand over *your* weapon. A matter of policy, you understand. It will be returned in due course.'

The knife clattered to the domestep.

'He said hand over, not drop on the ground.' Trooper Roa stepped forward and kicked the knife off the domestep into a dense shrub.

Hild glared at his young colleague. 'Leave it, Roa, we've more important things to worry about.'

Kaire was suddenly conscious of footsteps behind him.

'Good morning to you, troopers,' said Sannah brightly. 'Can you wait while I fetch a sunshield?'

'Two minutes,' said Trooper Hild.

The trooper dome was quiet when Hild and Roa returned triumphant. Their commanding officer had long since retired to his quarters, hoping to sleep during what remained of the day. The day-watch officer entered Sannah's details in the prisoner file and escorted her to the prison chamber. Kaire, who had insisted on accompanying her, took his leave and hurried to Fley's dome. No record or mention was made of his knife.

At five in the afternoon, the communicator woke Acting-Trooper-in-Charge Xan from a deep sleep. He was not amused.

'Good afternoon, sir,' said Trooper Lio. 'This is the day-watch officer reporting.'

'Cut the crap, Lio. What the Sun do you think you're doing calling me at this hour?'

'We have a new prisoner, sir.'

'And this warrants waking me?'

'Yes, sir, it's the storyteller.'

'What has that whore done now?'

'Murder, sir.'

'Murder!'

'Areth, sir.'

'Who brought her in?'

'Hild and Roa, sir, around two this afternoon.'

'Why wasn't I contacted immediately?'

'Er, I didn't want to disturb you, sir.'

'Lio, I'm gonna kick your arse.'

Xan lifted his hand to sever the connection. Adrenalin surged through his body as he anticipated the forthcoming interrogation. *I'll get her this time*, he thought, recalling previous accusations, her watertight alibis and smug smiles.

News of Sannah's arrest spread quickly and before long a crowd had gathered outside the trooper dome to show support for their storyteller. They were singing as Trooper Xan strode up the path, a haunting island melody that sent shivers down his broad back. Brown bodies parted at his approach but the singing continued, stirring long-suppressed memories. He hurried inside, struggling to check vivid images of a dusky island lover.

'Trooper Lio,' he bawled at the empty counter.

Lio appeared from a side door and followed Xan into the trooper-in-charge's chamber.

'Have Troopers Hild and Roa report immediately,' ordered Xan, settling himself at the work-module.

'Yes, sir.' Lio turned to leave.

'Just a moment. Can you tell me where the storyteller was arrested?'

'At her dome, sir.'

'Thank you, Trooper Lio. Dismissed.'

Reaching for the bottle of liquor Areth kept behind the work-module, Xan poured a large measure into a tumbler. He drank steadily, mulling over the regulations concerning Brown-skin prisoners. By rights, Hild and Roa as arresting officers should be present in the prison chamber when the trooper-in-charge conducted the first interrogation. Xan calculated it would take slow Hild at least fifteen minutes to don his uniform and make his way to the trooper dome, ample time for a solo visit with the prisoner. Sometimes protocol had to be overlooked. He drained his tumbler.

When Xan returned from the prison chamber, his full complement of troopers was milling around the reception area. 'News travels fast I see,' he shouted above the din of spirited discussion.

Conversation halted mid-sentence, the men jumped to attention.

'Troopers Hild and Roa, over here,' ordered Xan.

The remaining troopers moved towards the door.

'Stay where you are,' said Xan. 'No need to observe the conventions tonight. Our new prisoner is a special case, wouldn't you agree?'

'Yes, sir,' they chorused.

Xan cleared his throat. 'Thanks to Hild and Roa we have Sannah the Storyteller in custody, charged with Areth's murder.'

The two troopers swelled with pride.

'I have scanned the arrest report and commend you on the wealth of detail supplied. However, your colleagues have not had this opportunity, so I ask Trooper Hild as the senior officer to give a summary of events leading up to the storyteller's arrest.'

'Thank you, sir.' Hild retrieved his message board from an inside pocket and began to read. 'At eleven this morning, Trooper Roa visited the storyteller's dome to conduct a weapons search as directed by Trooper Xan. During the search, the storyteller remained in her bed. Scholar Kaire claimed she had been injured in a fall on the canal path and needed to rest. Trooper Roa suspected he was lying and decided to question the storyteller. Her responses were, he felt, deliberately vague. He also concluded her head and facial injuries were not consistent with a fall but had probably been sustained during a fierce struggle. Trooper Roa decided not to attempt an immediate arrest due to the presence of Scholar Kaire who, it must be noted, remained hostile throughout the visit. Trooper Roa then left the dome intending to return to the trooper dome for assistance. I was patrolling the paths near the marketplace when Trooper Roa approached and related his suspicions. I agreed there were grounds for arrest and because of the seriousness of the crime and the need to prevent escape, we resolved to return to the storyteller's dome immediately and apprehend her. This was accomplished without incident.' Hild paused and turned to Xan. 'The element of surprise worked wonders, sir.'

'It always does,' said Xan, a sneer playing around the corners of his mouth. 'Thank you, Trooper Hild, you may stand aside. I have some information to add.' He began to pace the floor, his hands clasped behind his back, cold grey eyes focused on the blank wall opposite. Suddenly he spun on his heel and facing his men he barked, 'Every rule has been broken, every recommendation ignored. For example …' He paused to scrutinise the now anxious faces. 'Our intrepid arresting officers did not communicate with the trooper dome at any time during this operation, nor did they acquaint themselves with the facts of this case. No, blinded by the desire to impress, they raced up the hill path, arrested the storyteller, and returned here expecting a commendation.'

Trooper Roa felt his cheeks burn; a trickle of perspiration ran down his neck.

'Truth is uncomfortable, eh Roa?'

The young trooper hung his head.

'I, on the other hand,' Xan continued, 'know the value of playing by the rules. I am also fully conversant with the facts of this case. I have studied the scene of the crime, interviewed Glena the Cleaner who discovered Areth's body, read the post-mortem report and spoken to the prisoner.'

He reached into his pocket, pulled out his message board and pressed the memory panel. 'Trooper Xan, Acting Trooper-in-Charge Village 10, Brown Zone, preliminary report concerning the murder of Trooper Areth, 3 August 2399,' he read, enunciating each word precisely. 'The murder occurred around 1 am in the victim's sleeping chamber. The post-mortem revealed, and I quote, "The injuries were consistent with a surprise attack. The deep scratches to the left cheek and bruising to the upper body were sustained earlier in the evening suggesting the victim had been involved in a fight prior to the fatal attack. High levels of alcohol in the blood confirm the victim would have been incapable of defending himself. This was a particularly brutal assault that continued after the victim's death."' Xan looked up. 'Now for my conclusions.'

He turned back to the message board. 'Examination of the murder scene revealed no sign of forced entry and nothing had been tampered with. The murder weapon has not been recovered. I conclude the victim admitted his assailant, who was known to him, shortly after returning from the inn.' Xan turned around and placed the message board on an adjacent counter. 'We know exactly the hour Areth left the inn, because Clar the Innkeeper called the trooper car to take him home. The innkeeper also confirms Areth had facial injuries but states no fights took place on his premises during the evening. So men, any questions before I give my orders?'

Hild and Roa exchanged anxious glances. The other troopers looked at the floor.

'Very well then.' Xan turned back to the counter, picked up the message board and began to key. 'These orders are to be carried out immediately,' he said, passing the message board to Trooper Lio.

Lio couldn't believe his eyes.

'Don't keep them in suspense, Trooper Lio.'

'Sannah the Storyteller is to be released without delay,' Lio read haltingly, 'and escorted back to her dome. She has been not only the victim of unjust action but also the victim of grievous bodily assault by person or persons unknown.'

Twenty pairs of eyes stared in disbelief.

'Troopers Hild and Roa, in my chamber now,' Xan ordered. 'The rest of you get to work. There's a murderer and a rapist on the loose out there. Find the bastard.'

Early the following morning, several prominent villagers, including Fley the Instructor and Payr the Healer, were taken into custody along with known troublemakers. They were subjected to intense interrogation, deprivation of food and a constant barrage of strong light. But after three nights, the identity of Areth's murderer remained a mystery and all denied knowledge of Sannah's assailant. Unfortunately Payr the Healer had omitted to take blood and tissue samples when she treated Sannah after the assault, vital evidence that couldn't be reproduced. Reluctantly, Acting Trooper-in-Charge Xan released the prisoners.

Privately, Xan suspected Scholar Kaire. High-ranking government officials were reputed to be jealous lovers and Areth had been murdered soon after the assault on the storyteller. It didn't take much intelligence to work out what had transpired. But as long as the storyteller maintained she didn't know the man who'd raped her, Xan didn't have a case.

He also had to consider the possibility of retribution from southern government officials if his suspicions proved baseless. More than anything else, Xan feared a transfer further north. He was already paying the price for his short temper and had five more years to serve in the Brown Zone.

Accordingly, seven nights after Areth's murder, Xan rescinded the emergency regulations and despatched the extra troopers he had drafted into the village to assist with the numerous interrogations.

CHAPTER 16

Life in Village 10 slowly returned to normal. Interrogation memories faded, villagers lingered once more in the marketplace to exchange news and gossip, and field workers reverted to standard working hours.

For Sannah, the anticipated rush to help instigate transport sabotage plans did not eventuate, allowing her time to heal. She had misconstrued the runaway prison builders' information. New intelligence received from contacts at northern prison domes advised the desert prisons would not be completed for some time. Fley and the other Line leaders began to consider a variety of options to disrupt the prison transfer.

By the time the new trooper-in-charge arrived, tension in the village had almost dissolved. Areth's brief reign of terror was seldom discussed in the marketplace and his murder had purged any desire for retribution.

From the first night, Trooper-in-Charge Gage made no secret of the fact he detested everything about the Brown Zone and had no intention of staying longer than was necessary. However, he was careful not to reveal his posting to Village 10 was the result of flouting inter-racial relationship laws. After five years without a reprimand from his senior officers, he had become careless, openly cohabiting with his long-term Asian lover and admitting paternity of her child.

Before leaving his previous post, Gage had received the official report of the recent murder and assault in Village 10. On arrival, he considered re-opening the murder case but discreet inquiries revealed the victim was unpopular with troopers and villagers alike. Surmising there was little point in expending time and energy pursuing the murderer, he consigned the file to the archive disc.

During the official welcoming ceremony in the community dome, Gage was surprised to discover a senior government official residing in the village, albeit temporarily. Envisaging pleasant after-work mornings in the company of this clearly cultured man, he checked the registration file and learned Scholar Kaire was visiting the Brown Zone to research the effects of the Nocturnal Life Project. The desire for agreeable fellowship was quickly replaced by anticipation of personal gain as a plan seeded in his mind. Gage knew very little about the NLP, having spent the first twenty years of his life in the White Zone and the remainder only a few kilometres inside the Asian Zone. But now he had plenty of time to learn as much as possible about the scheme. Once armed with this knowledge, he would suggest to Scholar Kaire they undertake a comparative study of the NLP and Southern Darkness Saving. The status gained from this joint project would be of immense benefit when applying for another southern posting at the end of his year's penance.

Gage soon realised there would be no difficulty persuading Scholar Kaire to extend his visit in order to conduct further study. Observing Kaire's interaction with the village storyteller, it was obvious he adored her. Initially this discovery saddened Gage, recalling as it did the pain of his forced parting from Li Lin and their son. But after a few weeks, he put the past behind him, and sought solace in the arms of the beautiful young woman who cooked and cleaned for him.

The villagers had feared the arrival of a new trooper-in-charge but it soon became apparent Gage preferred social activities to reinstating old rules and regulations. He also encouraged visits to the islands and the river villages, spoke of greater flexibility regarding working hours, and implemented a reward scheme for increased productivity.

This less structured and more lenient regime gave Sannah the opportunity to assume her new role of truthteller, at least unofficially. Determined to banish ignorance and lay the foundation for revolution, she decided to implement a series of Truth-Tales incorporating the scientific data Kaire had downloaded from Sky z59's databanks. Beginning in her own village, she planned to divulge these Tales to individuals and small groups in fields, on paths and behind dome doors.

Fley sanctioned the proposal but reminded Sannah that the Line couldn't consider wholesale action until every Brown Zoner knew the truth and was prepared to fight for freedom. The present priority must remain the desert prisons. They needed to ascertain occupation dates, which prisoners were to be transferred, and the method of transportation. Fley also stressed the importance of retaining an atmosphere of normalcy in the village, especially during Gage's first few months.

Inter-village relationships flourished following numerous visits to the islands and river villages. Several partnerships were arranged and in accordance with regulations, relatives and friends from throughout the Brown Zone were permitted to attend the ceremonies. Village 10 resounded with the buzz of festivity, much to the delight of Trooper-in-Charge Gage whose position ensured an invitation to every social function. The Women's Line used the ceremonies to organise meetings with friends from distant parts where information was exchanged, plans made and new members recruited.

Three months after his arrival, Gage was relaxing in his chamber at the trooper dome, feet resting on the work-module, one hand cradling a large tumbler of tropica, when the Brown Zone governor's face suddenly appeared on his monitor.

'Good evening, Governor An-il,' he said, hurriedly removing his feet from the work-module and slipping the tumbler out of sight.

'Engage communication shield, Trooper Gage.'

Gage pushed a panel beneath the work-module. 'Engaged, sir.'

'Good. I imagine you have read reports of the new desert prisons?'

'Yes, sir, I understand construction is ahead of schedule.'

'Well ahead, so currently I'm coordinating the transfer of several hundred political prisoners from northern prison domes to the desert. I've spent a great deal of time considering the best method of transportation. Brown Zone travel is always problematic: poorly maintained super-paths, tropical storms prevalent at sea—to say nothing of pirates. So I've decided to transport the prisoners by train.'

'On the main south-north line, sir?'

'Yes. I would prefer to conclude the train journey at Village 10 and then transfer the prisoners to riverboats, the New Valley River being navigable for some distance. But your villagers have a reputation for civil disobedience and I can't afford to take any risks. I realise you've only been trooper-in-charge for a short time, nevertheless I would value your opinion on the current state of affairs.'

Gage nodded. 'I can assure you, sir, civil disobedience is the last thing on my villagers' minds. They're preoccupied with ceremony and celebration. I understand the importance of keeping those under my control content and encourage a certain amount of festivity. As I'm sure you would agree, thoughts of rebellion are unlikely to surface when villagers are well fed and watered.'

Governor An-il laughed heartily. 'I doubt your villagers are drinking water, Trooper Gage, but I like your approach. Village 10 has been a perennial problem; now it seems you have discovered the solution. I'll forward the transfer details shortly. You will be supplied with additional troopers to escort the prisoners during the river journey and subsequent land travel. Any questions?'

'When is the transfer to take place?'

'Within a month. You will be advised of the exact date later.'

'Thank you, sir.'

'Good night to you, Trooper Gage.'

The governor's face faded. Gage waited for the familiar click before disengaging the communication shield. Leaning back in his chair, he contemplated a trouble-free prisoner transfer, and effusive praise from Governor An-il. An early release from the Brown Zone was now firmly within his grasp.

Kaire's burgeoning friendship with the trooper-in-charge ensured not only frequent invitations to Gage's dome but also unrestricted access to the trooper dome. One evening, on the pretext of a broken communicator and the need to send reports, Kaire was able to spend several hours using Gage's computer. It didn't take him long to override the online security system, gain access to confidential files and copy them onto his computer strip.

Three weeks before the political prisoners were due to begin their journey south, a small group of Line leaders visiting Village 10 for a partnership ceremony gathered in Fley's secure chamber. Plans had already been made to sabotage the train, but recent intelligence was causing concern. Troopers wearing the distinctive red uniform of the Security Unit had been observed travelling on the main south-north line and disembarking at far northern prisons. If the train were to be guarded by this elite group, the operation appeared doomed unless non-Line members in northern villages could be persuaded to take part.

After a lengthy and fruitless discussion, Fley suddenly clapped her hands and beamed at her co-conspirators. 'Wait a minute. We've overlooked the working parties. They're not far from the sabotage spot and I'm certain the older workers would assist. We just need to organise simultaneous breakouts.'

'But how do we contact them?' asked Fley's cousin Zira from Village 60. 'We can't risk sending instructions via communicator.'

'No need for a communicator, the escape instructions can be added to Sannah's Truth-Tale disc and hand delivered.'

'And how do you propose to gain permission to visit the working parties?' Zira asked.

'I don't. Scholar Kaire will deliver the disc. He's free to travel anywhere.'

'But isn't he a government official?' queried Suna from Village 6.

Fley nodded. 'And Sannah's devoted lover. She'll suggest he visit the working parties as part of his research. He's bound to agree, he hangs on her every word. The Truth-Tale disc will be concealed in his travelling robe. A coded communicator message will alert a trusted worker to remove it on his arrival.'

Maris leaned forward. 'Heddi's twins are very reliable, they're at Working Party 1.'

'And Sannah's daughter Pia can remove the disc at Working Party 2,' Fley added.

'Brilliant,' Suna exclaimed, 'we must communicate with Heddi at once!'

'Patience, Suna,' said Fley. 'One step at a time. First I need to speak to Sannah about the Truth-Tale disc.'

Maris reached out and clasped Fley's hands. 'We should have known your devious mind would come up with something.'

Laughter erupted, easing the tension pervading the tiny chamber.

An hour remained before curfew but the stallkeepers were already packing up their wares as Kaire crossed the marketplace. Business had been slow and most of the villagers had retired to their domes early, replete with the rich food and strong drink consumed at the partnership celebration. Kaire acknowledged the stallkeepers' greetings but ignored attempts to engage him in conversation, preferring instead to concentrate on his forthcoming meeting. A few hours ago, Fley's proposal had seemed feasible, but at this moment Kaire questioned his ability to convince Gage that a visit to the working parties would provide essential research material. The trooper-in-charge was no fool and a request to travel north only weeks before several hundred political prisoners were due to be relocated could easily arouse his suspicions. At the edge of the marketplace, Kaire paused a moment to steady his nerves before taking the well-kept path leading to the Gage's dome.

While his host busied himself in the kitchen, Kaire studied the programme cubes lining the walls. 'I had no idea you were a scholar,' he remarked as Gage emerged from the kitchen bearing a large jug and two tumblers.

'I'm hardly in your league.' Gage ambled over to the table, placing the jug and tumblers in front of Kaire. 'But I am interested in cultural matters and always endeavour to remain informed, even in this backwater.'

'You have an extensive range of programmes.' Kaire smiled. 'Perhaps we could view a couple together and discuss them when you have some free time?'

'It would be my pleasure.' Gage filled both tumblers, handed one to Kaire and said amiably, 'Your health, Kaire.'

'I drink to your health also and trust you may soon be travelling south. I do appreciate how difficult this posting is for you.'

Gage nodded and made himself comfortable on the floor-cushion opposite his guest.

The tropica burned Kaire's throat but he adhered to Brown Zone convention and drained the tumbler before speaking again. 'May I commend you on the quality of your liquor, Gage. The best I've encountered here in the north.'

'Thank you. Fortunately I've managed to find a decent supplier.'

'In Village 10?'

'No, River Village 2. I have an arrangement with one of the rivermen. I believe he buys it from a relative.'

'That is indeed good news. I must avail myself of his services.' Kaire paused, placing his tumbler on the table. 'I hope to travel further north myself soon. If now is an appropriate time, I should like to request permission to visit the working parties.'

'May I ask why you're interested in working parties?' asked Gage, staring at Kaire with curiosity.

'I feel my research into the NLP would benefit from observing and interviewing some adolescents.'

Gage snorted. 'Their attitudes are certain to be extreme.'

'I shall take that into consideration. I am fully conversant with the situation in the working parties, having conducted extensive research prior to embarking on this mission.'

'Of course, my apologies.'

Kaire nodded. *Sannah would be proud of my performance as haughty southern scholar*, he thought. 'I should explain my objective for northern travel is two-fold: people and produce, the two strands of my current research. As well as interviewing adolescents, I wish to see first-hand the progress being made in the north. Reports indicate recent crops have been excellent, with good yields and insect pests under control. If my visits corroborate this, I propose to recommend an expansion of the working party scheme on my return south.'

Gage frowned. 'Do we need additional produce? I thought the population in the south was decreasing.'

'That's correct, but …' Kaire paused. 'I can trust you not to repeat this information?'

'You have my word.'

'Thank you.' Kaire leaned forward. 'In government circles there is much talk of trade with the lands to our north. It is only a proposal at present but we are confident we can bring it to fruition before too long.'

'Trade with other nations? That would indeed be progress. I never thought to see such a thing in my lifetime.'

'So I have your permission to travel north?'

'Yes, permission granted. I'll arrange for a travel pass.'

Kaire sat back on the floor-cushion having exhausted Fley's suggested dialogue. 'Thank you, Trooper Gage. Now enough of *my* work, tell me a little about *your* career.'

Gage poured another drink for his visitor. 'I'm flattered you're interested in a military man, but allow me to fetch some fruit and cheese before we embark on further conversation.' He raised his hand in the direction of the wall monitor. 'Enjoy some southern music while I prepare the food.'

'Thank you, I do find the primitive sounds of Brown Zone music rather disconcerting.'

'My thoughts exactly.'

When Gage had left the chamber, Kaire poured the contents of his tumbler back into the jug. It promised to be a long morning.

CHAPTER 17

The solar train impressed Kaire. The sleek metallic tube, gleaming in the moonlight, was by far the largest piece of machinery he had observed on Planet Earth. Prudently, he suppressed his curiosity and refrained from touching the train's silver surface as he stood with Trooper Roa waiting for security clearance. Gage had insisted on assigning an escort for the journey to the working parties, advising the north was a dangerous place and it was unwise to travel alone.

'Security clearance complete,' announced a voice from somewhere above their heads. 'Please enter the train.'

Kaire deliberately took his time selecting a seat, his eyes darting over the interior of the train. The fittings comprised individual padded seats, small tables and lockers set in rows of four divided by a wide aisle. Once seated, he fiddled with the control panel set into the right-hand armrest and discovered a range of digital entertainment, a choice of refreshments both liquid and solid, plus the option of drug-induced dreams. The seats were roomy and comfortable with a wide choice of positions suitable for eating, sleeping or simply relaxing. Settling back to enjoy his first taste of Brown Zone luxury, Kaire hoped Trooper Roa, seated beside him, would not prove too much of an irritation.

Kaire and Roa were not the only passengers. Nearby, a group of young troopers milled around an older, obviously senior officer. There appeared to be some friction about seat allocation but eventually the senior trooper sorted out the problem and the youths settled down.

'Their first tour of duty, I imagine,' Roa muttered, his eyes fixed on the screen embedded in the seat in front. 'Stupid fools, you don't argue with a senior trooper.'

'Not if you have ambition, eh Roa?'

'You read my mind, sir,' Roa replied, turning away from the screen.

Kaire turned his head slightly. 'It isn't difficult to see through your thin veneer of nonchalance.'

Roa's cheeks burned.

'Ambition is an admirable trait, Roa,' Kaire continued. 'My advice to you is cultivate it and use every opportunity to elevate your position. I have always adhered to this philosophy.'

'It has served you well, sir. I'd be interested to hear about your professional life.'

'Another time, Roa, it's a long story. I would prefer to hear how you propose to structure your career.'

Roa hesitated. 'I, I don't have a firm plan, but I know my future doesn't lie in the Brown Zone.'

'You hope to transfer south in a few years?'

'Yes, sir, and I trust my strong work ethic and unswerving loyalty to government policy will ensure my success.'

Kaire smiled. 'I'm certain they will. But tell me, apart from the obvious advantage of promotion, what aspects of southern life attract you?'

'The landscape, sir.'

'The landscape?' Kaire repeated, baffled by Roa's response.

'Yes, sir. I believe it's quite beautiful in some parts, particularly the rugged coastline.'

'Indeed it is.'

'Have any forests survived, sir?'

Kaire struggled to recall the data Sannah had provided months before to support his southern identity. 'No, I'm afraid the forests vanished long ago. But there are small stands of trees in many areas. Overall, southern flora is more diverse than here in the Brown Zone.'

'Thank you, sir, I look forward to seeing and examining it,' said Roa, looking back at his screen.

The end of conversation, Kaire thought, relieved he would no longer have to feign familiarity with a landscape he had never seen. Touching the passenger panel, he selected a music programme. Soon strains of an ancient melody floated through his mind, beautiful but ethereal. Through half-closed eyes he tried to visualise the Sky music cell, but saw instead his young escort's face, lean slightly hollow cheeks, high forehead, thin bloodless lips, cold grey eyes.

Arrogant, ambitious and dangerous, he concluded, shuddering at the memory of Roa's recent visit to Sannah's dome. *And perplexing*, he added, pondering Roa's interest in the southern landscape.

A change of tempo dispelled the trooper's face, but as Kaire settled back to enjoy the music a familiar voice pervaded his head.

'Take care my beautiful pilgrim,' said Sannah over and over again, her words an unbroken current flowing fast beneath the music's smooth surface.

The following day, the train arrived at Coastal Terminal 6, a single dome surrounded by tangled grassland and sand dunes. For several minutes, Kaire and Roa stood beside the track anticipating the arrival of the promised trooper car from Working Party 1. Midday sun blazed in a cloudless sky, hot wind swirled dust over their feet, insects buzzed around their faces. Kaire quickly covered his nose and mouth with the end of his head-cloth.

'Don't say they've forgotten us,' muttered Roa, reaching for his communicator.

'I'll try the dome,' said Kaire. 'They may be waiting in the cool.'

But the dome entrance was sealed and judging by the long grass growing alongside it hadn't been used for some time.

'No one here, I'll try around the other side,' Kaire called back to Roa, still trying to raise someone at the working party.

Behind the dome, a battered trooper car was parked in a patch of shade. Inside, a trooper sprawled in the driver's seat, half asleep. Trooper Everr resented being roused from his bed in the middle of the day and made no attempt to stifle a yawn when Kaire approached and knocked on the window. The door panel opened slowly.

'Yes?' he queried as though he had forgotten the purpose of his journey.

'Scholar Kaire from Village 10,' Kaire announced, raising his hand in greeting. 'Trooper Roa is waiting by the train line.'

The trooper shifted in his seat. 'Trooper Everr.'

Kaire climbed into the car.

Trooper Everr also ignored Roa's formal greeting and offered no further information during the short journey to the working party. The trooper car, a smaller version of the one attached to Village 10, sped across grassland peppered with stunted wind-blown bushes towards a rocky outcrop devoid of vegetation. On reaching the ridge it lumbered to the top, faltering for a few seconds before ploughing down the other side.

Beyond the ridge, a different panorama revealed the symmetry of cultivation. Neat rows of crops and fruit trees, protected from harsh sunlight by open-ended cylindrical structures covered with shade-cloth; irrigation channels brimming with sparkling water; and behind them, three white domes: one large, two small, squatting on baked red earth.

The trooper car lurched to a halt outside one of the small domes. A small pad of sun-bleached stones marked the entrance.

'Make yourselves at home,' said Trooper Everr apathetically, pressing a panel to release the entrance door panel. 'Beds are located second chamber on the left. The working night begins at dusk. Breakfast is served at five in the large dome.'

Kaire and Roa scrambled from the car clutching their packs. Trooper Everr waited until they had entered the dome before turning his vehicle towards the other small dome.

'Some welcome,' remarked Roa scornfully. 'I expected a little civility from a fellow trooper.'

'And it seems he mistrusts us,' Kaire added, pointing to a beam of light above his head. 'I think he's sealed the entrance.'

Roa swung round on his heels. 'I won't be treated like a common criminal. Trooper-in-Charge Gage shall hear about this.'

'In the evening, Roa,' said Kaire wearily. 'Right now I need some sleep. Those young troopers kept me awake on the train despite the ear-guards.'

'Me too.'

Kaire smiled. 'Let's hope the beds are more acceptable than the welcome.'

At dusk the wind that blew in from the ocean during the day dropped suddenly and a blanket of humid air settled over the fields. Hordes of multi-coloured insects gathered in the hedges planted as windbreaks around the orchard and a high-pitched cacophony greeted the visitors as they emerged from the dome escorted by the surly Trooper Everr. Kaire covered his ears with his hands in a vain attempt to stop the excruciating pain.

'You get used to the evening chorus,' said Trooper Everr, 'same as the heat.'

'I'll take your word for it,' Kaire replied, 'though I don't intend to stay here long enough to find out.'

The trooper turned to Roa. 'Soft these twenty-four-hour southerners,' he muttered.

Roa nodded.

Inside the large dome, young workers sat on benches at long tables eating breakfast. Both males and females had close-cropped hair and were naked from the waist up. Kaire averted his eyes from rows of pert brown breasts.

'You get used to that too,' said Trooper Everr, steering the visitors towards the food table.

A dozen troopers, clothed in short, lightweight tunics and sandals, stood around a small table eating and engaging in noisy conversation. None of them looked up or raised their hands as Kaire and Roa approached.

'Visitors,' Trooper Everr announced indifferently. 'Scholar Kaire and Trooper Roa from Village 10.'

'Greetings,' an older trooper mumbled. A piece of masticated fruit slid from his open mouth onto the floor.

Roa cringed.

'Help yourselves,' said Trooper Everr.

Kaire looked around for a platter but couldn't find one among the debris of fruit skins so he picked up the long yellow fruit called banana. Apart from mango this was his favourite Earth fruit.

'Have a drink, mate,' said a voice beside him, thrusting a tumbler into his free hand.

'Thank you.'

'What you come here for, Scholar?' the trooper asked. 'Not much to see apart from crops.'

Kaire hastily swallowed a piece of overripe banana. 'I've come to interview members of the working party,' he explained, 'to determine their opinions of the NLP.'

The trooper laughed. 'The NLP don't make much difference up here, mate. It's too bloody hot all the time and any breeze we get drops on dusk.'

'I noticed. How do you cope with the climate?'

'I drink plenty of bloody tropica,' he answered without hesitation.

The other troopers roared with laughter.

'I reckon the alcohol's addled their brains,' Roa whispered in Kaire's ear.

Kaire nodded. 'How long have you been at Working Party 1?' he asked the tropica drinker.

'Three years.'

'That's a long time in such an isolated spot.'

'Oh it's not so bad.' The trooper grinned. 'There are some compensations.' He gestured towards a row of young girls.

Kaire smiled.

'I can fix you up with a couple if you like.'

'I trust the offer extends to my escort,' said Kaire, anxious to deflect Roa's attention from his own extra-curricula activities.

'Sure, mate.' He leaned towards Roa. 'Got just the thing for a young trooper.'

Roa recoiled from the draught of foul breath.

'Gotta go now,' said the trooper, noticing his mates were heading to the dome entrance. 'Another night in them bloody fields. See ya.'

'Moron,' Roa muttered.

Kaire refrained from comment.

At midnight Kaire made his way to the orchard, hoping to encounter some of the workers. He had spent the evening with Roa and Trooper

Everr, inspecting the workers' accommodation chambers beneath the large dome, viewing programmes promoting the working party scheme and surreptitiously examining the communications system. Inspections of the fields, orchard and irrigation systems were scheduled for after the midnight break. Trooper Everr had suggested a swim before lunch in a nearby lake but Kaire had excused himself, saying he had a headache.

At the far end of the orchard, a small group of girls lay spread-eagled under the fruit trees, cooling off under the sprinkler system.

'Mind if I join you?' he called.

'Not at all,' they chorused.

An older girl rose and walked towards him, long moist legs glistening in the moonlight. 'We welcome Scholar Kaire to Working Party 1,' she said formally. 'I am Line Leader Garna.'

Kaire gulped. Fley hadn't mentioned *this* in his briefing.

'And these are my Line workers,' she continued, indicating the other girls. 'We are responsible for the orchard. Later tonight I'll introduce you to the Line leaders from Fields 1, 2 and 3.'

'Thank you, Line Leader Garna,' Kaire replied, reproaching himself for hasty assumptions. 'I shall be pleased to meet your co-workers.'

He walked to a nearby tree and sat down on the damp earth. At once the other girls moved forward and arranged themselves in a semi-circle around him.

'Oh, no,' Garna said suddenly. 'I should have warned you about this red dirt—it stains terribly. Let me assist you with your robe before it's completely spoiled. It's such beautiful cloth.'

Before Kaire could answer, she had clasped his robe and was gently peeling the folds of fabric away from his sweat-soaked body. Soft fingers lingered, her warm breath fluttered, his blood boiled.

'Thank you,' he stammered, willing his erection to subside.

'He is a most beautiful man,' Garna informed the others as she folded Kaire's robe. 'I have never seen such pale, unblemished skin.'

Kaire blushed, covered the offending part with his hands.

'Don't be shy,' Garna chided. 'We're anxious to make your acquaintance. Visitors are a rarity here.'

Kaire bit his lip as ten pairs of velvet brown eyes stared at his naked body. Garna smiled, dropped the folded robe over his thighs and went to join the others.

'May I ask if you've come here to inspect the produce, sir?' asked a tough-looking adolescent.

Kaire smiled. 'I'm afraid I know nothing of fruit and vegetables, other than their taste of course. I'm here to conduct a survey on behalf of the government. I shall be seeking your opinions on the effect of the NLP here in the north. Interviews will take place in the large dome after the morning meal for the next three nights.'

'We'll do all we can to assist you,' said Garna, bowing her head.

'Thank you, I look forward to learning of your experiences here.'

A siren blared through the orchard sending the girls scrambling to their feet.

'Midnight break,' Garna explained. 'Will you join us for lunch?'

'I'd be delighted to, but first I must go and change.'

'I think you'd find a short wrap more comfortable in this heat. I'll borrow one from my brother and bring it to your chamber shortly. And of course I'll wash your robe,' she added smiling impishly.

But before Kaire could express his thanks, Garna had bounded away into the dark trees and he was left pondering if 'brother' referred to a blood relative or was just a friendly term used for male workers.

Over lunch Kaire learned that Tona, the owner of the blue wrap he now wore, and Garna were twins, as were four other members of Working Party 1.

'All six of us were born in the same northern village at around the same time but no one could explain the anomaly and only single births were expected,' Garna explained when Kaire, keen to uphold his position as high-ranking southerner, asked how this could have occurred given the Brown-skins' one-child policy.

'Perhaps the scanning equipment was faulty,' he suggested.

'Oh, I'm sure that would have been checked at the time,' Garna replied. She leaned towards him, making certain her thigh pressed against his. 'I like to think it had something to do with the heat and humidity up here,' she purred, her brown eyes roving over his pale face. 'A climate conducive to fertility.'

'You may be right,' he answered, crossing his legs to escape her warmth. 'I noticed the orchard trees here are heavy with fruit.'

'I am heavy with heat,' Garna whispered in his ear.

Kaire blushed, wondering if he would ever feel comfortable with the flagrant eroticism of these people. The incident in the orchard had also unsettled him. 'Later,' he murmured, anxious to maintain a friendly relationship with the young Line leader. Garna obviously held a position of authority within this community. Even the other Line leaders, to whom he'd been introduced before the meal began, had greeted her with the deference normally accorded a senior trooper. Fortunately, the siren decreed the end of provocative conversation and Kaire was left alone among the discarded flesh of overripe fruit.

The morning interviews proved an easy task. All the young workers were keen to take part in the survey and their comprehensive responses to Kaire's questions taught him a great deal about Australian government policy. Garna's twin, Tona, articulate and self-assured, was the last worker to be interviewed. As he packed up his voice scanner, Kaire noticed Trooper Roa had already left the chamber. Tona remained seated, evidently in no hurry to retire to bed.

'Your parents must be very proud,' said Kaire, 'to have both children promoted to Line leader after such a short time.' He had discovered the twins were just sixteen, much younger than they appeared.

'The quality of leadership runs in the family. Our mother is also a Line leader.'

Kaire considered Tona's use of the present tense. It could have been a mistake, though unlikely given the boy's obvious intelligence. 'Such women can be a formidable force,' he said, 'especially during difficult times. I believe this country could become great again if there were more people of the calibre of …' he paused, 'shall we say, Fley the Instructor of Village 10.'

The boy sat before him unblinking.

'Or Maris the Spotter of Island 1.'

The boy reached across to clasp Kaire's hand. 'It's stuffy in here,' he said. 'Shall we go and get some fresh air?'

Tona led Kaire across the fields and down a flight of steps into a small chamber built just below ground level. Two stone benches had been positioned against the wall opposite irrigation equipment. Lights from a control panel flashed patterns across the ceiling.

'What about the day patrol?' asked Kaire, taking a seat beside Tona.

'No problem. Up here the troopers don't care if we break the curfew. Day patrols were abandoned years ago, so I'm told. Escape attempts are extremely rare. There's nowhere to run to and no transport other than the trooper car, which is protected by a security shadow.'

Kaire nodded and turned away, considering his next move. He suspected the disc Sannah had sewn into the hem of his travelling robe contained more than Truth-Tales but his queries to that effect had met with stony silence. This had hurt, especially since he had acquired details of a forthcoming prisoner transfer for the Line. How long would it take to win Sannah's trust?

He considered the construction project he'd scanned weeks earlier, an underground penal complex to house all those that dared plot against the brutal regime. It would be impossible to escape from such a place, impossible to infiltrate. *Unless?* Fragments of thought coalesced in his mind.

'What would be the likelihood of a breakout if you had outside help?' he asked, turning to face the boy.

'None of us want to be here and I know of at least six guys that wouldn't hesitate to join me in any escape attempt.'

'You're aware it would be impossible to return to your families?'

'Of course. But there are other options. The lighter-skinned among us would probably travel south and simply blend in with the rest of the population.'

'And others like yourself?'

'There's always a place on a northern ship for one of us. We were once a sea-faring people, the ocean is in our blood.' The boy stared straight ahead, oblivious to thick walls and humming machines. A wide blue ocean beckoned—salt spray, fresh winds and freedom.

'And there is always Aotearoa,' said Kaire, hoping to gain some information about the mysterious place he'd overheard both Sannah and Fley mention when they thought he was out of earshot. Sannah's obvious agitation when he'd raised the subject beside that mountain pool had only fuelled his curiosity.

'Oh, Aotearoa,' Tona said wistfully. 'The last link in the chain, my people's islands, the land of my dreams.'

'It could become a reality.'

'Don't promise me something I know you can't deliver. The *Liberty* is lost and who knows how long it will be before there's another ship.' He turned to face Kaire. 'I'll do whatever it takes to help the cause but please don't mention Aotearoa again.'

Kaire patted the boy's arm. 'I'm sorry, I didn't mean to upset you.'

'I'm the one who should apologise. I should have known you wouldn't understand. You have led a very different life.'

'I have indeed,' said Kaire, wishing he could share something of Sky-life with this boy, who reminded him so much of the younger brothers he had left behind.

'So what do you want me to do?' Tona asked, interrupting Kaire's thoughts of home.

'By now your sister Garna will have removed a disc from the hem of my travelling robe. It contains vital information that must be shared with all workers. Have you access to a scanner?'

'No, but Garna should be able to "borrow" one from the trooper chamber. She moves in and out of there quite freely.'

Kaire smiled. 'I'm sure she does but I'd rather lend you mine. Just for today though, I'll need it for the interviews tonight. You can borrow it again in the morning.' He reached into the bag beside him, pulled out the scanner and passed it to Tona.

'I would risk anything for a chance of freedom,' said Tona wistfully, slipping the scanner into the pocket of his wrap. 'What life is this, forced to toil for years to provide food for indolent southerners? No offence,' he added with a smile.

'None taken.'

'The troopers have stolen my youth,' Tona continued, his tone betraying deep sadness, 'and the youth of all my generation. We'll never know carefree adolescence. At fifteen years we're taken from our villages, separated from family and friends, forbidden to communicate with our parents. We have to endure five years of callous treatment in an environment no one would willingly inhabit. That's enough to crush both body and spirit. How can we ...' He stopped mid-sentence and clutched his shaking knees.

'Fear is the real enemy,' said Kaire, putting his arm around the boy's tense shoulders. 'Have faith in the power of good, a free future awaits you.'

Tona leapt to his feet. 'Oh, Aotearoa,' he cried over and over again.

CHAPTER 18

Golden skin glowed in pale dawn light, long limbs stretched sensuously and a short red skirt rose and fell, revealing tantalising glimpses of firm flesh. The girl worked methodically, dragging a rake across a narrow path of white stones leading from Working Party 2's centre dome to a dirt track. Trooper Roa studied her every move, envisaging the full curve of buttocks, a soft pad of hair.

'Roa,' Kaire called from the trooper car. 'Come on, we're ready to leave.'

The fantasy dissolved. Reluctantly Roa climbed into the car.

'We are to view the fish farm before the morning meal,' said Kaire. 'The biologists have recently had great success with breeding disease resistant species.'

Roa responded by turning to the window for a last look at the girl.

'Attractive, isn't she?' Kaire remarked as they sped across the compound. He had already made the girl's acquaintance.

'Beautiful,' breathed Roa.

'Just like her mother.'

'You know her mother?'

'I've been a guest in her dome for some time.'

'That's Sannah's daughter?'

'Yes, her name is Pia.'

'*Pia*,' said Roa, savouring each letter. 'Perfection.'

'Love's young dream.'

'Who said anything about love?'

'It's always a possibility.'

'Not with a split, you know the rules.'

Instantly Kaire regretted his frivolous remark. 'How did you know Pia was a split?'

'Trooper Hild told me. He's been around Village 10 for years. He knew Pia's father.'

'Was he a southerner?'

'No, a split from a border village, so Hild said. But he could pass as White and used it to his advantage. Hild said he made many illegal trips south posing as one of us. Foolish man, he spent many months in prison domes.'

'What happened to him?'

'Oh, he died before Pia was born. A rare disease, Hild said.'

'How sad, growing up without a father. I never knew mine either.'

'I could've done without mine, the drunken lazy slob.' Roa's fist hit the door panel.

'Is everything all right, sir?' asked the driver.

'No problems, Trooper Ploe,' said Kaire. 'How far is it to the fish farm?'

'We'll be there in five minutes, sir.'

'Thank you.'

Roa sat hunched in the corner scowling, his agreeable morning mood ruined.

The fish farm did little to raise Roa's spirits. Located on the banks of a sluggish river, the place reeked of rotting fish and oozing mudflats. Biting insects swarming over the fishponds soon sought out the visitors, increasing their discomfort. Inside the farm dome, after a tour of the laboratory, a worker passed around a large platter of fish samples. Roa contemplated the slimy grey mess and his stomach lurched. But a glance at Kaire, who appeared to be chewing happily, convinced him he should try some. A single piece confirmed his suspicions. The new species might be disease-free but the taste was nauseating.

During the return journey, Trooper Ploe had to stop the car several times to allow Kaire to discharge the contents of his stomach. Back at the compound, Kaire retired to bed, too sick to conduct interviews. Roa took advantage of his absence to become better acquainted with Pia.

By evening, Kaire felt sufficiently recovered to proceed and sought permission to interview a group of workers during their working hours in order to make up lost time. The trooper-in-charge agreed and suggested Kaire set up his equipment at the edge of the fields. Trooper Everr, assigned to assist him, soon tired of listening to the same questions and wandered back to the main dome, giving Kaire ample opportunity to initiate an informal discussion on the youth working parties. Sannah had provided only a brief sketch of the rationale behind the scheme and he was keen to discover what propaganda the children had been fed prior to leaving their home villages.

Discussion soon degenerated into argument and he was about to silence them when Pia suddenly appeared. She hurried over to the young workers sitting on the ground at his feet, stood over them hands on hips.

'Quiet, you stupid kids,' she said brusquely. 'Do you want the troopers over here?'

'Sorry, Line Leader Pia,' they answered, hanging their heads.

Pia stepped back and turned to Kaire.

'I don't think teaching's my vocation,' he said before she had a chance to speak.

She smiled. 'Probably not, but I hear you're a good pilot.'

'Back to work now,' Kaire told the workers. 'Thanks for your time.'

'Any more interviews tonight?' Pia asked when the others had left.

'No, I'm going back to the dome now to collate tonight's information.' Kaire wanted to tell Pia he adored her mother and would do anything to help the cause she served but he remained silent, reluctant to be thought of as just another White man with a penchant for dusky flesh. How could he explain Sky-learned ethics to a girl raised in a society where skin colour determined every aspect of life?

'I'd better go and do some work now,' said Pia, as she finished helping Kaire pack up the equipment. 'Give my love to Sannah when you see her.' She ran off in the direction of the orchard.

Kaire picked up the equipment pack and headed for the path. Halfway between fields and domes, he heard footsteps and turning around saw a worker running down the path towards him. As she drew nearer, he realised it was Una, a first-year worker he'd interviewed earlier in the night.

'Is anything wrong, Una?' he called.

'Yes, I must speak with you, sir.'

'No need to run, I'll wait for you.' He stepped off the path onto a patch of grass.

She arrived breathless, perspiration running down her thin face.

'Sit down and get your breath back,' he said. 'I have plenty of time for talk.' Easing the pack from his shoulders, he squatted on the grass. Beside him the girl hugged her knees, small hands trembling against skinny legs. He recalled the brief interview, the way she'd stared at the ground, her monosyllabic answers. At the time, he'd presumed shyness; she probably hadn't encountered a senior government official before.

'Thank you for your contribution to my survey, Una,' he said, trying to put her at ease. 'I always find it helpful to hear what younger workers have to say.'

She lifted her head slowly, her large eyes focused fleetingly on his face. 'I, I think you should know, sir, that last day Line Leader Pia came into the first-years' dormitory and made us all listen to a disc. She called it a Truth-Tale.'

He sighed. 'Another tale purporting to be the true history of Earth's degradation,' he said in an exasperated tone. 'When will you people learn?'

'I found it very distressing, sir,' she continued, 'but I want to assure you I didn't believe a word of it.'

He smiled and patted her head. 'Thank you for telling me, Una, I'll organise a search for the disc and make sure it's destroyed. We don't want anyone else upset by lurid myths.'

'No, sir.' She lowered her eyes and plucked at a clump of grass.

'Is there something else, Una?'

'Yes, sir, but I'm afraid.'

'Afraid of trouble from your fellow workers?'

She nodded.

'You may speak freely, Una. Anything you say to me will remain confidential.'

She raised her head. 'I think you should know that wasn't the first Truth-Tale I've heard here, sir.'

'I see. The problem is obviously more serious than we thought. Can you remember any details?'

She paused a moment, then said brightly, 'I remember the Tale of Aotearoa because it was so incredible.'

'Would you like to tell me what you remember?' he asked gently.

She tilted her head, inhaled balmy night air. 'It goes something like this. Long ago when the ocean had already inundated the smallest of our islands and my people were crowded together on the few remaining islands, a group of young men and women decided to search for another place they could call home. After many weeks at sea, the travellers saw in the distance a landmass larger than they'd ever seen before. This land didn't hug the ocean like our coral islands, instead great mountains rose from dense forest to embrace the sky. Some of these mountain peaks even pierced the clouds. The travellers named the land Aotearoa, which means Land of the Long White Cloud. As they explored the land, they discovered a strange new world: vast lakes, boiling mud, mountains that belched fire.' Una paused and took another deep breath.

'It's certainly incredible,' Kaire remarked.

'Yes, sir.' She turned slightly light from the nearby field lamp illuminating her face and he noticed her eyes were shining. 'Apparently this land was empty of humankind. A paradise waiting for my people where they could live without fear of rising seas, tsunami and cyclones.'

'Would you like to believe in Aotearoa?' he asked gently.

She bit her lip, her brown eyes flashed fear.

Kaire laid his hand on her arm. 'There's nothing wrong with wishing the world were a better place.'

She managed a weak smile. 'I believe Aotearoa is the place where our spirits reside after death, the island of eternal sleep.'

He patted her arm. 'Thank you for talking to me, Una.'

'Thank you for listening, sir,' she replied and rose to her feet.

As shadows swallowed her slight figure, Kaire pondered her words, trawling his memory for details of a long ago Sky lesson. Volcanoes, boiling mud, long white cloud, descriptions he knew related to somewhere on Planet Earth. Suddenly he slapped his leg and exclaimed aloud, 'New Zealand.'

Stones crunched behind him the moment he resumed his walk to the dome. He resisted the urge to turn around.

'Wait, Kaire, please,' called Pia, running up behind him.

He stopped at once. 'What is it, Pia?'

Grabbing his arm, she pulled him off the path into the shadows. 'I heard every word she said. That girl could jeopardise the entire mission. We must get her out of the way until it's over. There's a holding chamber where workers are sent for punishment. You must tell Trooper-in-Charge Wyan that Una was insolent during her interview and order him to isolate her for several weeks.'

'There has to be a better solution. He'll increase security if he thinks there's any possibility of trouble. That's the last thing we want.'

'There's always the sick chamber,' Pia said after a lengthy pause, 'but it would have to be something contagious to warrant isolation for weeks.'

'Fish,' said Kaire, recalling the previous day. 'Mix some of the new fish samples in her food—they made me sick.'

'Good idea, but vomiting would only isolate her for a couple of nights. It needs to be a rash. The troopers up here are terrified of skin diseases.'

Kaire smiled and unfastened his robe. Red blotches dotted his pale chest. 'I didn't mention this before but I'm sure it's an allergic reaction to the fish.'

'We can't be certain Una will react in the same way, but it's worth a try.'

'Can you get hold of some samples?'

She nodded.

'And if it doesn't work?'

She hesitated. 'Then I'll have to think of something else,' she said turning away.

'Oh Pia, before you go, I'll need the disc back. Bring it to the orchard after the midnight break. And make sure Una overhears you mention the troopers have confiscated the disc and you're concerned about possible punishment.'

At the sick chamber Trooper Ome greeted Kaire informally before ordering Una to strip and lie down. His initial reaction to her rash was one of dread, hastily disguised, as though he wanted to convince both Kaire and himself there was no cause for concern. Skin diseases were common among youth workers, the result of heat and toxins in the soil, but Trooper Ome had never seen anything like this before. His scant knowledge of medicine, acquired during first-aid classes at military college twenty years earlier, did nothing to allay his fears.

'Where has she been working?' he asked.

'Field 2.'

'Potatoes and onions. No problems there at present. Has she eaten anything different in the last few days, fish for instance?'

'I think it highly unlikely. Who would want to eat the fish farm's produce?'

'I agree, their latest batch tastes like shit.'

'I vomited after sampling it but I didn't break out in a rash.'

Trooper Ome scratched his head. 'I confess I'm baffled. I'll have to carry out some tests. Unfortunately our equipment's rather primitive but I should be able to establish whether this is a new disease.'

'I could help you there,' Kaire offered. 'Village 10 medical dome is very well equipped. If you give me skin and blood samples, I'll take them back with me. You'll have an answer within a few nights.'

'Thanks, mate. In the meantime I'll isolate the girl just in case it's contagious.'

'Very wise.' Kaire turned to leave. 'Oh, I'd be obliged if you could bring me the samples soon, Trooper Ome, I leave tonight.'

'Of course. Goodnight to you.'

The path leading from the sick chamber to the main dome had long been neglected and Kaire's light sandals gave little protection from the rough ground. He winced as a sharp stone found its way between his toes. Bending down to remove it, he heard rustling in the tangled grass bordering the path.

'Who's there?' he called. The rustling ceased. He imagined it was a small animal.

Close to the dome's rear entrance, something or someone crossed the path behind him. This time he remained silent and increased his stride. He had almost reached the door panel when a hand touched him lightly on the shoulder. He swung around.

'Pia, what the …?'

'Sorry to alarm you, Kaire, but I had to see you before you left.'

'Not more problems?'

'No, I just wanted to thank you.'

'I told you I want to help your people.'

'This has nothing to do with the mission.' She glanced around. 'Come away from the light.'

'I have very little time.'

'It won't take long,' she insisted, grabbing his arm and pulling him off the path.

He wanted to protest he was Sannah's lover and could not, would not engage in sexual relations with her daughter, whatever the custom in these parts. It would be a betrayal of all they had shared.

'Pia,' he began, but she pressed her fingers to his lips and pulled him deeper into the darkness.

'Please excuse my haste,' she said when they were a safe distance from path and dome, 'but I'm supposed to be working and you're leaving soon.'

'Pia, I …'

'Please listen,' she interrupted. 'I only have a moment. I want to thank you for loving my mother.'

He breathed a sigh of relief.

'You are the partner she's been seeking all these years since my father's death,' Pia continued in a low voice. 'Oh, there have been many men and some she even called "lover", but none have moved her as you do. She even speaks of love.'

Not to me, he thought and almost spoke the words aloud. But he checked himself in time and asked instead, 'How do you communicate with her?'

'We have our ways, that's all you need to know.' She smiled. 'Some night when we have more time, you must tell me the story of your people. Sannah tells me you're not of this earth and yet you're human. I'm intrigued.'

Once more Kaire sighed, grateful to be spared the difficult task, for now at least.

'I must go.' She reached up to kiss his cheek. 'Goodnight, dear friend.' Tears threatened and she turned away, scrambling through long grass to the path.

Kaire watched her run across the baked earth until night swallowed her slight frame, thoughts of her mother pulsing through his head like distant stars.

CHAPTER 19

Kaire and Roa were to return south aboard a cargo train. It would be a slow journey, with the train stopping frequently to take on produce destined for southern markets. A small passenger module containing minimal seating had been attached to the train for their comfort. Roa wanted to sleep and suggested they select seats at opposite ends of the module for the first part of the journey. Making his way to the front seat, Roa set the seat to relaxation mode, closed his eyes and turned his attention to Line Leader Pia.

For several days her beautiful body had dominated his dreams. How he blessed Kaire's relationship with her mother—there was no way could he have competed with a high-ranking southerner. Trooper Ploe had arranged his first meeting with Pia in exchange for a sachet of a mood-enhancing drug called moonlight.

Moonlight, the natural variety, had also played a part in Roa's seduction strategy. For their second meeting, Trooper Ploe had organised a trip to the nearby lake, ostensibly to collect specimens for the fish farm. When they reached the lake, Ploe had announced his intention to drug-dream for a couple of hours and suggested Roa take Pia for a walk. 'The silver moon will guide your steps,' he'd said, digging the young trooper in the ribs.

At ease in his seat, soothed by the gentle probing of automated massage, Roa drifted towards dream.

Cool water dribbling over hot bodies, laughter perforating still night, wet garments clinging, warm hands exploring, soft grasses tickling naked flesh, soft moonlight bathing golden thighs. Silky, silky, coming, coming!

Semen oozed through Roa's lightweight travelling tunic. Hastily, he turned around and was relieved to see Kaire still slept. Reaching out, he pressed the control panel. Cleansing fluid soon erased tell-tale stains.

Night receded slowly. Four hours cocooned inside a small silver tube wasn't Roa's idea of fun. He peered through the tinted vision-strip, hoping to see signs of life: a village, a produce terminal, anything to relieve the boredom. Dense fog enveloped the land. He slumped back in his seat.

'Good morning, Roa,' Kaire called a few minutes later.

'There's nothing good about it, sir. The fog's so thick I haven't a clue where we are.'

Kaire rose and moved to the small seat beside Roa. 'We're approximately ten minutes from the first stop. I checked the navigation panel.'

'Now why didn't I think of that?'

'Your mind on other things, perhaps?'

Roa grinned. 'I can't get her out of my head.'

'I'm not surprised, she's a beautiful girl.'

'I've had beautiful girls before and walked away without a backward glance, but Pia's really got under my skin.'

Kaire laughed. 'Before you know it, you'll be applying for a transfer to Working Party 2.'

'Not sure I could stand the heat, if you know what I mean.'

'This is Weather Watch,' announced the automated information system, preventing further light-hearted conversation. 'An electrical storm is approaching your area. We expect severe wind squalls up to two hundred and fifty kilometres an hour, damaging hail and torrential rain. Return to your domes immediately. I repeat return to your domes immediately.'

'This is Tepp the Driver,' a human voice interjected. 'Please engage safety circuits. I have activated the emergency stop.'

Fingers pressed control panels. Roa's monitor responded instantly, but Kaire's remained blank.

'It must be faulty,' said Roa. 'Quick, go to another seat, you've got about thirty seconds.'

Kaire sprinted to the nearest seat and was about to press the monitor safety panel when the train screeched to a halt.

'The train will remain stationary until the storm has passed,' announced Tepp the Driver. 'Please remain seated with safety circuit engaged.'

'I hope we're not stuck here for long,' Roa called.

No response.

'Scholar Kaire, are you all right?'

There was still no response. Disengaging the safety circuit, Roa made his way carefully down the narrow aisle. Kaire slumped in a seat, his head resting against the monitor. Gently lifting the limp body, Roa watched in growing alarm as blood flowed from a gash on Kaire's forehead. He pressed the emergency panel.

'Please state emergency details,' Tepp the Driver said calmly.

'Scholar Kaire fell against the edge of the monitor when the train stopped. He's unconscious and has a deep wound on his forehead.'

'First-aid equipment is in the compartment above the seat. Press the green pad in the middle of the control panel.'

'Come and assist me, it looks serious.'

'I'm sorry, sir, but I can't leave the driver capsule.'

'Come at once, it's an order.'

'I'd be pleased to help you, sir, but the driver capsule is sealed and can only be opened at official stopping places.'

'That's ridiculous.'

'Stem the flow of blood, sir, then hold the wound together with your fingers and apply skin sealant, that's the red tube. I'll contact the physician in the next village and arrange for him to come to the train once the storm has passed.'

'Thank you, your advice is appreciated.'

'I'm pleased to be of assistance, sir.'

Roa followed the driver's instructions meticulously and soon the head wound resembled nothing more than a thin red line. But Kaire remained unconscious, which caused him concern. As a military escort, Roa was responsible for Kaire's welfare and failure to report additional injuries to the physician could result in a demotion or worse still, a transfer further north. Somewhat reluctantly, as Roa hated the thought of dealing with more blood, he unfastened Kaire's robe. There were no signs of injury on his neck, shoulders or chest, and Roa was about to press around the abdomen when he realised that as well as having no body hair, Kaire lacked a navel. Frowning, Roa ran his hands over the pale skin searching for a tell-tale ridge of scar tissue that could provide an explanation. But he found no sign of prior surgery and nor could he feel any foreign material beneath the skin. His hands moved lower. Everything else appeared in order so he decided to leave the navel problem for the physician to solve.

After checking the head wound remained sealed, he quickly pulled the edges of Kaire's robe together and looked around for the sash. It had fallen to the floor and was protruding from under the heel of his boot. Bending to detach it, his fingers brushed against the hem of Kaire's robe and encountered something hard. Curious, he lifted the thin fabric into the light. A slim square object about the size of an ID disc was embedded in the hem. Rough stitching above suggested it had been deliberately implanted. Without hesitation, Roa reached for the surgical scissors from the overhead tray and cut the threads.

A silver disc, similar but smaller than those he'd seen Kaire use for the interviews, slipped from its protective cover onto his outstretched palm. Military training had taught him concealed data could only mean one thing: Kaire had something to hide. *Perhaps scholar isn't the only role this pale-skinned southerner is playing*, he pondered, hurriedly retrieving the sash and fastening it in place. A quick glance at Kaire revealed no sign of imminent waking, so Roa stepped carefully into the aisle. Safely returned to his seat, he inserted the disc into his communicator.

The initial statement surprised him and he almost ejected the disc, thinking it comprised merely intimate messages designed to keep an absent lover faithful.

'Dearly beloved, I bring you words destined to touch heart and soul.'

But there was something unusual in the storyteller's manner of speaking that alerted far more than curiosity. The second sentence did not disappoint.

'As many of you know, I am Sannah the Storyteller from Village 10.'

Roa settled back to listen to the rest of the disc.

'Tonight I bring you a different tale, one some of you will not have heard before. This is a tale of greed, corruption and selfishness encompassing flood, fire, famine, war and dispossession. My time with you is short so this tale is only an outline of the truth you, my people, deserve to know. Comprehensive information with further supporting evidence will follow at a later date.

This Truth-Tale begins long ago in the time known as the Post-Industrial Era, a period of unprecedented advances in technology. By 2050 the developed world controlled global food production, water supply and fossil fuel usage. These nations possessed the technology to genetically enhance organisms, cure most diseases and alleviate global poverty and homelessness. But they also possessed sufficient nuclear weapons—or weapons of mass destruction as they were known—to totally destroy the planet several times over.

At the beginning of the twenty-first century, fear that other less stable nations might develop such weapons and cause global nuclear war preoccupied first world governments. Increasing acts of terrorism and the need to secure diminishing oil reserves led to first world invasions of several Middle Eastern countries. These wars dragged on for years, creating increased instability throughout the region. Victory eluded both invaders and invaded.

African wars dominated the second and third decades. Widespread poverty and disease combined with massive debt to the first world engendered both despair and hostility. Nations locked within boundaries created by former colonial rulers rose up against one another in an attempt to gain wealth, dominance and territory. Cities and towns burned out of control; chemicals seeped from damaged factories polluting waterways, pasture and arable land. The survivors left their ruined homelands and trudged all over the continent, searching for food, shelter and safety.

First world governments deplored the problems created by this flood of refugees: deforestation, agricultural collapse and epidemics of previously suppressed diseases, to name but a few. So after two decades it was decided this environmental degradation and an increased flow of illegal migration to Europe and beyond could no longer be tolerated. Aid to all African nations was withdrawn, refugee boats were turned around or sunk. Mass starvation and disease ensued, African economies collapsed.

The fortunate few fled to the first world where their wealth ensured a warm welcome.

But environmental damage and displacement of populations was not confined to the African continent. Now I wish to speak to you of our own region, our beloved Oceania. As you all know, it was at the beginning of the twenty-first century that our communities first began to experience the devastating effects of increased cyclonic activity and rising sea levels, which eventually led to the loss of our islands. Our people's subsequent struggle to find new homelands is also well documented. But what storytellers and instructors have never told you are what caused these environmental disasters.

The exorbitant burning of fossil fuels, massive deforestation and the release of huge quantities of chemicals and pesticides into the Earth's atmosphere all contributed to a phenomenon known as the Greenhouse Effect. From the late twentieth-century, all governments were aware of the need to curtail greenhouse gas emissions, especially those produced by coal-burning power stations and land vehicles—similar to the trooper cars—that ran on a substance called petroleum. Difficult as it is for us to imagine, first world families often owned two of these vehicles. Governments debated endlessly about restricting emissions but fearing a hostile response from powerful big business they lacked the courage to implement effective laws.

The Greenhouse Effect intensified rapidly during the twenty-first century as increased industrialisation in India, China and Southeast Asia raised living standards and billions more people began to acquire land vehicles and other energy-hungry machines. Once again the first world became alarmed and immediately threatened trade restrictions unless these nations restricted their emissions.

A familiar scenario developed—wars, starvation, disease, refugees. Familiar repercussions too, for despite diminished populations, damage to the environment was irreversible. The rest as they say is history, or, as we say in the Brown Zone, Tales.

In school domes throughout this zone, our children are taught, as we once were, the history of Pacific peoples in Australia. Instructors stress the generosity of successive governments, the 'open door' policy that welcomed environmental refugees from the devastated Pacific islands, providing them with housing, education, employment and healthcare.

Yes, these particulars are true but instructors fail to mention other government policies that determined the ongoing low status of our people. For example, the Migrant Settlement Scheme during the twenty-first and twenty-second centuries, which dictated where non-White immigrants might settle. Asians were permitted to live on the periphery of cities and towns; environmental refugees were assigned to rural areas north of a city called Brisbane. Government officials explained this was in the best interests of our people. A tropical climate would suit our lifestyle and allow us to live in small communities, grow familiar crops and fish the warm Pacific waters.

Island life recreated on the island continent, courtesy of a beneficent government, the advantages of South Pacific society plus the benefits of first world citizenship. Yes, in those days Australia was considered a developed country.

But our people were not told why Australians had abandoned the tropic north, although it soon became apparent. Increased cyclonic activity due to global warming destroyed crops and dwellings, floods inundated pastures, and run-off from mines polluted the rivers. Inflammatory and respiratory diseases flourished in the humid air, diarrhoeal diseases were commonplace, as was heat-stress. Large numbers perished but gradually our people adapted to this hostile environment and our communities, particularly those closer to the border with the Asian Zone began to thrive.

During the twenty-second century, rising seas continued to inundate low-lying coastal areas. Cities and towns were abandoned in favour of small villages as the central deserts expanded. Soil erosion, salinity and persistent drought threatened the viability of agriculture in all areas except the northeastern coastal regions. Government response was swift. In 2150, the area known as Queensland and northern New South Wales was re-named the Brown Zone and designated an agriculture-only region. Our people were informed they would now grow produce for the southern population, which by this time was predominantly White. Asian Australians still living in the south were relocated to the coastal regions between the Brown Zone and the area formerly occupied by the western suburbs of the city of Sydney. The Asian Zone became the manufacturing and industrial sector.

Stringent population control and euthanasia policies were introduced, justified by government as essential if the nation were to survive continuing climate change and environmental degradation. But Brown and Asian citizens were not told White Australians were exempt from these laws.

Successive governments have preserved this system of apartheid through denial of basic rights such as voting, land ownership, higher education and decent healthcare. My friends, my people, have you never questioned how Australia became an insular society, abandoned and ignored by the rest of the world? Did you blame it all on economic decline caused by exhausted mineral resources and lack of fertile soil? Have you never wondered why the Super Nations expelled Australia from the Global Trade Consortium?'

Roa silenced the communicator, he'd heard enough. Clearly the so-called Truth-Tale aimed to provoke civil unrest. Ejecting the disc, he speculated whether Scholar Kaire had instigated this propaganda.

'Safety circuits may now be disengaged,' announced Tepp the Driver. 'The storm has abated. The physician will be here in ten minutes.'

Roa peered through the vision-strip. Steam rose from the sodden earth, moisture dribbled down a fallen palm leaf.

'Kaire,' he called. 'Don't worry, help is on the way.'

Thankfully there was no response.

Returning to the seat beside Kaire, Roa replaced the disc in its hiding place and secured the hem with skin sealant.

On their return to Village 10, Roa had fully intended to mention the Truth-Tale disc to Trooper-in-Charge Gage, but he changed his mind when he found himself in deep trouble over Kaire's accident. Gage considered Roa should have swapped his seat for Kaire's instead of sending him in search of a working safety circuit. For failing to take adequate care of a senior government official, Roa was fined a considerable sum and confined to routine trooper dome duties for several weeks. Roa had no desire to further damage his career prospects by reporting the existence of subversive material when he couldn't even supply a copy of the disc. Kaire would be certain to deny its existence.

Kaire was kept under observation in the medical dome for a few nights, his lengthy period of unconsciousness following the accident considered an unusual consequence of a relatively minor injury. Routine tests revealed no underlying medical problems and the head wound was healing well, so Payr the Healer recorded 'collision trauma' in her medical report to Jules the Physician.

Once discharged, Kaire politely declined Gage's offer of accommodation down in the village and hurried up the hill path to his lover.

CHAPTER 20

In the northern region of the Brown Zone, another journey had just begun. A silver solar train comprising a driver capsule and six passenger modules sped through dry grassland dotted with low scrub. Since leaving Terminal 4, the train had made good progress, the storms and torrential rains of the previous week having passed out to sea and no further inclement weather was expected for at least five nights. By that time the passengers would be safe beneath desert sands, neither they nor their jailers concerned by weather conditions.

The mood remained calm in the passenger modules, prisoners subdued by the prospect of a protracted journey to an unknown destination. They had long suspected the far northern prison domes were to be closed. No new inmates had arrived during the previous year and routine maintenance had not been carried out. Prison troopers had refused to be drawn into discussion of possible alternative accommodation even for several sachets of the drug moonlight. Rumours abounded: removal to an island prison, further trials in the south, implementation of the death penalty. This latter, the prisoners now considered unlikely; Governor An-il would not have authorised a costly journey if they were to be eliminated.

Only one prisoner among the group of one hundred and twenty suspected the existence of desert prisons. Sami, a swarthy Tasmanian nicknamed 'Sunshine' on account of his golden hair, had been incarcerated in the north for just over a year, having been transferred from a southern prison for subversive behaviour. During his journey north,

Sami had overheard a conversation between two troopers. Careless words concerning prison construction beneath desert sands were spoken as their prisoner drifted in and out of sleep on the interminable stretch between Working Party 2 and 3. Like all Australians, Sami feared the desert and knew there would be no possibility of escape from these subterranean prisons. When he learned the inmates of Northern Prisons 3 and 4 were to be taken south, Sami began to plan his escape. Wisely he kept his suspicions to himself, reasoning a lone escapee stood more chance of success. A former solar train engineer, Sami had spent part of his training in the Brown Zone and knew this line, the major route in the region, ran parallel with the coast. If the prisoners *were* being taken to the desert, the final leg of the journey would have to be made by land transport. Sami planned to make his escape bid during the transfer.

The journey south terminated much sooner than Sami had expected. On a lonely stretch of track between Working Party 1 and 2, a trooper car burned fiercely. The car's occupants had already fled and were hiding along with other workers, villagers and Women's Line members, behind a shale bank running parallel to the track. Their intention was to halt, not wreck the southbound train. The navigation system would warn the driver of an obstruction ahead on the track and he would stop the train at a safe distance. The young workers would then enter the train through emergency exit panels on the roof, overpower the troopers and free the prisoners.

Conn the Driver received the warning but the train was travelling at maximum speed and halted less than a metre from the burning trooper car. The passenger modules swayed violently, flames licked the driver capsule and dry grass beside the track ignited, sending smoke signals high into the cloudless sky.

'Help, fire!' Conn the Driver shouted into the control panel. 'Release the door locks!'

At the small trooper dome alongside the nearest produce terminal, his plea fell on deaf ears. The sole trooper on duty slept soundly, an empty bottle of tropica lying on the floor beneath his chair.

Inside the passenger modules, security unit troopers peered out of vision-strips to determine the cause of the emergency stop, saw flames and panicked, unaware the train was designed to withstand enormous heat. The prisoners' welfare was of no concern—let them fry boil or suffocate, there were plenty more to take their place. Troopers in five of the modules pressed controls beside the door panels and jumped out, sealing the doors behind them via communicators. Racing away from the burning trooper car, they climbed over the shale bank where Worker Tona and his friends quickly deprived them of weapons and liberty.

In the sixth module, a young trooper repeatedly pressed the door controls with no success. 'Fucking thing won't budge,' he remarked to his colleague.

'We'll have to open them manually,' the older trooper replied, raising his communicator to release the security shadow.

The prisoners watched with interest as the two troopers, fast becoming breathless and red in the face, attempted to prise the doors apart.

'Perhaps I could help?' Prisoner Sami offered with his sunshine smile.

The two troopers exchanged glances.

'Thank you,' answered the older trooper.

Sami moved forward, seized the doors in his massive hands and pulled them apart.

'Your assistance will be noted in our report, Prisoner Sami,' said the younger trooper. 'Return to your seat now. We won't be stuck here long. Our colleagues will no doubt have requested assistance from the nearest produce terminal.'

Sami moved aside. The trooper smiled and quickly climbed down from the train.

As the other trooper moved forward, Sami sidestepped into the narrow opening, blocking the way. 'My freedom for yours,' he said calmly.

'Get out of my way White scum.' The trooper reached for his weapon.

Sami stepped backwards, pulling the door panels together as he fell. Landing in a patch of smouldering grass, he quickly rolled over and leapt to his feet. He was running towards the rear of the train when he almost collided with a tall half-naked girl.

Worker Garna had insisted on accompanying her twin brother to the sabotage spot and had been waiting with the others for the signal to storm the train when the troopers began to flee into the bush. No one had expected security unit troopers to abandon their prisoners—the punishment for desertion was death. The trooper car was now little more than a blackened wreck and posed no threat to train or passengers.

Sami extended an arm to halt the girl's progress.

Garna glanced at his red tunic with its black prison emblem. 'Let me pass,' she demanded, struggling to push his arm away. 'I have important work to do.'

Sami clapped his other hand over her mouth.

Line Leader Zira stepped from behind the train and ran towards them. She held up a small message board, which flashed the word SILENCE.

Sami released his captive and watched her sprint towards a shale bank a few metres away.

Zira paused to re-key, then held up her message board. 'I'm here to help you,' it read. Sami pointed to a small scar on his right wrist. She nodded, pocketed the message board and pulled out her knife. Sami clenched his teeth as she slit his skin and deactivated the personal detection device.

'How did you escape?' she asked, closing the wound with skin sealant.

Sami pressed a finger to his lips.

'It's all right. I've activated a sound screen to protect us from the other PDDs.'

Sami smiled. 'The troopers in my module were having a bit of trouble with the door panels, so I offered to help. I escaped after the first one had jumped from the train.'

'How many other troopers in the module?'

'One. I slammed the doors in his face.'

'What type of weapon is he carrying?'

'Standard issue, stun or destroy.'

'Which module?'

'The first one.'

She turned to leave.

'What happened to the other troopers?' asked Sami.

'My people apprehended them as they ran from the train.'

'So the fire was no accident?'

'No.'

'What happens now?'

'I've no time for questions, I must release the other prisoners in your module.'

'I'd be pleased to help.'

Zira rummaged in her money-belt for her spare eradicator and handed it to Sami. 'Use this to blast open the doors and deal with the trooper. Signal the prisoners to leave the train and proceed in a westerly direction. My people are waiting to take you all to safety.'

Sami nodded.

'We must get away from here quickly,' she added. 'The driver may have already contacted troopers at the nearest village.'

'Don't worry, it won't take me long.'

On a patch of stony ground behind the shale bank, several Line leaders stood guard while workers and villagers linked disarmed troopers together with metal wristbands. Suddenly a trooper broke free and raced towards a second trooper car parked nearby. Line Leader Zira raised her eradicator and was about to launch a beam when a worker chasing the trooper moved into her line of fire. The boy soon caught up with the trooper and pushed him to the ground.

'Just hold him still,' she called running towards the struggling pair.

A knife flashed in the trooper's hand.

'Watch out,' Zira yelled, aiming for the trooper's arm.

The eradicator beam missed its target as the trooper bent forward and stabbed the boy in the chest. A second beam found its mark.

Garna sprinted to her brother's side and shoving Zira out of the way took Tona in her arms. 'No, no,' she cried, sobbing bitterly. 'I failed him, I failed my twin.'

Zira kissed Garna's wet cheek. 'You're alive, that isn't failure. He didn't die in vain, his twin will know freedom.'

'What use is freedom now?'

'Freedom will mean living without fear, speaking your truth, always remembering the other with love.'

'Freedom is worth the risk,' said a deep voice nearby.

Zira looked up and noticed the prisoner whose PDD she'd deactivated standing a short distance away. 'Take care of her,' she ordered, easing Garna's arms from Tona's body. 'We have a long walk ahead of us.'

The access corridor leading to the long-abandoned mineshaft had been recently constructed by Line members behind a stand of trees that had regenerated despite toxic soil. Line leaders had already explained by means of message boards that all PDDs would be deactivated underground. Although they were now twenty kilometres from the rail track and at least thirty from the nearest village, troopers could well be searching the area before long. The driver capsule had proved impregnable and the terrified driver's incoherent answers failed to establish whether he had managed to contact the nearest trooper dome. Although the Line leaders knew he would face imprisonment for losing his passengers, they had no choice but to abandon him.

Troopers arriving at the stationary train would discover a burnt-out trooper car, a blackened driver capsule and patches of burnt grass but no other signs of violence or forced entry. If they looked behind the shale bank, they would find ten troopers linked together with wristbands around the trunk of a dead tree and the body of a young male worker. The bodies of the two troopers eradicated by Zira and Sami had been bundled into the trooper car belonging to Working Party 2. The young driver had orders to drive south for several kilometres before torching the car.

Underground, the atmosphere was dank, moisture dripping from cracks in the roof soaked into tunics and robes. Line leaders worked tirelessly, slitting skin, deactivating, re-sealing. There were no cries of pain or even grimaces; political prisoners were familiar with suffering. Sami stood to one side watching the proceedings, his thoughts focused on freedom.

'All PDDs deactivated,' said Line Leader Zira at last, wiping her bloody knife on her robe.

'Where are you taking us now?' asked Sami.

'I'll explain in a few minutes,' she answered, flashing him a brief smile before turning to speak to another Line leader.

The men waited expectantly. They were predominantly White southerners, imprisoned for seditious activities. Three men of Asian descent stood slightly apart from the others, the social mores difficult to relinquish. All the men directed their gaze to the Line leaders. They were unaccustomed to Brown Zone women and marvelled at their competence and authority. The few dark-skinned women they'd encountered previously had seemed immature and servile, gossiping incessantly, fawning over every White man who passed. So who were these female leaders and what did they intend to do with the men they had freed?

Line Leader Zira moved away from the crowd and raised both hands. Workers and other Line leaders turned to face her.

'We now enter Phase 2 of our mission,' she announced. 'Split into groups of six. No particular arrangement, stay with your friends if you wish. Two workers will accompany each group. You will be escorted to various safe places west of here.'

A ripple of fear spread through the lines of men.

'Don't be concerned. We're not taking you to the desert. You will be transferred to a permanent safe location as soon as possible.'

Sami stepped forward. 'We appreciate the need for caution but now that we're free, many of us will want to continue the fight against this despotic government. Will that be possible where we end up?'

'It will.'

'I don't suppose you can tell us where that is?'

'You suppose correctly.'

Footsteps rang on the metal ladder leading to the surface. Sami was one of the last to leave in a group comprising mostly young workers. Garna had left with Line Leader Zira sometime before, so Sami was astonished when she stepped out from behind a boulder as he emerged from the mine.

'What happened to the rest of your group?' he asked anxiously.

'Nothing, I just decided to wait and thank you for looking after me on the journey to the mine. If you hadn't held on to me, I doubt I'd have made it. Grief had done more than sap my strength, I wanted to lie down in the dirt and die.'

'I'm glad you didn't,' said Sami, reaching out to take her hand. 'Come, Garna, walk with me to freedom.'

CHAPTER 21

Below ground in the secret chamber, Sannah and Fley waited for news of the mission. Line Leader Zira had promised to communicate the moment she returned to her village. The four Line leaders directly involved in the train sabotage planned to part company from the workers, villagers and escapees a short distance from the mine. It was imperative the four women return to their home villages before the dawn curfew. Absences from work the previous night could be explained as sudden illness of the female variety. Troopers rarely questioned such absenteeism. But it was now two hours past curfew and Fley felt the fear rising in her.

'Anything could have delayed them,' said Sannah, reading her friend's mind. 'Someone would have contacted us if there had been problems.'

'I wish I could believe that.'

'What's happened to your customary optimism?'

Fley shrugged. 'I don't know, I just sense something's gone wrong.'

'Premonitions are usually my prerogative.' She patted Fley's hand. 'Why don't I contact Maris? She may have heard something.'

Before Fley could answer, a panel on her communicator began to flash intermittently. 'Someone's trying to get through.' She pressed several panels. 'Curse this old machine.'

'LLZ,' said a faint voice.

'LLF,' Fley responded. 'At last, what took you so long?'

'I had to visit a friend before returning to my dome.'

'Socialising before duty! What's the matter with you?'

'I had to break the news of her son's death,' said Zira calmly.

Fley closed her eyes and began to sway.

'LLF are you still there?'

Sannah leaned over and took the communicator from Fley's hand. 'Your news distressed her. Have you any details?'

'I'm not at liberty to say. The boy's father still has to be informed.'

'I understand. Any other problems?'

'No, all went well.'

'Excellent,' said Sannah, but the connection had already closed. Line Leader Zira didn't trust her cousin's ancient communicator.

'Such a waste of a young life,' Fley said softly.

'He knew the risks.'

'We all know the risks, Sannah. It doesn't lessen the tragedy.'

'Come on, it's time to get some sleep. You look worn out.' Helping Fley to her feet, she led her down the narrow passage to the door. In the sleeping chamber, music blared from the monitor. Fley raised her hand. Silence enfolded the two women.

At dusk, Sannah left Fley to prepare for another night in the school dome and headed home. She made slow progress and almost came to a standstill when she reached the steep hill path. Her head throbbed, Fley having spent hours speculating on the consequences of sabotage, asking endless questions for which Sannah had no answers. *A waste of words and energy*, she thought, but perhaps talk had helped calm her friend's agitated spirit. Eventually total exhaustion had compelled Fley to rest, but for Sannah sleep did not bring peace. Dark dreams disturbed her brief sleep, dreams filled with images of dead children. She'd woken with a start, convinced troopers were surrounding the bed, threatening to kill her daughter Pia.

The hill path seemed interminable; every few minutes she was forced to stop and catch her breath. Pain stabbed her right side, stars floated before her eyes and it took immense effort to fill her lungs. Not far from her dome, she slumped against a smooth boulder convinced she could go no further.

'Coo-ee, coo-ee,' called a familiar voice.

She didn't have the strength to reply.

Kaire shook her gently. 'Sannah, what's happened? Are you ill?'

She opened her eyes.

'Sannah, tell me what's happened.'

'I have risked everything,' she said wearily, 'my life, her life, your life. And for what, a few hundred words, another tale of the past? To think I believed this Truth-Tale could begin to change our future. I'm astonished at my own naivety.'

Kaire gathered her in his arms. 'Come on, you're exhausted.' He helped her to her feet. 'This is neither the time nor the place for talk.'

Back at the dome, she allowed herself to be led downstairs to the sleeping chamber where she slouched like a drowsy child as he stripped off her robe and eased the dusty sandals from her feet. Her eyes were already closed when he tucked the cool sheet around her shoulders.

A few hours before dawn, Kaire perched on the edge of the bed while Sannah ate the food he'd prepared. All of a sudden she pushed the platter away and leaning towards him confided, 'I wanted to be Sannah the Truthteller, wanted *my* voice to spread the word. Not next week, not next month, but right now! I should have waited until after the sabotage, until we had a new ship. I should have kept quiet. What if my Truth-Tale fell into the wrong hands? Not only the Line but hundreds of my people would be at risk.' She clutched his shoulders. 'I'm going to destroy it now before more lives are endangered. It was stupid to make a permanent record. My people have always preferred the oral tradition, it's part of our cultural heritage.' She paused for a moment, then pushed him away and leapt out of bed. 'Truth will be told in every corner of this land,' she cried, brown eyes blazing, 'whispered at close of night by mothers to weary children, passed from worker to worker in field and marketplace, confided by lovers in the afterglow of passion. Truth will be told.' Rushing over to the robe-rack, she grabbed the travelling robe Kaire had worn for the journey north and rushed out of the chamber.

Kaire shook his head and fell back onto the pillows.

In the kitchen, Sannah picked up a small knife before entering the store. Spreading Kaire's robe on the floor, she felt along the hem for the disc. Soon her fingers touched the disc cover and knife in hand she bent to slit the stitches.

A film of skin sealant covered the opening. *Why hadn't Kaire used the thread I'd supplied?* she thought, cutting the fabric and releasing the disc. Lifting a large jar, she placed the disc underneath the hard edge and ground it into dust. The debris she carefully swept up and tossed into the kitchen waste tube.

Only then did she remember his travelling robe had been cleaned and pressed at the medical dome. Seizing the robe, she raced across the living chamber and down the stairs.

'You fool!' she cried, bursting into the sleeping chamber. 'Why the Sun did you leave the disc in your robe?'

'What are you talking about?' Kaire mumbled sleepily.

'Whoever took your robe to clean it had discovered the disc and listened to it.'

'How can you possibly know that?'

She thrust the robe in his face. 'Look, the opening's been re-sealed with skin sealant.'

'I can see that but there's no need to worry, it was Payr who took my robe away.'

'Healers don't clean robes. Payr would have passed it to one of the laundry workers.'

'They are your people,' he answered defensively.

'But their supervisor is an informant.'

'If the supervisor had found the disc and handed it over, why haven't I been ordered to the trooper dome?'

'I've no idea, but I don't trust Gage. When he hears about the break-outs and the train sabotage, he could easily become suspicious of your northern travels.'

'It's a chance we'll have to take.'

'I won't take any more chances, the consequences for Pia could be horrendous. I won't expose her to their barbaric practices.'

'So what do you propose to do?'

'We must leave the village immediately and …'

'You know we can't leave now,' he interrupted. 'That would be tantamount to admitting we were involved. Think of the repercussions for the young workers. Pia and the other girls will be in enough trouble as it is once the troopers realise stealing the cars wasn't a prank and the boys aren't coming back.'

She grasped his shoulders. 'Let me finish. We must retrieve your transporter and go to Working Party 2. You have the authority to demand Pia's immediate release. Any excuse will do.'

'Such as?'

'Say you need her for some research.'

'And when I've secured Pia's release?'

'I want you to take us to Aotearoa.'

'New Zealand?'

She hesitated, surprised by his knowledge. 'I believe Aotearoa was known by that name long ago,' she answered warily. 'It's a small country, primitive by your standards but safe because of its isolation from the rest of the world. A number of my people live there, the government is sympathetic to our cause.' She sighed, released him and slumped back on the bed. 'Please take us to safety.'

He looked thoughtful. 'Would I be welcome in Aotearoa?'

'Of course, why wouldn't you be?'

Leaning forward, he placed his white hand on her brown arm.

She smiled. 'Skin colour is irrelevant over there. Aotearoa is a haven for anyone fleeing oppression.'

'Then we'll leave just before dawn. I'll program a direct route now.'

'I'll go and pack a small bag,' she said, sliding off the bed.

'No, we take a little food and water that's all. Everything must appear normal when the troopers come looking for us.'

She nodded and reached for her robe.

Climbing the stairs to join Sannah in the kitchen, Kaire heard strains of song in an unfamiliar language but a melody he recognised, the same one the island women had sung in honour of his visit. He leaned against the railing and looked beyond the narrow confines of domes, paths and fields to the vast reaches of space. 'Stars keep us safe on our journey to Aotearoa,' he prayed fervently.

CHAPTER 22

Morning mist veiled the crown of the hill. At its base, Sannah and Kaire halted for a few minutes to moisten their parched throats. The journey from Village 10 had been uneventful apart from a heavy shower that briefly slowed their progress. After sealing the water flask, they scrambled through the thick foliage prevalent on the lower slopes. Halfway to the summit they veered north, following a rocky ridge devoid of vegetation. Stones and soil slid beneath their feet and a strong wind flung dust in their faces. Heads bowed, they trudged towards the steep gully where Kaire had abandoned the transporter.

'We'll stop up there,' Kaire called, indicating a cluster of low bushes in the distance. 'I need to check our position.'

'What's wrong with right here?' Sannah queried, needing a break.

'Flying sand could distort the reading.'

The sparse foliage afforded little protection from the wind. Pulling the communicator from his backpack, Kaire pressed the navigation panel but nothing registered. 'I don't understand. It's never failed before. The transporter should be around here but the readings give no indication we're anywhere near the gully.'

'The land seems different,' said Sannah, scooping up a handful of dry soil. 'I'm sure there were more bushes up here before. There must have been a dust storm or a rock fall recently.'

'Maybe, but that doesn't explain why I can't pick up the transporter's location.'

'We could have climbed the wrong ridge.'

'Impossible, the communicator can't change navigation settings. We're simply retracing our steps.'

'If we climb a bit higher, we might be able to see the gully. The mist's clearing.'

'We can give it a try.' He shoved the communicator into his backpack. 'So much for advanced technology.'

They climbed in silence, Sannah slightly ahead, her robe flapping in the strong breeze. After a while she stopped and turned to scan the hillside.

'Over there,' she called, pointing northwest. 'I can see the gully.'

Kaire hurried to join her. 'Yes, this is the place. But I can't see the transporter.'

'It wouldn't be visible from here. The gully's far too deep.'

'Then what are we waiting for?' he cried, seizing her hand and pulling her forward.

They stood on the rim staring at altered terrain. Rocks littered the gully floor, part of the opposite bank had collapsed, drifts of sandy soil hugged protruding boulders.

'Do you think the transporter's buried under there?' asked Sannah.

Kaire reached for his communicator. The navigation panel remained blank. 'I don't know. It could have been swept down the gully by the force of the rockslide. Or …' he hesitated, reluctant to speak the probable truth. 'Or it may have been annihilated.'

'Annihilated, is that possible?'

'Yes, it's a lightweight surface transporter. It wasn't designed to withstand avalanches.' He sat down heavily, clutching his communicator. Automatically his fingers played over the control panel as if movement could restore the readings, his mind refusing to acknowledge the continuing absence of data. Sky training had not prepared him for a situation like this.

'I'm going back down,' Sannah announced after a long silence. 'We must find shelter soon.' She began to scramble down the bank into the gully.

'Why are you going down that way?' he called after her.

'If we follow the gully, the transporter could be visible further down.'

'Wait for me,' he said, stowing the useless machine.

Near the foot of the gully, pieces of shattered passenger bubble protruded from a mound of sand. Dropping to his knees, Kaire began to dig frantically with his bare hands.

'Stop it!' Sannah cried. 'Do you want to injure yourself?'

'I must find out if it can be repaired.' He pulled out a long cylindrical object. 'See, here's part of the drive mechanism.'

Kneeling beside him she said firmly, 'We can't excavate the transporter with our bare hands. We need help. We must contact Fley, she'll arrange for a team of villagers to meet us here.'

He raised his head. 'I thought we agreed not to contact anyone.'

'What other options do we have?'

'None I can think of.' He pulled the backpack from his shoulders. 'I just hope the wretched machine works this time.'

Fley was enjoying a meal when the minuscule alarm hidden in her day-robe began to pulse against her skin. Reluctantly she made her way to the concealed chamber.

'LLF,' she said into the old communicator.

'Listen carefully,' said a familiar voice.

Fley sighed and sank down on the hard bench. 'I think you have your codes mixed up, friend, and I can tell you I'm not impressed. It's been a long night in the school dome and my legs are killing me.'

'I'm far away and need your help,' said Sannah.

'Far away? What are you talking about? Have you been drinking?'

'Coordinates being transmitted now,' Kaire interrupted.

'Received.' Fley studied the figures and pondered what Sannah and Kaire were doing out in the hills.

'We need at least six strong villagers with portable digging equipment,' said Sannah, 'and by portable I mean capable of being carried over a long distance. Can you arrange it?'

'I should think so. The troopers are somewhat preoccupied at the moment.'

'Trouble?'

'A fire in one of the grain stores.'

'We have an avalanche here.'

'I see,' said Fley, completely baffled now but unwilling to ask further questions and increase the risk of detection. 'I'll contact you when arrangements have been made.'

'Hurry,' said Sannah as Kaire terminated the communication.

A small cave at the base of the hill provided shelter from the blazing sun. The day passed slowly. They slept intermittently, taking it in turns to watch for signs of trooper activity. Nothing stirred save a few insects hovering over the dry grassland beyond the cave. Towards evening they walked to a nearby small creek crossed on the outward journey. The water was shallow and tepid but sufficed to wash off the dust. Sannah did not refill their water bags, even though supplies were low. Drinking untested water in the Brown Zone could prove fatal.

A warm wind dried their skin as they retraced their steps. Near the cave entrance, she sat down on a flat rock and tilted her face to the darkening sky. Beside her, Kaire stood stiffly, tapping his foot against a stone.

'It'll be some time before the villagers arrive,' she said, reaching for his hand. 'Come sit beside me and watch the night sky.'

'No, I think I'll go and see if I can uncover more of the transporter.'

'And what do you propose to use for digging equipment?'

He studied the ground for a few moments. 'A rock will have to do.'

She bent over to retrieve her sandals.

'You don't have to join me,' he said, stroking her hair. 'You look tired, stay here and rest.'

'Thanks.' She smiled. 'Leave the communicator here. It'll save you carrying it.'

Kaire nodded, hitched up his robe and set off towards the gully.

A high-pitched sound roused Sannah from sleep and she peered into darkness expecting to see a posse of troopers marching towards the cave. An equally startled rat scuttled past her feet. The noise intensified. Grabbing Kaire's backpack, she fled into the night. Her flight ended before she had crossed the small patch of grass in front of the cave and laughing at her foolishness, she pulled out his communicator and pressed the panel.

'At last,' said Fley. 'I was beginning to fear the worst.'

'Sorry, I fell asleep. Is everything organised?'

'Yes, but you must return to your dome at once.'

'Friend, I have something to tell you,' said Sannah, her voice quivering with emotion. 'I'm not coming back, we're travelling to the other side.'

'You have to come back,' Fley replied. 'Pia has been arrested.'

'Where is she?' cried Sannah.

'We don't know yet.'

'I'm on my way.' Sannah closed the communication. Wearily, she picked up the backpack and began to climb back to the gully.

Down in the village, the night progressed as usual: stallkeepers were busy setting up in the marketplace, villagers gossiping in dome doorways, troopers exchanging small talk on path corners, impatient for their shift's end. Sannah slipped unnoticed into Fley's dome and made her way downstairs as arranged. The concealed panel behind the robe-rack opened as she approached. The narrow passage was dimly lit but she could see Fley sitting on a bench in the chamber.

'I came as soon as I could,' she called. 'It's a long walk from the hills.'

'Good thing you're fit.'

Sannah bent down and kissed Fley on both cheeks before joining her on the bench.

'Tell me about the arrests.'

'We heard the news direct from Working Party 2. Worker Tanna managed to transmit a message to Zira. It was brief but thanks to the data piracy programme Kaire set up during his visit, we were able to intercept the subsequent trooper report. Five girls have been arrested: Pia and two others from Working Party 2 plus two from Working Party 1.'

'Are the arrests in any way connected with the train sabotage?'

'We don't think so. Problems arose at Working Party 2 because the girls' attempts to distract the troopers weren't wholly successful. The boys only got away with the trooper car when two youngsters started a fire in a storeroom. Fortunately in the ensuing chaos, one of the girls managed to disable the main communicator, which prevented the troopers calling for immediate assistance. Initially, according to the report, the troopers assumed the theft was an isolated incident, a worker prank. But when they discovered the same thing had occurred at Working Party 1 they became suspicious and called in senior officers.'

Sannah nodded. 'Do we know how the girls are coping?'

'They're currently being transported to the border station, where officers from the young workers department will question them. Parents are to be present at the interviews.' Fley laid her hand on Sannah's knee. 'So you see I had no choice but to demand you return home.'

Sannah managed a half-smile.

'Gage is expecting you to report to the trooper dome this evening. He knows you've been away from the village.'

'How?'

'He contacted me when you didn't respond to his message about Pia's arrest. He asked if I knew where you were.'

'What did you tell him?'

'It sounds ridiculous, but it was all I could think of at the time.' She hesitated.

'Go on, I promise not to laugh.'

'I told him you'd gone into the bush behind your dome with Kaire to collect loveweed.'

'Loveweed! Do you think we need an aphrodisiac?'

'Of course not, but I figured Gage just might swallow the story. With luck he'll let you off with a caution.'

Sannah smiled. 'Thanks, that was a brilliant excuse.' She rose from the bench. 'I'd better go and get it over with. I'll call on my way back.'

Trooper-in-Charge Gage did not acknowledge Sannah's presence. Dismissing the young trooper who'd admitted her to his chamber, he continued to stare at his monitor. Sannah stood at a respectful distance from his work-module.

'Ah, storyteller,' he said after several minutes. 'Returned from your wanderings I see. No doubt you're aware of the rules regarding unauthorised excursions?'

'Yes, sir.'

'Then I won't waste my time listening to whatever excuse you've concocted to justify breaking those rules. This time I'm prepared to overlook your transgression, but I warn you if it happens again I won't be so lenient.'

'Thank you, sir, I assure you it won't happen again.'

Gage nodded and turned back to his monitor.

'May I leave now, sir?' she asked tentatively.

'No, you may not,' he replied without lifting his gaze from the screen. 'Do you think I ordered you to the trooper dome simply to discuss your carnal appetites? No doubt your friend the fat instructor has already informed you your daughter has been arrested?'

'Yes, sir, but I don't know why she's been arrested.'

'Bring that chair over here,' ordered Gage, 'this could take some time.'

He watched her bend to lift the chair, moistening his lips with the tip of his tongue. Positioning the chair close to his work-module, she sat down and smoothed her robe with her hands.

Gage looked down at the screen. 'Pia, daughter of Sannah the Story-teller of Village 10,' he read slowly, 'is charged under Section 2 of the Working Party Security Act, this third night of December 2399. The accused will be interviewed by Youth Workers Department officers at the Brown Zone border station within one week.' He raised his head. 'You will be transported to the border station on Wednesday afternoon to attend the interview. Report here at 1600 hours.'

'Yes, sir.'

He pressed the pad beneath his right hand. The monitor disappeared from view. 'No need to concern ourselves with any more legal jargon,' he remarked pleasantly, leaning back in his chair. 'I just want to know why your daughter broke the rules.' He smiled. 'And I'm sure you can help me, Sannah.'

'I'd like to help you, sir, but I still don't know what Pia has done. I'm not familiar with Section 2 of the Working Party Security Act.'

'Of course you're not,' said Gage with an ingratiating smile. 'Well, to put it in simple language, Pia has been charged with aiding and abetting a breakout.'

'I see. I had no idea, sir.'

'Didn't you?' he muttered under his breath, tapping the work-module with his nails. 'Pia and two other female workers attempted to seduce three troopers while a group of male workers stole the trooper car and made their escape.' He fixed his gaze on Sannah's face. 'That's just the sort of exploit a woman with your prodigious sexual appetite might suggest to her daughter, isn't it?'

Sannah struggled to retain her composure. 'I might suggest a liaison,' she answered carefully. 'Troopers are renowned lovers, but I know nothing of any breakout.'

Gage sighed. 'The same thing happened at Working Party 1. Bit of a coincidence don't you think?'

Sannah shrugged.

'Both incidents suggest outside involvement,' he continued. 'It's highly unlikely female Brown-skins aged fifteen, sixteen and eighteen devised such a plan by themselves.'

'Oh, it's possible, sir. At that age the hormones do tend to take control.'

Gage thumped the work-module with his fist. 'Don't play games with me, storyteller. It might have washed with Trooper Wurn but I'm not desperate to get between your legs.'

Sannah felt her face flush crimson.

'Truth burns, eh storyteller? Just like a trooper car on a rail line.'

'I'm sorry, sir, I don't follow you.'

Gage propelled his chair backwards. Rising quickly, he skirted the work-module and yanked Sannah to her feet. 'You think you're so clever, storyteller,' he said, his breath stinging her face, 'with your glib tongue and your sugar-sweet smile. But I'll corner you one of these nights, just you wait and see. Now get out of my sight.'

'Yes, sir,' she replied and fled as fast as she dared through the trooper dome and out into the relative safety of the street.

CHAPTER 23

Beneath the main dome of the border station, a group of Brown Zone parents sat on long benches in a corridor, waiting anxiously to be called into the interview chamber. An armed trooper stood at the chamber door staring straight ahead, his large boots planted like stone pillars on the bare concrete floor.

Inside the chamber, perched on a hard plastic seat that protruded from the rear wall, Sannah waited for Pia's interview to begin. The two Youth Workers Department officers sitting stiffly behind monitors hadn't exchanged a word for what seemed an eternity. In the centre of the chamber, Pia sat cross-legged on the floor, the red prison robe tight around her neck.

One of the officers rose quietly, walked around the work-module and approached Pia. A tall, well-built man, he moved with unexpected grace, the tread of his boots barely audible on the stone floor. 'The prisoner will now stand.'

Pia scrambled to her feet, smoothing coarse cloth over her thighs.

Lifting a well-manicured hand to his mouth, Officer Reyi gave a small cough before addressing the prisoner. 'Pia, daughter of Sannah the Storyteller of Village 10, you are charged with aiding and abetting a breakout at Working Party 2 on the twenty-first night of November 2399. Do you understand the charges?'

'Yes, sir,' Pia answered confidently.

'How do you plead?'

'Not guilty, sir.'

He turned to face his colleague. 'Officer Como, please read the statement made by Trooper Ome.'

'Statement by Trooper Ome of Working Party 2, twenty-third night of November 2399,' he began, delivering the data in a slow deliberate fashion reminiscent of a child learning to read. 'I had not long finished my shift and was relaxing in my chamber when there was a knock on the door panel. I checked the security screen, saw it was Worker Pia and released the panel. When she entered I noticed she was carrying a small platter. She said she had made me a special treat to celebrate the recent good harvest. I asked what she had made and she replied, a coffee cake. That's my favourite cake and a rare treat in these parts, coffee being so expensive. As a friendly gesture, I invited Worker Pia to stay and share the cake with me. I also offered her a drink. For a short period we ate, drank and discussed the high yields. Then Worker Pia moved closer to me and began to speak of more personal matters.' Officer Como paused and cleared his throat. 'Her words and her close proximity aroused me. I attempted to hide my condition but failed to do so as I was wearing only a thin day-robe. Worker Pia suggested she relieve my discomfort. I agreed.

'Not long afterwards, the siren sounded so I dismissed her and hurried to the main dome. A fire had broken out in one of the store chambers. It took some time to extinguish the blaze. As we were organising teams of workers to clear the chamber of debris, we realised few male workers seemed to be around. A roll call revealed ten male workers were missing. A short time later, we discovered the trooper car had also disappeared. Somehow the workers had managed to deactivate the security shadow protecting the car. Further investigation revealed they had also tampered with the main communicator, preventing us from alerting other troopers.

'When we had repaired the communicator and were waiting for assistance, we interviewed the remaining male workers. All denied knowledge of the trooper car theft or any escape plans. The female workers were subsequently interviewed and corroborated the male workers' story.

'Later, during conversation with my colleagues, it transpired I was not the only trooper to have been visited by a female worker that morning. Consequently three female workers were arrested and charged with aiding and abetting a breakout.'

The officer looked up. 'Data terminates here, sir.'

'Thank you, Officer Como.'

A brief silence ensued, and then Officer Reyi turned back to Pia. 'Prisoner Pia, do you acknowledge Trooper Ome's statement as a true record of events?'

'I do, sir.'

'In that case, do you wish to change your plea?'

'No, sir. I plead not guilty to the charge.'

Officer Reyi sighed. 'Then perhaps you could tell me why you went to Trooper Ome's chamber?'

'To give the boys time to steal the trooper car. It was a prank, sir. The boys just wanted to see if they could pull it off, they intended to return later in the day. At least, that's what they told me.'

'Were you aware that workers from Working Party 1 had planned the same, er, prank at the same time?'

'No, sir.'

Turning on his heel, Officer Reyi strode to the work-module, leaned over the monitor and conferred with his colleague in a low voice.

Pia began to fidget with the hem of her robe.

After a few minutes, he returned to the prisoner. 'You plead ignorance of the male workers' intention to abscond permanently, Prisoner Pia, but that does not excuse your part in the proceedings.' Placing his hand on her shoulder he said in a fatherly tone, 'You have been very irresponsible, but if you agree to cooperate I'm prepared to be lenient on this occasion.' He smiled.

'I'll do whatever I can, sir. I realise how stupid I've been.'

He nodded. 'You are acquainted with Trooper Roa from Village 10, I believe?'

'Yes, sir, I met him recently when he visited my working party.'

'And would you say Trooper Roa finds you attractive?'

She blushed. 'I think so, sir.'

Removing his hand, Officer Reyi stepped back a pace. 'The department believes Trooper Roa is in possession of vital information relating to the breakouts, but he seems reluctant to share it with us.'

Instantly Pia adopted an astonished expression.

'Pia,' he continued, noting her reaction. 'I want you to employ your, er, considerable charms to coax this information from Trooper Roa.'

'I'll do my best, sir,' she answered coyly.

'Oh, I don't think you'll have to try very hard. No doubt Trooper Roa possesses the customary sexual appetite of the young. It won't be a chore as no doubt it was with the ageing Trooper Ome and coffee cake is unlikely to be on the menu.' Smiling at his witticism, he turned abruptly, returned to his seat and conferred quietly with his colleague.

Sannah shifted on her seat, disconcerted by this revelation. Had Trooper Roa discovered the Truth-Tale disc on his journey north with Kaire?

Officer Como rose to his feet, preventing further speculation. Sannah sat up straight, aware a verdict could be imminent.

'Prisoner Pia, you are henceforth released into your mother's care,' Officer Como announced in an officious tone. 'Sannah the Storyteller, step forward.'

Sannah hurried across the chamber to the work-module.

'Sannah the Storyteller, you are to begin training your daughter in the art of storytelling. As you are aware, there is a vacancy for a storyteller on Island 1 due to that unfortunate drowning. The evidence against Pia is inconclusive. Your trooper-in-charge will be informed of her release immediately.'

'Thank you for your clemency, sir. Training will commence as soon as we return home,' Sannah replied graciously.

He nodded.

'May I ask a question, sir?'

'You may.'

'Won't the villagers think it strange Pia has returned home when she still has eighteen months to serve at the working party?'

He tossed her a mocking smile. 'I shall make it known the department has waived this final work period so that Pia can begin training for the storyteller vacancy. That should forestall the usual Brown Zone gossip.'

'Thank you, sir.'

The officers exchanged glances.

'Interview with Pia, daughter of Sannah the Storyteller now terminated. Get going before I change my mind.'

Sannah and Pia hurried to the door.

'Oh, and Worker Pia,' Officer Reyi called out as they were about to step into the corridor. They turned around and noticed his smile had vanished. 'You would do well to acquire the information I need quickly; otherwise you may find yourself back in a working party for an indefinite period.'

CHAPTER 24

Light rain began to fall as the stallkeepers set out their wares. Some quickly covered their merchandise while they erected makeshift canopies; a few, notably the robe-seller and the potter, packed up and returned to their domes. The marketplace was almost deserted— Thursday evening always a bad time for trade. Villagers received their meagre pay every Saturday; by Thursday most had only enough tokens left to purchase essentials.

At the rear of the marketplace, Trooper Roa leaned against a low wall cursing the colleague who'd assigned him this shift. He detested Thursday market duty: there were so few villagers to monitor and the stallkeepers were sullen. Now rain threatened to make the remaining work hours even more miserable. Looking across to the baker's stall, he decided he might as well seek shelter.

The delicious smell of fresh bread wafted over him as he stepped under the awning. 'Good evening, stallkeeper.'

'There's nothing good about it, Trooper Roa,' Ingle the Stallkeeper replied. 'Not many customers about.'

'Well I'm buying,' said Roa, pointing to a long brown roll dusted with seeds. 'I'll have one of those, I'm starving.'

Ingle picked up the roll with a pair of tongs and handed it over. 'Have it on me,' he said as Roa reached for his money-belt.

'Thanks, I'm going to enjoy this. Pity I can't wash it down with a beer but we're not allowed to drink on duty.'

Reaching under the stall, Ingle extracted a small flask. 'I can offer you a swig of domemade fruit juice,' he said pleasantly, 'or you could purchase some at Creo's stall.'

Roa took the flask. 'Thank you, stallkeeper.'

Ingle smiled. 'Excuse me, I have another customer.' He turned to serve a young woman waiting a few paces behind Roa. 'What will it be today?'

She moved forward as Roa stepped aside. 'Three brown rolls and a white loaf, please Ingle.'

Tongs clattered to the ground. 'Pia, my dear child,' said Ingle. 'It is you, isn't it?'

Roa's half-eaten roll fell to the ground as he swung around. 'Pia, what the Sun are you doing here?' he cried, reaching out to embrace her.

'Good evening, Trooper Roa,' Pia replied, using her basket to create a barrier between them. 'I've returned home for a while.'

Roa withdrew to a respectable distance, grateful Pia had behaved discreetly. A trooper did not embrace a villager in a public place. 'I'm pleased for you, Pia,' he said. 'I'm sure the storyteller is delighted to have you back in her dome. I must leave now, perhaps we'll meet tomorrow at the Tales?'

'Yes, I'll definitely be there. I'm an apprentice storyteller now.'

'Really? Till the Tales then.' Roa turned to leave.

Ingle the Stallkeeper waited until Trooper Roa was out of earshot before moving to Pia's side and embracing her warmly. 'We heard such terrible news, we didn't expect to see you here in the village for many a long night.'

Pia smiled. 'They made a mistake, Ingle, so I've been released, not only from prison but also from the working party. When Sannah has trained me, I'm going to be the storyteller on Island 1.'

'Congratulations on both counts. It's not often troopers admit their mistakes.' He looked around before asking in a low voice, 'What really happened at the working parties?'

'I can't say anything here, Ingle, but I'll tell you the whole story one of these nights.'

Ingle turned back to his stall, selected his best products and placed them in Pia's basket. 'The bread's on me,' he said, pushing the tokens back into her hand. 'The sight of your beautiful face has made my night.'

'Why thank you, Ingle,' Pia answered coyly.

He grinned and blew her a kiss.

Towards the end of his shift, Trooper Roa returned to the trooper dome. Entering via a side entrance, he removed a small sachet of moonlight from his locker before making his way to the main chamber.

'Evening, Jull,' he said loudly to the fat trooper slumped behind the duty officer's console.

Trooper Jull's head jerked upright and his sleep-filled eyes struggled to focus. 'Evening, Roa,' he mumbled, his mouth split in a yawn.

'It looks as though you could do with a break, Jull. I'll take over for a while if you like. There's nothing going on out there.'

'Thanks, Roa, I could do with a bite to eat. Sure you don't mind? You're due to finish soon.'

'Another hour won't make any difference. Besides I could do with a sit.'

Trooper Jull struggled to his feet.

'Oh, just one thing, Jull. Could you open a file for me? I need to check on a former prisoner.'

'No problem.' Jull resumed his seat. 'Who are you interested in?'

'Pia, daughter of Sannah the Storyteller.'

Fat fingers pressed a panel. 'Here it is.' Jull levered himself out of the seat and staggered out into the small chamber that served as the staff kitchen.

Roa smiled to himself as he adjusted the monitor; the expensive moonlight could be kept for another occasion. Silently he thanked the Moon that lazy, incompetent Jull had been on duty this evening. First-year troopers weren't supposed to access prisoners' files.

The file contained only a summary of the incident at Working Party 2, so Roa scrolled through details of Pia's arrest to a section headed 'Report of interview with officers of the Youth Workers Department.' Once again he gleaned little information, the report consisting of a precis rather than a transcript of the proceedings. But the subsequent section headed 'Declaration of Intent' provided all the data he sought.

'Prisoner Pia is to be released from custody into her mother's care,' he read, 'to begin training as a storyteller. As Pia has cooperated with Officer Reyi, she will not be punished at this time for her involvement in the breakout at Working Party 2 on the twenty-first of November 2399.'

'Pia perfection,' he murmured. 'Home for me.' Leaning back in the chair and licking his lips, he envisaged her honey-golden flesh and savouring its delicious sweetness.

After the Tales that morning, the villagers appeared in no hurry to leave the community dome despite the imminent curfew. Some huddled in small groups, low voices and sombre expressions testimony to serious concerns. Others sat quietly, staring at the now empty dais. Near the entrance, Trooper Roa waited impatiently for Pia to finish her conversation with Eran the Recorder. After what seemed an eternity, the two women kissed goodbye and Pia walked towards the door.

'Greetings, Pia the Apprentice Storyteller,' he said formally, stepping into the aisle to block her progress.

Pia raised her left hand. 'Greetings, Trooper Roa. How did you find the Tales today?'

'Sobering, a timely reminder to us all.'

'Us?'

'Troopers are only human, Pia. We're also subject to temptation. We all needed to be reminded of the importance of loyalty to the government. It appears treachery is alive and well in the Brown Zone at present.'

Pia blushed. 'Stealing the trooper car was only a prank. Stupid and irresponsible, yes, but not what I'd call treachery.'

'I agree, but sabotaging a train and freeing prisoners is another matter.'

'You think immature boys were responsible for that?'

He hesitated, unwilling to appear foolish. 'Not really, it's just a rumour going round the trooper dome.'

'There are always rumours going round the Brown Zone. Well I must be going, good morning to you, Trooper Roa.'

'I'll walk with you as far as the hill path,' he said keen to prolong their conversation.

'Isn't it out of your way?'

'Yes, but I enjoy your company, Pia.'

She smiled sweetly. 'Come on then, or I won't get home before curfew.'

Outside the community dome they encountered Trooper Jull sprawled on a bench. 'Fancy a drink, Roa?' he asked.

'I'll see you at the inn later,' Roa answered. 'I'm just going to escort the apprentice storyteller to the hill path.'

'How gallant of you,' said Jull facetiously, his small pale eyes wandering over Pia's flimsy robe.

'Women appreciate good manners, Jull,' Roa answered in a low voice before turning back to Pia. They began to walk up the path.

'Especially storytellers,' Jull called after them.

'What was that about storytellers?' asked Pia.

'Jull said Sannah's an especially talented storyteller.' He turned to face her. 'I agree with him, you're lucky to have such an accomplished teacher.'

'Yes, and I'm going to do my best for her.' She sighed. 'But I'll never be as skillful as she is.'

'You'll surpass her,' he said confidently, edging towards her until his tunic brushed her robe.

'You flatter me, Trooper Roa.'

'It's true, you have a perfect voice and a brilliant intellect. I foresee an outstanding career.'

'Don't be ridiculous, I have to prove myself first.'

Deliberately he moved several paces to the right and stared straight ahead.

'Sorry, I didn't mean to offend you,' said Pia in a little-girl voice.

'I'm the one who should apologise,' he said returning to her side. 'I've been overly familiar. Forgive me.'

Pia struggled to stifle a laugh. 'Don't be so formal, I thought we were friends.'

He smiled. 'Yes, we are friends, and to prove it I'm inviting you to Clar's inn for a drink and a meal.'

'Thanks, but you know how slow service is there. I'd never get home before curfew. Why don't you come to my dome? I'd be pleased to share the morning meal with you.'

'I'd like to accept but …' He fiddled with his tunic. 'To put it bluntly, Pia, I could do without the company of a parent.'

Pia laughed. 'Oh, you don't have to worry about that. Fley's invited Sannah and Scholar Kaire to eat at her dome this morning. I doubt we'll see them today, Fley's renowned for her generous meals. They won't make it back before curfew.'

He bowed deeply. 'In that case I accept your offer graciously,' he said in mock-formal tone.

Pia grinned. 'Race you up the hill path, I'm starving.'

The taste and texture of beautifully prepared food faded as Roa's lips brushed a golden cheek. Smooth as good wine, her skin slid beneath his open mouth as he skimmed towards moist lips, drinking greedily. Tentatively, he tested the heat behind her white teeth with the tip of his tongue and reassured, plunged into sweet warmth.

The fragrance of her lingered long after he had descended the hill path and returned to his chamber in the troopers' quarters. Unable to sleep, he replayed every detail of their morning over and over again. How long before he could revisit the source of such exquisite pleasure? One night? Two nights? An hour away from her seemed an eternity.

Pia had no such thoughts or questions and she slept well. Youthful beauty and sensuality ensured the task set by Officer Reyi would soon be accomplished. Roa was already besotted, she could tell. Following her mother's example, she was quickly learning to play more than the role of storyteller.

CHAPTER 25

Trooper Roa stood before his commanding officer, legs trembling, stomach churning, heart pounding. He had been summoned to the trooper dome in the middle of the day, a sure sign of the seriousness of the impending interview. Gage had not yet spoken and continued to stare at his monitor, even though Roa had been standing in front of him for at least ten minutes. When at last Gage raised his eyes from the screen, he appeared to be studying the wall opposite. After clearing his throat and drumming his fingers on the desk for another interminable period, he finally made eye contact.

'Trooper Roa, I need to ask you a few questions,' said Gage, flexing his thick fingers. 'There are some strange rumours circulating regarding your recent visits to the working parties.'

'What rumours, sir?' Trooper Roa asked tentatively.

'They concern a disc observed at both working parties. Did you notice it by any chance?'

Trooper Roa looked uncomfortable and shook his head.

'Are you sure?' Gage persisted. 'It has been suggested you delivered it.'

Trooper Roa looked down at his feet.

'I'm well aware troopers occasionally pass discs from parents to young workers in return for, shall we say, favours,' Gage continued in a supercilious tone. 'The Youth Workers Department usually turns a blind eye. Unfortunately they believe this particular disc contained detailed instructions for the breakouts. One of the younger girls arrested was most forthcoming and certain you were the one passing the disc around.'

'That's an absolute lie, sir. I did not take a disc to the working parties.' He shuffled his feet and twisted his hands behind his back. 'But ...' He hesitated, well aware what he was about to say would make him appear not only incompetent but downright stupid.

'I'm waiting, Trooper Roa.'

'Yes, sir.' Moving his hands to his side, Roa took a deep breath. 'When I was attending to Scholar Kaire's head injury on our return journey, I discovered a disc concealed in the hem of his robe. As he remained unconscious, I removed the disc and returned to my seat to examine it.'

Gage leaned forward. 'What did it contain?'

'An audio file, sir. Sannah the Storyteller relating what she called a Truth-Tale. I would call it anti-government propaganda. There was nothing about breakouts but I can't be sure I heard it all.'

Gage looked thoughtful. 'Where is the disc now?'

Roa bit his lip.

'Where is the disc, Trooper Roa?'

'I, er, I had to put it back, sir, before Kaire, er, woke up.'

Gage drew his hands together and cracked his knuckles.

'I don't believe you. Any other trooper would have reported this immediately.' Rising slowly, Gage walked around the work-module and slammed his fist under Trooper Roa's chin. 'Bring me the disc. I won't have the Youth Workers Department sniffing around here undermining my authority. You have twenty-four hours. Dismissed.'

Outside the trooper dome, Roa stopped briefly to drink from the tap used to wash mud from boots, crossed the marketplace and took the path leading to the northern edge of the village. He was heading for the storyteller's dome, hoping to gain entry on the pretext he needed to see Pia. Somehow he'd have to find an opportunity to search for this Truth-Tale disc. But as he raced towards the hill path he realised arriving at this hour would arouse intense suspicion; even the most ardent lover would baulk at the thought of climbing Storyteller's Hill in midday sun. Reluctantly he turned around and headed back to his quarters.

It was late afternoon when Trooper Roa arrived at the storyteller's dome, rivers of perspiration streaking his cheeks and tunic. Pausing at the entrance to catch his breath, he wiped his face with his hand.

'Pia, it's Roa,' he called through the sound-grill. 'Open the door panel.'

There was no response even though he knew she slept in the living chamber. 'Pia, please open the panel,' he called again.

The door slid open. Pia stood yawning as she secured a sheet around her naked body.

'Roa, what the Sun are you doing here at this hour?'

'I had to see you,' he answered breathlessly. 'I ran all the way.'

'I'm flattered, but why the rush? You look as though you haven't slept all day.'

'I haven't,' he answered forcing a grin, 'too many thoughts of you whirling in my head.'

She smiled, stepped forward and kissed his lips. 'Come in and sit down. I'll fetch you a cold drink.'

'Make it water,' he said as she turned towards the kitchen, 'and bring a tumbler for yourself. I've brought something special for us to share.'

When she returned, he extracted a small phial from his pocket and held it up. 'Essence of fireweed!' she cried, her eyes dancing with delight. 'I haven't tasted that for ages. We're in for a fun time.'

'I thought you'd appreciate it,' he said, dividing the phial contents between the two tumblers. 'Are you sure your mother won't mind you drinking before work?'

Pia shook her head. 'We're in luck. She and Kaire won't wake for hours. They didn't get to sleep till late.'

'Socialising or what?'

'Surely I don't need to explain,' she answered coyly.

He laughed. 'To a magnificent evening,' he said, raising his tumbler.

'To a magnificent evening,' she repeated.

He watched her drain the tumbler in one swig, a Brown Zone custom. Smiling at her over the lip of his tumbler, he took care not to allow any liquid to enter his mouth. Then he placed the tumbler on the floor, snuggled up to her and waited for the potion to take effect.

'Beautiful fireweed,' Pia murmured minutes later, her head lolling on the floor-cushion.

'Beautiful,' he echoed, kissing her flushed cheek as she slipped into a deep sleep.

At the bottom of the stairs he paused, took another phial from his tunic pocket and set his stun gun to active mode before entering the sleeping chamber. Sannah and Kaire slept soundly, naked limbs entwined. Creeping towards the bed, he sprinkled the phial contents over their faces and withdrew to the doorway. After a few minutes, he checked their breathing had slowed and began his search.

He examined every piece of clothing, looked under the bed, the lamp, the stool. In the adjoining bath chamber he inspected towels, mat, even tubes of wash-gel. Finding nothing he trudged back up the stairs.

An hour passed.

In the kitchen he searched shelves, cupboards, drawers. He opened the cooler, picked up wedges of cheese, peered into pitchers and tore apart a half-eaten loaf.

Another hour passed.

He entered the store chamber, plunged his hand into each jar, inspected every centimetre of the floor and lifted abandoned pots layered with dust.

In the living chamber, Pia stirred and kicked the empty tumbler with her foot. It rolled across the floor, collided with the table and shattered. Hearing the crash, Roa backed out of the store and raced to her side. Seizing the remaining tumbler, he grabbed her shoulders and forced the contents down her throat.

'I'll find your Truth-Tale,' he muttered, pushing her limp body back down on the floor-cushions. 'I'll find it if I have to tear this dome apart.'

'Truth,' Pia murmured. 'The Skyman knows the truth.'

'Who's the sky man?' he demanded, shaking her roughly.

But the fireweed had already taken effect and her response was incomprehensible.

'Sky man, sky man,' Roa mumbled to himself as he charged around the chamber, looking in and under the few pieces of furniture. Suddenly a new idea surfaced and he stood motionless, staring at the ceiling. In places the surface showed the spidery cracks of age but he could see no sign of a deliberate cut in the plasterboard. Nevertheless, he shifted a stool to the centre of the chamber, clambered up and began to examine the ceiling with the palms of his hands. Almost finished, he overbalanced and fell heavily against a pile of program-packs stacked against a wall. Cursing under his breath, he struggled to his feet and was straightening the packs when he noticed a small black strip protruding from one of the sleeves.

There were no markings on the plastic strip and when he held it up to the light he couldn't see the thin lines normally found on identity tags or encrypted files. He slipped it into his tunic pocket.

'Pia,' called Sannah from the bottom of the stairs. 'What are you doing up there?'

Roa forgot about the stool lying on the floor, the broken tumbler, the empty phial of fireweed and headed for the door.

'There's no need to rush away,' said Sannah from the top of the stairs. She noted the disarray, her daughter sprawled on the floor-cushions, and Roa's flushed face.

'I swear I didn't take advantage,' he blurted out. 'We just had a few drinks and fell asleep. You startled me when you called out and I knocked over the stool.'

'There's no need to explain,' she replied, amused by his agitation. 'I know perfectly well why you're here. Pia is eighteen years and at liberty to choose her lovers without interference from her mother.'

'I'll be going then, I'm late for duty.'

'Do call again, Trooper Roa,' she said pleasantly.

He nodded and headed for the now open door panel. On the dome-step he turned around and said brightly, 'Would you please thank Pia for a magnificent evening?'

'Don't worry, I'll relay your message,' Sannah called after him as he sprinted away from the dome.

Sannah closed the door and walked over to her sleeping daughter. The empty phial had rolled against the adjacent floor-cushion. Snatching it up, she held it under her nose. 'Fireweed,' she exclaimed and began to stroke Pia's forehead with her free hand. 'Oh my, dear daughter, you're going to have an appalling hangover.'

Once more Trooper Roa stood before his commanding officer, fear pulsing through his veins. All he had to show for hours of searching was a plastic strip of indeterminate worth. He had hoped to access its data in the privacy of his chamber but when he slid the strip into his computer nothing happened. There remained no alternative but to hand it over to Gage and hope he could unlock the contents.

'Goodnight, Trooper Roa,' Gage said amiably as though they were about to begin a pleasant chat. 'I trust you have brought me the disc?'

'No, sir, but I found this hidden in a program-pack in the storyteller's dome.' He passed the strip across the work-module.

Gage held it up to the light. 'Evidence, I hope.' He looked up at Roa. 'And the kiss of life for you, eh Roa?' With a flourish he pressed the strip to his lips.

'This is Commander Breta,' said a voice not unlike Scholar Kaire's. 'Proceed with your report, 323.'

The strip fell from Gage's fingers onto the work-module.

'The girl Pia has been released from detention and allowed to return to her home village,' said a second voice, definitely Kaire's. 'I am monitoring the situation.'

'Good. What news of the woman Sannah?'

'She has destroyed the Truth-Tale disc.'

'Does this mean the long-term objective has been shelved?'

'No, they have reverted to the oral tradition.'

'How fortunate you forwarded a copy, I found it fascinating.'

'I thought you would, Commander.'

Gage and Roa exchanged glances.

'Plans are underway for more missions,' Kaire continued. 'Sky equipment is proving useful.'

'Excellent, although I'm not sure I entirely agree with your unorthodox methods.'

'Do I have your permission to continue?'

'Absolutely. I haven't received such engrossing reports in years. The blue globe was certainly worth the detour.'

'I could spend months here, there's so much to discover.'

'You don't have unlimited time, 323. I want you to undertake more extensive assignments. NZ could be interesting.'

'Yes, Commander, but as I reported previously, NZ had to be aborted due to transport problems.'

'Any word on the reconstruction?'

'No.'

'Follow it up, 323.'

'Yes, Commander. End of report.'

'Sky z59 disengaging pilot contact.'

The two troopers stared at one another, each unwilling to break the silence pervading the chamber like dense fog.

'It seems we've been deceived,' said Gage after several minutes. 'I imagine Kaire works for the Security Department. I wonder how long he's been engaged in this Blue Globe investigation?'

Roa shrugged. 'It was a clever disguise, sir, saying he was researching the effects of the NLP.'

Gage nodded. 'And then managing to form a liaison with the storyteller. Brilliant.'

'Do you think that's what his commander meant when he said unorthodox methods?' asked Roa.

'Probably.' Gage reached for the computer strip, waved it over his monitor and passed it to Roa. 'Return this to its hiding place as soon as you can. Kaire must not suspect I've blown his cover. We'll continue to treat him as a scholar. He obviously has his reasons for not telling me the true nature of his visit. Meanwhile I want you to keep both Pia and her mother under surveillance. I need further evidence of their complicity. Report to me nightly on my private communicator.'

'Yes, sir.'

Gage leaned forward. 'There could be a promotion in it, especially if you can unearth evidence linking this Truth-Tale disc to the working party breakouts and the train sabotage. Why should the Security Department get all the glory, eh Roa?'

'I hope you won't disapprove of my unorthodox methods, sir?'

Gage laughed. 'Roa, the whole village knows you're burning for Pia.'

'I'll pay another visit to the storyteller's dome at the end of my shift, sir.'

'Good. Now go back to your chamber, you look as though you could use some sleep.'

'I sure could, sir,' Roa replied and turning on his heel, marched to the door panel, head held high.

CHAPTER 26

Trooper Roa became a frequent visitor to the storyteller's dome. Usually he came bearing gifts: a bottle of perfume, a phial of fireweed, a sachet of the drug moonlight. But occasionally he arrived empty-handed, disregarded his primary role, and spent hours luxuriating in Pia's silky flesh.

Their relationship progressed unhindered, as Sannah was preoccupied by Women's Line business and absent most evenings. Kaire also spent many hours down in the village, listening to programmes in the trooper-in-charge's dome. Gage seemed very keen to further cultivate their friendship.

Pia revelled in her burgeoning love affair, the first sexual intimacy she had experienced. Roa was the perfect lover: romantic, considerate and accomplished in the erotic arts. Night and day she yearned for his beautiful body, the real reason for her presence in the village pushed to the back of her mind.

Whenever she lay supine on floor-cushions, high on moonlight or fireweed, Roa recorded their conversations on a tiny communicator sewn into the neckband of his tunic. Gently he directed her drugged mind towards Truth-Tales and sabotage. Often her responses were muddled but he still managed to glean snippets of useful information. Gage was delighted and began to construct a profile of the storyteller's nefarious activities.

After several weeks, Gage possessed a large file but still lacked sufficient evidence to arrest Sannah. He spent many a sleepless day pondering ways to acquire irrefutable proof of her involvement in the breakouts and the train sabotage. Eventually he came to the conclusion a drug lacking the side effects of moonlight and fireweed could be the catalyst he needed. But how could he obtain such a drug without drawing attention to his unauthorised investigation?

Early one evening, sitting at his work-module, drinking strong coffee in an attempt to clear his sleep-deprived brain, Gage remembered an incident during his previous posting. He reached for his personal communicator.

'Medical dome,' said a pleasant female voice. 'How can I help you?'

'Medical Officer Jani, please,' Gage answered.

'Certainly, who shall I say is calling?'

'Trooper-in-Charge Gage, Village 10, Brown Zone.'

'Transferring you now, sir.'

'Good evening, Gage,' said a familiar voice. 'How's life in the Brown Zone?'

'I won't answer that question, Jani,' said Gage wearily. 'My list of complaints would take hours.'

Jani laughed. 'So what can I do for you, or is this a social call?'

'I need to pick your brains, Jani.'

'Go ahead.'

'Do you know of any narcotics that induce a high but don't distort speech patterns or memory?'

'Yes,' Jani replied without hesitation. 'I can think of several fitting that description.'

'Good, thank you.' Gage waited a moment before adding, 'I would prefer not to order these drugs through the usual channels.'

Jani hesitated. 'I don't think I can help you there,' he said finally. 'My senior medical officer would be reluctant to supply dangerous drugs to another village without authorisation.'

'Remember the Starlight incident Jani?' asked Gage, knowing full well the young medical officer would not have forgotten an oversight that could have ended his career.

'Of course and I'll never forget the help you gave me.' Jani coughed. 'What quantity do you need?'

'A small amount. The patient is a young girl, eighteen years, slight build. I leave the choice of drug to you.'

'No problem. Is the matter urgent?'

'No, just send it on the train, marked confidential.'

'I'll organise it tonight.'

'Thank you, Jani. Goodnight, give my regards to your partner.'

'Yes I will. Goodnight, Gage.'

Gage closed the connection and slid the communicator back into his pocket. Yawning, he set his chair to the reclining position and settled down for a nap.

Three nights later, a parcel arrived at Gage's dome. It contained a small quantity of the drug LC24-10 and a large quantity of southern delicacies prepared by Jani's partner. Gage generously invited Scholar Kaire to share the latter.

Trooper Roa next met his lover outside the community dome after the Tales. He suggested a walk by the river and hinted at a special gift to be bestowed when they were safely hidden from prying eyes.

Early morning sunlight enhanced the beauty of golden skin. Pia stretched out on the grass fringing the steep riverbank, the folds of her white robe spread around her like a cloud.

'When can I see this special gift?' she asked, bending one long leg so her robe fell open from the waist.

'Later,' Roa murmured, unable to resist sleek thighs and the promise of velvety moistness.

Warm breeze, sunshine and the afterglow of passion suppressed all thoughts of the phial of LC24-10 hidden in Roa's tunic. Half asleep, he lay beside his lover, conscious only of the buzz of insects and the slap of water against the bank. The first curfew siren startled them both.

'Oh no,' cried Pia, scrambling to her feet and hurriedly fastening her robe. 'I won't get home before curfew. I'll have to spend the day at Fley's dome.' She slipped on her sandals and blew him a kiss. 'See you, lover.'

'Wait,' he called, jumping to his feet. 'I've got a better idea.'

She returned to his side. 'It'd better be good.'

Seizing her hand, he said breathlessly, 'Pia, I long to spend the day with you, share my bed with you, wake up in the afternoon with you beside me. Come back to my chamber, please.'

'What about the other troopers?'

'They won't care, probably won't even notice if we slip in the back entrance.' He squeezed her hand. 'Please, Pia.'

'I don't suppose it can do any harm.' She fiddled with her robe. 'So long as you're certain you won't get into trouble?'

'Positive,' he answered with a grin. Tugging her hand he led her away from the river towards the village.

Clouds gathered in the late day sky, wind stirred patches of dust and sun-dried leaves. Below her dome, Sannah stood on a rock scanning the hill path for her errant daughter. She wasn't impressed by Pia's behaviour; the girl should have known better than to spend the day in a trooper's sleeping chamber. The late hour had been a tame excuse; she could easily have gone to Fley's dome.

Stepping down from the rock, Sannah began to walk down the path. Memories of her long-dead partner surfaced as she pondered Pia's affair with the young trooper. Her relationship with Pia's father had been intense, passion ruling every aspect of their few years together. Passion for each other, passion for freedom, passion for truth; each segment interlocking until life had become a multi-coloured garment, vivid as a rainbow.

Heavy raindrops spattered her skin and a streak of lightning zig-zagged across the sky. She began to run, her sandalled feet pounding the well-trodden path. How could she have been so blind, so preoccupied with Women's Line business and her own love affair not to have regis-tered Pia's total absorption with Trooper Roa? The ramifications could be disastrous; she knew only too well how secrets could be spilled in the heat of passion. Had Pia forgotten the reason for cultivating a relation-ship with Roa? The Youth Workers Department expected results.

Far below she glimpsed a solitary figure, a white robe fluttering in the freshening breeze. She waved but there was no answering gesture. Stepping off the path, she perched on a flat boulder to await Pia's arrival.

Clear as the birdsong that once greeted dawn, Pia's sweet voice echoed through Gage's living chamber. She spoke at length of Truth-Tales, stressing the need to spread the word quickly; she expressed hope young workers would be chosen to assist in future; she referred to special tasks assigned to Line leaders and acknowledged their pivotal role in arranging missions. But despite the plethora of information, she failed to name names, mention 'prisoners' or 'trains' and made no reference whatsoever to her mother.

Gage silenced the communicator. 'You've done well, Roa,' he said, turning to his young trooper. 'Even without named conspirators we now have sufficient information to make further inquiries. Discreet inquiries,' he added with a smile.

'I'll assist in any way,' Roa said eagerly.

'Thinking of that promotion, eh Roa?'

'Well yes, sir, but my primary aim is to find those responsible for the train sabotage.'

'Excellent.' Gage toyed with a piece of fruit he had prepared for breakfast. 'I want you to recall your visits to the working parties. Can you think of any unusual incidents?'

Roa scratched his head. 'Nothing that sticks in my mind, sir.'

'Did you sit in on Kaire's interviews with the workers?'

'Sometimes, and if I was busy another trooper accompanied him.'

Gage nodded. 'We can be reasonably certain Kaire gave Pia the Truth-Tale disc. I imagine Sannah asked him to deliver it. But I don't think we can presume he passed it to workers at Working Party 1. That would have compromised his position.'

Roa frowned. 'Then how did they find out about it?'

'Think, Roa,' ordered Gage, pushing the fruit into his mouth.

'I've got it!' he cried after several minutes. 'One night I overheard a group of female workers giggling about Kaire's encounter in the orchard with a girl called Garna. The girls mentioned Kaire's beautiful pale skin. I didn't take much notice at the time, you know what Brown women are like, sir, can't keep their hands off White men.'

Gage smiled knowingly. 'Go on,' he said through a mouthful of chewed fruit.

'Garna was a real beauty,' Roa recalled, 'long legs, full breasts and …'

'Get to the point, Roa,' Gage interrupted.

'Sorry, sir.' He frowned, labouring to recollect other details. 'I remember now, at lunch I asked Kaire why he was wearing a blue worker's wrap. He blushed and mumbled something about red mud in the orchard. He said Garna had taken his travelling robe to clean it. She must have found the disc and listened to it.'

Gage smacked his lips. 'Excellent. Can you recall anything else about this girl?'

Roa thought for a moment and shook his head.

'Pity. 'Ah well, a little interrogation should loosen a few young tongues, eh Roa?'

'Yes, sir. Will we be visiting the working parties?'

Gage turned away slightly. 'Leave the details to me. I'll keep you informed. In the meantime I want you to continue your visits to Pia. But go easy on the moonlight and the alcohol, I don't want an irate mother on my domestep.'

Roa grinned. 'I'll think of another present to take Pia, sir.'

'I've got just the thing,' said Gage, easing his body from the comfort of the floor-cushions. He walked into the kitchen and returned carrying a small bowl. 'Crystallised fruit,' he explained, handing Roa the bowl. 'Brown women love it.'

'Thank you, sir,' Roa replied gratefully. His relationship with Pia had already cost far more than he had anticipated.

CHAPTER 27

The following night, Gage began his journey to the working parties. Officially, he was going to visit his sick mother, so made certain he was seen boarding the southbound train. At the border terminal he changed out of his trooper uniform and transferred to a northbound produce train.

Soon after arriving at Working Party 1 he received unwelcome news. Worker Garna had absconded along with nine male workers and was now presumed dead. The trooper-in-charge explained that during the search for the escapees a burnt-out trooper car had been discovered containing human remains. Security Department officers had advised the troopers not to take the two charred bodies back to the working party for forensic testing. In the department's opinion, deceased workers did not warrant such attention or expense.

Despondent, Gage continued his journey north. At the next stop, he stepped from the train into blistering heat and a strong wind blew stinging sand into his face. A sullen trooper escorted him to Working Party 2 and deposited him inside a large dome, telling him to wait. An hour passed before another trooper appeared. He suggested Gage visit the eating area, as the trooper-in-charge would be busy for at least another hour. Gage demolished a hearty breakfast while he waited. Two hours passed. Then a young worker, who said her name was Una, approached him and announced the trooper-in-charge would see him now. She led him to a small chamber at the rear of the dome.

The door panel slid open. 'Come in, come in,' called the trooper-in-charge.

Gage approached the work-module. 'I am Agriculture and Fisheries Officer Nisu,' he announced formally. 'I bring you greetings from …'

'No need for the formal drivel up here,' the trooper interrupted. 'Sit yourself down and tell me what you want to do during your visit. Your communication didn't specify. I'm Wyan, by the way.'

'Pleased to meet you, Wyan,' Gage replied.

'Drink?' Wyan pulled a large bottle of tropica from a drawer.

'It's a little too early in the evening for me, thank you.'

'Never too early up here.' Wyan smacked his lips. 'A good way to start the night, I always say.' He filled a large tumbler. 'Now, what would you like to do first, Nisu?'

'If it's no trouble I'd like to speak to your senior workers, discuss their experience of recent crop production.'

Wyan wiped his mouth with the back of his hand. 'Bit of a problem there. I only have two experienced Line leaders at the moment, no doubt you heard about the breakout?'

'Yes, dreadful business,' murmured Gage, his spirits rising as he recalled Pia's remarks about Line leaders and special assignments.

'I lost two Line leaders,' said Wyan, 'and six other male workers. And if that wasn't enough, two of my best female workers, both Line leaders, were arrested.'

'In connection with the breakout?'

'Yes, though lucky for one of them the charges were dropped.'

'So when can I see her?'

'You can't. Pia's been allowed to return home. Village 10, I think.'

'I see,' said Gage thoughtfully.

'Strange business that,' Wyan remarked, 'not what I'd have done under the circumstances. But then who am I to question what the Youth Workers Department does?' He paused to take another swig. 'I'll arrange for my two Line leaders to see you during their lunch break. Meanwhile have a look round and talk to some of the younger workers. You'd be surprised how much they know about crops. I'd never let on but some of them could teach me a thing or two.'

Gage smiled. 'Thanks for your help, Wyan.' He rose to leave. 'Perhaps

I'll start by talking to the girl who showed me to your chamber. I think she said her name was Una.'

'That's right. She should be in the food preparation area now. I'm keeping her on light duties at the moment, she's been sick.'

'Nothing contagious I hope.'

'No, an allergy to something she ate, we suspect—probably fish. But she won't admit to eating fish. I don't blame her, mind you. Taking stock from the fish farm is a punishable offence.'

'I almost forgot about the fish farm,' said Gage hurriedly. 'When can I see it?'

'Any time, just ask me and I'll arrange for Ploe to take you over in our new trooper car.'

'Thank you. Goodnight, Wyan.'

'See you,' said Wyan, turning to his monitor.

Gage had almost reached the door when Wyan called out. 'Meet me for lunch, Gage, we can share a bottle.'

'Sure,' Gage replied with a smile. 'I've no problem with drinking after midnight.'

Gage located Worker Una in a small store adjacent to the food preparation area. She was absorbed in stacking shelves and didn't notice his arrival.

'Goodnight, Worker Una,' he said warmly. 'May I speak with you?'

The girl jumped, dropping the bag of flour she was holding, and swung around. Wide brown eyes gleamed fear-bright in a thin sallow face.

'Sorry, I didn't mean to startle you,' he said gently. 'I just want to talk to you about crops.'

'Er, which ones?' she stammered, twisting the hem of her short wrap with trembling fingers.

'Whatever you like,' he answered, puzzled by her agitation. 'I'm Agriculture and Fisheries Officer Nisu. I'm up here to discuss current issues in crop and fish production.'

'I don't know much,' she mumbled. 'I've only been here a few months.'

'Nevertheless, I'm sure you've gained valuable knowledge during your time here and the department would be grateful for your input.' He smiled. 'Why don't we find a seat and you can tell me all about your work?'

'There's no one in the eating area at the moment,' she ventured.

'Sounds a good place to me. Lead the way Worker Una.'

She managed a limp smile and walked out of the store.

After twenty minutes feigning interest in Una's experience of potato and onion production, Gage decided to introduce a different slant. 'I understand you've been sick,' he said, concern etched on his face. 'Have any other workers have been ill recently?'

'No,' she answered quickly, averting her eyes.

'That's good. We wouldn't want our crops to cause sickness down south.' He paused, giving a small cough. 'There's some I could mention,' he continued softly, 'who would like to see the work of the department discredited. You should hear the tales.'

'Tales?' she queried in a small voice.

'Rumours about diseased fruit, toxic fish, mouldy vegetables, that sort of thing. They're known as Truth-Tales, perhaps you've heard of them?'

A thick sheen of fear glazed her face. 'I didn't believe it,' she blurted out. 'I told that official I knew it was all lies, I told him I was forced to listen to that disc.'

'Disc?'

'The Truth-Tale disc, the one the storyteller sent to Pia.'

Gage looked puzzled. 'Pia, she was a Line leader here, wasn't she?'

'Yes, sir, but she's gone now. She was arrested after the breakout.'

'What do you know about the breakout, Una?'

'Nothing, sir, nothing I swear. I was asleep in the isolation chamber when it happened. Trooper-in-Charge Wyan knows I was there. Besides I told him I would never get involved in anything like that.'

Gage touched her arm. 'Don't worry, I believe you. Now about this Truth-Tale disc. I don't suppose you can remember which crops it dealt with?'

'The storyteller didn't talk about crops,' Una exclaimed, then covered her mouth with her hands.

'It's all right, Una, no one is going to punish you for telling the truth.

In fact, I'll see you're rewarded for helping me. Take your time. Try to remember names, dates, instructions.'

'I'll do my best, sir.'

Alone in the small chamber he had been allocated, Gage pulled out his communicator and listened again to Una's words. He could barely contain his delight; even without the Truth-Tale disc he now had sufficient evidence to arrest both Sannah and Pia. If necessary, Worker Una could be called as a witness, although he hoped her recorded evidence would suffice. Under duress she could prove more of a liability than an asset. He was also concerned Una would break down and confess her betrayal to her friends. Replacing the communicator in his pocket, he left the chamber and hurried to Wyan's chamber.

'Officer Nisu to see Trooper-in-Charge Wyan,' he announced at the sound-grill.

'Come right in, Nisu,' said Wyan, releasing the door panel. 'No need to stand on ceremony. Drink?' he queried as Gage entered the chamber.

'A small one, thank you, Wyan.'

'To healthy crops,' said Wyan raising his tumbler.

'To healthy crops,' echoed Gage.

Wyan drained his tumbler in one gulp.

'I've come about Worker Una,' said Gage.

'She's a good little girl,' Wyan murmured, bloodshot eyes fixed on the tropica bottle.

'Yes, I'm sure she is, but I've been studying her medical records and I think it prudent she be removed from here immediately.'

'Whatever for?'

'She has a severe allergy to the crops grown here. If she returns to fieldwork it could recur.'

Wyan smiled, revealing stained yellow teeth. 'No problem, she can continue with domework.'

'The department would consider it wasteful to employ such a productive worker in food preparation,' Gage countered in an officious tone.

'What do you suggest I do with her then?'

'I imagine such a diligent worker would be welcomed at Orea River.'

'Come off it, Nisu, you know the department wouldn't sanction it. She's far too young for mine work.'

'I was thinking of surface work,' said Gage quietly.

'Good one, Nisu, I'll contact the department.' He turned to his communicator.

'Oh, one other suggestion,' said Gage quickly. 'Why not send her back to her home village until the transfer arrangements have been made? She could do with a break—she became ill again a few hours ago when I was interviewing her, as I'm sure you know.'

Wyan frowned. 'No, I didn't know.' He drummed his fingers on the desk. 'I'd better isolate her again, just to be on the safe side.'

'I could save you the bother,' said Gage, leaning across the work-module. 'I'll be returning south in a few hours. Why don't I take her with me and drop her off at the trooper station nearest her village?'

'You're not worried about catching something?'

'She has an allergy, Wyan, I read the medical report.'

Wyan smiled. 'So you did.' He turned to his communicator. 'Trooper Ome, fetch Worker Una from her dormitory and bring her to my chamber.'

A produce train sped south through dry grassland and remnants of open eucalypt forest. Cocooned within its cylindrical body, two passengers reclined in padded seats. One, a trooper, closed his eyes and envisaged southern vistas: a rocky headland, saffron sand, a mother and child frolicking in blue water. The other, a young girl, slept soundly, her dreams filled with memories of a loving childhood dome.

Noonday heat brought torrential rain, like hammers pounding sleek metal and pitting dry trackside soil. The passengers stirred. Minutes later, sunlight blazed from empty skies, the damp earth steamed. The train slowed, coming to a halt beside a small white dome. A silver door panel slid open, and the young girl was disgorged into harsh sunlight. Small sandalled feet stepped towards the white dome. A trooper emerged as she neared the entrance, motioning the girl inside.

The train continued on its journey. Inside the small passenger module, the trooper closed his vision-strip and settled back for a good day's sleep. But sleep did not bring peace. Graphic images seared his dreaming brain: sweat-soaked mine workers screaming accusations, a small child drowning, a mother sobbing. No one heard the dreamer's cries; no one saw the ruddy cheeks streaked with tears. Oblivious to human distress, the train raced on towards the Brown Zone border.

CHAPTER 28

Still wide awake at midday, Sannah sat up in bed hugging her knees, wishing she could stop Fley's message about the girl from repeating in her head. The information had come from a reliable source and discreet inquiries confirmed Una had returned to her home village, but it seemed implausible troopers would send a first-year worker home because of a food allergy. *Perhaps Pia would be able to shed some light on the matter?* she thought, making a mental note to ask her daughter if Worker Una had exhibited any unusual behaviour or sickness. It was also possible Kaire would remember her, although he'd made no mention of health issues at the working parties, other than the vomiting he'd experienced after sampling a new species of fish.

Beside her Kaire stirred. Careful not to disturb him, she lay back on the pillows, hoping sleep would come before long.

'What's the matter?' asked Kaire, sliding over the sheets until their bodies touched.

'Nothing, I just can't get to sleep.'

'Worried about Pia and Roa again?'

'Not really, I had a good talk to Pia about keeping her distance emotionally.'

Kaire snuggled in, kissing her gently. 'It won't be long before the transporter's repaired, my love. A new life awaits you and Pia in Aotearoa.'

Grateful for darkness, she pondered how to tell him only Pia would accompany him on the journey to Aotearoa. Important work remained to be done and she had decided to stay in the Brown Zone, whatever the outcome. She had been part of the Women's Line for twenty years, taken countless risks. To leave now would be an act of cowardice.

'It means so much to me to know you'll be safe when I have to leave Planet Earth,' he murmured, his lips soft against her cheek.

'Perhaps one day we'll be together again,' she said wistfully, thoughts spiralling skyward. 'After your next voyage, you could return to Earth and take me back to Sky. I'd love to experience space travel.'

Every muscle in his body tensed, his lips froze on her face.

'Don't you want to take me to Sky?' she cried, pounding his chest with her fists. 'Are you afraid a woman like me wouldn't be welcome in your advanced society?'

Fingers pressed her shoulder, nails dug into her flesh.

'Put the lamp on, Sannah,' he said in a voice she hardly recognised. 'The time has come for you to hear *my* Truth-Tale.'

She waved her left hand towards the lamp and watched a warm glow illuminate Kaire's pale face.

'There should be no secrets between lovers,' he said, throwing back the sheet and pointing to his smooth abdomen. 'This isn't the result of an accident or surgery. All Sky Explorers are born this way. It is, you might say, our badge of office. I don't mean I'm some sort of android. I'm as human as you are but I was created in a laboratory, not as a result of sexual intercourse and pregnancy.'

'Why didn't you want to tell me?' she asked, puzzled by his reticence. 'Even a deprived country like Australia possesses such technology.'

'You don't understand, I'm trying …'

'Yes I do,' she interrupted, anxious to allay his fears. 'Brown Zoners don't have access to artificial wombs but I believe they're often used by wealthy southerners.'

Kaire reached out and took her hand. 'Listen to me, Sannah. I'm trying to tell you I'm a clone.'

She pulled her hand away, shook her head rapidly, revelation vying with disbelief. 'No that's not possible, human cloning was outlawed centuries ago and all reference to cloning technology erased from databanks the world over.'

'That doesn't stop scientists experimenting, especially when faced with the demise of their own people. We had no choice—most Sky

People are sterile. If we are to find our new Earth, we need thousands of Sky Explorers.'

She took his hand and held it against her breast. 'I appreciate your honesty but I assure you it doesn't make any difference to me.'

'But it does make a difference to me.'

'How can it? No one here knows. You won't suffer the same fate as those first clones. You won't be ostracised and forcibly sterilised.'

He sighed. 'It means I can never return to Sky.'

'Why ever not?'

'The old Earth problem, no room.'

'So you keep exploring till you die?'

He inhaled slowly through parted lips, turned away from mellow lamplight. 'Our ships are programmed for a seven-year voyage. After that, the Sky Explorers transmit a final report, program the ship to return to Sky and take the end-capsules.'

'You commit suicide!'

'Once our mission has been completed.'

'But you're so young at the end of your voyage. You would only be thirty-three years.'

'Space-life is short, Sannah; a totally artificial environment has a negative effect on the human body. Even naturals rarely survive beyond fifty years.'

'So why don't your people return to Earth?'

'We don't belong on Earth, we are Sky People and proud of it. Stars, moons and the silence of space nourish our spirit.'

She clutched the sheet with her free hand. 'Then why are you here?'

'You know why.'

'A pilgrimage to your ancestral home I can understand. Why you continue to stay and risk your life is incomprehensible. Our struggle against oppression is not yours, Kaire.'

Fingers lifted her chin, eyes studied her face as though it were unfamiliar territory.

'I stay because I love you,' he answered softly. 'That's why I had to tell you the truth.'

She pulled away and sank back on the pillow. 'This is not the time for love. There are far more important issues to consider.'

'I can wait.'

She sighed, exasperated by his naivety. Did he imagine the two of them were participants in some heroic drama battling injustice and brutality? That love will conquer all, even in the Brown Zone? She wanted to grab his pale arms, shake his shoulders, and demand he face facts. Instead she swallowed her irritation.

'Time may be limited, Kaire,' she said quietly. 'How long will it be before your southern identity is exposed as fraudulent and you're thrown in a northern prison?'

Beside her his body jerked involuntarily. 'You tell me. I know nothing of Brown Zone security systems.'

'The Security Department will be on high alert following the train sabotage, and recent arrivals in the Brown Zone could be among the first to be investigated.'

'I'll do a data search on Gage's files this evening, see if anything turns up.'

Sannah reached out and rested her hand on his shoulder. 'Promise me you'll get out of here at the first sign of trouble.'

He nodded. 'You have my word.'

Raising her hand, she waved it over the lamp. 'I must try to sleep, otherwise I'll be yawning all through the Tales.'

Darkness enveloped the chamber. Stretching out on her back, she became aware of a hand stroking her arm and warm breath bathing her skin. Eyelids closed, limbs relaxed, breathing slowed. But beneath the surface fear lingered, a current of unanswered questions.

The community dome was packed, villagers eager to observe the interaction between their storyteller and her daughter. It was Pia's first appearance on the dais and although she would play only a minor role today, nerves threatened her usual equanimity.

'No one will judge you harshly,' Sannah had assured her as they descended the hill path just before sunrise. Glancing at Pia now perched on a stool beside her, she hoped a modicum of confidence had returned.

A sudden commotion drew both mother and daughter's attention to the audience. In the rows nearest the dome entrance, villagers were rising to their feet and heads turned towards the open door.

Immediately the trooper on duty climbed onto his seat, demanding quiet in loud menacing tones. Dark shapes suddenly filled the entrance and slid over the domestep.

Villagers gasped as Trooper-in-Charge Gage and Trooper Roa, eradicators flashing in their hands, marched down the aisle, heavy boots striking the concrete floor like hammers. As the two men approached the dais, Sannah and Pia rose from their stools, stood side by side, fingers linked.

'Sannah the Storyteller and Pia the Apprentice Storyteller,' said Gage, making a show of leaping onto the dais. 'I hereby arrest you for seditious activities.'

'No, no, no!' the villagers cried in unison.

Gage swung around. 'Silence!' Striding to the edge of the dais, he fired an eradicator beam into the domed ceiling. A shower of plaster pitted robes and head-cloths.

'Move, storyteller,' ordered Trooper Roa, prodding her thigh with his eradicator and pushing her towards Gage.

Head held high, Sannah crossed the dais and stepped down into the aisle, taking care not to trip on her long white robe. Pia followed a short distance behind, Roa's eradicator pressed into her back.

Kaire stepped into the aisle as they reached the third row and stood facing Gage, legs apart, arms crossed over his chest. 'This is an outrage, Trooper-in-Charge Gage!' he shouted. 'I demand to know what evidence you have concocted against these innocent women.'

Gage grasped Kaire's arm. 'Don't put emotions before duty, man,' he said quietly. 'It's not worth it, you lovesick fool.' Lifting his hand, he pushed Kaire aside. Troopers and detainees continued down the aisle, watched by rows of silent, frightened villagers.

Over the succeeding week, Sannah and Pia were interrogated daily, sometimes singly, sometimes together. The format always followed the same pattern: two troopers arrived in the dead of day, dragged them from the hard narrow platforms that served as beds, and marched them down a flight of stairs to a tiny chamber buried deep in the earth. Here, Gage and the two troopers indulged in both verbal and physical abuse, determined to break the women's spirits by any means.

After seven days, prison robes were blood-spattered and bodies were battered, but torture had failed to elicit any useful information. Eventually Gage was forced to accede to Sannah's demand for a trial before the Brown Zone governor, her prerogative as an experienced storyteller. Youth Worker Department officials would try Pia, her offences having taken place at a working party.

After reporting the situation to Officer Keo at the Security Department, Trooper-in-Charge Gage retired to his dome for a well-earned break. Interrogations plus a week of broken days had left him jaded.

Several nights passed before Kaire dared descend to the village. He hadn't risked contacting Fley via communicator; most likely Gage would be monitoring every communication in and out of her dome. He decided to take a chance Fley would respond to his call through the sound-grill. At least they could exchange a few words on the domestep via message board. He timed his arrival for an hour before dawn, knowing the school night would have finished and Fley should be at home. A full moon guided his steps behind the school dome and over the low wall into Fley's yard. Moments later, Fley was hurrying him below ground to the concealed chamber.

'Any information?' he asked once she had sealed the door panel and taken her customary position on the left-hand bench.

Fley looked up and noted his gaunt face. The strain of the past few nights was beginning to tell.

'Just a message from Zira. Her niece Yani has been investigating a young worker's sudden departure from Working Party 2, supposedly on account of a food allergy.'

'Una!' Kaire exclaimed, sinking down on the bench opposite Fley. 'You know this girl?'

He quickly explained his meeting with Una and her subsequent removal to the isolation chamber prior to the breakout.

'Pia's said nothing about this and you obviously haven't mentioned it to Sannah.'

'I thought the problem had been solved.'

Fley sighed loudly and shook her head. 'Oh Kaire, when will you learn to be wary?'

He bit his lip and stared straight ahead.

'I imagine Una told her trooper-in-charge about the Truth-Tale disc,' Fley continued, 'and was sent home as a reward.'

'Then why haven't I been questioned? Una knew Sannah had sent the disc to Pia. If she mentioned this to the troopers, surely they'd have suspected I delivered it, even if I did so inadvertently?'

Fley shrugged. 'I don't know, obviously Gage has his reasons. We both know his men are keeping you under surveillance. Perhaps Una decided not to betray Pia. Further investigations may reveal the truth.'

'And how do you propose to uncover the truth? I imagine Una will be well guarded in her home village.'

'Our methods are not your concern,' said Fley firmly.

'Not my concern!' Kaire retorted, jumping to his feet. 'The woman I love and her daughter face long years in prison and you say it's not my concern!'

'It's a matter of security. You can't be forced to tell the troopers what you don't know.' She reached across the narrow chamber and touched his wrist. 'Sit down, Kaire, how can I speak to you when you're pacing the floor?'

He slumped on the bench. 'I apologise, my emotions are in turmoil. I'm terrified of the consequences for Sannah and Pia.'

'Fear is the real enemy,' said Fley gently. 'When the fear rises up in us we make mistakes. A careless word, a reckless act, that's all it takes to jeopardise the work of years. You must try to conquer fear. It's the only way to accomplish anything here in the Brown Zone.'

Tears stained his burning cheeks. 'I'll try, I promise,' he stammered.

She smiled. 'You can do it.'

'It's not easy for me,' he continued, his voice calmer now. 'Sky is a safe environment—there's no poverty, violence or disease. Planet Earth was a rude awakening.'

'But we thank the Moon you landed in the Brown Zone, Kaire. I can't tell you how grateful we are for the help you've given us.' She paused, then added, 'But we wouldn't want you to feel compelled to stay.'

'I have no choice,' he answered without hesitation. 'Now I share your people's fears and hopes and want to help heal the sickness endemic in this ruined land.'

'And Sannah?'

'She is all I ever wanted: lover, friend, teacher, nurturer. Heart and soul I have given her and would give my life if it should prove necessary.'

They sat in silence for a few minutes, each engrossed in private contemplation. Suddenly Fley clapped her hands and said brightly, 'I have an idea. If you agree, of course.'

The first flush of dawn tinted the sky as Kaire walked down the path leading to the trooper-in-charge's dome. On the way, he had stopped at the marketplace to purchase fruit, cheese and a bottle of Gage's favourite liquor. Fear rumbled around his empty stomach as he neared the dome and he half-hoped Gage wouldn't be home or be otherwise occupied, anything to delay this encounter. But his hesitant greeting at the sound-grill was answered promptly.

'Good dawn to you, Kaire,' said Gage, ushering him into the living chamber. 'This is indeed an unexpected pleasure.'

Kaire managed a weak smile. 'I, er, I need your advice, Gage,' he said, having decided to dispense with small talk, 'on a rather delicate matter.'

'I'd be happy to assist, do sit down.'

'I don't expect you to listen on an empty stomach.' He handed over the basket he found in Sannah's store.

Gage peered into the basket. 'Delightful, I'll fetch some platters and tumblers. Be with you shortly.' He disappeared into the kitchen.

Kaire arranged himself on a floor-cushion, making certain his shaking knees were concealed beneath his robe.

'An excellent choice of liquor,' Gage remarked on returning from the kitchen. 'Creo's stall, I presume?'

'Of course, he makes the best in this village.'

'And charges the highest prices.'

Kaire nodded.

'Your health, Kaire,' said Gage, raising his tumbler.

'And yours, Gage.'

Gage drank quickly, reached for the bottle and poured another small measure.

Kaire took two small sips before placing his tumbler on the table. 'I've been rather foolish,' he began, addressing the floor as though he were too embarrassed to look Gage in the face, 'over a woman, I'm afraid.'

Gage smiled indulgently. 'I thought as much. On what other subject could I possibly advise a scholar of your calibre?'

Kaire looked up. 'When I visited Working Party 2 recently, at Sannah's request I delivered a disc to her daughter Pia.'

'What's known as the Truth-Tale disc?'

Kaire nodded. 'Although I must stress I didn't know what it was at the time. I presumed, naively I know, that it was simply a communication from mother to daughter.'

'It didn't occur to you to listen to it during the journey north?'

Kaire shook his head.

'Rule number one for a security officer, I would have thought.'

Kaire frowned.

'Come, my friend,' said Gage quickly. 'There's no need to continue this charade. I've known for some time you're working for the Security Department.'

'How the Sun did you find out?' Kaire asked indignantly, hoping his tone adequately disguised his confusion.

'I've had the storyteller and her daughter under surveillance ever since Pia was unexpectedly released from custody. One of my men has been most diligent, even if his methods are, shall we say, a little unorthodox.'

'Trooper Roa had no right investigating me.'

Gage smiled. 'I assure you it was unintentional. On one of his visits to Pia, Roa discovered what he thought was the Truth-Tale disc.'

'Impossible,' Kaire interjected.

'I know that, your report stated as much.'

'My report?'

'Let me finish.'

Kaire sat back on the floor-cushion, hugging his trembling knees.

'When Roa brought me the object he'd found among the storyteller's program-packs, I discovered it was a micro-communicator,' said Gage smugly. 'I must say, Kaire, I've never seen anything like it before.

Brilliant technology, it could easily be mistaken for one of those figure strips our recorders use.'

At last the fog in Kaire's brain began to clear. 'It appears we have a problem with our latest device,' he said quietly. 'I'm supposed to be the only person able to access it.'

Gage beamed. 'We troopers aren't as stupid as you security people seem to think.'

Kaire leaned forward and toyed with a piece of cheese. 'Now that you know my, er, identity,' he began, 'I think we should begin this conversation again.'

'Very wise, and perhaps you can start by telling me if your concerns are real or was that story about the Truth-Tale disc just a ploy to foster your scholarly guise?'

'My concerns are very real,' Kaire answered looking directly at Gage. 'I've behaved like a lovesick adolescent and allowed my relationship, or should I say obsession, with the storyteller to impair my reason. I've filed deficient reports and in some instances completely overlooked basic tasks. To answer your earlier question, yes, of course I listened to the Truth-Tale disc before I handed it over to Pia but—and this is where I fear repercussions—not only have I somehow mislaid the copy I made but I also inadvertently sent a read-once-wipe file to my commander.'

Gage remained silent for a moment, one hand resting on his chin. 'I understand your dilemma, especially now the storyteller has destroyed the one piece of evidence that would have ensured a conviction.'

'I've tossed and turned for many days considering my options,' said Kaire miserably. 'What would you do in my position?'

Gage made a show of considering the problem. 'If we work together, we can uncover evidence that will link those troublesome women to more than the Truth-Tale disc and working party breakouts.'

'You refer of course to the train sabotage.'

'Yes, I'm convinced there's a connection between the breakouts and the sabotage.'

'As am I,' said Kaire forcefully. He paused. 'It was unfortunate our witness didn't shed any light on the matter.'

'You know about Worker Una?'

'Of course.'

'She may reveal more at the trials.'

Kaire sighed. 'I doubt it. It's highly unlikely such a young and excitable girl would have been entrusted with vital information.'

'I agree, but Pia's another matter. We know she was involved in the distraction of troopers prior to the breakout so she must have known of the sabotage plans. The problem is how to extract the information. Standard interrogation methods have failed completely.'

Kaire bit his lip, fighting to suppress distressing images of prison chamber torture. 'There is another more subtle method we could employ,' he suggested.

Gage raised his eyebrows. 'Go on.'

'Pia trusts me. She believes I'm in love with her mother and would do anything to prevent either of them spending long years in prison. The safe delivery of the Truth-Tale disc confirmed my allegiance, so it wouldn't arouse any suspicion if I offered to assist them further.'

'What have you in mind?'

'Acquisition of counter-evidence to secure their acquittal.'

'And how the Sun will that help us?'

Kaire smiled. 'Naturally I shall need assistance with this task, and who better than their fellow conspirators.'

Gage frowned. 'If you know the names of the other conspirators, why haven't you had them arrested?'

'I don't have any names but I do have my suspicions. After all, a storyteller and her daughter could hardly devise a plot of this magnitude on their own. Sannah would never divulge any names; she's lived too long in the Brown Zone to completely trust a southerner, even if he has professed undying love. But Pia is young, idealistic, pliable. If I could spend some time with her alone, I'm convinced she would give me the names.'

Gage leaned forward, his hands clasped under his chin.

'And this is where you come in,' Kaire continued before Gage could reject the idea or suggest an alternative. 'As trooper-in-charge you have the authority to release Pia into my care until her trial.' He smiled. 'This gesture should convince both Sannah and Pia that I'm even prepared to use my southern privileges to help them.'

'Excellent,' Gage exclaimed. 'And my name will be mentioned in the report to your commander?'

'Of course, my friend. I empathise with your desire to leave this cultural desert.'

Gage rose to his feet. 'I suggest we adjourn to the trooper dome,' he said, his face a picture of self-satisfaction. 'We have business to conduct.'

CHAPTER 29

Sannah was thankful to remain the sole prisoner in the claustrophobic chamber, even though she had no idea why Pia had been released and allowed to return home until her trial. High on Storyteller's Hill her daughter would be safe, protected by Kaire from trooper brutality. Up there, Pia could wander beyond thick chamber walls, feel warm earth beneath her feet, the splash of raindrops on her skin. Time would heal raw prison wounds, although for Sannah the memory of bloodstains on Pia's robe after that first interrogation remained raw. Maternal outrage had led Sannah to raise her fist to the trooper who'd escorted Pia back to the prison chamber. She would have punched him in the face had Pia not pushed her down on the bed and whispered, 'No, Mother, violence is not solved by violence.' As soon as the trooper departed, they had embraced one another and wept.

Now she wondered if mother and daughter would ever be reunited. This evening she'd had little time to ask questions when Gage appeared in the prison chamber. He'd muttered something about influential friends, grabbed Pia and left the chamber. When Kaire arrived soon after, ostensibly to fetch Pia's sandals, he'd only had time for a fleeting embrace and a few whispered words of encouragement. She imagined Pia would be safely out of the country by the trial date. Repairs to Kaire's land transporter would soon be completed and his ship was only a few days' journey west. Fley would arrange permission for the Sky-ship to land at the settlement in Aotearoa. A new life for Pia and the man who called himself pilgrim. If only she could escape the prison chamber, freedom could be hers as well.

The *Liberty's* replacement would be completed in a few months and there were various safe havens where she could shelter until then. She could make her way north to Fley's cousin, Zira. Her village was close to the mouth of a river suitable for sea craft and Zira had often remarked that the local spotters and troopers were fairly lax. The Line's new ship could easily slip into those waters.

A glance around the prison chamber jolted her back to reality. *Liberty* was not hers to determine. Storyteller or truthteller, she couldn't conceive the tale of Sannah's bid for freedom. Armed troopers stationed in the corridor outside the door guarded the chamber night and day. Gage had drafted extra men from the surrounding villages and not one of them had a friendly face. And apart from troopers, the security screen hummed incessantly, a constant reminder of confinement.

She fingered the bruises on her legs, pondering whether there would be more interrogations? Her body and her will were strong but she dreaded the thought of Gage's slimy hands on her skin, his strident voice, and the gleam in his bloodshot eyes as he applied the latest instrument of torture. She knew Gage wouldn't rest until he'd secured sufficient evidence to ensure her conviction, for despite his cruelty she had revealed nothing worthwhile. The secrets of the Women's Line were safe with her; she wouldn't be named in future Truth-Tales as the weak link in the chain. A storyteller's trade was the spoken word, but she understood the power of silence.

The night after Pia's release, a stranger joined the long queue in front of Ingle the Baker's stall. Shuffling forward, the woman scanned the marketplace, ignoring the chatter swirling around her like mist. After a few moments, she raised her hand and called out a greeting. Eran the Recorder waved back but continued walking towards the fruit stall. The stranger waited patiently, an empty basket hanging over her arm.

Soon Eran reappeared, accompanied by Kaire. The stranger smiled as they approached the baker's queue. 'This is my cousin, Tiwa the Robemaker from River Village 2,' Eran informed Kaire.

He nodded. 'I am Scholar Kaire.'

'Greetings, Scholar Kaire,' Tiwa answered, raising her left hand.

'What brings you to Village 10?' asked Kaire officiously.

'An appointment at the medical dome,' Tiwa answered. 'I came in on the riverboat this morning.'

'Make sure you return home promptly,' said Kaire.

'Yes, sir.'

The queue moved forward a little.

'It's a long wait for bread tonight,' Eran remarked. 'Ingle must be even slower than usual.'

Tiwa smiled and stepped closer to Kaire. 'Excuse me, sir,' she said politely, lifting the sleeve of his robe and rolling the fabric between finger and thumb. 'I couldn't help noticing the quality of your robe.'

'Naturally I have access to excellent fabric,' Kaire answered in a supercilious tone.

'Really, Tiwa,' said Eran, slapping her cousin's fingers. 'How many times do I have to tell you it's bad manners to touch other people's robes?'

'Please accept my apologies,' said Tiwa, stepping back.

'There's no need to apologise,' Kaire replied. 'It's a pleasant change to meet a Brown Zoner genuinely interested in her work.' He smiled. 'Now I must bid you goodnight, I have a report to transmit.'

He crossed the marketplace at a leisurely pace, pausing several times to greet a villager or trooper before turning onto the path leading to the inn. In the distance he could see Clar the Innkeeper sitting on an old bench just outside the door. Reluctant to stop now, Kaire increased his pace and passed the inn with a brief wave of his hand.

Reaching the relative safety of the hill path, he slowed down and slipping a hand into his robe, released the tiny cloth package Tiwa had clipped into his sleeve. A protruding thread caught his eye so he pulled it gently, easing the neat seams apart. Soon a wafer-thin disc emerged from bright fabric. Grasping the disc between finger and thumb, he slotted it into the concealed aperture on one side of his communicator.

Inside Sannah's dome, Kaire only allowed himself a few mouthfuls of water before rousing Pia from her makeshift bed in the living chamber and leading her into the stand of small trees at the rear of the sloping yard. They sat side by side on dusty ground between the trees, their eyes focused on Kaire's communicator screen.

'LLF to SKY,' said a familiar voice, 'message to be relayed only once, repeat only once. Message will self-delete on completion.'

Text appeared on the screen, wrapped around at normal reading speed.

'In four nights,' they read, 'a senior storyteller will visit us. Both villagers and troopers are to be seated in the community dome by midnight. You must sit adjacent to the small door on the left-hand side of the dais. Just before the end of the Tales the community dome will fill with smoke. Leave via the small door and make your way to where the canal crosses the river. A craft will be waiting to take you upstream. LLF will make no further contact.'

Text dissolved and Kaire was about to eject the disc when Fley's voice stayed his hand.

'Dear friends, may moon and stars go with you,' she said unsteadily.

Beside him, Pia sniffed back tears.

The disc slipped into Kaire's hand. He rose quickly, searched around for a small rock and smashing the disc into tiny pieces, scattered them over the ground. Pia paid no attention to his actions; she had retreated to text-based reality. Hunched over her knees, she envisaged the community dome, the small door, the little-used path leading through fields to the river. She could almost feel the flat-bottomed punt skimming over the surface, night breeze and spray cooling her hot skin. But she refused to visualise smoke or fire.

In her eighteen years she had experienced many natural disasters: flood, famine, swarms of pestiferous insects, cyclones, tsunami. Such phenomena were expected in twenty-fifth century Australia and Pia, like other Brown Zone children, had learned the hard lessons of survival at an early age.

Bush fires also raged during dry spells and had decimated the remaining open eucalypt forest in most of the Brown Zone, but even a fleeting thought of smoke or flames evoked indelible and traumatic images for Pia. Fingers of fire snaking through dry grass. Her grandmother's voice shouting, 'Run Pia, run!' Five-year-old legs stumbling through tangled undergrowth. Mother's arms pulling her to safety.

The child's grazed skin had healed quickly and heavy rain soon engendered new green growth, concealing hillside scars. But Pia had never forgotten the screams of pain or the blackened body cradled in a trooper's white arms.

'Freedom,' said Kaire, reaching out to take her hands.

She pushed the memory away and said softly, 'Life, liberty.'

They got to their feet, twirled round and round the trees, disc dust and dry earth flying through the air until the two of them fell in a heap, exhausted.

CHAPTER 30

Sunshine filtered through smoke-filled sky, ribbons of yellow light illuminating the eerie aftermath of fire. Charred produce littered marketplace stalls, awnings hung in blackened ribbons and water trickled across soot-stained paving.

Outside the community dome, exhausted troopers and villagers surveyed the damage in silence. They had worked relentlessly during pre-dawn hours to prevent the fire spreading to the rest of the village.

The injured had received first-aid promptly from medical staff attending the special session of the Tales. Those requiring further attention had now been carried to the medical dome, which fortunately escaped damage. Injuries were for the most part slight; smoke inhalation affecting several small children and a few elderly bones broken during the scramble to leave the community dome.

The school dome had also been spared but no children would sit within its walls for many a night. Fley the Instructor had paid a high price for her voracious appetite, her plump legs unable to outrun fleet flames. Now she lay on a cold slab in the mortuary chamber beneath the medical dome, her only companion old Fen the Stallkeeper, whose limbs had also failed him.

Inside the trooper dome, Trooper Hild crawled on hands and knees sponging blood from a corridor floor. His arms moved mechanically from side to side, stopping every few strokes to wring out the sponge in a bucket of water. He refused to allow himself the luxury of thought. There would be time enough later to reflect on atrocities.

In the reception area, young Trooper Lio drooped in a chair, eyes closed, arms resting limply by his side. He knew he should rouse himself but felt incapable of action. Like a disc jammed in a communicator, his mind could only replay the horror of recent hours.

When the community dome had begun to fill with smoke, Lio, who was sitting on the left-hand side near the dais, had followed Scholar Kaire and Pia out of a nearby exit. The door opened onto a path leading in one direction to the canal and the other back to the marketplace. Kaire and Pia had turned to the right and Lio had been tempted to join them, the canal being a sanctuary, but duty decreed that he head for the marketplace where he could be of some assistance fighting the fire. But as he emerged from behind the community dome, the emergency signal had blared from his communicator and he found himself summoned to the trooper dome instead.

The scenes that greeted him would remain forever in his memory, dark shadows tormenting daydreams, entering unbidden into night thoughts. In the corridor just outside the prison chamber door, he'd found his friend Roa slumped against the wall, a large knife protruding from his blood-soaked tunic. Lio had fallen to his knees and was checking for signs of life when Gage emerged from the prison chamber, active eradicator in one hand, long-handled knife in the other.

'Leave him Lio, save your energy for the living wounded.' Gage gestured towards the prison chamber.

'In there?' Lio queried in a small voice.

'Yes, and a couple of corpses if my aim was accurate. But I'm not concerned with their health; they're prisoners and need processing. Get to work.'

Stunned, Lio had remained on his knees.

'Get up at once! You're a trooper, not a snivelling villager.'

Somehow Lio had managed to stand up and stagger into the chamber where he found four men huddled together on the floor, their blood-spattered robes testimony to excessive ferocity. Nearby a fifth man sagged beside a stool, intestines spilling from a gaping hole in his abdomen. Lio's stomach heaved and bile filled his throat. Swallowing hard, he turned his head and saw Prisoner Sannah lying naked on a low platform, her wrists and ankles shackled to iron rings. Lio stared incredulously—such instruments of torture belonged in a museum, not a twenty-fifth century prison chamber.

'What the Sun are you waiting for?' Gage shouted behind him. 'Take their details.'

Dazed, Lio walked over to the four men.

'Remove any dead to the yard,' ordered Gage, kicking the fifth man, 'and when you've finished with the living, report their capture to Officer Keo of the Security Department.'

Lio nodded.

'And get Hild to clean up this mess.'

'Yes, sir,' said Lio, finding his voice at last. He activated his communicator. 'Name, rank and village,' he asked in what he hoped was an authoritative tone.

'Mayo the Innkeeper, River Village 2,' answered the man closest to the door.

But before Lio could enter the data, Gage pushed past him, knocking the communicator out of his hands.

'Cover your filthy carcass, woman,' Gage cried, releasing Sannah's bonds and throwing her prison robe over her body. Turning to Lio he said brusquely, 'I'm taking the female prisoner to a high-security prison dome. When you've reported to Officer Keo, contact Scholar Kaire and inform him of this matter.'

'Where shall I say she's being held, sir?'

'That's my business,' Gage retorted, seizing Sannah's arm and coupling her wrist to his with an electronic restraining band. 'Ancient or modern, there's nothing like bondage to raise the body temperature, eh storyteller?' he asserted, his face contorted with hatred.

Lio winced as once more he witnessed the fear in Sannah's eyes and heard the maniacal tone of Gage's voice. *Who knew what lurked beneath the surface of a rational man?* he thought, opening his eyes to banish appalling images. Getting to his feet, he ran across the chamber to the main communication console. Earlier there had been no response from Scholar Kaire's personal communicator or the storyteller's dome, but Lio was fully aware he must make contact soon or face an insubordination charge when his superior officer returned. He keyed in the details and waited patiently.

'Communication failure,' the computer reported after a few minutes. 'Suggest possible equipment breakdown.'

'Medical dome,' Lio instructed.

'Village 10 medical dome,' a voice responded instantly.

'Trooper Lio here. Can you tell me if Scholar Kaire and Pia the Apprentice Storyteller were among those admitted this morning?'

'One moment, I'll check.'

Lio drummed his fingers on the console.

'No, Trooper Lio. Have you tried the marketplace? The clean-up is still going on I believe.'

Lio yawned; he could do with some sleep. 'Thanks, I'll try there.'

At the marketplace Lio asked around but it appeared neither Scholar Kaire nor Pia had been among those helping extinguish the fire or clean up the damage. One of the stallkeepers thought she'd seen them walking towards the school dome earlier in the morning so Lio set off to check. The schoolyard was empty and a look at the security data revealed no one had entered the school since before midnight. Glancing at the clearing sky, Lio sighed and began the long trek to the storyteller's dome.

Mid-morning sun blazed from a cloudless sky, heating dry soil and naked rock. Three figures climbed steadily up a boulder-strewn hillside, ignoring the hot sand invading thin sandals to burrow between the toes. Sweat dripped from burning faces, damp robes clung to weary limbs but they pressed on towards the summit.

At last they reached their destination, a deep gully carved from the hillside by innumerable storms and avalanches.

'Liberty,' cried Kaire, raising his arms to the boundless sky.

'Life,' Pia added, her smile wide as a crescent moon.

The third member of the party clambered down into the gully. 'Give me a wide river and a riverboat any night,' the river villager said as he lifted the camouflage cover from Kaire's restored transporter.

Far from the hills where Kaire and Pia rejoiced, Sannah languished in a tiny chamber below ground in a high-security prison. Freedom had seemed so close the night Fley had paid her one sanctioned visit to the trooper dome prison chamber prior to the fire. Fortunately, Trooper Hild left prisoner and friend alone for a few minutes while he fetched Sannah's food, which had given Fley time to write an outline of the liberation mission on her thigh with the tiny pen a body search had failed to find.

The mission had failed because no one, least of all Sannah, had considered Gage to be a particular problem. In all her previous dealings with him, he'd seemed nothing more than a typical trooper, arrogant and domineering with the usual White superiority complex. That he lacked Wurn's sense of humour and genuine warmth had seemed no cause for concern. Wurn had been an unconventional trooper-in-charge in many ways, a good man whose affection for her had seemed sincere. She remembered with pleasure the many tender caresses they'd shared in her dome.

If it were not for her hopeless situation, Sannah would have laughed at the way her sensuous body had betrayed her in the end. Liberty would have been a certainty had Gage not chosen to indulge in bizarre sexual practices with his prisoner.

Sannah had known most of the troopers would be attending the special session of the Tales that night, for when Hild had brought her lunch just before midnight, he'd said only Trooper Roa would remain in the trooper dome. Throaty laughter had echoed around the chamber as Hild related Roa's annoyance at being chosen for prisoner guard duty.

Roa had no need for such emotion now; she had seen his mutilated body when Gage dragged her away from the prison chamber. A just reward for duplicity, some would have said, but all she saw was another young life wasted and she had wept not for Roa alone but for all the damaged youth of their sad nation.

Initially she hadn't been alarmed by Gage's unexpected visit. She'd heard him dismiss Roa from guard duty and send him to the main communication console to retrieve an important report. Gage had greeted her cordially, sat down on the bed and begun to talk of village matters such as crop yields and storm damage. In retrospect, she had to admit he'd cleverly lulled her into a false sense of security, but there was no way she could have foreseen what followed. Even if she had, there was nothing she could have done about it.

Then, in the middle of detailing plans for a second produce terminal, he had dropped to his knees and begun groping about under the bed. When she'd asked if he'd lost something, there had been no response.

She'd heard the sound of a panel opening and had looked towards the door, thinking it was Roa bringing the report, but the panel remained closed. She'd turned back to see Gage still on his knees, pulling the narrow bed away from the wall.

'Why don't you let me help you look for whatever it is you've lost?' she'd suggested. Again, he hadn't answered, so she'd moved closer to the bed and peered over. Where the bed had stood was a narrow opening of indeterminate depth and she'd shuddered, envisaging nights entombed in black earth. But Gage had more surprises in store and she'd watched in horror as a wooden platform with iron rings set into each corner emerged from the pit.

'Are you familiar with the Dark Ages?' he'd asked, sitting back on his heels.

'Is it another term for the Nocturnal Life Project?' she'd quipped, trying to make light of this latest torture instrument.

He'd laughed, a croaky sound that rattled in his throat like stones rolling down a hill. 'A good try, storyteller.' Then he'd leaned forward and lifted a small box from the centre of the platform. 'In the Dark Ages, prisoners were chained to their prison walls with chains such as these,' he'd remarked, casually pulling several lengths of metal links and clasps out of the box.

'No!' she'd cried, backing away.

'Don't be afraid, I have no intention of using them for that purpose. We're more humane in this enlightened age.' Slowly he'd let the chains slip through his hands onto the bed. 'Come, storyteller, surely a woman of your experience can imagine another, shall we say, more gratifying use for these relics?'

'Yes, sir,' she'd answered with as much composure as she could muster. 'But my experience of bondage is limited to leather.'

'You'll find this infinitely more exhilarating.' Joining her on the other side of the bed, he'd drawn a clammy hand across her cheek before attaching lengths of chain to her wrists and ankles.

Blood boiling, she'd forced herself to smile, knowing it would be wise to appear a willing participant in his sadistic game.

Stretched taut like a carcass, she'd endured his vile language and probing fingers for what seemed an eternity. In order to minimise injury, she'd tried to remain calm, but when he rammed into her, a scream escaped, resonating around the chamber like a wounded animal. The moment his force was spent, he'd pulled away, wiped himself on her robe, straightened his tunic, and returned to his position on the bed as though nothing had occurred.

Unable to see the expression on his face, Sannah could only speculate on his next move. Powerless and humiliated, she was ripe for further torture but a sudden commotion in the corridor outside had reminded her that the rescue mission was imminent. As Gage leapt up and headed for the door, the panel had flown open and five river villagers brandishing knives rushed into the chamber. Almost immediately an eradicator beam had struck one of the men in the chest and he slumped to the floor. In the melee that followed, all she had seen was the yellow streak of eradicator beams and blood trickling across the floor. Gage had soon regained control, his superior weapon and combat skills easily overpowering the intruders.

Alone in the pitch-black cell, as light was only permitted during meals, she imagined Gage would be rewarded for his courage in taking on and routing five armed men. She could picture him now, strutting around the village prior to his return south. If only she had a knife and the opportunity to remove a small appendage. She would leave the rest intact; death would be too generous a gift. And she almost laughed out loud as she devised a new tale to recount the fall of Gage the Sadist.

But deep down she knew such a tale would never be told, for whatever the outcome of her trial, she would never be permitted to practice her craft again. Storyteller or truthteller—what did the label signify if her voice had been silenced forever?

CHAPTER 31

Judge Moy-il dismissed the young trooper who had escorted him to the chamber set aside for judicial use during the trial and sealed the door panel. The chamber was small and a faint odour of overcooked vegetables lingered in the humid air. He set the climate control before easing his weary bones into the single comfortable chair.

The preliminary session of the river villagers' trial had passed without incident. A makeshift court chamber erected beneath a large canopy in the marketplace had proven adequate, the recorders and prosecuting officer efficient. Evidence against the accused was conclusive, no challenge could be mounted, and the judge was expected to pass sentence the following night. He had already warned the villagers crowding the public area he would not be lenient and resolved to demonstrate the full extent of his authority.

The judge had anticipated a certain amount of dissension during this particular trial. The atmosphere in Village 10 was tense, the troopers exhausted. The recent fire had left innumerable scars, both physical and psychological. The villagers remained traumatised, and the removal of their beloved storyteller to a high-security prison dome had only exacerbated the situation. But insurrection could not be tolerated under any circumstances, and to make this absolutely clear Judge Moy-il had insisted on holding the trial in Village 10, rather than at the border station court dome.

After a few minutes rest, he extracted a flask from an inside pocket and poured himself a measure of southern spirit. Resisting the urge to drain the tumbler, he drank slowly, rolling each mouthful around teeth and palate in an attempt to banish the disagreeable taste he'd experienced since lunch.

After the evening session Judge Moy-il had retired to the inn for lunch, preferring a crowded venue to a solitary meal in this claustrophobic chamber. How he wished he had chosen to eat alone, far removed from the danger of indiscreet conversation. Conjecture or certainty, he could not ignore what he had overheard. Now he would have to interview not only Trooper-in-Charge Gage but also all the other troopers stationed at Village 10. It was imperative he ascertain if any of the men had actually witnessed the incident they were discussing with such ebullience over a liquid lunch. Gage was a fool if he *had* indulged in sadistic behaviour with a prisoner, especially one to be tried before the governor. Sannah the Storyteller had a reputation for outspokenness and would be certain to raise the issue at her trial.

But even if the talk in the inn was just malicious gossip, the judge knew he would have to advocate an immediate transfer for Gage to prevent further unrest. The innkeeper could also have overheard the troopers' conversation; he had been nearby at the time.

Replacing the cap on his flask, he lifted his wrist and spoke into his communicator.

Judge Moy-il looked up from his monitor and smiled as Gage entered the chamber. 'Sit down, this won't take long.'

Gage bowed slightly and sat down in the solitary chair facing the judge.

'I've read your report detailing the attempted release of Prisoner Sannah. An excellent report by the way, but I need clarification on a couple of points.'

Gage nodded.

'Your report states you went to the prison chamber a few minutes before the five river villagers burst in. Did you suspect trouble that night?'

'No, Your Eminence, it was pure coincidence I happened to be there.'

The judge turned to his monitor and simulated reading for a few moments before raising his head and looking directly at Gage. 'Unfortunately I have received conflicting information on that point.'

Gage twisted uncomfortably. 'I fail to see how that's possible, Your Eminence. I was the only trooper in the trooper dome at the time.'

'Why was that?'

'My men were in the community dome listening to a visiting senior storyteller.'

'I see. Then I'm sure we can clear up this matter promptly.' The judge cleared his throat. 'It's been suggested you went to the prison chamber that night with the intention of having sexual intercourse with Prisoner Sannah. Are you aware this is an offence under the Detention of Villagers Act?'

'Of course, Your Eminence, but I strongly deny this allegation.'

'Idle talk in the inn, I imagine. We both know how liquor loosens the tongue.'

'Yes, Your Eminence,' Gage replied with renewed confidence. 'More than likely my men had overindulged. They were probably celebrating the capture of the five river villagers.'

'Understandable.' The judge sat back in his chair. 'If the gossip were true, I would be willing to overlook it on this occasion, considering what followed. You showed immense courage tackling five armed men.'

'Thank you, Your Eminence.'

'But it wasn't only sex you wanted, was it? You chained the prisoner's wrists and ankles to iron rings set into a platform. A platform you had erected beneath the prison chamber floor on your arrival in Village 10. This constitutes torture, Trooper Gage, torture and rape.'

'No, no, these are blatant lies!' Gage shouted.

'Or the product of an overactive imagination,' the judge continued in a slightly bored tone. 'Perhaps the stress of long hours fighting a fire, the need to release tension.' He paused and keyed a few sentences into the file open on his monitor. 'A particularly vicious joke, Trooper Gage,' he said, raising his eyes from the screen. 'I urge you not to take action, your men have had an exceptionally difficult time recently.'

'Yes, Your Eminence, there's bound to be trouble when popular villagers are arrested. Sannah the Storyteller and her daughter were extremely well-liked.'

'Daughter? What daughter?' The judge didn't wait for an answer. 'That's right, *two* Village 10 women were arrested in connection with the train sabotage. Tell me, Trooper Gage, where is the other prisoner?'

Gage studied his boots. 'Missing, Your Eminence.'

'You mean she escaped during the fracas with the river villagers?'

'No, she was attending the Tales the night of the fire.'

The judge slammed his fist on the work-module. 'Is it common practice in these parts to allow prisoners to attend Tales?'

'No, but in this case I deemed it necessary to release her last week, under supervision, of course, until her trial.'

'Necessary?'

'I believed given a certain amount of freedom, Pia would lead us to others involved in the recent insurrection.'

The judge smiled. 'A sensible decision. Has the prisoner's supervising officer reported anything useful?'

'Kaire's not one of *my* officers, Your Eminence. He works for the Security Department and reports directly to a Commander Breta. He's been staying in the village for some time, working on the Blue Globe project.'

The judge nodded. 'To return to the question of the missing prisoner, what has Officer Kaire to say on the matter?'

'I haven't heard from him and I fear the worst, Your Eminence,' Gage answered, his face a mask of concern. 'One of my men saw Kaire and Prisoner Pia running towards the canal during the fire. It's possible they became disoriented due to the smoke, stumbled into the water and drowned. The canal's choked with weed at that point. I organised a search directly after we had cleared up from the fire, but no bodies have turned up.'

'The Security Department won't take kindly to the loss of one of their officers, Trooper Gage.' The judge drummed his fingers on the work-module. 'However, there is another possibility. Officer Kaire may have decided to remove Prisoner Pia to a safer location and neglected to inform you.' The judge lifted his wrist. 'A word with the Security Department should put both our minds at rest.'

Commander Ethan, a high-ranking officer, proved extremely helpful and provided detailed answers to all inquiries. The judge was careful to restrict his own responses to either monosyllables or discreet comments and kept the wrist-communicator pressed to his ear. When communication terminated, he lowered his arm to the work-module in slow motion, stretching each finger in a ritual exercise.

'I have grave news, Trooper Gage,' the judge said at last, pausing to pass a hand over his brow. 'No Security Department officers are currently working in this section of the Brown Zone and the Blue Globe project does not exist. Furthermore, the name Kaire is unknown to the department and a Commander Breta is not, and never has been in their employ. Commander Ethan searched the national security database and found no trace of a Kaire or Breta in the entire country.'

The judge leaned forward and fixing on Gage with an icy stare said curtly, 'Trooper Gage, you have been duped. No doubt Pia and her deliverer, whoever he may be, are well away from the Brown Zone by now. If you had paid more attention to your duties and less to your perverse sexual preferences, this would not have occurred. There will have to be a full investigation. I have no alternative but to detain you here until arrangements can be made to transfer you to a military prison.'

'But I listened to Kaire's report to his commander,' Gage protested. 'One of my men stole his communicator.'

'Save your excuses for the investigating officers.' The judge turned back to the monitor. 'Trooper Lio, in here now.'

The door panel opened immediately.

'Trooper Lio reporting, Your Eminence.'

The judge looked up. 'Trooper Lio, your former commanding officer is under arrest and is to be detained here, possibly overday, until I have organised an escort to the nearest military prison. This chamber will have to serve as temporary accommodation for him. I have no desire to disturb the other prisoners by placing him in their chamber. Please arrange for all equipment to be removed. I shall implement a security screen immediately. And as an added precaution, a trooper is to be stationed in the corridor near the door at all times.'

Lio bowed. 'Yes, Your Eminence, I'll see to it at once.'

Judge Moy-il rose and traversed the chamber without a glance at the snivelling Gage. 'I am relocating, Trooper Lio,' he announced from the doorway. 'If you need me, I shall be at the inn. Clar the Innkeeper serves excellent liquor.'

'He does indeed, Your Eminence. I recommend his tropica.'

'Thank you, Trooper Lio,' said Judge Moy-il as he swept from the chamber in a cloud of purple cloth.

Lio moved over to the work-module and picked up the monitor and an empty tumbler.

'By the Sun I'll see you suffer for your loose talk,' Gage hissed, 'and I'll sever more than your wagging tongue.'

Empty threats, thought Lio and he hurriedly left the chamber, eager to be away from the despicable man who had fooled them all with his façade of geniality.

CHAPTER 32

Kaire guided the transporter westward over smooth rock and patches of dry grass. The metalworker from River Village 3 had carried out an excellent repair job, he thought, so far the engine had performed well despite the sweltering conditions. During this first day's travel, Kaire had decided to maintain a steady pace and if possible, avoid surges of acceleration or deceleration. Difficult terrain lay ahead: a wide expanse of ever-changing dunes, their red sand particles blown about by the hot winds continuously sweeping the central desert, the unexpected tangle of sun-dried vegetation, the pitted surface of a dried up river. All could prove problematic for a vehicle already weakened from lengthy burial. Fortunately the return journey to the ship would take less time than the initial three-day trek. This time he had set the scanner on a direct route west to evade troopers or desert prison builders.

No Line leader had made contact, leaving Kaire to assume the mission had proceeded as planned. Sannah would be sailing north by now, on her way to rendezvous with the Asian ship that would take her to Aotearoa. Opal the Technician from Island 1 Spotter Station had arranged Sannah's passage with the ship's captain, in exchange for overlooking an encroachment of a Brown Zone fishing zone. Kaire would have preferred Sannah to travel in *his* ship, but Fley had insisted on separate escape routes. He smiled as he envisaged troopers wasting endless hours combing the village and surrounding area for the escapees. How long had it taken Gage to discover Scholar Kaire didn't work for the Security Department or any other Australian government agency?

A glance at the console monitor wiped the smile from his face. Behind him, Pia sat bolt upright, arms folded against her chest, eyes fixed on the monotonous landscape. News of Fley's death, relayed by a passing riverman as they travelled up river, had devastated Pia and all Kaire's attempts to comfort her had failed miserably.

Sunlight struck the patched passenger bubble, sending streaks of shadow over Pia's face and shoulders. Kaire longed to break the silence, to distract her from the pain of tragedy, but a further glance at the monitor showed a face so cloaked in grief he abandoned the idea and turned instead to the console readings.

'Can we stop?' she asked suddenly.

'Why, are you feeling ill?'

'No, but I'll wet myself if we don't stop soon.'

'Use the black tube to your left.'

She looked down. 'No way am I using that thing.'

'All right, we'll take a short break.'

The moment he released the passenger bubble, Pia sprang out and raced behind a nearby boulder. Climbing out of the pilot bubble, Kaire stretched his legs before watering the arid earth. Only when he'd returned to his seat, did he notice the emergency signal flashing on the console.

'Pia,' he yelled, pressing the panel.

'LLF to SKY,' announced an unfamiliar voice.

'That's not possible,' he answered cautiously.

'LLZ using LLF equipment,' explained Line Leader Zira. 'I'm here for the end of life ceremony.'

Kaire sighed with relief. 'Go ahead, LLZ.'

'The mission failed,' Zira declared in a matter-of-fact tone. 'I repeat, mission failed.'

'Where is she?' Kaire cried.

'Location suspected but not confirmed.'

'What happened?'

'A trooper in the prison chamber.'

'He knew about the mission?'

'No, he was there for another purpose.'

'Torture?' Kaire asked, keeping his voice low as Pia climbed in behind him.

'Yes.'

Kaire shuddered. 'Is she hurt?'

'Not as far as we know.'

'What's up?' Pia appeared, leaning over his shoulder.

'The mission failed,' he said.

Fingers gripped his robe.

'Are you still there?' asked Zira.

'Yes,' he hissed through clenched teeth, struggling to contain anger and fear.

'Continue your journey as planned, directions for the landing site will be communicated when you reach your ship. Another mission will take place as soon as we have confirmation of locale.'

'What are the chances of success?'

'Fairly high. They won't be expecting a second attempt.'

'I wish I had your confidence.'

'Success is imperative if our work is to continue. Further interrogation could uncover vital information.'

'How dare you!' Pia shouted, sinking her fingernails into Kaire's neck. 'Sannah would never betray the Line.'

'Take care of her,' said Zira, closing the connection.

Gently Kaire eased Pia's hands from his neck. 'We must go now,' he said, stroking her fingers. 'Sit down so I can close the bubble.'

'Not unless you promise to take me back to my people immediately.'

'That would be senseless, Pia. You'd be arrested the moment you set foot in the village.'

'I'm not that stupid. Take me to Zira's village. It's far to the north and won't be under surveillance. I can work for the Line there. I can't desert them now.'

'Zira wasn't communicating from her home village, she's at Fley's dome for a ceremony.'

'The end of life ceremony,' said Pia quietly. 'Fley had no partner or child. Zira was her closest relative.'

He patted her shoulder. 'Please sit down, Pia. We've a long journey ahead of us. Think positive—Zira was confident the second mission will succeed.'

He felt her body tense.

'The troopers aren't complete idiots, they'll have taken her to a high-security prison. How can another mission succeed?'

'Miracles can happen, Pia.'

'You really believe that?'

'Without hope we die,' he said, massaging her taut shoulders with the tips of his fingers. 'That's what my people believe, what sustains us as we search for a new world to call our own. Do you think it's easy living on a rusting space station, year after year, generation after generation, never knowing how long the ageing structure will remain intact? Do you think it's easy watching wave after wave of young men and women leave their home to wander through uncharted space, never to return? Those are the issues *my* people face, Pia, every day of their lives. Faith in the future, faith there will be a future, that's all we have on Sky.'

She covered his hand with hers and squeezed briefly before releasing him and sitting back in her seat. Kaire closed the bubble.

'Take me to your ship, Skyman,' she ordered in a tone reminiscent of her mother, 'and as we travel tell me what to expect. The Brown Zone education system hasn't prepared me for sky flight.'

'Certainly, Earthwoman,' Kaire replied, activating the powerful thrusters. 'We should reach the ship in approximately twelve hours. There will be no further stops.'

Pia looked down at the black tube and grimaced.

'Sustenance will be taken at four-hourly intervals, and please ensure fluid intake is adequate.'

Kaire steered his vehicle along a dry creek bed to the base of a low ridge cloaked with wind-swept bushes. The transporter climbed slowly, straining to push through the foliage. On the other side of the ridge, a featureless plain stretched to the horizon but he knew beyond the waving brown grass, swirls of burnished sand decorated an immense desert. Camouflaged among those sand patterns, his beautiful Sky-ship waited to take them to the new world of Aotearoa.

CHAPTER 33

In the central chamber of the border station court dome, the trial of Sannah the Storyteller was drawing to a close. All prosecution witnesses had been heard and their testimony corroborated. It remained for the prosecuting officer to summarise the evidence against the accused.

Governor An-il sat on an immense padded chair, a scarlet robe arrayed like a fan around his ample body. Golden slippers, glistening in harsh artificial light, peeped from beneath his robe. To his right, a monitor rested on a moveable rod; to his left a similar rod supported a tray containing a silver jug and tumbler. The two recorders, young men wearing the pale green robes of their profession, perched on low stools behind a communication console while the prosecuting officer, elegant in navy with silver flecks, stood behind a monitor opposite. Sannah squatted, cross-legged on the floor in the centre of the chamber, guarded by an armed trooper.

The senior recorder stood. 'Night four, trial of Sannah the Storyteller of Village 10, Brown Zone. The prisoner will now stand.'

Sannah struggled to her feet. She wore prison garb: a short red tunic made of coarse cloth and soiled white sandals. An electronic wristband pulsed against her left arm, dried blood caked her legs and a yellow bruise decorated her right cheek. The trooper pushed her roughly into a small circle engraved in the floor. Stepping away from the monitor, the prosecuting officer turned to the governor and raised his left hand.

'You may proceed with the evidence summary,' Governor An-il said gruffly.

The prosecuting officer bowed. 'Thank you, Your Excellency.' He stepped back to the monitor. 'Four witnesses have given evidence against the accused. In view of the complexity of this case, I propose to deal separately with each witness's evidence.'

The governor nodded in agreement.

'Prosecution Witness 1, Worker Una formerly of Working Party 2, now resident at Orea River mine,' the prosecuting officer read from the monitor, then paused as though waiting for text to appear on a palm-sized message board. 'This witness informed the court of matters relating to the distribution of the Truth-Tale disc. Her testimony confirmed all workers at Working Party 2 listened to the disc. The witness denied prior knowledge of the subsequent breakout at Working Party 2 or the train sabotage. Further inquiries have corroborated her statement. Witness 1 also verified the Truth-Tale disc was delivered to Worker Pia, the accused's daughter, by the man known as Scholar Kaire, the accused's lover.'

'Quite a family affair,' the governor remarked loudly.

The prosecuting officer acknowledged the statement with a slight nod of the head. 'Have you any questions before I proceed to Witness 2, Your Excellency?'

'No questions, proceed.'

'Prosecution Witness 2, Trooper Gage, formerly Trooper-in-Charge of Village 10, currently held …'

'Please refrain from including superfluous information,' the governor admonished. 'Proceed with the testimony.'

The prosecuting officer nodded. 'Witness 2 stated Scholar Kaire delivered the Truth-Tale disc to Working Parties 1 and 2. Auditory evidence in the form of a report Scholar Kaire made to a Commander Breta was also supplied. This report supports our hypothesis that Scholar Kaire collaborated with the accused in the planning of the breakouts. The report also refers to the accused's involvement in future northern missions. Unfortunately, the copy made of the report was of poor quality so we have been unable to decipher some parts. However, Witness 2 also provided a digital recording of discussions held with Scholar Kaire concerning the accused. The discussions, conducted over several nights, confirm the link between the breakouts and the train sabotage.'

'We have her now,' muttered the governor.

'Pardon, Your Excellency?'

'Nothing. Please continue.'

The prosecuting officer gave a slight cough. 'Witness 2 also reported on the arrest and subsequent interrogation of the accused. Despite extensive questioning, he was unable to extract further proof of guilt.'

The governor frowned. 'And I understand interrogation by Security Department officers has also proved unproductive?'

'That is correct, Your Excellency.'

'Sannah the Stubborn,' the governor retorted.

The two recorders turned to one another and smirked before exchanging whispered comments.

'Silence in my court,' the governor bawled.

The recorders shrunk back behind their monitors.

'If I may now proceed to Witness 3, Your Excellency?' the prosecuting officer asked haughtily.

The governor inclined his head.

'Prosecution Witness 3, Cron the Driver, formerly of Village 30, now resident at Orea River mine. As you may recall, Your Excellency, this witness was the driver of the sabotaged train.'

'There's nothing wrong with my memory, officer,' said the governor irritably. 'Continue.'

'Witness 3 supplied evidence concerning the perpetrators of the train sabotage. His testimony states they were predominantly Brown males aged between fifteen and eighteen years. This is consistent with the description of the workers that absconded from the working parties. Witness 3 also reported seeing a woman of about thirty-five years, who appeared to be organising proceedings.'

'A Brown-skin?' the governor asked, leaning forward.

'I can't recall, Your Excellency. I'll have to refer to my files.'

'Proceed, I have no wish to delay matters.' The governor sat back in his chair, a self-satisfied smile coating his thick lips.

'In that case, Your Excellency, I shall proceed to the last witness. Witness 4, Security Officer Keo of Brown Zone Security Department. Witness 4 furnished details of forensic testing he ordered carried out recently on human remains found in a burnt-out trooper car not far from the train sabotage scene. Testing proved the victims were troopers, not workers as previously thought. Witness 4 affirmed the official Security Department view that the train sabotage was part of an extensive plan to free political prisoners before they could be sent to the new prisons in the northwestern desert.'

'That is my view also,' the governor remarked.

The prosecuting officer offered a small smile. 'Here ends the summary of witness evidence, Your Excellency.'

After a short silence, the governor stood with difficulty, the voluminous robe impeding his progress. 'All rise, this court will adjourn for twenty-four hours to allow me to consider all aspects of this case. I shall present my judgment at that time.'

The following night, Governor An-il kept everyone waiting. The recorders passed the time playing computer games while the prosecuting officer, having slept badly, slumped in a chair beside his monitor. On the floor, Sannah attempted to stretch her legs but was rewarded with a swift kick from the trooper standing guard behind her. She longed for the trial to finish: the verdict a foregone conclusion; the twenty-four hour adjournment to mull over the evidence a pointless delay.

At last Governor An-il sailed into the chamber, scarlet robe billowing. The senior recorder waited until the governor had settled before emerging from behind the communication console.

'Night five, trial of Sannah the Storyteller of Village 10, Brown Zone,' he announced in a monotone. 'His Excellency Governor-An-il presiding.' He returned to his seat behind the monitors.

The governor cleared his throat. Sannah glanced up, noted his bulbous red nose, and pondered how much liquor he'd consumed during the adjournment.

'Prior to presenting my judgment, I shall issue instructions concerning Prosecution Witnesses 1, 2 and 3,' the governor declared, his voice gritty as a Brown Zone sand storm. 'Recorders, please note my instructions are to be carried out immediately following this trial.'

'Yes, Your Excellency,' the senior recorder answered promptly.

'Prosecution Witness 1,' the governor began, lowering his voice slightly. 'Worker Una is to be relieved of her duties at Orea River mine and returned to her home village. There she will undertake training in the village produce store.' He paused to smile in Sannah's direction. 'This government rewards cooperation.'

The recorders exchanged furtive glances.

'Prosecution Witness 2. I recommend leniency in the judgment and sentencing of Trooper Gage at his forthcoming trial. He showed intelligence, tenacity and great courage in the pursuit and capture of those who seek through nefarious activities to destabilise the government.'

To emphasise this last point, the trooper kicked Sannah in the shin and she winced in pain.

The recorders nudged one another and laughed.

'Silence in my court,' the governor bellowed. 'Prosecution Witness 3. Cron the Driver is to be relieved of his duties at Orea River mine and revert to his position as driver on the south-north line. He is to be commended not only for his cooperation but also for the composure and perception he exhibited both during and after the sabotage of his train.' Looking up, he glared at Sannah for a moment before turning to address the recorders. 'Please arrange for reports of these "rewards for cooperation" to be publicised at forthcoming Tales throughout the Brown Zone.'

'It shall be done, Your Excellency,' the senior recorder replied.

A long silence followed, broken only by the flow of water from jug to tumbler and the governor's slow sipping. The prosecuting officer crossed and uncrossed his legs; the recorders' fingers hovered expectantly above their console.

'I shall now proceed to judgment of the accused,' the governor declared at last. 'Prisoner Sannah, step forward to the sentencing block.'

Sannah rose stiffly and walked over to a small raised platform fashioned from black stone situated directly in front of the governor's chair. Stepping up, she stood perfectly still, arms by her side, head held high.

'Sannah the Storyteller,' the governor began, 'you are accused of numerous crimes. Namely: the production and supply of subversive material to Working Party 1 and 2; the conception of plans for breakouts at said working parties; organising the sabotage of a train carrying political prisoners; and harbouring an enemy of the government known as Scholar Kaire.' He paused to clear his throat. 'I have heard comprehensive evidence from four witnesses and studied auditory evidence from Troopers Lio, Hild and Xan of Village 10. Every piece of this evidence is irrefutable, Prisoner Sannah. I am convinced you did not act alone, but as you refuse to name your co-conspirators you must bear full responsibility for these crimes. Therefore I have no choice but to pronounce you guilty on all counts.'

The prosecuting officer gave a discreet smile while once again the young recorders grinned foolishly. Only Sannah remained impassive.

'Prisoner Sannah, do you have anything to say before I pronounce sentence?'

'Yes, Your Excellency, I wish to address the court on the subject of truth.'

'I should be most interested to hear your views,' the governor answered with a touch of irony. 'Proceed, Prisoner Sannah.'

'Thank you, Your Excellency.' Moving one foot to the edge of the block, she turned her body slightly. 'I wish to define my occupation. As storyteller for Village 10, Brown Zone, I have fed my people a steady diet of lies over the last twenty years. I have lied about past events, current policy and future direction. The government sanctioned each and every one of these lies.'

Murmurs of incredulity rumbled around the chamber like distant thunder.

'Can you believe it?' the junior recorder remarked to his colleague. 'She continues to condemn herself.'

'Silence in my court, let the prisoner speak.'

'Thank you, Your Excellency. Now, however, I am proud to call myself Sannah the Truthteller. At last my people are learning the true history, not only of this nation but also of this planet we call Earth. Before long every man, woman and child in the Brown Zone will understand how and why this beautiful planet was desecrated. Greed, arrogance, concern for profit rather than conservation, apathy, egotism—these are some of the words my people hear in Truth-Tales. Yes, Your Excellency, your assumption is correct. I did not act alone. Others before me have known and passed on the truth and others after me will continue the process. For truth is like the ocean, sometimes it laps our shores, sometimes it storms our defences, nightly it ebbs and flows, but no human being can ever curb its motion.'

Silence pervaded the chamber as words sank deep. All eyes remained focused on the speaker, standing tall on the sentencing block, her eyes gleaming like dark jewels, her face glowing.

'I hear your words, Prisoner Sannah,' said the governor after a lengthy pause, his voice unusually benign, 'but tell me, do you imagine this knowledge will in any way alter the harsh reality of life on Earth at the beginning of the twenty-fifth century?'

'It's never too late to make amends, Your Excellency.'

'Wise words, woman, but it seems you are incapable or unwilling to take your own advice.' He snorted loudly and when he spoke again his voice had reverted to its normal gruffness. 'At no point since your arrest have you shown any remorse for the damage your Truth-Tale has caused. Lives have been lost, lives have been diminished, crops neglected, property destroyed. At this moment scarce resources are being used to track down escapees, including your own daughter. And as for your lover, Scholar Kaire, the Security Department is expending enormous sums in their efforts to locate him.'

Sannah laughed out loud, then winced as the trooper rushed forward and slapped her face.

'You find my words amusing, Prisoner Sannah?'

'No, Your Excellency. I laugh with joy because the Security Department will never find Kaire. You see, Your Excellency, Kaire is no southerner. He isn't even a native of Earth!'

'Is there no end to your lies, woman? No, don't answer, I've heard enough.' Rising with uncharacteristic speed, the governor strode over to the sentencing block and seized Sannah by the chin. 'Sannah the Storyteller of Village 10, Brown Zone, in view of the gravity of the offences and as a deterrent to other would-be truthtellers, I have no alternative but to impose the maximum penalty. I hereby sentence you to death. Sentence to be carried out in twenty-four hours in the marketplace, Village 10.' He dropped her chin and gestured to the trooper. 'Take her away.'

CHAPTER 34

So it was almost over—Sannah, Storyteller and Truthteller, would never see another sunrise tint her beloved ocean, feel salt wind on her face, hear waves pound a moonlit beach. Thirty-eight years she'd lived on the shrinking green rim of a heartbreak land, a land that once held such promise for so many of Earth's dispossessed.

In her short life she'd known flood, drought, cyclone, famine and disease, to name but a few of the natural disasters that frequently plagued Australia. She'd also experienced the unnatural disaster of apartheid and its attendant violence and oppression. In many ways it had been a grim existence.

But she refused to allow the tenebrous cloak of Brown Zone life to dominate her few remaining hours. Now was the time to remember rays of light—beauty, joy, serenity, love—for these she'd known in abundance. The beauty of moonlight, clouds and raindrops; the joy of small footprints in sand; the serenity of sleep after passion; the love of mother, father, partner, daughter, friends—unconditional love, dazzling, all-encompassing. And during those last traumatic months, the love of a stranger who'd come to her from the star-studded canopy of space.

Despite recent events, she still possessed hope. Did she foresee a miracle, villagers storming the marketplace, snatching her away from the death block? No, that would have been an implausible scenario, nor would she have wished any more of her people to give their lives for her freedom. Her hope was a beacon lighting the way to liberty, a future free from oppression, a future where all the people of the nation could work together to repair the ravages of centuries and recreate the golden land.

As the welcome mantle of darkness enshrouded Village 10 once more and a siren announced the beginning of another working night, Sannah rose from the bed in the trooper dome prison chamber to which she'd been moved after the trial and knelt on the cold stone floor. Quieting her mind, she entered the still small space where words could enter unbidden or wing their way to others waiting in deep silence for guidance.

'Pia, my beloved daughter, I bequeath you my hope. Nourish it and watch it grow strong; then the flame of hope will blaze and diminish the darkness.

'Kaire my love, my beautiful pilgrim, your hope and your faith brought you to Earth. Not for you the flight into uncharted galaxies, the ceaseless quest for new worlds. Pour your hope and faith into the fire; join my people in their quest for freedom. Then your pilgrimage will not have been in vain.

'Women of the Line, don't weep for me; I am resigned to my fate and go gently to the Island of Eternal Sleep. Rejoice in the knowledge the Line remains unbroken and remember no one can silence the voice of an entire people.

'Farewell my people—open your hearts to receive this last unspoken message.'

Silence cloaked the crowded marketplace; stalls stood unattended, produce neatly displayed, undisturbed. There would be little trade this dark night. On the western perimeter, villagers gathered in front of a newly erected stone block guarded by two troopers, their eradicators pointed at the crowd. Suddenly the sound of an approaching car distracted them and their heads turned slightly. The villagers remained motionless, even small children kept their eyes fixed on the block.

A silver trooper car eased to a halt, released its door panels and disgorged five passengers. Three troopers in full riot gear marched towards the block while a fourth followed at a discreet distance, dragging Prisoner Sannah by the wrist. She was barefoot, her body swathed in a black robe and head-cloth. On reaching the block, the trooper released the electronic wristband and pushed her forward. She stepped unwaveringly onto the rough surface and turned to face her people. Then with a sweeping gesture, she unwound the head-cloth designed to protect her from seeing the eradicator beams and dropped it to the dusty ground.

A sigh rippled through the crowd and the humid air stirred a little as a hundred white robes began to sway, waves of light streaming into an ocean of darkness. Light penetrated, warmed chill depths. Two hundred lips parted and song flooded the ebony sky. Singing in perfect harmony, the villagers melded old islander lyrics and the hope of a displaced people.

May stars and moon guide you tonight
May your craft berth softly on the shore
May warm earth cradle your spirit bright
May your heart-fire blaze evermore

Island of Eternal Sleep
Free and safe our Sannah keep

May the salt wind carry our song
May your spirit soar with each line
May you hear every voice grow strong
As the liberty path we climb

Island of Eternal Sleep
Free and safe our Sannah keep
Island of Eternal Sleep
Free and safe our Sannah keep

Impassioned voices saturated the marketplace. No one heard the strident sounds of the troopers' condemnation, no one saw yellow eradicator beams, no one watched a body fall. But every villager caught a whiff of salt air; every villager felt the pull of Pacific Ocean currents.

High above the blue ocean, a Sky-ship hovered, silver fins shimmering in bright morning sunlight. In the front passenger capsule, Pia sat beside Kaire, her face pressed against the window. An island appeared through a gap in the cloud, and she gazed in awe at grey mountain peaks, turquoise lakes and a green, living forest.

The ship's communicator began to flash and hum.

'Kauri 378 to Sky z59.323,' announced a stranger's voice.

'323 receiving you, Kauri 378.'

'Welcome to Aotearoa, you have permission to land at the settlement.'

'Thank you. Have you any news of the mission?'

Desperate for information about her mother, Pia turned away from the window.

'Repeat,' said Kaire, 'have you any news of the mission?'

'Mission aborted, repeat, mission aborted.'

'Why?'

There was no response.

'Kauri 378, I repeat, why?'

'We will discuss the matter on your arrival.'

'I demand you tell me now.'

'Sannah's trial was a sham, the verdict a foregone conclusion.'

'Then we have no time to lose. Tell the Line leaders to find out where the troopers have taken her and organise another rescue mission.'

'There won't be another mission, Kaire. The death penalty was carried out last night before the rescue team could reach her.' The speaker paused. 'I'm so sorry.'

Pia's high-pitched scream failed to reach Kaire's ears—he had already collapsed against the console. The Sky-ship lurched and dipped earthward.

'Attention, Pilot Kaire, correct your position immediately. Craft heading for mountain. I repeat, craft heading for mountain.'

Automatically, Kaire's hands touched the console and the Sky-ship began to gain height.

'Craft now on course, landing in three minutes.'

Pia leaned over and shook Kaire's shoulder. 'Take me away from this blighted planet!' she cried. 'Take me to Sky.'

'No,' he answered curtly, pushing her hands away. 'Sky z59.323 preparing to land.'

'But I have no future down there,' Pia asserted. 'They killed my mother, nowhere on Earth can I be free of that memory.'

'Didn't you hear Sannah's message?'

'What message, when?'

'Two nights ago when we were waiting in the desert for Line instructions. It came like a warm wind rustling golden leaves, words of encouragement, words of love. I didn't want to believe it because …' he hesitated, swallowing hard to clear the lump in his throat, 'because she said farewell.' He reached for Pia's hand and clasped it firmly. 'We mustn't give up, Pia. We can't turn away from all Sannah and Fley worked for. Together we can become a beacon of hope lighting the path to liberty. Together we can help restore a ruined nation, make its people proud to be Australian.'

Sniffing, Pia wiped her tears with the back of her free hand. 'My legacy,' she said softly, 'a new world rising from the ruins of the old.' She sat back in her seat. 'Take me to Aotearoa, Skyman,' she ordered in a tone Sannah would have been proud of. 'There is much work to be done.'

Silver fins dipped and the Sky-ship slipped through a long white cloud.

ACKNOWLEDGMENTS

I wish to thank all the writers I have met over the years, especially those at Mordialloc Writing Group for encouraging me to pursue my dream of becoming a professional writer.

Many thanks also to my publisher at Odyssey Books, Michelle Lovi, for having faith in my story and enabling me to share it.

ABOUT THE AUTHOR

Originally from England, Sue worked after graduating (B.A. University of Queensland, majors in English Literature, Drama and French) in university libraries until taking early retirement in 2008 to concentrate on creative writing. Since then she has written: *Sannah and the Pilgrim;* several short stories, articles and poems, which have been published in magazines and anthologies; a feature film script *Feed Thy Enemy* (based on a true story) set in Naples in 1944 and 1974, and a second novel *Safety Zone*. Her current project is a sequel to *Sannah and the Pilgrim*—the working title is *Pia and the Skyman*.